Dorie LaValle

Mary DesJarlais

Minneapolis, Minnesota

Minneapolis, Minnesota

THIRD EDITION DECEMBER 2022

10 9 8 7 6 5 4 3

ISBN: 978-1-959770-67-1

Book design by Gary Lindberg

Praise for Dorie LaValle

DesJarlais...gives her readers a seamless blend of murder, thrills, passion and friendship in a small town, with a pitch-perfect sense of time and place.

Mary Ann Grossman, Saint Paul Pioneer Press

An implicit theme of the book is that if people associate the Roaring '20s with flappers and jazz clubs, many women led far less glamorous lives. A friend tells Dorie: "The men in my life never looked at me as something of value. They only saw me as something pretty to touch.

Janice Harayda, Minneapolis StarTribune

LOVE LOVE LOVE this new writer. Genealogical fiction is a new trend and Mary did a great job. Taking a person in her family history and making up a story surrounding them was genius but the writing and word usage was like having your cake and eating it to. I can't wait to hear more from this writer.

Mickey Mikeworth, Amazon review

DesJarlais pushes the reader to decide--is Dorie a victim with the intelligence to survive or is she better suited for the Mafia?

Linda O, Amazon reader

I expected to like this book, I didn't expect to LOVE it. The author... kept me turning the pages far into the night.

Sandy Janssen Barry, Amazon reader

... took off right from the start. It had everything, mystery, love, heartache and action. I would recommend this book for both women and men. There is a lot of true history...as well.

Apple, Amazon reader

I simply could not put it down the first time I opened it. Highly recommended.

Maribella, Amazon reader

I couldn't put it down. How difficult to be a woman in the early 20th century when needing to take care of herself and her business were necessary. I would recommend this book to all readers.

Lucille B, Amazon reader

A great first book!

RE Krause, Amazon reader

Great character development, interesting story line, and well told.

Anonymous review

I could not put this book down. My dad was visiting while I was reading it and he picked it up and read it the whole visit. He went home and bought his own copy so he could finish it.

M. Bearce, Amazon review

The characters are compelling and the story unfolds in an almost organic way, much like life.

Jessica Looman, Amazon review

Each chapter is filled with surprise. History, passion, mobsters, forgiveness, morals and a dose of religious references.

Lynn, Amazon review

For Kevin Schieffer (1959-2015)

I was honored to be your alpha and omega love. I still marvel when the universe opened that small window, allowing us to find each other at the unlikely age of fifty. I'm beyond grateful for our mostly lovely (sometimes bittersweet) five-year run. Thank you for your dogged assistance to edit and promote this novel. You pushed me to start a second book and I will forever miss the way you would take the laptop from me and say, "Let's see what your crooked little mind has cooked up now." Keep the good ideas coming. I'm forever on the end of your chain of stars

Dorie LaValle

Mary DesJarlais

Part 1

1

The Problem

A tease of warm winds gusted across the snowy potato fields. Snowmelt dripped from the porch roof, drumming a hollow ping against the collapsed gutter, while barn cats sunned themselves on the bench of the hay wagon. Sun, angled low in the afternoon sky, pierced the porch windows, warming Dorie's shoulders as she stood on the planked floor swiping the paintbrush across the kitchen door and concealing the gouges and greasy fingerprints Louie always left each time he moved the cases of moonshine into the cellar.

Winter had worked itself into her bones that year. An ice storm hit on the first day of November followed by chains of slate-colored days, weeks of below zero temperatures, and nightly blankets of new snow that narrowed the paths to the barn and sheds.

As February wore on to an end, Dorie felt chilled and weary in a way she hadn't remembered in the twenty-eight previous winters. Today, the spring air filled Dorie with new vigor, and she painted in efficient strokes, pulling the brush back and forth as the smell of paint mixed with the wet of the yard. She also knew that, at any moment, the air currents might shift and cool, causing the paint to thicken and bubble. In Dorie's experience, nothing that felt this good ever lasted very long.

Dorie plucked a loose boar bristle from the paint and wiped the smear across the newspaper photograph of President Coolidge. One thing she couldn't deny was that the harsh winter had been good for business. Five nights a week her kitchen bustled with farmers who came to drink, share stories and play music until their sweaty faces glowed and Dorie's sleeve was fat with the roll of bills. For the first time in her ten years of married life, the taxes were paid, there was ample food in the pantry, and she had money left over for hats, perfumes, and milled soaps.

This afternoon, Louie was off delivering pints to the men forced to imbibe on the sly. Dorie hummed, "I'm the Sheik of Araby," and reveled in the absence of his prattle. She suspected Louie enjoyed these delivery days even more than she did. Even though he had only three stops, it would be several hours until he was due to stumble back home. Typically, each grateful crony was guaranteed to share his good fortune. She smiled, stood back to survey her efforts, and then smoothed out a dribble. After she finished with the door, she had a mind to rid the porch of the tangle of ropes, broken crates, and the sorghum buckets Louie used to make his birdhouses.

Last July, Louie had cut a rounded hole in a pail and then crimped and folded the top third shut. He twisted a length of wire to fashion a hanging loop, painted the whole thing green and hung it in the pine tree at the edge of the drive. It would have ended there had her sister Obeline not stopped over that day on one of her rare visits and ranted and raved about it as if he had assembled an entire house. He gave Obeline that first birdhouse, and then talked endlessly about how he could sell them to everyone in town! It did Dorie no good to argue that birds lived in barns, and people in these parts were poor as dirt and not apt to part with a nickel to buy an old bucket. Moonshine made far easier money than farming potatoes or making birdhouses, she assured him, but he continued to collect buckets, stacking them on the porch by the door where she was forced to see them every day. She clenched her teeth every time they toppled over with a noisy series of clanks.

At the sound of an automobile engine, Dorie turned to see Victor's Model A lurch to a stop in the muddy drive. She balanced the paintbrush across the top of the can and rubbed her sticky fingers on a rag. "Imbecile," she muttered. Victor wasn't due to make the delivery until after dark. She stomped across the porch and propped the screen door open with her hip.

"What if someone sees you?"

Dorie watched as Victor stepped from the car into the slush. Last spring, when Dorie could no longer make enough moonshine in her kitchen to keep up with the demand, she brought Victor Volk in as a partner. Victor had grown up in Osseo, but often wandered to other parts, picking up odd jobs, and, just when everyone had written him off as gone for good, he would return, broke but full of stories of his travels. Together, they decided to build a still out in the woods behind Buzzy Johnson's abandoned farm.

He pulled a white handkerchief out of his pocket and mopped his brow. Victor always told her they were connected in some strange way because they shared the birthday of January 1, 1900. "What a great day to be born!" he would tell everyone who would listen. Victor was far different from any of the men in Dorie's life, all of whom were dark and compact in stature. Louie called him Victor the Viking because he stood six feet tall with blond hair and white eyelashes in contrast to his very blue eyes. Once last summer when they were out at the still, Victor took off his shirt as he moved the jugs of moonshine, and Dorie was surprised to see that his chest was smooth and hairless. She was even more shocked to find herself wondering what it would be like to put her palm against his pink skin.

When he looked over his shoulder at the empty road, she yelled again. "Pull into the barn for now. Louie'll be back later to help unload." Cold winds scurried in from the north. Dorie held her dress down with one hand and rubbed the gooseflesh on her arm with the other. Why would he take such a risk?

Victor turned back toward Dorie as the wind pulled open his jacket, and she saw his shirt was stained bright with blood. "Dorie, help me," he mouthed. Dorie ran down the steps and put her arms out to steady him. Together, they stumbled in the slush. When she reached for the metal porch handrail, the cold bit her skin. She looked over her shoulder as Victor had just done to see if he'd been followed. The back of his car was full of jugs.

She pulled open the screen door as his knees started to buckle. With each heavy step, her legs trembled. As she dragged him into the porch, her arm skidded across the fresh paint on the back door. As soon as they made it into the kitchen, she hooked a ladderback chair with her foot and pulled it under him before he slumped over on the table.

Dorie's hand moved over her heart as if the pressure would slow the wild beat. She ran to the back porch and grabbed the old quilt from the wicker chair and took it out to Victor's car to throw over the cases of moonshine. The car smelled strongly of sweat and spilled moonshine.

She ran back into the kitchen and touched his shoulder. When he opened his eyes, she realized she had been holding her breath. The kitchen felt suddenly cold, and, as she closed the window, the glass rattled in its frame.

"A man was out there," Victor whispered. "He must have watched me load up."

"Take off your jacket." He sat up some. When she tried to work his arm out of his sleeve, he groaned loud enough to make Dorie jump.

She eased the suspenders from his shoulders but hesitated to lift his shirt, soaked bright red now, from the tails to the shoulder. Dorie went to the pantry to get Victor a glass, poured him a good dose of his own moonshine, looked at it for a moment, and then poured a second shot.

She set the glass on the table near his arm and nudged him. "Drink?"

Victor winced and shook his head. The dried blood on his arm stuck to the oilcloth on the table. His skin was gray, and there were beads of sweat on his upper lip. *What if he dies right here in my kitchen?* Dorie wondered. She wished Louie was there to help but knew he would only squeeze his hands into worried fists. Worse yet, he would keep drinking and then the crying would start. Then she would have a bleeding man and a crying drunk, so that would be no good.

She swallowed a mouthful of the drink and listened to the loud ticking of the clock Mother had brought from France. As the warmth settled in her belly, she put the teakettle on the stove to boil and pulled one of Louie's clean shirts from the mending basket. First she cut some notches in the shirttail and then ripped it into long strips. Victor's eyes were closed, but she watched the steady rise and fall of his back.

Dorie wasn't afraid of blood. One time, her father had carried a farmhand into their kitchen whose arm had been torn off in a thresher. Three years ago, Del Otis had stepped into a rusty bear trap and had languished in the woods for days before his wife finally found him. Dorie had helped Martha load Del, the trap, and the gangrenous mess of his leg onto a hay cart to get him help.

No, it wasn't the blood. Dorie was afraid of getting caught.

There would be questions. She couldn't lie and say Victor was a stranger. The stash of moonshine in the cellar would be safe because the linoleum sheeting covered the trap door. The car she could hide in the woods. What scared her most was thinking about the man who shot Victor. Hopefully, it was just someone who wanted to steal the delivery. Last fall, Victor had told her that someone had hid a punctured keg of oil in the car. Luckily, Victor made the discovery and dumped it in the cornfield before he could be tailed to the still. To date, that had been their closest scare. Dorie had heard stories of crooked federal agents and mobsters running operations, but those incidents were far away in the big cities like St. Paul and Minneapolis. Not in Osseo. As her heart fluttered a queer beat, she wondered if she should get her gun out of the potato bin.

"Did he follow you, Victor? Did he have a car?" Victor didn't answer.

When the teakettle started to hum, she poured the boiling water into a mixing bowl to soak the linen. Dorie squatted next to Victor's chair and started to cut the shirt from his body. The strips fell to the floor with wet slaps. Drops of blood splattered on the linoleum with irregular edges like miniature suns. She wondered when the ground would be thawed enough to bury this bloody mess in the woods.

Dorie squeezed the hot water from one of the cloths and dabbed a ragged bullet hole the size of a nickel. Victor reared up, "Sonuvabitch."

"The wound needs cleaning, Victor. Drink."

She sniffed but didn't smell any bowel. There was a smaller hole in his lower back. That meant she wouldn't have to dig it out, but she wondered what damage its course might have caused. The wet strips turned water in the bowl bright pink. "It's important to prevent infection." Her voice sounded strange—a warning to Victor of what was to come. The moonshine would kill germs.

With her weight against his shoulder, she flooded the wound until his pants were soaked and the bottle was empty. *The wild screams of a man were very different from the labor cries of a woman*, she thought. The alcohol smell burned her nose and throat. When Victor finally passed out, his arms were outstretched, and his head tipped back. Dorie sat on the floor staring at Victor's muddy shoes.

When her legs felt sturdy enough, she stood and folded more shirt scraps into thick squares and pressed them over the wounds, holding them in place by tying the long strips tightly around his ribs. If the bleeding didn't stop soon, the bullet hole would have to be cauterized.

What now? What if someone came looking for the car? Should she move him to one of the bedrooms? Everything about him was heavy. She pushed his shoulders forward so that he was leaning against the table and draped another of Louie's shirts over his shoulders. Dorie decided to tell any visitors that Victor came to the house all liquored-up and passed out right at the table. She watched the bandages redden.

The sun disappeared behind some furious looking clouds, and she shivered in her damp housedress. She pulled some wood and kindling from the bin and stuffed the stove to feed the fire. At every noise, she startled, picturing Victor's shooter at the door.

She scooped the wet strips and the remains of Victor's shirt into the enamel wash bowl, and then poured the last of the hot water into her bucket. As she rubbed the mop head with lye soap, she saw her nails were rimmed with blood.

Even after mopping, the kitchen still reeked of moonshine and blood, so she put the skillet on the stove, dropped in a dollop of lard and started chopping three large onions. The knife made loud *thwacking* noises against the cutting board. Her eyes and nose ran. Soon the kitchen was filled with the smell of frying onions. When she felt a tug on her apron she startled, and the spoon clattered to the floor.

"Victor, you scared the living daylights out of me! What is it?" She turned and pushed his blond, limp hair from his eyes.

"Dorie, you have to go out to the shack." Victor licked his lips. He was trying to catch his breath as if he had run a long distance. "I shot him." He closed his eyes and whispered, "Find him before someone else does."

2

The Plan

When Dorie heard Louie's truck pull into the driveway, Victor had been asleep, slumped over the table, for two hours. She had boiled a turkey carcass for soup. The ritual of chores and noise soothed the quiet of the afternoon. Victor snored lightly and sometimes whimpered in an almost musical pitch.

A tired ache throbbed under her breast, deep in the ribs, where she must have pulled a muscle when she helped Victor into the house. Louie whistled, "Since Ma Is Playing Ma Jong," as he made his way along the icy sidewalk. Dorie had a small moment of hope, like a bubble rising from the bottom of Eagle Lake, that when Louie heard the news about Victor, he would hold her hands and tell her he had a plan to keep them all safe. Dorie shook her head, knowing it was the fatigue, or maybe the moonshine, making her think crazy thoughts about the possibility that the husband she sent to town that morning would return to her a changed man.

"Doreee," Louie sang her name. "What's Victor's car doing here? I didn't expect him 'til tonight." He stomped his boots on the braided rug on the porch as he hung his hat on the hook. The wind briefly lifted the wooden door, and then slammed it tight. "Dorie?"

Louie hid one hand behind his back. His face was flushed, whether from the drink or the wind, she couldn't tell. His eyebrows sprouted wildly over his green eyes. His hair seemed grayer at the temples than she remembered, and he needed a haircut too, she realized. He never went to the Osseo barber for a cut. Instead, he always waited until she sat him down on a stool in the kitchen and trimmed his hair. If it weren't for her, he would probably let it grow down his back in a tangled mess of waves.

"I have a surprise for you." His wiry body thrummed with excitement.

It was candy. Every time he went to town he bought candy. Only the variety of candy changed, and even then, it was always ribbon candy, licorice, or lemon drops. Dorie would have preferred perfume or silk stockings, and she used to tell him this, but he continued to bring candy, so she stopped asking.

When he walked into the kitchen, his face creased with confusion. "Victor?"

"Victor's been shot."

The small wax bag fell to the floor. Lemon drops rolled across the linoleum sheeting, stopping where Dorie had just mopped Victor's splattered blood. Louie circled the table and stared at Victor.

"Where? Who?" He rubbed his thumb against his index finger.

Dorie wiped her hands on the apron and shrugged. "He showed up not long after you left for town. He said someone was waiting for him at the shack. He hasn't been awake much since I cleaned the wound."

"I told him to be more careful."

"I want to move him into the spare room. Then, I want you to get the delivery to the cellar before any of the regulars come tonight."

Louie bobbed his head in agreement. He usually did whatever she asked. In the first days of their marriage this was pleasing, and she would invent things for him to do around the house. It was so different from her father, who never listened to any of the ideas from his wife or six daughters. As the years went on though, it began to feel like she was directing the actions of a simpleton child.

Dorie squatted next to Victor and slung his arm across her neck. "Get on his other side, like this." She braced her legs.

Victor groaned. "Oh, Dorie," he said as his head lolled forward, pressing against her temple. The flannel shirt she had thrown over his shoulders fell to the floor, and the bare skin, the weight of him, felt like an embrace. She held her hand over the bandages to keep them in place, and then suddenly Victor clamped his hand on top of hers, pinning her fingers against the wetness.

"Take it easy, Victor," Louie said. "We're just takin' you to bed so's you can rest up."

As they made their way through the arch of the dining room, Victor stumbled and vomited a thin stream of yellow bile.

"Maybe we should call Doc Pitzer," Louie said.

"We can't. There'll be questions. Before you know it, the sheriff will be out here." She was thinking about the dead man at the still.

"But what if he—"

She couldn't see Louie's expression but heard the wetness in his voice.

Dorie cut him off. "He won't. I'll take care of him."

She clipped the edge of the table with her hip as they shuffled toward the bedroom. She pictured tomorrow's bruise staining her skin like a peony bloom.

Once in the bedroom, she yanked back the blankets just as Victor fell heavily to the mattress, pinning her arm for a moment. The metal headboard slammed against the wall. It was a small bedroom containing a single bed, a small serpentine oak dresser with an oval mirror, and a small nightstand. On the wall was her wedding photograph. Guests occasionally slept here, but mostly Dorie used the bedroom as an escape from her chain of sleepless nights.

She pulled the shade to darken the room and started thinking of things to do: cut up more bandages, heat a water bottle and get another quilt from the attic—anything to keep her mind from what might be waiting out at the still.

"Go on," she said, pushing Louie toward the door. "Get that delivery to the cellar while I change his bandages."

"Shouldn't I wait 'til dark? I could hide his car in the tool shed and move the jugs later." He shifted his weight from foot to foot.

"We need to use Victor's car this afternoon." Dorie hesitated and then undid the belt and buttons of Victor's trousers. "Yank on the cuff," she instructed Louie.

Victor's muscular thighs and calves were sparsely covered with reddish-golden hair, but it was his feet she found herself staring at as she peeled off his woolen socks. Victor had the most beautiful feet she had ever seen. She had the urge to laugh because she had a mostly naked Viking in her bed, and she was staring at his toes, so nicely proportioned, each one simply a smaller version of the largest. There were no corns or bunions or crooked shapes or sprouting hairs. Each nail was perfectly squared.

Louie cleared his throat as she quickly pulled the quilt up over Victor's shoulders.

"Go on now, Louie. It's best if he sleeps."

Dorie scooped up the clothes, watching Victor's face in the dim light.

"Why do we need Victor's car?" Louie whispered as she shut the bedroom door.

"Victor told me he shot a man at the shack—he might be dead." Something pounded thickly in her ears as she said this.

Louie's bloodshot eyes went wide, and he turned and walked to the kitchen. He rubbed his palms together as if he was trying to remove something sticky. "I don't want nothing to do with touching any murdered body. It's bad luck."

Dorie grabbed his sleeve, spinning him around. "I'll tell you about bad luck, Louie. If a body is found, how long do you think it'll take for someone to mention Victor's name, and then mine and yours?"

"That body don't prove nothin' about who shot him. People will think he was a hobo. Nobody's gonna give a thought to a dead hobo," Louie said as he poured himself a tumbler of moonshine.

Dorie realized she was clutching Victor's trousers hard enough to make her arms ache. "What if he's not some hobo? What if he's a fed? Then he'll have some kind of badge. People will come looking for a fed."

Louie crouched, picking up the scattered lemon drops. "I still think we should wait. Look at the sky, for cryin' out loud. It's gonna snow tonight or probably tomorrow. I say, let the snow cover him up."

"Goddamn it, Louie." Dorie threw the clothes on the table. "I have to go out there. What if there is a body? What if he's not dead, and he's making his way to the road right now as we're talking?"

Dorie stomped to the stove, using the lid of the stockpot to carry the steaming turkey carcass to the sink. She watched her hands tremble.

Louie came up behind her, his fingers plucking at the fabric of her housedress as he spoke. "Say this fella's dead. What if his spirit's hangin' around out there in the woods? What if we bring it home with us?" His voice was a boozy, hot whisper in her ear.

Dorie wanted to shove him out of the way. He was always touching her like that, picking at her in a desperate way. It felt as if he were trying to steal small bits of her to hold, like the candy, in his hand.

"Just move the delivery," she said through clenched teeth.

"Okay, Dorie," he agreed and drained the glass. "I'm sorry I can't—"

"I'll take care of it myself, Louie." She cut him off. She had had enough of his teary apologies to last her whole life.

"Anyway," he said as he shrugged into his overcoat, "someone should stay here and look after Victor."

3

The Body

Dorie threw a shovel into the back of Victor's Model A. The battering winds flattened her dress against her legs. The sky, so clear and blue only hours before, was now a murky shade of gray, going darker at the edges like something rescued from a fire. She leaned into the car and retrieved Victor's heavy wool overcoat, slipping her arms into the silky lining and her gun into the deep pocket. The sleeves hung over her fingertips. When she tipped her head forward, her auburn curls tumbled over her face until she stuffed them under Victor's fedora. She pushed the spark lever down, ran to the front of the car, and with both hands swung the crank around until the engine coughed twice and caught. Dorie slid behind the wheel, her teeth chattering—whether from nerves or cold, she couldn't tell. Louie's face appeared in the kitchen window. As soon as she was gone, he would probably run out to the shed and start working on another of those damn birdhouses. Meanwhile, Victor could bleed to death.

The hell with Louie, she thought, pressing down on the gas pedal as she turned on the main road.

Last summer, Victor had moved the still to the wooded acreage at the edge of the old Johnson farmstead. Buzzy Johnson had died two years earlier, and his widow followed him on the anniversary of his death. She'd had some problems with the taxes, so the bank was holding the deed until someone paid up. Victor's cousin worked at the bank and had promised to alert Victor if someone started showing any interest in buying the place. Chances of a sale were slim because the Johnson farm, like most of the places in the area, was composed primarily of gravel and poor soil that challenged each owner to produce a profitable crop.

Fat snowflakes glanced off the windshield. Dorie hoped the snow would hold off until she figured out if she was going to find a dead man, a wounded man, or no one at all. She passed the Emerson farm as Margaret set the flag on the mailbox. Dorie pulled Victor's hat low over her eyes, shielding her face with her hand. She had seen Margaret last week in Benson's Dry Goods Store in Anoka. As soon as Dorie had caught her eye to call out a greeting, Margaret dropped her bolt of cloth, spun around, and headed for the front door. Dorie wanted to call out, "Tell Howard I have his delivery of preacher's lye ready!" but Margaret was moving faster than those stumpy legs should have been able to carry her. Dorie turned the wheel, maneuvering the muddy ruts, and headed south on the small road that bordered the two farms. She looked for a parked car that might belong to a stranger.

She turned at the break in the trees that signaled the entrance to the still, slowly now, going more by feel than memory. It was darker here in the midst of the pines. Victor liked the pines because they masked the smoke. It was farther than she remembered, but just when she thought she had chosen the wrong path, the shack came into view.

Dorie popped the car out of gear and coasted to the edge of the building. Victor wasn't much of a carpenter, and this place reflected that—just a few two-by-fours covered with large pieces of rusted tin and scrap wood. The whole thing would probably blow over in a wind. She didn't fear the things that haunted Louie—boogie men and lurking creatures with scales and talons coiled in the trees ready to pounce on lost children—but instead knew the real dangers of thieves and gypsies. She shivered to think of Victor all alone out here as he prepared a batch. She climbed out of the car, listened to the knocking sounds of the engine as it cooled and watched her breath bloom in thin clouds. She fingered the gun in her pocket. Where was the other car? How had the stranger gotten here?

Burlap bags still covered the mash boxes that held the fermenting corn. She could smell the manure Victor had packed around the boxes to keep them warm and hastened the fermenting process, despite the cold. At first everything appeared as it should.

Her eyes followed the icy path to the shed. That's where she saw the first stains of blood—dark frozen blotches in a dizzy chain that lead into the gloom of the shack.

Dorie shivered. What if someone was watching? She turned around in the soft sound of the woods, hearing only the water running in the creek behind the shed and birds chirping. A sudden movement caught her eye. She raised her hand to her mouth and her gun blindly in the direction of the motion. A deer, poised and quivering, stared at her for a long moment before it crashed away through the fallen needles. Dorie's legs trembled as if the connections that held muscle to bone had liquefied.

She leaned a shaking hand on the doorframe. The mixture of sugar, fermenting corn, and manure filled her nose and throat. She held her breath and ducked inside.

In the shadows, she made out the shape of a lantern and struck the match she found in Victor's pocket to light the wick, spilling oily yellow light around her. Fat sacks of sugar and corn had been slit and overturned next to jugs of moonshine. That's when she saw the smeared bloody handprint.

Dorie scrambled to her feet and ran out of the shack, filling her lungs with cold air. She made her way up the slope behind the shack, sliding on the patches of ice and pine needles. The fermenting pot sat undisturbed on the grate atop the circle of boulders. A length of copper tubing that coiled from the pot into the six-foot-high worm box was still intact. The intruder hadn't had time to wreck the still, if that was his goal.

Behind the worm box, she spied a pair of black shoes pointed toward the tops of the trees. She moved closer, watching for any movement.

Dorie flexed her stiff fingers around the butt of the gun and circled around to the back of the box. A man was lying on his back, his muddy coat flung open to the sky. His shirt, like Victor's, was stained red and his too-white face was marked by a smear of dried blood across his forehead. She studied his features and knew she didn't recognize him, but she could almost see him lifting a black eyebrow as he flirted with a woman. His short, thick hair was matted with leaves and needles, his hands and nails caked with mud and blood. He must have been trying to climb up the hill. A gun lay inches from his hand. *Where was his car?*

She met his cloudy, fixed gaze. Dorie wondered why he didn't look more surprised by death. Snowflakes began to fall all around them, and the ones that landed in his eyes didn't melt.

Dorie pocketed her gun and knelt next to the body. She slipped her hand into his trousers and pulled out a sterling silver money clip, thick with bills and adorned with a faceted garnet, as well as a neatly folded handkerchief monogrammed with the initial "D." In the other pocket, she found a pocket watch on a chain and was startled to find it was already after five o'clock. It would soon be dark. She slid his belongings into Victor's deep pocket but put the man's gun into his own coat.

Now what? She had hoped to find his car and drive him out to the quarry, cover him with boulders at least until the thaw, but she decided she couldn't risk being caught in Victor's car. Her nose ran, and her toes felt numb. She headed back to the shed, grabbed the ax that was propped there, a length of rope and an empty burlap bag. Pulling the sled, she made her way up the slippery incline back to the body. She grabbed both his hands and lifted his torso onto the flatbed of the sled. Next, she picked up his ankles and swung his legs over.

She panted and was warmer than she had been all afternoon. She tried to tell herself this was really no different than the time after the blizzard when she had to move the calf carcasses.

The rope scratched her palms as she started tugging the sled up the hill. Head down, she concentrated on watching her boots, trying to think only of the next step, but then she couldn't help but steal looks at him, curled on his side, his arm thrown over his face, reminding her of Louie sleeping off a night's drink.

As she struggled up the hill, daylight dimmed. Soon she would be working in the dark. She realized she should have brought the lantern, but it was too late to go back for it, and she knew it would be hard to manage both the lantern and the sled.

She moved parallel to the stream as it widened, and the muscles in her shoulders pulled tight like the rope in her hands. The woods smelled of wet, rotting leaves. She stopped, looped the rope around her waist, and pulled her load like a sled dog.

In a few minutes, the south side of Eagle Lake came into view, the shore studded with pale dried grasses and broken cattails.

She scanned the lake until she spotted the dark circle of thin ice. Spring fed was how Louie explained why his favorite fishing lake never warmed, even during the hottest summer days, nor completely froze during the coldest of winters. No one ever put up an icehouse on this part of the lake for that reason. She untangled herself from the rope. When she reached for the ax, she realized it was wedged under his shoulder, and for one crazy moment she had the urge to apologize to him for the discomfort.

She stepped out onto the ice, listening for a telltale cracking. Cold seeped through her rubber boots and her shoes, drilling into her bones. She walked quickly to the dark, gray circle, and knelt at its edge. Her numb hand brought the ax down again and again, sending chips of ice and snow flying in her face. After she pried out the first loose chunk, she used both hands to make the hole bigger until she had made a ragged scar in the ice large enough, she judged, to accommodate his body.

She returned to the shoreline, back to the body on the sled. She couldn't clamp her jaws hard enough against the chattering of her teeth. She used the shovel to pry up small boulders, filling the burlap sack, stopping to test the weight and then adding a few more. She laid the heavy sack in his lap. Not trusting the ice to hold the weight of two bodies and a sled, she grabbed his ankles and pulled him off the sled toward the glistening hole. The muscles in her arms shook.

Tired and cold, she had the urge to curl up next to him, this dead, nameless man… to spoon against him like a sated lover and drift into the darkest sleep. She didn't stop though, not even long enough to curse that coward Louie. Over her shoulder, she saw the edge of the lapping water. She dropped his ankles and bent to loop the rope from the bag around his leg, tying a clumsy knot. When she heaved the bag into the water, his leg jerked as the rope pulled taut, and her heart pounded.

Dorie fell to her knees and the frigid water soaked the coat. Louie's claims that the spirit may be hovering somewhere in the woods came to mind. It seemed like she should say a prayer for the dead stranger. Instead, as she slipped his body into the water, she said, "Have mercy on my soul."

4

The Infection

In the middle of the night, Dorie heard Victor calling her name. It felt as if he was reaching into her thick, clotted dreams with both hands, yanking her back into this world. She blinked and shivered in the cold bedroom, struggling into her dressing gown. Two days had passed since she slipped the dead man into the lake, and she still couldn't get warm. A slice of moonlight divided the bed she shared with Louie. He slept, the blanket pulled high over his bony shoulder. As she pulled her hair out of the back of her robe, he snuggled toward the heat of her ghost-shape. She liked him best this way—sleeping. It was easier to recall the tenderness she once felt toward him.

Victor hollered again. It sounded as if he were arguing with someone. Dorie's feet quickly found the worn dip in each stair and then met the cool air in the dining room. His wail felt like an icy finger running the length of her spine. She pushed open the bedroom door and found him thrashing in the twisted sheets. In the amber glow of the lamp, his blond hair was wet and matted, his cheeks bright red. As she leaned over him, his hands flew up to hold her face with fingers so hot Dorie imagined they might leave a branding print. His blue eyes darted like loose marbles rolling in a pan. She placed her palm against his forehead as he yelled, "Watch out, he's got a gun!"

She knew it was the fever bringing dream-demons into the room, but when she jerked her head to look, his thumbs dug painfully into her cheekbones.

"Victor, it's Dorie. You're safe. There's no gun." She pushed his slick hair away from his forehead. His eyes focused and locked on hers, and she wondered for a moment whether he could hear her heart tumbling. Suddenly, his hands fell heavily to the sheets.

"Dorie, am I going to die?" Tears trailed along his temples.

"I need to cool you down. I'll be back."

Dorie ran to the kitchen and pulled the enamel pan from beneath the sink, slipped her feet into Louie's boots, and headed out into the backyard.

The cold wrapped around her legs, swirling up through the thin nightgown. She held the icy rail and stepped into the fresh snow on the stairs. The air of purple-blue night hung crisp and still. She used the shovel to knock the thick icicles that hung from the porch roof, stepping back as they impaled the fresh drifts.

With numb fingers she gathered and stacked the icicles in the basin as the snow worked its way over the tops of her boots, melting against her ankles. She hurried back to the kitchen and pulled the pile of old socks and rubbing alcohol from under the sink, and then ran back to the bedroom.

Victor's eyelids fluttered, revealing the whites of his eyes. The silence unnerved her more than the hollering. When she set the pan at the foot of the bed, his teeth clenched, and he reared off the pillow, his body bucking and shuddering. A thin stream of drool oozed from the tight corners of his mouth. She had heard that people could bite through their tongues during a fit like this, but she didn't see any blood in his spit. Even if she had, she doubted her ability to pry open his jaws. "Don't die. Don't die," she said to the beat of his head against the pillow. The fit seemed to go on forever, and she counted through her tears. Finally, when she reached ninety-three, he let out a long hiss of a breath and relaxed.

Dorie untangled the wet sheets from Victor's heavy thighs and dropped them to the floor. With shaking fingers, she packed the socks with icicles and placed them around his legs, torso, and arms. The rubbing alcohol made a hollow noise as she poured it into the enamel pan. She wrung out a cloth and began to wipe his face and neck. His eyes were closed, but he responded with a low growl as the alcohol glistened and ran in rivulets over his ribs, pooling in his navel.

The bandage over Victor's wound was sticky with yellow pus. As she exposed the wound to the air, the smell of rotting apples filled her nose and mouth.

Infection.

Maybe Louie was right—maybe she should have called Dr. Pitzer right away, but most of the time he charged three dollars for a handful of quinine pills that he dispensed for everything from gout to bellyaches. To Dorie, it seemed as if his presence was incidental to whether people lived or died.

Truth was, she didn't like him any more than he liked her. Last fall when she went into town to buy a dress, she saw him speaking to a group of people in the park across from St. Vincent de Paul church. She saw him before she heard him, watched the crowd sway and raise their hands as he spoke. He was in his seventies now, waiting, Dorie heard, for his replacement to arrive, but as his final days of service wound down, he had become vocal about his hatred for the use of alcohol. Dorie commented to Louie that he seemed to be grooming himself for a new vocation of preacher.

His starched white shirt had billowed across his rounded shoulders, and his pants hung low over his shoes. "Evil, evil," he had intoned. "Drink is pure evil that spreads the devil's seed, destroying families, health, and minds."

Dorie had stood at the back of the crowd and stared at his pale, folded hands. Doc Pitzer always held his hands in front of him as if he were ready to release a white dove, like a circus performer.

The people had stood in that hot September sun, fanning themselves with church bulletins, murmuring their agreement. "It's our duty to find these lawbreakers and drive them out." Spit flew from his lips as he yelled.

Dorie had snorted then, loud enough to catch his eye, loud enough to turn the heads of most of the women standing in front of her. She had walked away just as she had when he had told her with a sneer "Your hips are too narrow, an unnatural condition for birthing children."

No, she didn't want ol' Doc Pitzer in her house, those watery brown eyes looking at her as if to say "See what happens when you scoff at God?"

Her arms were heavy as she finished changing the bandages. She put her lips to Victor's forehead to gauge his fever. He was still warm, but the heat had eased for the time being. She pulled up her sewing rocker next to the bed, wrapped the quilt around her shoulders and rested her throbbing head on the damp bedding next to him.

She drifted, not quite asleep, when she felt his warm hand move through her hair, finding the base of her neck where his thumb stroked slow circles.

When she opened her eyes, Louie's face was just inches from her own.

"What?" she asked as she sat up, untangling Victor's fingers from her hair. He stared at her so strangely that she began to feel guilty about something she couldn't name.

"I woke up and didn't know where you were," Louie whispered.

"Wound's infected," she said by way of an answer. Victor was still warm when she placed her palm on his forehead. "He's running a fever."

"Maybe we should call someone."

"I told you, I don't want that old temperance bastard lecturing me and calling in the sheriff." The bed was soaked with sweat and melted ice, but Victor was resting now, so she decided to change the bedding later. She motioned Louie out of the bedroom to the kitchen.

"I wasn't talkin' about Doc Pitzer." Louie fingered the worn lapels of his plaid robe. His flat hair looked like it had been rubbed in lard.

Dorie moved to the stove to put the kettle on for coffee. "Who then?"

Louie pulled out one of the kitchen chairs and sat down. "You know Emil Erickson's daughter? The one who went off to college a few years back?"

Dorie nodded.

"What I heard is that she was going to school to be a doctor, but when her mother took ill last year, Emil brought her home to help with the younger children." His hands shook as he spoke. When he caught Dorie's stare, he pulled them under the table. "She might be able to help some."

Dorie spooned the coffee grounds into the pot and considered this. If Erickson's daughter wasn't yet a real doctor, then maybe she could buy her cooperation.

"I've heard people have been sending for her to catch babies and help with all kinds of doctor matters," Louie added.

When she grabbed him by the shoulders, he flinched. "Hurry then. Get dressed. After breakfast, I want you to drive over to Erickson's. Just say someone's sick. Don't talk about the shooting. I'll send some money with you." The money clip from the dead man was still in Victor's coat pocket. It seemed right that his money should help pay to save Victor's life.

"Don't you think I should just call her?" he asked.

"No, it'd work better if you just show up. She'll have a harder time saying no. Besides, they might not have a car."

Louie didn't answer. In the early morning light, his skin and eyes had a yellowish cast. Dorie turned back to the stove and began slicing thick pieces of ham to put into the skillet.

"But what if she won't come?"

Dorie knew he was afraid. She palmed a brown egg from the basket and had the urge to throw it in his face. First he suggested the idea, and now he balked at following through. She wanted to tell him to clean himself up and look presentable for a change—shave, trim his hair, put on a clean shirt—but there wasn't time for that now. She hoped Emil's daughter would have a soft spot for the pitiful, bloodshot look of Louie.

"Tell her it's important," she said finally. "Tell her a man's having fits from high fevers. He might die."

"Fits?" He tugged on his earlobe.

"Fits," Dorie repeated. "You don't want to see one of those. It was like an evil spirit had entered him." She couldn't resist the urge to scare him and turned around, adding the cooked potatoes to the pan so he wouldn't see her smile.

"Okay, Dorie, I'll go." He stood and started to walk out of the kitchen. Dorie was already thinking about making new bandages and changing Victor's bed when she felt him at her side again.

"It was a good idea, wasn't it?" She heard his fingers scrape the stubble on his cheeks. Water for the coffee began to boil. "To call Erickson's girl."

"Yes," Dorie sighed, "it was a good idea."

5

Lenny

Dorie was in Victor's room when Louie returned with Emil Erickson's daughter. She heard his muffled accounts of Victor's condition as they made their way to the back bedroom. Emil's daughter didn't look at Dorie but placed her leather satchel on the chair next to the bed and immediately began to examine Victor. "I'm Helena, but you can call me Lenny," she said as she pulled his eyelids open.

"Lenny," Dorie repeated. She couldn't stop staring. Louie had told her that Emil's daughter was twenty-five years old, but she looked as if she should still be walking to the high school. She was short, about five feet tall, and wore men's gray pleated trousers. Her wavy blond hair was cut chin-length in a bob style that Dorie had only read about in movie magazines.

She plucked the bandage from the oozing wound and tossed it into the pan under Dorie's arm. "Infected gunshot wound. Did your husband shoot him?" Dorie opened her mouth to deny the accusation, and then she saw the half-smile pulling at the corner of Lenny's wide mouth. "Or did you shoot him yourself?"

"No, it's nothing like that."

"Did the bullet go through him?" she asked.

Dorie nodded. "I think so."

"Help me lift him. I want to see that wound."

Dorie pulled on Victor's arm, turning him on his side.

"Mmmm, has he been awake much?"

"Not since the fever set in last night, and then he was calling out some nonsense about someone else being in the room." Dorie didn't want to mention the part about the gun.

Lenny held up a limp, wet sock and raised both brows as a question.

"I was trying to cool him off. I packed the socks with ice. It was all I could think of to cool him down."

"Clever," Lenny said. "Most people smother the patient with blankets, trying to burn the fever out." She curled her short hair behind her ears, and Dorie noticed the spray of pale freckles across her nose and cheekbones.

"First thing we need to do is get some fluids in him. See this?" She pinched the skin on the back of his hand. When she let go, the skin stayed puckered. "He's all dried out. I'll bet he hasn't used the bed pan lately, has he?"

Dorie shook her head. She hadn't thought about that.

"Make him some tea while I clean out the wound with hydrogen peroxide." Dorie smiled. It was a relief to have someone else in charge. What she wanted to do was collapse into the rocking chair and invite Lenny to minister to the ache that pounded behind her eyes.

"I'll take a cup too, if it's not too much trouble," Lenny called after her.

Dorie pushed past Louie, who lingered in the hallway.

Dorie poured dumpling batter on top the bubbling stew. She heard voices coming from the bedroom. Hopefully this meant that Victor was over the worst of it now. Lenny had spent most of the day tending to the wound while Dorie dribbled teaspoons of broth between Victor's chapped lips.

Suddenly, black dots swarmed her eyes, smothering the bright sunlight in the kitchen and the chattering voices. She let go of the spoon and blindly grabbed for something to hold onto, but her fingertips slid over the smooth enamel of the stove. Just as she seeped into blackness, she felt someone's arms catching her, easing her to the floor. She was confused and she called out, "Victor?" wondering how he was able to get out of bed in his weakened state.

"It's Louie." His voice was slow and whispery thin as if it came a great distance across the potato field.

When Dorie opened her eyes, she stared at the edge of the gray, wool braided rug, imagining she could make herself small enough to crawl into the rough furrows, away from the sharp smell of ammonia that stung her nose and throat.

"Wake up now, Dorie," Lenny commanded.

She focused on Lenny's teeth, which seemed abnormally large and white.

"We're keeping you busy today, Miss Lenny," Louie said. He knelt above Dorie's head, patting Dorie's cheek. She wanted to twist away from his touch as she did from the smelling salts. Lenny pulled her up and helped her to the kitchen chair. Her housedress was damp, and she shivered.

"Louie, could you heat up the coffee?" Lenny asked. He nodded, and Dorie watched him shuffle to the stove. He snapped three matches before he got one to catch and light.

Lenny's hand rested on Dorie's when she whispered, "Is there any possibility that a baby might be causing the fainting spell?" Her hazel eyes held Dorie's gaze.

Dorie glanced at Louie. "No, there's no chance of a baby coming. I've just forgotten to eat." This was the truth. The sun sliced through the kitchen window, and Dorie watched the dust motes fall about them like snowflakes.

"What about these cuts here? How did this happen?" Lenny examined the various scrapes and nicks on the backs of Dorie's chapped hands. Dorie stared too as if seeing her injuries for the first time since she slipped the dead body into the lake.

She held Lenny's gaze. "Hard work is all." She pushed her hands under the table.

"Mmmm, hard work." Lenny repeated.

"How's Victor?" Dorie asked.

Lenny ran her fingers through her blond waves. "The infection had a good hold of him, but he's strong. I've flushed out the wound and dressed it with gauze. I'll leave some with you. It's more sanitary than using cloth."

Dorie bit her lip and wondered if her linen bandages made the wound go bad.

"Don't worry! Really, you've done a good job nursing him up to this point. I just wish there was more we could do for him."

They watched Louie set out three cups and saucers on the table. "Keep him drinking and flush out that wound." Lenny spun her empty cup.

"It's important," Dorie paused as she plucked a wad of bills from the sleeve of her dress and pushed them across the oilcloth near Lenny's hand, "that you don't mention this to anyone." Dorie could feel her heart beat in some queer place high in her throat. All at once, her head was clear, and she realized she was ravenous.

Lenny picked up the bills and smiled. “Of course. Say, Louie, do you have anything handy to make that coffee a little more Irish?”

6

The Recovery

Dorie swished the pearl-handled razor into the warm water, leaving an eddy of soap and whiskers. Victor grinned as Dorie leaned closer. She studied his face as he pretended to scrutinize her work. He had lost weight in the two weeks since the shooting. Now his pink, shiny skin seemed to be all cheekbones and jaw, angled like the limestone rock at the swimming quarry. And then there were those eyes, so blue she had to turn away.

"Stop that," she said, meaning the smile. "I'm apt to cut you." She tried to be stern, but she couldn't manage it. It was good to see him sitting up, and she loved how the soapy smell in the room had replaced the sour air of sickness.

"Stop what?" He let his hand rest lightly on her hip. At his touch, something unwound in her belly. She elbowed his hand away.

"You forget I'm holding a razor." She wiped the blade on the towel so he wouldn't see her shaking hands.

"You'd never hurt me," he answered.

"Is that so?" She pushed his chin upward and moved the blade up his jaw line with deft movements, enjoying the sharp, scraping sounds.

"Dorie, you're not as hard-boiled as you want everyone to think. I know your secret." His Adam's apple trembled.

"Shhh. Don't talk," she said. Her hand held the back of his neck. Did he sense her terror that his death would leave her with only Louie to run the business? Or did he know she nearly jumped out of her skin every time one of the regulars came knocking at the door? She licked her dry lips and swallowed, making a clicking noise she was sure he could hear.

"Dorie," he whispered, his lips near her ear.

She flinched then, a small movement, but the tip of the razor disappeared for a second into the skin. Instantly, a trickle of blood ran a crooked path down his neck.

"Damn. I told you not to move." She pressed the towel against the cut, wondering if she would be stanching his blood for the rest of his life.

Did he really know her secret? Last night she dreamt she was in the kitchen with some of the regulars. Sam and Otto sat around the table while Freddie De Mars leaned against the counter. Dorie was telling a story about the time she had scared off some gypsies with her papa's shotgun when Victor strolled in to join the group. His hat pushed high off his forehead, he smiled as he ran a coin, end over end, back and forth across his knuckles. Suddenly everyone but Victor disappeared from the room. There was no sound as he pulled her to him and kissed her with a long, slow kiss that she had never had outside of this dream world, but it was a kiss she somehow knew. Then, the men reappeared all around her, back in their places, slapping cards on the table as Freddie plucked out a tune on his banjo. Everything was the same except for the trace of moisture on her lips. She awoke in a sweaty tangle of sheets and didn't sleep again that night.

"Anyway, I don't have any secrets." She couldn't tell him of the dreams or her fears of the sheriff or FBI pounding on her door. It was never good if a man knew too much about what was in a woman's head or heart. She lifted the towel and saw that the bleeding had stopped.

"I know you care about me." He held her wrist delicately, his thumb pressed against the thudding of her pulse.

"Of course I do," she answered. "I need you to help me run the business. If you died, do you think Louie could make the moonshine as well as you do? I'd end up selling eggs or better yet, birdhouses!" She pulled out of his grasp and busied herself picking up damp towels along with his soiled nightshirt.

"When I was in the fever, I had dreams," Victor said.

Dorie bit the inside of her cheek as she picked up the enamel water basin.

"I was held under water," he whispered.

Dorie gasped and faced Victor as the soapy water sloshed over the basin lip, wetting the front of her dress. She pictured the body she had released, gently bobbing in the frigid current against the muddy lake bottom.

"Then, I could breathe again and felt you working over me. I saw your tears, and I knew you wanted me to stay."

"Dreams, Victor. A fever delirium is all." Dorie's throat clamped tight, making it hard to swallow. She turned to leave, not trusting herself to the threatening tears. She watched him in the mirror her parents had given her for a wedding present. As he struggled into the clean shirt, a sheen of sweat broke out across his upper lip.

"I know what I know, Dorie," Victor called out after her.

Her hand closed over the doorknob. She had the urge to press her lips against his forehead, just as she had done to test his fever. She took a shaky breath, and when she pulled open the door, Louie pitched into the bedroom and tumbled to the floor.

7

The Visitor

Dorie smiled, enjoying the moment when the regulars all hung on her next word. They reminded her of ravenous dogs as she moved the full pan of scraps back and forth in front of their slobbering maws. She never sat at the table with the men who came to drink in her kitchen, instead preferring to circle the table and tell her jokes.

"Come on, finish the story!" the Schumacher brothers begged.

Dorie rolled her eyes and said, "Naw, you've heard this one before." She waived her hand at them and turned around as if to leave the room.

"We haven't heard it!" Sam cried.

"All right then." She took a deep breath and delivered the punch line with a flourish. "Then the farmer's daughter said, 'But I haven't even gotten to the milking yet!'"

Otto's greasy fingers slammed the empty glass to the table. He threw his head back and opened his mouth. Dorie could see his bad assortment of missing and crooked teeth, reminding her of bits of broken china. For a moment, no sound came out at all, and then his brother Sam joined him in an identical wheezy laugh.

Dorie opened the top button on her dress and mopped her neck with the lilac-scented handkerchief she always kept in her sleeve. The kitchen was warm tonight with the musky scent of cattle and sour milk she always associated with the brothers. They looked like twins, even though they weren't, with their round, red faces, and not more than two dozen wispy long hairs sprouting from each of their heads. Dorie liked them because they were efficient drinkers. Their dairy herd was stricter than any wife, calling for them to be up at four in the morning. Sam and Otto would be schnockered up and out the door by eight o'clock, she predicted.

Louie laughed with them, even though he had heard the story many times before, and poured them each another shot. Sam wiped his runny eyes and nose on a sorry-looking handkerchief. Dorie kept careful tabs on the drinks. Otherwise, Louie, in his own friendly stupor, was apt to wave them off at the end of the night.

"Dorie, I think that story is about you!" Otto chuckled and pulled on his large, pink ear. "Hey, fellows, it's Victor Volk. What's wrong? You're looking under the weather."

Victor shuffled slowly into the kitchen, wearing Louie's robe, the sleeves riding high on his forearms. He was still pale but smiled broadly at the group.

"What's ailing you, Vic?" Sam asked. He pushed a chair toward Victor with his boot.

Dorie and Victor had agreed earlier not to tell anyone about the shooting. While most people in the area were familiar with stories of FBI raids, gangster ambushes, and robberies, Dorie was worried that even the regulars might be scared off by the news of Victor's run-in at the still.

Victor grimaced as he slowly lowered himself onto the chair. "Appendix," Victor said simply, patting his side. "First, Dorie cut me open like a buck, right here on the kitchen table, and then she reached in and yanked it right outta me."

Dorie rolled her eyes at him and swung a dishtowel at his face. "Liar."

"Trouble was," Victor winked broadly at Otto, "my appendix didn't need taking out. She was just mad at me cuz the delivery was late."

The brothers howled their approval.

"I bet she threw it to the goat," Otto snorted, his pink face bright with mischief.

"No, she fried it up for Louie's dinner," Sam broke in, slapping the table.

"Whee, that's a good one, boys," Louie said as he poured Victor a shot.

"So, boys, how close are you to calfin' time?" Victor turned the conversation without answering their question.

"Oh, we have plenty of weeks left—not like last year when we lost the early ones in that spring blizzard," Otto answered.

Dorie moved away from the table and busied herself with some dirty glasses. It wasn't their laughter and foolishness that bothered her—it was

Victor. She was unable to look at him without her heart thudding and her mouth going dry. But none of this made any sense. This is just *Victor*, she had to remind herself a dozen times a day. For over two years he had helped her make moonshine, and she had thought of him only as a part of the business—of no more or less importance than the corn or the sugar.

She certainly had never felt this way about Louie, not even on her eighteenth birthday when she wed him at St Vincent's.

"His parents left him that farm," her mother had argued, "and, after all, it's not about happiness or love, like the silly girls today talk about. Marriage is about getting through life and raising children." And when her mother died a month later, Dorie knew she didn't want to be chained to the care of her failing father. While she didn't have any feelings of love for Louie, she was eager to escape for something different.

On Camille's deathbed, she had spoken to Dorie in hushed tones of obedience and duty. As a child, Dorie had been whipped often for her rebellious ways, so she understood the concept of compliant behavior. The duty part she figured out on her wedding night when Louie groaned and heaved above her on the gray, rough sheets of his dead parent's bed. She had bitten the inside of her cheek to keep from laughing at the silliness of it all. Thankfully, his tap, tap, tap on her shoulder occurred only occasionally. When it did, Dorie was free to let her mind wander and plan the next day's chores.

"Tell us another tale, Dorie," Louie implored. "The one about the Indian maiden and French trapper."

She realized then that she had been drying the same glass over and over. Dorie was oddly relieved to see Louie smiling and happy. Part of his jovial mood was due to the hooch and the company, she knew, so it wouldn't last beyond the evening. Still, it was a welcome change from the last two weeks when he had sullenly haunted her like the thin February shadows, appearing soundlessly in rooms and hallways. It had gotten to the point where she imagined him in the room. She would spin around and wonder how she could constantly see the ghost of a man who wasn't dead.

"On nights when the full moon flowed over the pines, the maiden would find stacks of the finest pelts—beaver, fox, mink—outside her tent," Dorie began. "She knew they must have been a gift from the most cunning hunting spirit. As the maiden gathered the soft pelts to her face, she would sing her thanks to the moon for—"

Dorie froze at the sound of a knock at the door. She looked up to see Victor's frown and spun around to see a man standing on the porch. He brought his hand near his face to peer inside, and his breath clouded the panes. She felt herself checking her hair, smoothing her dress with trembling fingers.

She threw her hip against the swollen storm door, and it opened with a sickening crack.

He tipped his hat forward. "Ma'am?" he said in a low voice.

"Yes." She squeezed the doorknob so hard it felt as if her knuckles would burst through her skin.

"I'm traveling and was told that a man could buy a drink here." He brushed away the snowflakes that had settled along the brim of his hat.

Dorie strained to study the details of his face in the hazy yellow light. The moment felt like one of her dreams, where a faceless man arrived at her door.

"Who sent you?"

"A fellow at the train station. I don't know his name."

"You're alone then?"

"Yes, ma'am."

If what he was saying was true, then it was Jake Bates who had directed him here. She had entertained travelers many times before, but since the shooting she suspected everyone of being a gun-toting fed or a thief. She cursed her lost nerve and believed she was no longer able to look a man in the eye and see what was in his heart.

He smoothed his black hair with a big hand. There were dark circles under his eyes, which might have been just shadows. He smiled then, a half smile really, his full lips parting slightly as if for a kiss.

"I can pay you well," he said.

"Dorie, what are you thinking? Let the man in—" Louie shouldered past her, pushing her against the door. He clapped the stranger on the back. "Come on in!" Louie pumped his hand and pulled him into the kitchen. A rush of cold air and the caress of his cashmere coat along her arm sent a chill up Dorie's spine.

She clenched her teeth. Damn Louie. She wanted to strangle him. He would let in the devil himself. Not for the money, of course. It was the companionship of the drink he loved.

"Louie LaValle," he said with a hand on his chest. "Over there is Sam and Otto Schumacher. My wife, Dorothy—you can call her Dorie—and Victor Volk is our big Viking."

"I didn't catch your name," Dorie said.

"Salvatore D'Agostino." The name rolled from his lips. "From Chicago." There was that half smile again.

"Glass, Dorie?" Louie asked.

She walked to the cupboard, and her hip grazed the handle of the potato bin. She pictured her gun nestled in the back corner and wondered why this stranger felt so dangerous.

"Salvatore, what brings you so far from home?" Victor asked.

"Call me Sal. I'm here on family business."

"What do you do in Chicago?" Otto asked.

"My family, they run a grocery store."

Dorie set a glass in front of Sal, and Louie poured a generous shot. "We won't be servin' long. I'm tired, and it's getting late," she warned.

Dorie raised her eyebrows at Victor. She wanted to ask him if the visitor jarred his memory of the day of the shooting. "I'm not taking in any renters either."

"No, Mrs. LaValle, I don't need a room. Just a drink, like I said."

"We're just two old bachelors who ain't much for fancy housekeeping and all, but you're welcome to stay with us anytime," Otto said.

"That's good. I might be spending some more time around these parts."

"What about the grocery business brings you here?" Victor asked. Dorie noticed that Victor hadn't touched his drink.

"It's a legal matter for Francesca, my wife. Her uncle and aunt died, and they had no surviving children, so the farm was left to her, but we're not farmers. We'd like to sell the place, but the bank says there are no buyers and some matter of unpaid taxes. I dunno. It's all a confusion." Sal shrugged and pushed back the long section of hair that had fallen over his eyes.

Dorie tasted bitterness at the back of her throat. She moved behind Victor's chair to study Sal's face directly. "Your wife's relatives? What was the name?" Dorie asked. She concentrated on keeping the muscles in her face smooth.

Sal wiped his lips with the back of his hand and smiled. There was a slight space between each of his peg teeth. "His last name was Johnson. His given name was Bernard, but Francesca said he always went by—"

"Buzzy," Dorie finished for him. Her heart tumbled as if it had come loose from its resting place and was now able to move freely around her chest.

"You're related to Buzzy Johnson!" Louie clapped him on the shoulder. "We knew Buzzy." He motioned to the Schumacher brothers. "A good man that Buzzy. A shame that consumption got him."

"Buzz helped us on more than one occasion birthin' calves. That man had a way with animals," Sam said.

Louie raised his glass. "To your wife's uncle, Buzzy Johnson, a fine man."

The men clinked their glasses.

This prompted Sam to compose his own toast. "Ahem," he said as he blinked his watery eyes. "Here's to love. Here's to caring. Here's to friends and pickled herring."

"Amen," Otto added.

Dorie joined in their toast, hoping the moonshine would ease her frantic thoughts. Did Sal know the man who shot Victor? If Sal had been looking around the Johnson place, had he seen the still?

"How long have you been in town?" Dorie asked.

"I said I just arrived on the train today, Mrs. La Valle," Sal answered. He held her gaze without blinking. There was a fine sheen of sweat across his face. Dorie tried a little half smile of her own as she leaned over the table to pour him another shot. "Call me Dorie, please. This is your first visit to our town then?"

"Yes." Sal brought the glass up to his lips. His eyes traveled slowly up and down her body. Once, as a child she had been startled while weeding in the garden when a fat garter snake had slid across her bare foot. Sal's look felt just like that snake's touch, and she had to grip the chair to keep from jumping back.

"We were not able to come for the funerals." He smiled and tossed back the shot. "You know how the grocery business can be. Besides, Francesca was with child at that time."

"How are you getting around town?" Dorie asked.

"From the train, I hitched a ride out to Buzzy's. I've been using his Tin Lizzie. It's been in the shed since he died, but it runs pretty good."

Maybe Sal was related to the dead man, or maybe they worked for the same boss. She wondered if Victor's cousin at the bank could find out if Sal was really related to Buzzy or not.

Dorie turned her head at the sound of breaking glass. Victor stared at the liquid as it ran across the linoleum. "Oh, Dorie, the glass. I'm sorry. Clumsy oaf. I must have hit it with my elbow." He bent over to retrieve the shards, but went white at the effort.

"Stop," Dorie said.

"Let me get that," Sal offered. Instantly he was kneeling next to Dorie, balancing the thick, wet pieces in the palm of his hand. Dorie wiped up the moonshine and the tiniest glittering bits with her towel. She stared at Sal's maroon silk tie. No man had ever worn such an elegant tie in her kitchen.

Dorie wanted them all gone. She wanted to be away from their voices and their smells. She wanted to stomp around in the wintry air, clear her head, and figure out what part of Sal's story might be close to the truth. She gripped the towel and felt the glass grit bite through the thin weave.

She stood up quickly. "Drink up. Time to go," she said.

"Ah, Dorie. Sal just got here," Louie complained.

"I'm tired. It's time."

The Schumacher brothers produced identically dingy handkerchiefs, cinched to hold their coins.

"It's ninety-five cents for you Otto. Sam, you owe two bits."

She heard glass clanking against metal as Sal deposited the broken glass in the basket under the sink. He stood, pulled a money clip from his pocket, and peeled off a five-dollar bill. When he moved his thumb away from the clip, Dorie recognized the heavy sterling silver and the inset garnet. It matched the one she had taken from the dead man, the one now resting in the drawer of her buffet.

"For your kindness to a traveler," Sal said as he pressed the bill into her palm. "Dorie," he whispered.

8

Trip to the Bank

Dorie warmed her left hand inside her red fox muff as she maneuvered the Model T over the icy ruts. The side curtains snapped with each gust of wind that surged across the glazed fields. She exhaled frosty plumes and tried to burrow her chin deeper into the matching fox collar of her coat, squinting against the sun's relentless glare.

"You sure you're feeling up to this?" Dorie hollered over the flap of the side curtains and the chugging of the engine.

Victor nodded. This was Victor's first outing since the shooting, and Dorie stole little looks at him as she watched the road. His cheeks and nose were red with cold, but he looked healthy. He had insisted on accompanying her to Osseo to see his cousin at the bank.

"I think we should blow up the still," Victor said suddenly. "Louie has some sticks of dynamite left from taking out those stumps last spring. It will look like a fed job—"

The thought of going to the still made Dorie's teeth chatter. "I don't want to go back there. Someone could be watching. I say we leave it and start up in a new place in the spring. It won't be long, another month or so."

"God, Dorie, I didn't mean for you to go back there. You've done enough already." Victor clenched his hands into fists.

He didn't say it, but he was referring to the body she had slipped into the lake. Last night, after Sal and the Schumacher brothers had left, and Louie had stumbled up to bed, Dorie had led Victor into the parlor and said, "I need to tell you the real story about the man who shot you." It was the first time she had spoken about that afternoon. When she had come home that day, half frozen, bleeding from cuts and scrapes, Louie had poured her a cup of coffee, but he had never asked what happened. Until that moment, Victor hadn't remembered anything about the afternoon he was shot, including how he managed to get himself to Dorie's. He listened carefully as she told him about the bloodstains, the shed, the body, and how she had dragged it to the lake. When she had finished talking, he folded her in his arms, and she relaxed against his chest, listening to his fierce heartbeat.

The memory made her blush, and she was grateful for the cold air on her face. "Sal's admitted to being at Buzzy's place. He's probably already seen the still."

"So what? He can't connect us to the still," Dorie said.

"Of course, he can! He was sitting in your kitchen drinking our moonshine last night!"

The wheels caught a rut, and the car skidded toward the ditch. Dorie pulled hard on the steering wheel. Suddenly, Victor's hand clamped firmly over her own until the car corrected itself. Fear, liquid and hot, surged though her arms and legs and pooled in her chest.

Victor leaned in closer, his nose brushing against her fox collar. "That was exciting."

She couldn't look at him. "I might not be the only person making moonshine. Maybe we can say the still was Buzzy's operation!" She passed Gunnar's mahogany-colored horses huddled together at the edge of their pasture, heads low as they nibbled a mound of hay.

Victor laughed. "You know our still doesn't look like something a dumb farmer would hook up for his own use." He leaned in closer, and she didn't push him away.

"Sal can't prove it's ours unless you hung a sign that says *Victor And Dorie's Moonshine Mill*," she teased.

He returned a tired smile. There were a few lines around his eyes now, and she fought the urge to press her lips to them. Why was she having these thoughts?

"If Sal has seen the still, then he might have seen the blood," Victor said as he began to run his thumb lightly along her jaw line.

Dorie shivered again. "There's no body to find. No one knows you've been shot except me, Louie, and Lenny." He shifted again, his fingers finding the back of her neck. "What if Sal's a fed?" she continued breathlessly. "Maybe he's got someone watching the place right now. What would happen if they caught you waltzing around the shack with sticks of dynamite in your pocket?" She realized she was coming up on the Osseo Feed Mill at the edge of town. "Move over now," she nudged him with her shoulder. "We're in town."

For a long moment, he didn't respond. Dorie concentrated on shifting the gears and glanced away from the sight of the St. Vincent de Paul church steeple.

"Anyway," she began to ease Victor's silence, "let's go find out what your cousin knows about the mysterious Salvatore D'Agostino before you start blowing things up, eh?"

Victor retreated suddenly, his warm hand pulled away from the nape of her neck. Dorie eased up on the gas and guided the car to a halt in front of the Farmer's State Bank. Victor grabbed her outstretched hand and rubbed it between his own before bringing his cupped hands to his mouth and blowing warm breath over her fingers.

"Fine. You win for now. Next time we're alone, I won't let you off so easily."

He raised one blond eyebrow as if to challenge her and continued warming her hand. Dorie struggled to focus on Ingeborg and the bank.

Dorie didn't trust banks. It wasn't natural, she thought, to hand a stranger all your money in return for a little book with a notation. Blame her worries on her Grand-père Madore, who had told her tales of outlaws and bank robbers for bedtime stories. Pierre had witnessed the Northfield bank robbery of 1876 and reveled in telling how he had crouched on the floor as eight outlaws, including Frank and Jesse James, shot the cashier in the heart when he said he couldn't operate the lock. When the townspeople heard the gunfire, Pierre told Dorie, they attacked the gang with rifles and rocks, killing or wounding six of the outlaws. Only the James brothers escaped unharmed.

No, banks were too vulnerable. Dorie kept her money close to her, hidden in empty tea tins in the barn, the sheds, and the cellar. Sometimes, for no reason she could understand, a breathless feeling would come over her, and she would drop whatever she was doing and run out to one of her hiding places. Then she would pull the rubber bands from the rounded bundles and examine and count each bill until her heart slowed its frantic beat, and she felt safe again.

The sun glinted through the leaded glass door of the bank, throwing wavy liquid prisms across the dark pine floor. She followed Victor past the tall oak desks toward the cashier window. "There's Ingeborg. Let's get in line," Victor said, taking Dorie by the elbow.

Dorie's dislike of banks was compounded by her dislike of Victor's cousin. Ingeborg Nelsen was in her late thirties, although in Dorie's opinion

Ingeborg appeared years older. Her mouth was pulled into a perpetual frown, framed by two large creases. She was too skinny for Dorie's taste, no bosom or hips to speak of, and she wore an endless array of faded black dresses. Dorie watched Ingeborg through the bars of the cashier's window. She licked her thumb prior to pulling each bill its full length through the tight grasp of her other hand. Dorie thought it looked like one hand was fighting the other. *I want the money*, one hand would say. *You're not going to get it*, the other one would answer.

Ingeborg's narrow green eyes darted as she caught sight of Victor standing in line. Victor waved at Ingeborg and then grinned at Dorie. He knew of Dorie's feelings toward Ingeborg, and yet he had never warned her to think Christian thoughts, as Louie would have, when she admitted she wanted to tie Ingeborg down, henna her nest of graying hair and burn every one of those hideous black dresses. He had only laughed and agreed that Ingeborg was a little odd. Then he explained how Ingeborg's husband, Karl, had gone missing for years during the war. When he was finally declared dead, she donned widow's attire. Later, it turned out that Karl was alive, although suffering from mustard gas poisoning, but Ingeborg continued mourning for a husband who was only partially returned to her. Dorie experienced a momentary twinge of sympathy for her. After all, didn't her own husband sometimes behave like a mustard gas victim? Still, in Dorie's mind a useless husband was no excuse for letting your looks go.

"Gosh sakes, Vic, I'd thought you'd fallen off the face of the earth!" Her eyes flickered over Dorie, who adjusted her fur collar. "Mrs. LaValle."

Dorie nodded.

"A little trip, is all," Victor answered. "But I'm back now, and I need to discuss some business with you."

"Well, you might have told someone. Mrs. Hamm didn't have any idea where you were. If your rent hadn't been paid ahead, she could have thrown your belongings into the street." Twin lines between her eyebrows deepened as she scolded him.

"You know I missed you dearly. I was going to send you a postcard, but I'm not much of a writer." Victor looked down at the hat in his hand, sheepish, remorseful.

Dorie rolled her eyes and watched Ingeborg soften, relieved that Victor could so easily charm his viperous cousin.

Ingeborg looked Victor over more carefully now. "Didn't you eat while you were away? You're looking awfully thin."

"It was slop, I tell you. Not fit for pigs—nothing like your *gasetek.* Oh, how I've missed that." Victor leaned against the counter.

"Well, then, why don't you take me to Sunday services, then stay for dinner?"

Dorie tapped her foot impatiently and broke in. "We need to know if a fellow named D'Agostino has been in here asking about Buzzy Johnson's property."

Victor threw a panicked look over his shoulder, but she felt impatient, and the lobby had mostly cleared of customers since they'd arrived.

"That's why I was trying to get you at the boarding house. You asked me to let you know if anyone came in askin' about the place. Let's go where we can talk." Ingeborg yanked the shade down and flipped a closed sign across the bars.

Dorie wasn't sure exactly what Ingeborg knew of their moonshine business. Surely, by now various town gossips had filled her ears with stories about Dorie's wicked ways. As for Victor's involvement in the production, Ingeborg most likely believed that her cousin was innocent or duped. Victor had gone to live with Ingeborg's family after his mother died, and everyone knew she had always turned a blind eye to the antics of the poor, motherless boy.

Ingeborg nodded to Mr. Farrell, the bank president, who looked over his spectacles and stroked his lush mustache as he watched his cashier escort customers into the private room. Dorie noticed that Ingeborg had the beginnings of a dowager's hump. "I'll just say you're inquiring about a loan," she said quietly.

Victor pulled out a chair for Dorie. When he sat down next to her, he pressed his thigh against hers. Dorie started to sweat in the small, windowless room. Much to Dorie's irritation, Ingeborg sat on Victor's left side so that Dorie had to lean around him to see Ingeborg's pinched face.

"Now, Vic dear, what business do you have with Mr. D'Agostino?" She placed a chapped hand over Victor's. She was still wearing her yellowed, rubber counting thimble. She probably wore it to bed, Dorie thought.

Victor moved his chair back from the table, breaking contact with Dorie's leg. "Well, first tell us what you know about him."

"He came here with a copy of Buzzy Johnson's will, saying his wife had inherited the place." Ingeborg absently touched the lace at the throat of her dress. "He caused quite a stir."

To Dorie's surprise, Ingeborg blushed.

"A stir, how?" Dorie asked.

"Well, he was from *Chicago*, and he wore the most beautiful suit." She spoke to Victor as if he had asked the question. "He was most handsome."

"What else?"

"The paperwork seemed to be in order. I assisted Mr. Farrell, who explained to Mr. D'Agostino the matter of the unpaid taxes."

Dorie slumped against the chair. So far the story matched everything they had been told. She realized she had been holding every muscle in her body as tight as a tin roof. Sal wasn't a fed or in the mob. He was just a guy who ran a grocery store and had inherited a run-down gravel farm.

"So, Vic, why are you interested in that old place, anyway? Have you found some pretty, young girl to settle down with?" She raised a thin eyebrow at Dorie.

Victor laughed. "Now, Ingie, that's my secret for now, but you'll be seated in the front pew should I ever decide to tie the knot."

Ingeborg smiled at Dorie, who had the urge to box her ears.

"Fine. I'm sure there are too many girls to count, as usual. Still, I don't see you as much of a farmer, Vic."

Dorie hated the way Ingeborg sang the word "Vic."

"You never know, " Victor said sagely. "Actually, I ran into D'Agostino just last night, and we were talking about a fair sale price. I wanted to check out his story with you to make sure he was being honest and all. Frankly, I wondered if he won it in a poker game or something, but if you say—"

"He's still in town? I would have thought someone would have seen him around. He was here, let's see, in the beginning of February. That was a month ago."

"I think Sal must have gone home to Chicago for a while because he said he just arrived yesterday."

Dorie was bored. She wanted to get away from Ingeborg's sharp chatter. There was a long list of things to get at Hessian's Dry Goods—fabric, thread, peanut butter, and flour. It had been so long since she'd been to town. Maybe she and Victor would lunch together at Schieffer's Diner.

"Sal? Who's Sal?" Ingeborg interrupted Dorie's list.

"Salvatore D'Agostino," Victor answered. "That's the fellow's first name."

"Oh, no. I distinctly remember his first name. It was Eugene," Ingeborg said. She continued dropping her voice to a whisper. "I'll never forget it. He kissed my hand and told me to call him Geno."

9

The Diner

Schieffer's Diner was located exactly in the middle of Main Street in Osseo. During the winter months, farmers gathered there at one time or another during the day to commiserate about sick cattle, the price of seed, and the aggravations of malfunctioning machinery. This time of year, there was an urgency about them, the way they jiggled a heavy boot or drummed fingers on the tabletops. They placed bets on the first day the ground would be ready to plow. They waited impatiently for spring.

Dorie loved the gleaming wood booths and tables at Schieffer's and the comforting smells of roasting meat and baking breads. When she first realized a profit from the moonshine business, she insisted that she and Louie take a meal here at least once a week. What a luxury to be relieved of the duty, if only for one day a week, of fixing a meal. She always sat near the windows as it gave her another chance to show off a new hat or frock.

This was the first time she had been there with Victor. Dorie added two heaping teaspoonfuls of sugar and cream to her cup. She stirred too quickly, and the creamy brew sloshed over the rim into the saucer. When the bell on the door jangled announcing another customer, the spoon slipped from her fingers, clattering against the table. Every sound was like something jagged scraping against her brain. She hid her trembling hands under the table and wondered if she were developing a case of nerves like her Aunt Juliet.

"We will figure out a plan, Dorie," Victor said calmly.

Dorie said nothing, but shivered as another customer opened the door, sending a blast of frigid air swirling around her ankles.

"We will put our heads together and outsmart this Salvatore D'Agostino, or whatever his name might be."

"You know what I think? Sal was looking for his missing brother. I know you don't remember him, but there's a strong resemblance." She didn't say his name aloud, but it felt like bitter medicine on her tongue: Eugene D'Agostino. The dead man whose face floated into her dreams now had a name and a family concerned enough to travel over six hundred miles to find him.

Victor waved a hand. "All those Dagos look alike to me."

Dorie shook her head. "I didn't tell you this, but I took a money clip that afternoon at the lake. It matches the one Sal had last night."

"Really—"

"There you go," Ginger said as she set Victor's plate delicately in front of him. Dorie's own plate would have landed in her lap if she hadn't brought up her hand to block it.

"Enjoy, Victor," she said as the swing of her hips brushed against his elbow.

Dorie compared her doughnut to Victor's. She tested its freshness with her finger. Hers was dry and stale, while Victor's appeared to be fresh out of the fryer.

She was suddenly reminded of making beignets with her sister Alice. She couldn't have been more than five years old at the time, because she had needed to stand on the red stool while Alice dropped dollops of batter into the bubbling grease. Alice had turned each beignet with a wire strainer. Dorie said they reminded her of ducks bobbing on a pond. Long strands of Alice's hair escaped her bun and stuck to her cheeks and neck in wet waves. Dorie fanned her with an apron, making Alice laugh. One by one she had caught the beignets in the strainer, draining them for a moment in the air before she flicked her wrist, sending them tumbling to the white, towel-covered platter. They were bumpy and golden, clotted in funny shapes like sweet potatoes. It was Dorie's job to dust them with powdered sugar by tapping the sifter with her finger. Alice didn't speak, but Dorie felt her strong hand on her shoulder as she supervised. When she had finished, Alice poured steaming chicory coffee into Mother's china cups. Next, she bunched her apron around the handle of the pan and poured steaming milk into each cup. When Alice nodded, Dorie filled her mouth again and again with the crispy, sweet warmth.

"You're studying your doughnut like a gypsy reads tea leaves."

She looked up at him. "Sorry, what were you saying?"

His hand moved across the wooden tabletop as if to cover hers, but then retreated. Instead he folded his napkin into accordion pleats. "Maybe they're related, but as far as Sal knows, his brother's only missing right now. Hell, he mighta run off with some dame."

"If Sal thought his brother ran off, then why did he end up in my kitchen on his first night in town? He most likely saw the blood out at the still and asked some questions that led him to us." She gripped the cup tightly, willing the warmth to travel through her body.

"Don't jump to conclusions. There's no body." He dropped his voice to a whisper. "If he comes to us again, of course, we don't let on we know anything about what Ingeborg told us, but we might set the idea in his mind that Geno met up with some kind of trouble. Maybe we warn him to be careful of all those rusty bear traps hidden all over Buzzy's place, or we mention the thieving bums who camp in the woods." Victor tore into his doughnut with gusto.

Dorie stared at the delicate frost that had formed along the inside of the diner window.

"I wish you remembered something about that day you got shot," she whispered under the chatter of the diner. "They don't seem like two-bit robbers, so why?" She stared at his strong fingers and blushed as she remembered his promise not to let her win the next time they were alone. "There's so much we don't know about Sal. I hate the idea of waiting for him to come after us." Dorie squirmed as the tension coiled and tightened through her shoulders and neck.

"Then let's get out of here," Victor said suddenly. "I've always wanted to see California. Come with me." He licked the sugar from his thumb.

Dorie stared and gasped. Leave Osseo? Her business? She had never traveled farther than Minneapolis. Her heart stuttered.

"It's sunny and warm there all the time." He flashed that smile that made the skin crinkle around his eyes. "Let's leave this mess with the D'Agostinos behind us."

And Louie, she thought… *leave Louie behind too*. She pictured him making birdhouse after birdhouse, forgetting to eat, drinking the rest of her stash of moonshine until it ran out.

"You're a lunatic, Victor. I'm a married woman," she hissed at him.

Victor held her gaze for a long moment, and she saw a tiny muscle twitch along his jaw.

"Yeah, you're right," he said in a rush. "I was just talking crazy nonsense."

"Coffee, hon?" Ginger refilled Victor's empty mug. He grinned that same smile at her, and Dorie felt something heavy clench in her stomach.

"Where were we before I made my little joke? Oh, yeah, a plan. I say we bring him to us and find out what he knows. I doubt he suspects a lovely woman such as yourself would have anything to do with his brother's disappearance."

"How?"

"We'll leave a message for him at the boarding house—invite him back for drinks tonight." He pushed back the shank of blond hair that always fell over his left eye.

"Then what?"

"You'll charm him."

"Me?" Dorie tasted something bitter at the back of her throat.

"I saw him looking at you last night." Victor looked at her over his coffee cup. "It won't be hard."

10

Osseo

Dorie entered Hessian's Dry Goods store and made her way to the section of fabric bolts. She fingered the red-and-cream checked cotton, calculating how much yardage it would take to replace her faded kitchen curtains. While she was not the seamstress her sister Jeanette was, she frequently sewed curtains, tablecloths, and pillows, trimming them with elaborate embroidery.

"Elsie? George?" she yelled out, "it's Dorie LaValle."

"I just got a new fabric in this morning I know you'll love," George hollered out from the back storeroom.

Dorie liked George Hessian and was relieved that his regular clerk, Elise Goetz was nowhere to be seen. George always ordered lavender soaps, perfumes, and special chocolates, all things she loved, knowing Dorie was one of the few customers who paid her tab in full. George had never been out to her place to drink, but if he disapproved of her business, he certainly never voiced any objections.

George parted the storeroom curtains, waving the bolt of fabric high about his head like a victory flag. His age was a mystery to her. He had been running the dry goods store since she was a girl, and his appearance had never changed. A mass of snow-white waves framed his unlined face. George had a stocky, powerful build with arms thick as oak branches. He even stood tree-like, his feet planted apart like old roots, bracing as if he were expecting a windstorm.

George spread out the lovely fabric… a delicate Swiss dot, the color of the lilac bush that bloomed near her barn. She had sketched a picture of the dress she wanted weeks ago—before all this trouble had started with Victor and Sal. The idea came from the occasional, precious fashion magazine—another luxury courtesy of George. She made them her own by taking a sleeve from one, a neckline from another.

"This will look lovely with your eyes, no?" George said draping the material across her shoulders.

"I'll take five yards, and thread to match. What do you have for buttons?" She didn't want to reuse buttons from one of her old dresses. She wanted something new and special.

"The minute I saw it, I knew." George tapped his temple. He began to measure out the yardage. Dorie couldn't wait to stop at Maggie Rougier's dressmaking shop. She shook with excitement. She'd order a hat too, something with lots of plumes and tulle. This is what she needed—a chance to be alone, some new things to lift her spirits. She didn't want to worry about the D'Agostinos or remember Victor's hurt look when she told him she wouldn't go to California.

"What else for you today?" George slid the shears back into his canvas apron that hung under his belly.

Dorie consulted her crumpled list, her mind momentarily blank. "Peanut butter, a pint will do." George moved the lid from the top of the barrel and plunged the scoop into the oily mixture. As he filled the wooden container, Dorie inhaled deeply and could almost taste the creamy spread on a warm slice of bread.

"A few pickles, a sack of flour, some brown sugar, oh, and a bar of lavender soap." The soap she hoarded for her own use, leaving Louie her batches of lye soap.

While George bustled around the store, gathering items from high shelves and from under the counter, Dorie admired the organization of the store. She liked the stacked tins, spools of every color of ribbon, and the tempting smells.

She pictured a store of her own with fragrant soaps, leather gloves, chocolates and silk hosiery. Of course, it wouldn't be in this town, where the women sneered at her. Not where women made do by fashioning dresses out of flour sacks and wore threadbare, darned undergarments. No, it would have to be in a big, fine city like Minneapolis where the women would know the importance of surrounding themselves with fine things.

"Dorie, anything else for you today?"

She blinked and shook her head. The vision of her imaginary store vanished in the bright sunlight flooding through George's windows. The fabric was wrapped in paper and tied with string. Her other purchases were tucked neatly into a crate.

"You have been so wonderful, George. What's my total?"

"Two dollars and sixty-five cents," he answered quickly. Like Dorie, he computed all sums in his head. As Dorie counted out the bills from her purse, she wondered if she could talk George into joining her business. She might have to do just that if Victor decided to go to California without her. What was holding him here in this small farming town of endless, terrible winters?

An ache gripped her chest, as awful as pneumonia, and at the moment, she realized she couldn't let Victor leave.

George began to sing in a baritone voice, *"Every little beat that I feel in my heart, seems to repeat, what I feel at the start. Each little sigh, tells me that I adore you."*

The notion of Victor's absence left her feeling weak and sick. Dorie swayed.

George peered over his spectacles at her. "Are you unwell? I sing too loud, maybe, huh?"

She had feelings for Victor—something more than a just a business arrangement, more than a friend.

"I'm fine, George, really, but there's one more thing. Could you get me a bag of Bull Durham?"

George nodded and quickly snared the yellow cloth bag with the pole, its yellow tag fluttering in the air like the beat of her heart. Dorie pressed some coins into his large palm as he tucked the bag into her crate.

"Is Louie doing any business in town or would you like me to put these things in your car?"

Dorie bit her lip. She had thought Victor would have met up with her here already. "If you don't mind settling them in the car, George. That would be lovely. Here, I'll take the fabric and thread directly to Maggie's."

As Dorie headed for the door, George's rich voice carried over the store. *"Anyone can see why I wanted your kiss. It had to be, but the wonder is this. Can it be true? Someone like you, could love me?"*

Dorie hummed along.

Outside, she squinted against the mid-day glare of the sun and glanced up and down Main Street hoping to glimpse Victor's broad shoulders. She didn't want him to see her looking for him, so she hurried down the sidewalk, clutching her fabric and notions close to her body against the damp air. Water dripped from the eaves of the post office, making a row of pockmarks like bullet holes in the white ice.

She passed Mrs. Setzler, who eyed her, said nothing and then turned her head sharply as if something of great interest had caught her eye across the street.

Dorie didn't know why she bothered with manners at all. What was the point? This was the response she received from most of the women in the town. She snorted. This was the treatment she received even from her own sisters.

She paused outside Claude Feltault's studio and remembered the last time all the sisters had gathered here to have their portrait taken. Her fingers counted back. Could it really have been seven years since they were all here together?

Dorie sat peacefully before Claude's mirror as she prepared herself for the session. She applied real rouge to her cheeks rather than rubbing rose petals on her cheeks as her sisters did. She continued to pull the heavy, silver brush through her long hair, even as her sisters called for her to hurry. Dorie listened to their chatter in the next room. They were so happy to be together again. All morning they had been hugging and whispering. Her sisters wouldn't admit it, but Dorie believed they were happy to be away from the drudgery of their men and children and farms.

"Dorie, Claude's waiting!" Jeanette poked her head around the velvet curtain and scolded her. Dorie bit her lips so they would look full and red and followed her into the studio.

Claude Feltault looked through the lens, shook off the camera cloak from his shoulder, and then came forward to take Dorie's hands in his warm, dry palms. Claude always smelled of tobacco and something spicy like cloves.

"So beautiful," Claude murmured.

One by one he arranged the Bibeau sisters, a ritual he had been performing for years. Claude tilted Minnie's chin this way and adjusted her necklace. At last he came to Dorie. He took her by the shoulders, moving her so that she faced him. His thumb followed her collarbone through the lace of her dress.

"Dorie," he whispered. He turned and headed back to his camera.

"Yes, it's always about Dorie," Minnie hissed.

Dorie bowed her head at the memory. Suddenly, a shape rippled next to her.

"Are you thinking of having your portrait taken?" A dark voice circled and settled around her.

Dorie turned her head. "Mr. D'Agostino, you startled me." Dorie didn't recognize her own voice.

He tipped his hat. "I apologize then."

"No. I mean, I'm not having a sitting with Mr. Feltault. I was just remembering the last time my five sisters and I met here. It was ages ago."

Sal put his hand over his heart in mock surprise. "Five sisters? Tell me," he said, his lips curling into that half smile again, "who is the most beautiful sister?"

Dorie found herself blushing despite the damp air. She stepped back because he didn't. She remembered Victor's suggestion that they invite Sal over for drinks.

"Well, if you won't confess, I'll have to look at the portrait and judge for myself." As he said the word confess, Dorie felt the blood pound in her ears. She clenched her teeth to keep them from chattering and smiled.

"Fine. Why don't you come by the house tonight, say about seven?" She kept her hands hidden in her muff.

Sal tipped his hat again, and nodded. "Seven," he repeated.

She felt him watching her as she continued down the street, and his gaze felt hot against her back. She counted each footstep, feeling awkward and unsteady. When she said "sixty" aloud, she glanced quickly over her shoulder, but he had vanished. She no longer felt like going to Maggie's.

Victor came out of the barbershop. The sight of him, clean-shaven, his blond hair slicked back and dark with tonic caused Dorie to gasp. Had it only been a little more than an hour since she'd seen him? She quickened her pace.

"Victor!" She slipped her arm through his and began to babble about Sal. "He's coming tonight, Victor. Let's go over our story. How much should we tell Louie?"

"I'm going back to Mrs. Hamm's," Victor interrupted. "I should've sent word to her."

Dorie pulled her arm from his and adjusted her packages.

“I’m well now. It’s time I stayed at my own room. I can never thank you enough Dorie, for all you’ve done for me.”

What had happened to the teasing mood of the morning? He was mad at her. She’d embarrassed him by refusing his offer to leave town.

“You must stop by tonight. Sal will be there, and I don’t know what to do.”

“Maybe I’ll come by later. That’s better, don’t you think?”

He’s not going to come. She pictured him back at the boarding house, dumping out the dresser drawers full of clothes into a suitcase, leaving behind what didn’t fit. He would catch the first train that was going west, out to California, away from the cold, and Sal, and… her.

11

Another Night With the Regulars

Freddie DeMars was a smiler. Even his lush brown mustache was waxed to mimic the shape and position of his happy mouth. He smiled so much that when Dorie first met him she thought he was a simpleton. How could anyone be so cheerful all the time?

As he pulled the bow of his fiddle across the strings, the loose sole of his boot flapped a beat against Dorie's linoleum floor, and there was that smile looking like it had been affixed to his face with two tacks. His flannel shirt was worn thin at the elbows and frayed along the collar where it rubbed against his beard. His overalls were pinned and patched with large, clumsy stitches. It must be the music that lifted his heart, she decided, because he certainly didn't have much to be happy about. His wife had died in childbirth, leaving him, a poor dairy farmer, to raise five young children.

Louie clapped his hands along to the beat of Freddie's music. He closed his eyes and lifted his sweaty face upward as if feeling the sun's rays. Dorie heard a light tap against the kitchen window. Her heart fluttered with anxiety and excitement— Sal or Victor? Louie sprang from his chair and opened the door, greeting Anton Selznick. He was alone. Dorie rubbed her arms to ease the chill that had chased across her shoulders.

Anton was in his eighties. Cursed with arthritis, his back was stooped, his joints twisted and swollen. He lived with a son and daughter-in-law at the edge of Osseo, and they faithfully took turns dropping him off at Dorie's once a week. His watery, bright eyes were always bloodshot. Anton drank more and more these days to ease his terrible aches.

"Dorie, my dear. You look lovely tonight," Anton said. Dorie helped him to a chair, easing his heavy coat from his shoulders. She thought Anton's shoulders felt like a burlap sack filled with river stones and sticks.

"Always a charmer, Anton." She poured him a healthy shot and looked away as he cupped the glass in his curled hands. All the while, she was listening for the sound of Victor's car in the drive. Maybe it was better if he didn't come tonight since she could never tell him she had feelings for him. She was tied to sadness, this failure of a farm, and Louie.

She checked her shadowed reflection in the kitchen window. Despite Anton's compliment, everything felt wrong tonight. Her favorite dark-green dress with the tiny pearl buttons pulled tight against her neck and bust. Her hair piled high on her head refused to stay fastened. Tendrils escaped, and there were lumps at the crown. Even her skin was sallow looking. She thought of going to her room to apply more rouge when she heard Sal's voice booming on the porch.

"Dorie, Louie, it's me... Sal," he sang.

Dorie put her ice-cold hands to her cheeks and had the urge to flee. Grab the money from the tins and leave. No satchel, no note. If she could just slide an arm into the sleeve of her coat, it would start the motion she needed, only she couldn't turn away from her reflection in the window. She was a child again, running away from the sounds of her sister's voices. Often, she set off barefoot and empty-handed across the hot field, the gravel biting her feet, the sun prickling over her shoulders. She talked out loud to herself about finding a family that would pamper their foundling with a trunk of new dresses and music lessons and would never make her eat beets or potatoes ever again. Eventually, Minnie was sent to fetch her, scuffing her boots across the dusty field as she dragged her home.

"Dorie, our friend Sal is here," Louie's insistent voice poked at her. She took a deep breath, pulling all her muscles tight. "I'll get it," she said. Her hand trembled reaching for the door handle. Sal grinned at her through the glass. She knew he had been drinking already, but where had he gotten it?

He stared at her from underneath heavy lids. His coat was open, and he moved his thick fingers up and down the front of his shirt.

"Bella Dorie." He steadied himself against the doorframe. His face was dark with new beard growth, and even in the chill of the porch she could detect boozy sweat mixed with musky, unwashed scent.

"Sal, I already poured you a drink!" Louie called.

As Sal brushed past Dorie, his face slid close enough for her to feel his breath against her ear.

"Excuse me," she said, wishing she'd never invited him here. She turned her attentions to Anton, poured him another drink, and mopped the splatters on the oilcloth with a clean towel.

"I don't believe Louie has made the proper introductions. Our guest is Salvatore D'Agostino, all the way from Chicago. He was related to Buzzy Johnson by marriage. He's thinking about selling the farm." Dorie turned up both palms. "Anyway, our fiddle player here is Freddie DeMars, and this is Anton Selznick."

"Where's Victor tonight?" Sal asked.

"Oh, Victor," Dorie shrugged her shoulders. "He was talking about taking a trip again. Victor comes and goes with the wind, that one does." At the mention of his name, her breath quickened.

"Anton here sees things," Louie said, squeezing his eyes shut tight as he tapped a finger against his temple. "He sees things regular folk don't—like when floods are gonna come or where lost things have gone."

"Is that so Anton? I had a Nona that could do much the same thing. My grandfather wouldn't do business with someone my Nona didn't approve of." Sal sat heavily on the chair next to Anton and scratched his chin. "I respect that."

"Have you lost anything, Sal?" Freddie asked.

Dorie cut Freddie off. "Anton is here as a guest. He's not here to perform parlor tricks." Her heart stuttered as she pictured Anton describing Geno's watery grave.

Anton chuckled, his bent fingers tapping Dorie's hands as they rested on his shoulders. "This one, she takes better care of me than my own daughter-in-law. Salvatore, my talents have been greatly exaggerated. It's really more of a feeling anyway—not like seeing pictures in books. I'm wrong more times than I'm right. Hell's bells, if I were better at it I could get a job with the travelin' circus. Come see the Amazing Anton!" He gave a wheezy chuckle. "I'd have money and see the world. Maybe I'd even get myself one of those dwarf girlfriends. Hee, hee, hee."

Sal snorted along with Louie and Freddie, who swayed slightly in his chair. "That'd be perfect for your tiny pecker, Anton," Freddie giggled behind his fiddle.

Anton's hands still covered Dorie's. If he'd heard Freddie's comment, he gave no indication. "I'll tell you what I do know as well as I know the ache in my bones. This wonderful woman here is filled with deep love and passion."

Freddie slid the bow across the strings, a few bars of a love song whose words Dorie couldn't remember. Her cheeks burned. She knew she didn't flush in the manner of delicate heroines. Instead, her skin grew blotchy and uneven, and this only increased her discomfort. Dorie bit her lip. Freddie clapped Louie on the back while Sal flashed his now familiar leering half-grin. He lifted his glass and shook the last drop above his open mouth to the tip of his protruding tongue.

Dorie spun around, moving blindly to the icebox. "Food, Anton? How about a little something to eat?" She filled her arms with sausages and cheeses—something to keep her hands busy. The food tumbled to the counter. She yanked open the metal bread box, removed the loaf of bread she had baked that morning, and began slicing. She liked the feeling of the heavy bone-handled knife. It fit perfectly against her palm.

"So, boys, do you know anyone who wants to buy a property?" Sal asked. "My family's in the grocery business. We're not farmers. If I pay the back taxes, do you think I've got a chance of selling it?"

As Freddie began to talk about Bill Dubay's interest in leasing the land, Dorie glanced up to find Anton looking at her, his wild sprouts of eyebrows raised in a question. She smiled back at him. What did Anton see? Did he know her feelings were for a man other than her husband? It was strange to think of the ownership of feelings. Freddie thought Dorie longed for Louie. Sal probably had notions that she longed for him. God only knew what Louie thought. She was glad then that Victor wasn't in the kitchen. She might not have been able to breathe if he were there.

"Buzzy's land, with the woods included, is about a hundred acres or so, is that right?" Louie asked.

"The banker, he said it was a hundred five," Sal replied.

Dorie pulled a plate down from the cupboard and piled it high with chunks of sausage and Swiss cheese. The sharp smell of fennel was comforting. She sliced thick hunks of bread and slathered them with butter.

"The woods behind Buzzy's? I wanted to ask you about that. I found a still out there, Dorie. Is it yours?"

Dorie startled at his words and the serrated edge of the knife sliced a white smile across her knuckle. When Dorie flexed her knuckle, a torrent of blood ran, across her thumb and around her wrist like a bright red bracelet. Dorie grabbed a flour sack and wrapped her hand over the sink.

"Dorie? Is that your still at Buzzy's?" Sal asked.

Her finger throbbed a beat. *Louie, remember—hold your tongue*, she screamed in her head.

"Sal, I'm not the only one with a still! Folks around here make their own. Maybe it was Buzzy's!" She stared as the dripping water mixed with the splatters of blood in the sink.

"Buzzy's been dead for two years now. This still looks like it's been used since then. Besides, it's, how would you say... a big operation."

"You know, Sal, the woods are full of bad things—thieving gypsies, bad spirits. You should be careful out there alone," Louie said slowly.

Dorie let out a breath she had been holding. She could see him struggling with the rehearsed line. Thankfully, the others would think his hesitancy was from the drink. Dorie had threatened to make him go into the woods and dismantle the still if he wouldn't help her with the story. Louie rested his face on his palm now, his sallow loose skin bunching up to close one eye. He had done his part. She couldn't expect any more help from him.

Dorie set the heavy plate on the table. "Louie's right. The woods are dangerous. When Del Otis went rabbit hunting last year, he stepped into an old rusty trap that someone had forgotten. He was caught out there for days, hollering, delirious by the time his wife, Martha, found him." Dorie leaned in closer to Sal, breathing through her mouth now so to avoid the smell of him. "By that time, gangrene had set in. We had to take off the leg below the knee." Dorie shuddered dramatically. "I can still hear his screams." When the white towel in her hand began to stain red, she hid it behind her back.

"I say watch out for wolves," Freddie said as he grabbed a hunk of sausage and bread. "There's a mangy pack of 'em out there—must not be enough for 'em to eat because they got one of my goats in November. Oh, and Rich Matsch said he found his dog all tore up." Freddie made a clawing motion at his throat.

Dorie nibbled on the smoky sausage and watched Sal. They were planting the idea that something could have happened to his brother out there alone in the woods.

"I'm not afraid," Sal said, pulling back his jacket to reveal a pistol tucked into the waistband of his pants.

"Good for you then." Anton raised his glass to Sal. "Fire away," he chuckled.

Looking at the black, oily gun against Sal's white shirt, Dorie's vision blurred for a moment. She pictured Sal's brother, Geno, so like him physically, poking around the still when Victor happened to drive up that afternoon. Geno would have had a gun tucked into his trousers just like Sal now… the gun he'd used to shoot Victor. She shuddered again.

"Dorie, you look unwell. Is anything wrong?" Anton asked.

They were all staring at her now, heads cocked, bleary eyes squinting. "I'm clumsy tonight. I've managed to nick myself is all." She held up the stained towel. "I'm going to tend to it." Dorie rushed out of the kitchen, through the parlor up the dark stairs to her bedroom.

She closed the door behind her and leaned her forehead against the cool wood, smelling the beeswax polish mixing with the stale smell of her own panic.

She moved to the dressing table. With her left hand, she awkwardly poured some water from the pitcher to the basin. The muscles in her arm began to tremble. The pitcher wobbled back and forth, striking the edge of the basin, chipping the lip of the pitcher.

Dorie cradled the pitcher against her right forearm and eased it to the dresser top. She ran her finger over the chipped edge. The missing piece resembled a tiny hoof print.

In the dim light, she unwrapped the towel and examined her wound. The bleeding had stopped. A dark-red band of dried blood ran across her knuckle. She flexed her finger, and the blood began to seep again before she plunged her hand in the water. This one would be tough to heal.

The rolls of washed bandages she had used to bind Victor's wound sat in a basket on the floor. Dorie plucked one from the basket and began to unwind it, revealing a pattern of rusty bloodstains.

She pictured him dozing on the train, his body jostling slightly with the rhythm, moving farther and farther away from her. Would he dream of her? She caught sight of her tear-stained face in the oval mirror over the dressing table. Who was this sad, weepy woman? What good were any of these tears? She wound the bandage around her finger.

More likely Victor was in a poker game in the baggage car, smoking and squinting slyly over a hand of cards. Maybe he was flirting with a young girl in the dining car, offering her a first taste of moonshine from his flask as he ran his fingertips along the back of her neck. He was free to do that after all. Who could blame him?

The cut throbbed a wicked beat now as she cinched a clumsy knot using her teeth. The pain was good. It cleared her head of silly romantic notions.

She poured more water from the pitcher into her lilac-scented handkerchief and dabbed her temples before she held it to the back of her neck. She knew she had to get back to the kitchen before Louie blabbed something. Dread, heavy and sharp-edged, crouched in her chest.

With her left hand she felt her way down the narrow staircase toward the sound of Freddie's fiddle and the stomping of boots. Maybe she could keep Freddie playing the rest of the night. That way there would be less talk and fewer questions.

She saw his shoes first. Polished gleaming tips sticking out from dark flannel trouser cuffs. Standing at the base of the stairs, she watched as he fingered, like a thief, the framed pictures and figurines she had arranged on the buffet. As she moved behind him, he lifted the sterling silver framed portrait of her sisters. His blunt thumb smeared the glass. Dorie cringed as if she had been touched and then thought of his brother's money clip stashed in the drawer with the silver.

"Well, you found the portrait of my sisters that you wanted to see," Dorie called out.

Sal, still holding the frame, turned to face her. "You took so long. I came to check on you."

"I'm bandaged."

He took her injured hand in his own and put his lips to her palm. Dorie pulled her hand away and held it close over her thudding heart.

"Tell me their names, your sisters." He held the photograph out to her. When Dorie reached out for the frame, Sal didn't relinquish his hold.

"From this end, there's Minnie. She is the eldest. Then Obeline, Jeanette, and Alice. I'm standing next to Frannie."

"You're the youngest then?"

"Yes." She tried tugging the frame from his grasp.

"And the most beautiful too." His speech was thick and more heavily accented now.

Privately, she had always believed this to be true, but she squirmed to hear the words come from his mouth. She busied herself rearranging the articles on the buffet.

"It's true then?" he asked. A shank of dark hair fell over his eyes. The oily pomade reminded her of her father.

"That I'm the most beautiful?" Dorie shrugged. "It's only an opinion—something of no weight or value." She concentrated on the crystal bobs that swung from the lamp. Sal shifted his weight, knocking the buffet and tipping the figurines. The crystals swung wildly and clinked against the lamp.

"What's true is you're full of longing and passion, like that old coot Anton claimed."

Before Dorie could reply, his hot, large palm clamped the back of her neck, his thumb digging painfully under her jawbone. In the next instant, his mouth, slick with boozy spittle, completely covered her own, blocking her nostrils as if he were attempting to eat her whole, like a snake. She pushed against him, and her injured finger bent painfully against her chest. She tried to cry out, but she was suddenly suffocating on the bitter taste of his tongue. Dorie squirmed but was held fast by that horrible hand. The portrait crashed to the floor. Glass shattered, and shards bounced off her shoes.

The fiddle stopped abruptly, followed by a shuffle of chairs. "What happened?" Louie fumbled with the latch to the pocket door. Dorie stepped back, wiping her mouth with the back of her hand. The door rattled in its track as it opened.

"I'm a stumbling drunk," Sal said. "I knocked over a picture frame, Louie. Let me give you something to repair it." Sal flicked the hair from his eyes and pulled his money clip from his pocket.

Louie was already waving him off. "Naw, not a bother." Louie, who had broken plenty of Dorie's treasures over the years, was quick to give redemption to a fellow clumsy drunk. The glass crunched under Dorie's shoes.

"Sal was just leaving. Louie can you fetch him his coat and hat?"

Sal ran his tongue over his lip. He leaned against the buffet to steady himself.

"We have an extra bed if you want to stay," Louie offered.

"No," Dorie said sharply. "Time to go."

Louie nodded and pulled nervously at his eyebrow.

Dorie tasted blood in her mouth. Couldn't Louie see what had happened? Her hair had been pulled from the clips, and her face burned. No, all he could see was that she was sending home his drinking partner. His good time was over until tomorrow.

12

Insomnia

Dorie stood over Louie where he lay sleeping on their bed, his arm flung over his chest. He made no sound at all. She held her breath and leaned in closer to his open mouth, her hair spilling across his arms and chest. Was he dead?

Suddenly he gasped a thick, clotted noise, like a drain giving way. Dorie reared back and realized that one day she might find his lifeless body.

He had looked sallow tonight, unhealthy. Maybe she should order some California Fig Syrup, guaranteed to clean out the bowels, the magazine ad had promised. This terrible winter was to blame, without a chance to be out in the fresh summer air working the fields.

In the summers, Louie's face, neck and forearms always tanned the shiny, reddish brown of a chestnut. The first year they were married, Dorie remembered him as a tight bundle of a man, springing off the tractor before the final plume of exhaust had disappeared. One day he had rushed toward the stoop where she sat in the shade snipping green beans. Even baggy overalls couldn't disguise his bow-legged canter. He turned and dashed back to the tractor, retrieving armfuls of Queen Anne's lace mixed with sprigs of wild chicory and seemed oblivious when his straw-brimmed hat blew from his head and tumbled to the ground. When he reached the shade, he relaxed his squint, revealing delicate fans of white lines around his brown eyes.

Her feelings for him that summer were gentle, not love mind you, but it was just easier to have him around. In those days, she didn't experience any anger or irritation. Now those feelings flared constantly and poked at her. It was the drinking that pushed down the best part of Louie. Was it her fault that he drank with such gusto?

Yes, it had been her idea to sell the moonshine. God knew the potato farm was sending them straight to the poorhouse. Now they paid their taxes on time, had food on the table, and she had some nice things to wear. If children were ever to come, they would be plump from good food. When they got sick, she could afford to call a doctor right away and pay for the proper medicines. If they were girls, they would have lovely dolls and matching ribbons for their hair.

Dorie sat at her dressing table and picked up a tin of face cream. She hadn't forced him to drink, but she recalled the look in his eye as he tasted that first awful batch she had made in the kitchen in the days before Victor. After all, she didn't drink very much. Oh, a shot or two when the regulars were here. A nip in coffee on a cold winter day was nice, but she didn't crave it or shake for it or look at a glass as lovingly as Louie did. She breathed in the comforting smell of lanolin and tried to push away thoughts of guilt.

She couldn't sit still. Her foot swung back and forth as if connected to some kind of motor. The tin clattered as she tossed it on the dressing table. Louie snored. She could light a stick of dynamite right here in the bedroom, and he wouldn't stir. She swung the thick mass of her hair over her shoulder and braided it.

Leaning closer to the mirror, Dorie lifted her top lip and examined the two cuts from Sal's revolting kiss. They looked smaller than they felt. She wished a horse would bash in Sal's teeth. She smiled at that thought even though it hurt her lip to do so.

She had lost some money tonight when she threw Sal out and ordered Louie to send the others on their way. Not wanting to play the gracious barmaid any longer, she had stormed up to her room and hoped they all heard the slamming door. Within the hour, she heard them leave and hoped Freddie had helped Anton get safely home. Had Louie even collected any monies tonight?

Dorie stuffed her feet into her green felt slippers and pulled her dressing gown from the hook on the door. The kitchen must be a mess. Better to clean it up now while this craziness chugged throughout her veins. She couldn't climb in bed next to Louie and believe that sleep would simply come like a mother's cool comforting hand on her forehead.

Chilled air met her as she made her way down the stairs. As she cinched her dressing gown tighter and rubbed her arms, the clock chimed the half hour—it was only 9:30. This was the time she usually wrapped things up with the regulars.

Dorie LaValle

Why was it so cold? Had that imbecile Louie neglected to fill the coal stove? Lately he seemed to have lost the threads of the day-to-day routine. Every day it was the same: "Remember to feed the stove at night so we don't freeze to death in our beds," she would remind him. "Ah, yes," he would answer, one finger pointing up at the heavens, his reply sounding like a single word. And still the next day, with the thermometer hovering at zero, she would have to instruct him again.

She hurried to the front room and saw the coals burning hot and orange through the eizenglass window. She moved closer, reveling in the pocket of warmth that surrounded the stove, smelling the slight sulfur odor.

When she turned toward the kitchen, she felt a chilling draft and saw both the back door and the porch door standing open. Wasn't it just like Louie to forget to latch the doors after the guests? Dollar bills fluttered around the floor with each icy gust.

The north winds had picked up, pinning the screen porch door against the metal handrail. Just as Dorie was about to reach for the handle, another gust of wind kicked it shut. The screw eye was torn from the wooden frame, and it dangled from the hook. Splinters surrounding the hole looked like the petals of a dried daisy.

Snow had begun to drift in—a light powdery drift on the threshold of the porch floor. Dorie picked up a length of rope that hung on the hook near the broom. She tied it around the door handle, but couldn't find anything close enough to anchor it. The porch was a shambles of barn coats, shovels, crates, and piles of knotted frayed rope, empty lanterns, and dented pails. She sighed—more chores that would have to wait until morning. She hurried back to the kitchen and slammed the door shut hard enough to rattle the panes.

Empty glasses were overturned on the table. She bent to retrieve the curled bills Freddie and Anton had left for payment amongst the crumbs. It was cold enough to see her breath. The windowpanes over the sink were painted with hoar frost. She tucked the money into her dressing gown sleeve and threw some wood in the cook stove to heat up some old coffee and water for dishes.

She busied herself clearing the dishes, wiping the table and sweeping the floor of food and grit tracked in on the bottoms of their boots. Comforted by the order, she poured herself a cup of coffee, rested her lower back against the counter, and listened to the house creak in the battering winds.

The bottle of moonshine was empty. If she was ever going to get to sleep tonight, she'd better get another one up from the cellar. After she had moved the table and chairs out of the way, she rolled up the linoleum sheeting and pulled the metal ring of the cellar trap door, propping the door against the red metal stool.

Dorie lit a candle nub as she descended into the chilly cellar. She counted the ten steps because she couldn't see them well. The flame flickered over the jars of last summer's beets, tomatoes, and cucumbers. The cold from the dirt floor caused her to shift from foot to foot. She snatched a bottle from the case and scooted up the uneven stairs just as the flame extinguished.

She shivered at the top of the stairs. When she turned around, Sal was leaning next to the counter, in the same spot where she had rested only minutes before. "What are you doing here?" she asked even though she knew the answer to the question. Her heart fluttered in her throat.

"I got all the way back to Buzzy's, but I suddenly felt bad." He rubbed his lower lip, and Dorie stared, remembering that crushing kiss. Her tongue traced the fresh cut.

"I came back to make things right again between us." He moved a step closer. Dorie clutched the neck of the bottle.

"What do you mean, make things right?" How best to get rid of him? If she was at all agreeable, he might take that as encouragement. The bottle slipped in her sweaty hands.

"You got mad at me, just when we were starting to get along. I didn't like that." He shook his head. "It made me sad." A muscle flexed in his lower jaw.

"Well, Sal, you forget I'm married. I'm not a young girl who can kiss a different suitor in the parlor every night." Her voice quavered.

"Ah, Louie. What kind of husband is he to you?" His voice leaned on the word husband.

Dorie flushed, the roots of her hair prickled.

"Aren't you married?"

"Francesca," he repeated, pursing his lips. He stepped closer and clamped his hand on hers, the one that held the bottle. His index finger rubbed the length of hers.

Was it possible to fill him with enough booze to put him to sleep or kill him? Did she dare take a swing at his head?

"Let's invite Louie down for another drink. He'd be happy to know you've come back to share our company."

"Yes, why don't we call Louie down? Oh, Louie, Louie," he bellowed, his lips close enough to her ear to leave a spray of spittle. She flinched as the sound bounced around the empty house. "Louie, it's your great friend, Sal."

What were the chances she could reach around him and pull her gun from the potato bin? She pulled her muscles tight to keep her knees from buckling.

He yanked the bottle from her hand, pulled the cork out with his teeth and spat it on the floor. He took a long pull. How much could he drink?

"He's not answering his new, great friend Sal. I'm thinking he's already in dreamland, no?"

She stepped away from him, but he moved with her like a dance partner.

"Your husband is not going to come down and discover the lovers in the kitchen. What do you think about a kiss now?" he whispered wetly into her ear.

The bone-handled knife, the one she used to cut the meats and cheeses was still in the sink with the dirty dishes. How many paces away, four or five?

Dorie swallowed a dry, painful click. She locked eyes with him but no longer trusted her own voice to answer. She shook her head and bit the inside of her cheek to steady herself. Everything about her felt loose and quivery. The clock in the parlor chimed.

Sal took another drink and set the bottle on the table. "Maybe I'm not so good at this. Maybe I offer the wrong thing." He pulled his money clip from his pocket, thick with bills, and shook it under her nose. "You love money. Is it money you want?"

Don't look at it, she told herself. The thin taste of her own blood, salty and sour, filled her mouth. Suddenly, he grabbed her wrist and jerked it back and up toward her shoulder.

Dorie screamed, a pain like touching an electric cattle fence shot through her left shoulder. He was standing close now, a terrifying embrace. She felt him swollen and stiff against her hip.

"This hair," he held up her braid. "I wanted to touch it since that first moment I saw you."

When he yanked at the ribbon fastened at the tip of her braid, her head snapped in response. His fingers crawled its length until they were completely woven into the hair at the base of her neck. When she struggled against him, he pulled her wrist up higher toward her shoulder blade.

Yell for help, she thought, but to whom? To Louie passed out in the bedroom or to God, who routinely looked away from her? Her nose ran, making it hard to breathe.

That dreadful mouth was on hers again, forcing her sore lips open as she tried to twist her head away. She bit down hard on his lip like it was a piece of gristle, hard enough to shoot a pain up through her jaw into her own ear.

Sal yelped and leaped back, releasing Dorie from the crushing mouth and the tangled grip on her hair. She wobbled and clawed blindly at the air for something to grab on to.

"You bitch!" He wiped his bloody mouth with the back of his thumb. His eyes widened when he saw his own blood. "Is this what you did to my brother before you killed him?" Sal pulled an empty money clip from his pocket—the one she had hidden in the drawer of the buffet.

"I found it in the woods," Dorie blurted out. This was true enough.

"Yet you saw mine that first night here in your kitchen and you didn't say, 'Oh, Sal, such a strange thing has happened. I found a money clip in the woods that matches yours. Let me show you.'" He mimicked her voice.

Dorie sniffed. "I didn't tell you because I wanted to keep the money for myself."

"And what were you doing out in the woods by the still you claim not to operate?"

Not one clear thought, not one lie came to her at that moment. Hot panic bubbled in her stomach.

"I think you killed my brother after you took the money he came here to hide. I've looked everywhere, but I can't find it."

Hidden money? Dorie blinked hard trying to make sense of what he was saying. She edged backward, trying to get to the sink.

"My brother came here to hide the money from our moonshine heists. Where is it? Where's my brother?" He was yelling now. His bloodshot eyes bulged, his arm swinging. She could see the gun he kept tucked into the waistband of his pants. What good was a knife against a gun? Her hip brushed against the counter.

He was moving toward her again. Dorie stumbled over the rolled linoleum, and her elbow clipped the counter. Sal grabbed her hair and wound it slowly around her throat. Her face slowly tilted up toward his as he pulled.

"Where... is... my... brother?"

Even if she wanted to confess, she wasn't able to do it now. She couldn't swallow, couldn't breathe. A terrible pressure was building, moving up her face. Her eyes felt as if they would burst from their sockets. She tried to swipe at his face, but her arms wouldn't respond, dead things hanging at her sides. Sal's face seemed to pull back from hers, surrounded by a black halo. It was like looking down the wrong end of her father's telescope. *What will Louie do when he finds my body?*

Suddenly, he released her, and she crumpled to the ground, banging her head against the cupboard door as she fell. As she gasped for air, she heard groans and scuffling. Dorie rubbed her eyes against the pain.

Victor was in the kitchen. He had his forearm wrapped around Sal's neck, and Sal clawed at it, his tongue protruding. Was this real? The pair spun around the room, flailing arms and scuffling legs, Victor's blondness against Sal's dark features, going purple now. Then, Sal brought a fist forward and rammed his elbow back into Victor's gut. Victor released his hold and fell to his knees, groaning, and tipped over on his side. He was close enough to her that she could have reached out to move the shank of hair from his eyes. Sal stood over them breathing hard as he pulled the gun out of his waistband.

"It's no bother to kill the two of ya." Sal grinned. "At first, I thought Victor here had done in my brother. Then I realized that everyone here does your bidding anyway, Dorie."

Victor lay curled on the floor, eyes closed, his face as white as the day he sat slumped and bleeding over her table.

"I shot your brother," Victor said through clenched teeth. "Dorie had nothing to do with it."

"How much time do you think you gain with that confession? Maybe I'm so mad I kill you first, or maybe I kill Dorie, and you can watch her die."

This was how it was going to end. She and Victor would bleed to death in her kitchen. There were no deals to be made after these confessions.

The screen door blew open again, slamming against the handrail. Sal looked toward the door, head cocked, frowning. Dorie crouched and lunged for Sal's legs, wrapping her arms around his knees as she propelled the both of them toward the open cellar door. Her eyes shut tight. The world was all sound. Sal's cry of surprise, the clattering of his gun across the floor, the thick, heavy tumble of his body down the steep steps, the crack of splintering wood, and finally, the sounds of breaking glass. When Dorie opened her eyes, she was left holding one of Sal's expensive shoes.

13

Another Body

A little after midnight, Dorie drank another cup of strong coffee laced with moonshine. The wild shaking of her hands had eased to a slight tremor. She propped both elbows on the kitchen table, resting her forehead against her palm because it felt like her neck might snap under the strain of holding up such a heavy weight. She pictured her head bouncing off the table, rolling across the floor, coming to rest by the wood stove. She giggled raggedly at the thought. Victor looked up over his coffee with a worried, bloodshot glance. With one finger he lightly traced the rounded bone of her wrist.

Dorie watched as his tongue felt the contours of his swollen, split lower lip. He shifted in his chair, holding a hand across his side. She hoped all that fresh, healing tissue hadn't ruptured. In the quiet of the kitchen, Dorie took stock of her own injuries. Her shoulder felt like a piece of rotted, torn linen. Her index finger throbbed whenever she brushed it against anything. The back of her head ached from where she had bumped it against the cabinet. As Victor closed the trap door and rolled back the linoleum, she found two large clumps of her own hair that Sal had yanked out by the roots.

They were alive. She wished she could ignore the fact that there was a man with a broken neck sprawled on the floor of her cellar.

"Victor," she said. He looked startled and she realized they had been sitting in silence for nearly an hour. Her voice was hoarse, her words cracked and dried like old timber. "Why did you come back tonight? I thought..." Should she tell him of her imagined scenarios?

"I said I'd stop by tonight. I thought it was better to show up toward the end of the evening." The chair creaked as he moved. "Lately it's hard to spend time here with you, Dorie, in the home you make with Louie." His fingertips moved to the inside of her wrist where they rested precisely on the beat of her pulse.

Tell him now, a voice in her head urged. Her throat ached from where Sal's fingers had dug into her windpipe and for what she felt for Victor. "You saved my life. If you hadn't come, I'd be dead now." It was all she could manage to say. She had never told any man she loved him. In books, the lovers always had a perfect moment to express their love—after a moonlit carriage ride, or in the parlor, the suitor on bended knee offering flowers or baubles. It wasn't right to tell him now—both of them raw and bedraggled.

"We're in this together, Dorie. We saved each other tonight," Victor said. He leaned closer. "Tell me what happened."

Dorie sighed and tried to concentrate on the evening's events. Was it only a few hours ago? Time seemed to have stretched and pulled itself out of shape, hanging loosely like worn elastic.

Slowly Dorie began to tell him about Freddie, Anton, and Sal arriving, and how they had told Sal about the dangers in the woods. She focused on the white half-moon of Victor's thumbnail and recalled Sal's unwanted kiss. As the words tumbled from her mouth, it seemed odd to be telling Victor about Sal's advances, and yet when she saw the muscle in his jaw contract, she was comforted by his outrage. His hand covered hers completely now, a firm pressure, and it encouraged Dorie to tell him how she had thrown the lot of them out early.

"I couldn't sleep. When I came back downstairs, I found both the back door and the porch door standing wide open. I didn't think much of it—I figured it was Louie's absentmindedness. I went down to the cellar for another bottle, and when I came up, he was standing right there." Dorie pointed. "He had a mean drunk on. I don't know how long he'd been in the house, but he'd rooted through the buffet and found Geno's money clip." Dorie touched her fingers to her throat. "He was mad enough to kill me, and he ranted on about some money that Geno had come up here to hide. He accused me of killing Geno and taking his money. He tried to strangle me with my own hair. That's when you came in." The words rushed out with her tears and Victor's clean, pressed handkerchief appeared in her hand.

"Brave Dorie."

"I didn't feel brave. I couldn't get to my gun or the knife in the sink. Worse yet, no story or lie was enough to make him stop." The clock chimed once.

"So, what do we agree on?" he asked.

The porch door flew open for the third time that evening, and Dorie flinched.

"No sheriff. I've managed to keep him at bay this long. I'm not going to invite the devil to dinner if I don't have to."

"But Sal tried to kill you. The sheriff isn't going to question your story. You would be telling him the truth. Sal came here late at night and attacked you, Dorie. His finger marks are all over your throat."

Dorie touched her throat as if the bruises were palpable things with edges or texture. "Then he'll wonder how this stranger from Chicago came to be in my kitchen in the middle of the night. Why was my cellar door open at this hour? I'm sure he's heard talk about my business. This will be the excuse he needs to arrest me." Dorie could feel the acid rise of panic. "Even I can't think of a good enough story to explain these things. Can you?"

"Could we pay him off?"

"Maybe, but what if he won't take a bribe? I can't chance that."

Dorie reached for her coffee. To her horror, her hands were shaking more than before. She grabbed the cup and squeezed until her knuckles went white, willing them with a stern look to behave, as if they were naughty children. "When is the last time you had something to eat?"

Eat? Dorie blinked and tried to remember the last time she'd sat down to a meal. She shrugged.

Victor stood slowly, his arm pressed to his side, and made his way to the icebox. "Do you have eggs?"

Dorie nodded.

Victor scooped a dollop of lard from the crock and released it into the cast iron pan with a whack of the spoon. After he lit more kindling in the stove, he began to dice a small onion and some leftover cooked potatoes. Dorie tried to stand, but Victor motioned her back into her chair. "Sit. We need strength as well as our wits about us."

No one had cooked for her since she was a small child. Victor threw a handful of onion into the sizzling lard. He lifted the pan away from the flames to keep them from burning. She liked that his back was to her because she was able to study the breadth of his shoulders without detection. From the time she spent nursing him, she was well acquainted with the exact contour of the muscles in his arms. She liked the clean, squared off line of his fresh haircut. His ears, she noticed, fit close to his head, delicately curved and pink like the inside of a clam shell.

He added eggs, stirring the mixture with a fork. Dorie watched, amazed. Of course, Victor would know how to cook for himself, although she had never stopped to consider it before. She had assumed he had taken all his meals at the boarding house, in town, or at Ingeborg's.

He dumped the mixture from her cup down the drain and refilled her cup with hot coffee. Sleepy with contentment among the smells of grilling onions and potatoes, fresh coffee, and the vision of Victor's movements, Dorie smiled, wishing the awful night's events were only a dream that would drain away when she opened her eyes.

When he set the plate of steaming eggs in front of her, her mouth watered. Victor placed a chair close to Dorie's and straddled it. He leaned his chin on his forearm and waited.

Dorie felt awkward. First he cooked for her, and now he was going to watch her eat?

"What? I have to feed you too? Are you getting me back for all the meals I took in bed? Fine. If that's the way you want it." Victor picked up a forkful of steaming eggs and brought it to her mouth.

"Wait," she said as she took the fork from him. "I can do it." The moment she slid the fork in her mouth she knew she had never tasted anything so good. Why was that? Eggs were eggs, after all. Onions were just onions. She smiled and nodded her approval, even though it hurt to swallow. "This is wonderful, but you've made enough to feed a couple of hired hands." When she looked up from the plate, Victor had produced his own fork, poised now in mid-air.

"I was waiting for you to ask."

They ate the eggs without further conversation, only the sounds of clinking silverware and the occasional slurp of coffee. Dorie felt stronger as she ate. Her cluttered thoughts arranged themselves in orderly rows. Victor fed her the last chunk of potato from his fork and cleared the table.

"Better?"

"Much better. Thank you, Victor."

"A plan then, right, Dorie?"

She looked at him. Neither wanted to be the first to ask what they were going to do with another body.

"The lake?" she said finally. She had done it once to keep them safe, and she would do it again.

Victor shook his head. "I think we need to move tonight, and the moon's only a sliver. It'll be too dark in the woods, and I don't want to risk using the lantern. Besides, there's bad weather starting." Victor held her chin, moved her face so she had to look him in the eye. "I'm on the mend now. I can do this myself."

A rush of blood thudded in her ears, nearly drowning out his words.

"Could we stash the body someplace until the ground thaws? It's already March. In six weeks or so we could bury him."

He squinted with concentration. "What if he mentioned to someone that he was coming here?"

"He admitted that he and his brother pulled heists. I don't think he talked to anyone here in town."

"Listen, if Sal disappears just like his brother, how long till another D'Agostino brother finds his way to us?" Victor moved to the stove and put on more water to boil.

He was right. Dorie didn't think she could stand any more visitors landing on her doorstep.

"Let's move him to Buzzy's. We can make it look like he had an accident. Maybe he fell out of the barn loft when he was poking around. Maybe someone robbed him," Victor said as he put the skillet in the sink. Sleet pelted the windows. "And there's no reason why Dorie LaValle's name would ever have to be uttered," he added.

"He had suspicions about you—us. What if he wrote home or sent a telegram saying as much?"

Victor shrugged.

There seemed to be so many ways to get into trouble. Could she live the rest of her life as she had lived the last month, waiting for a knock on her door? A fed? The sheriff? Another mobster from Chicago?

"So someone needs to find his body soon, and there should be no questions about his death." She was thinking out loud now, pacing around the kitchen. She saw the ribbon Sal had ripped from her hair lying on the floor. She must look a fright what with a swollen lip, wild hair, and no rouge. She turned away from Victor to smooth the front of her dressing gown, tighten the sash, and plait her hair.

"You look lovely." His hands were on her shoulders.

She turned around and leaned against his chest so he wouldn't see her blush. How odd to be pressed so close against the bodies of two men in one night in the same room! At the thought of Sal, she shuddered violently against Victor, as if someone had flicked her spine with a whip.

Victor wrapped his arms around her shoulders and rubbed small circles across the center of the ache in her back. This wasn't Sal's touch that made her sick, worlds away from Louie's desperate pawing. Victor's reddish-blond fairness, the tone and strength of his muscles, even his smell was unique. Despite the late hour, Victor still smelled of soap and the sharp tang of shaving tonic. If she could only pluck this perfect moment and shake off all the bad things clinging to it.

She moved out of his arms because it was hard to breathe, and she liked that feeling of hovering on the edge. "Buzzy's car is outside," she began. The idea came to her fast and clear. "Let's drive Sal's body to that stand of pine trees at the edge of Buzzy's drive. We'll make it look like he missed the turn and smashed the car. 'Crash broke his neck, poor fellow,' they'll say."

Victor smiled broadly and kissed her forehead with a noisy smack. "You are the most clever woman I know, but I want to do this alone. I owe you, and you've been through enough tonight."

"If there's a storm coming, you can't walk all the way back here, or all the way back to the boarding house. Either way it's too far."

"But—"

"No." She held up her hand. "I'm going to get dressed. Wait for me, and we'll haul the body out to the car together. I'll follow you out to Buzzy's and afterward drop you in town, if you want."

He looked as if he was going to protest but didn't dare.

"Your wound, the side is sore?"

Victor gave a nod that was neither yes nor no.

"I'm banged up some too, but between us we'll get this over and done with."

His pale brows creased.

"Victor, you said it yourself. We're partners. If you're feeling guilty about his death—forget it. He brought this on himself. I'm not going to feel sorry, and you shouldn't either." Saying it out loud made it seem true.

"No, it's not that." He came close and slipped his arms around her easily as if he had already spent a lifetime doing it. "You've saved my life for the second time in so many weeks. There are things I've meant to say, and it occurs to me to put the words here." He cupped both of her ears. "Trouble seems to be coming hard and fast. In case something happens, I need—"

"Wait," she put two fingers to his lips, minding the split. She was surprised at their softness. "We both have things to say, but not here." She faltered, unsure of how to explain herself. She didn't want the words, whatever Victor had to say, to be tainted by the presence of Sal's body. It was like his black spirit might seep into the moment she was sure to remember for the rest of her days. She shook her head. Now she was starting to sound like Louie.

"We'll talk later, I promise, but for now we have a chore to do," she said and pressed her hand against the warmth of his chest.

14

The Blizzard

"Buzzy's car won't start, and we've already got a few inches of snow," Victor said, his face bright red with cold. "Where does Louie keep the jug of denatured alcohol?"

"In the shed next to the barn," Dorie answered as she knelt next to Sal. "The one with the green door. The horsehair blanket should be hanging on the hook. Throw it over the hood once you get it started."

She had worried how they would get Sal's body up from the cellar, but elbow grease was all it took. Victor cinched a rope around Sal's ankles, and they pulled him up, inch by inch, ignoring the sickening thuds as his head made contact with each step.

Victor went out to start the cars while Dorie changed her clothes. She found Sal's coat stuffed behind the settee. She pictured his thick fingers rifling through her things, pulling open the drawers in the buffet. What had gone through his mind when he discovered his brother's money clip? Would he have shot her as she slept? She had the urge to scour anything he might have touched with lye soap.

It might look odd to the sheriff if Sal's coat was thrown on the seat next to him, especially in this weather, but dressing him was harder than it looked. When she pulled Sal into a sitting position to put each arm into the sleeve of his coat, his head flopped backward, and she swore she could hear the delicate crunch of shattered bones as his head lolled. She paused for a moment, slid her fingers in his pocket, and pulled out that money clip. At first she took all the bills, but then thought better of it and replaced half of them and slipped the clip back into his pocket.

Even though she knew he was dead, she wanted to hurt him, poke his glazed eyes, bend his fingers backward, and gouge his skin. The feeling left her both sick and thrilled. She didn't want to look at that face, that terrible mouth.

Breathing hard, her chemise felt damp with sweat under Louie's wool long johns. She was wearing Louie's pants too. She had learned how hard it was to move a body in a day dress. Experience was making her an expert. She had caused Sal's death, to be sure, was glad he was dead, but she didn't feel like a criminal.

She pulled on her heavy wool sweater, worked the buttons while her knuckle throbbed, then pulled her braid from the back of the sweater. She wrapped the muffler around her neck and pulled the rabbit-lined hat down low over her ears. Victor came in as she was shrugging on the heavy overcoat.

"Got 'em both running," Victor said and then blew into his fingers. "I'm wondering if we should put this off until the storm passes, maybe tomorrow night?" They both looked down at Sal's body.

"I'll jump right out of my skin if he has to stay here," Dorie blurted.

"We can move him out to one of the sheds—"

"No. Please, let's just do it and get it over with. In an hour we can put this all behind us."

Victor nodded grimly.

First, Victor rolled Sal onto his back, got behind him, and then grabbed him under the arms. Dorie threw Sal's hat on his lap and bent to grasp his ankles.

"Wait. Where's that shoe?" Dorie scanned the kitchen until she spied it on the seat of a chair. It was a new shoe, she noted, buffed to a creamy shine, the leather barely broken in across the square toe. She untied the laces, opened the tongue wide and pushed, but his foot wouldn't slip in.

"I'll get Louie's shoe horn. Where is it?" Victor asked, easing Sal's shoulders to the floor. Dorie didn't answer, but clenched her teeth and wiggled the shoe back and forth, pulling the wool stocking tight until the heel finally slid in. She tied a loopy knot.

"Ready?"

Dorie nodded and placed one of Sal's feet under each arm and stood with Victor's movement. He backed his way through the porch, checking over his shoulder. Sal's head rested at an odd angle against Victor's chest.

The running lights on Buzzy's car carved a golden path across the snow. Dorie's shoulder muscles burned and the pain crept down to her fingertips. She shifted both of Sal's feet under her left arm, struggling to keep her footing as the wet snow pelted her face. Sal's body grew heavier. She pictured him laughing as he watched them, adding invisible stones on top of his body with each step.

Victor pulled his hat low over his eyes. He paused to shift Sal's weight in a movement that looked like an obscene hug. They didn't speak, but their white clouds of breath mingled and vanished into the falling snow. When they reached the car, they dropped Sal's body. Victor leaned his lower back against the door and panted.

If Dorie had worried about the cold, her fears were wasted. Sweat ran in rivulets down her back. Meanwhile, Victor yanked and muttered curses at the frozen passenger door. Finally, he climbed in the driver's seat and kicked it open. The car rocked and settled with each blow until the door gave way with a noisy crack.

Victor spilled out of the seat and began to heave Sal's body into the car. Dorie couldn't stand to watch the crazy bob of Sal's head, so she went back to get his hat from where it had fallen near the steps. She shielded her eyes from the blowing snow and watched as Victor worked without complaint. By the time she made her way back to him, he had stuffed the body into the front seat. Sal's legs were curled on the floor, his head resting on the seat. Dorie tossed in his hat. Victor slammed the door that now refused to latch.

"It appears Sal doesn't want to go for a ride tonight," Victor grunted as he repeatedly threw his weight against the door.

"We'll have to tie it shut." Dorie hurried back to the porch to retrieve a length of rope. Mittens clenched between her teeth, she knotted the rope around the handle and flicked the remainder across Sal's body. "You'll have to hold it as you drive." Dorie turned and headed for Victor's running car.

"Wait, Dorie, I don't want you to go out to Buzzy's. Look. The snow's falling heavy here. It'll be dangerous," he called out to her. His face was hidden in the shadows.

She ran back to where he stood. "But what will you do after you leave him out there? How will you get back?"

"I'll hole up in Buzzy's barn until this thing blows through."

Horrified, she pictured him wandering in circles, trudging through the snow that would deepen and drift, first past his knees and then over his hips. She shivered as her sweat began to cool.

"No! I'm following you!" She wanted to brush away the snow that gathered on his bangs.

"Dorie, you always believe that things will be much easier than they really are. It's part of your charm, but it makes me crazy sometimes, too."

"Then it's settled. I'm following you." She turned and ran for Victor's car.

She heard him call, "Is there any stopping you?" but pretended the question was lost in the swirling snow that fell between them.

Was he angry now? All she wanted was to be with him! Dorie swiped the glass to clear the snow that had fallen since Victor had started the car. By the time she had decided to run and tell him she was more worried about his safety than her own, he had already started to pull around the drive.

"Pushy women are always unattractive," her mother's voice jumped into her ear. Was she being forward? Which was more distasteful: insisting they move Sal's body tonight or the murder itself? Dorie sensed she was operating under a whole different set of rules now and smiled at the imagined conversation.

"Murder is a mortal sin." Her mother had pressed her lips together.

"Indeed," her sisters would agree. "We can't say we're surprised at the way things have turned out."

"Get out of the car and walk," she hollered at her phantom family as the gears engaged, the jostling motion sending shooting pains through her shoulder.

Snow whipped around the outside of the car like sheets snapping on a clothesline. Snow swirled around the inside too, sneaking in between the cracks of the side curtains. Dorie could hardly distinguish between the motion of the car and the swirling snow. She followed Victor's lights, afraid to blink or ease up on the gas pedal. She'd rather follow him into the ditch than be left behind.

March blizzards usually came fast and hard, easily burying fences, stranding cattle in the fields, and then just as quickly, the accumulation would melt away by the end of the week. She gripped the steering wheel until her arms felt numb. Each time she saw the back end of Buzzy's car shift and slide, her heart mimicked the movement. Luckily, crazy fear was keeping her warm enough.

How far had they gone? Would Victor be able to see the stand of trees marking the turnoff? God knew he had driven out to the still more times than she could count, but this snow made it seem as if she were escorting Sal's body on a never-before traveled road. It felt as if they were headed to the edge of the world, some black eternity that was just beyond the blurred light. When she finally arrived there, she wanted to roll him out the door, dusting off her hands as his body tumbled into what she imagined as an eternal dark abyss.

With bare fingers, she scratched at the frost forming on the windows until they went numb. She squinted against a pain pressing behind her eyes—a headache from fatigue, moonshine, and worry. She remembered when she was a child of seven or eight, standing at the window, peering out into a storm, waiting for Grand-père Madore to return home from work.

The snow had fallen steadily all day. By late afternoon her mother had begun to pace and mutter, "Where is Papa Madore?"

"Surely he'll stay in town," Minnie said.

"Yes," added Obeline. "He's having dinner and whiskey at Hackemuler's. At this very moment he's sitting by the fire drying his stockings."

"No. He's walking home as he always does," her mother countered, and Dorie knew this was true.

At dusk, Mother had gathered her daughters in the parlor to say the rosary. Kneeling behind Obeline, her sisters followed the pious example, heads bowed, lips moving, their fingers caressing each bead. Dorie had slipped out of the room and made her way back to the front parlor. She would not say any prayers for his soul because she knew he was coming home. She pressed her forehead to the cold glass until the pain was a brilliant white. She saw it then—the glowing tip of his cigar. Holding her breath, she waited until she was sure. "It's Grand-père," she shouted, her relief like something boiling over on the stove. When he finally made it up the drive, wading in snow up to his waist, and into the chaos of the kitchen, he said, "What's the fuss? It's only a little weather!"

It's only a little weather," she repeated aloud. Why, in three months' time she and Victor would be swatting mosquitoes on the stoop, exchanging laughs, and talking of this March storm. It was an odd thing. When she pictured that future spring night, she could see the shadow of moths battering themselves against the porch light, smell the lilacs on the cool breeze. Why she even knew what dress she would be wearing—the red-and-white checked cotton with the lace-trimmed collar and cap sleeves. She could see Victor clearly too. He would have stripped down to his undershirt, his suspenders dangling loose over his hips. His cheeks and nose would be pink from the sun. A barn cat would rub against his leg as he rolled a cigarette. What she couldn't picture was Louie. She couldn't hear him, couldn't smell him. Was she seeing her future like one of the gypsies?

Did her vision mean that she might someday be divorced? She didn't know anyone who had gotten divorced, but she knew of many women who made their escape in other ways. Mrs. Cardinal probably shot her husband after he had beat her one time too many, although no one uttered their suspicions aloud. "He was cleaning his shotgun in the barn and it musta gone off," Mrs. Cardinal reported to the sheriff. The neighbors knew, however, that he always performed that ritual at the kitchen table. Then there was Mrs. Hazlack, who died after the birth of her eleventh child at the age of twenty-nine.

Divorce. She wasn't worried about muddying her reputation. The moonshine business had done that already. But what would happen to Louie? She wished he were a stray dog at the door she could ignore until he ambled over to the next farm, finding a family to take him in and give him a plate of scraps. She pictured him alone, forgetting to eat or bank the stove. He would most likely drink his way through the remainder of the moonshine stock left in the cellar and then move on to the vanilla in the pantry. And then, in desperation, he'd turn to the jugs of denatured alcohol used for the radiators. How long would he last? A matter of months? She shook her head. No. She wouldn't be responsible for his certain death too. That was too much.

What about Victor? If only she could shrug her way out of this life and make new choices. Was it even possible for a woman to do that?

Hypnotized by her own thoughts and the snow beating down on the windshield, Dorie gasped when Buzzy's car suddenly turned left and vanished. She punched the brake hard enough to cause Victor's car to lurch and slide. The motion brought her back to her childhood, to the rope swing on Eagle Lake. She would run to catch the fat, prickly knots between her hands and knees, swoop over the steep bank into the rush of sun and shadows, her stomach dropping just before she released her grip, hanging there for the longest moment before she fell into the cool water.

Only, this time there was no refreshing splash into the lake. Dorie's head snapped forward striking the steering whee, and then back against the seat just as the car came to rest.

15

Buzzy's House

She struggled into an upright position and jumped out of the car into the raging snowstorm. The back end of the car rested against the shorn-off mailbox post, the back wheels sunk deep into the fresh powder, while the front wheels reared up into the air. Curls of steam rose from the engine.

Where was Victor?

Turning around, she called his name, stumbling over the icy ruts hidden under the new snow. How much had fallen? Six inches, eight? She heard a distant hiss and moved toward the sound, her arm extended like a blind person. Snow pelted her face, and she wiped her blood-clogged nose with the back of her mitt. Right now, she would give one of her tins stuffed with rolled bills for a lantern.

"Victor, answer me!" Dorie called. The wind blasted her words into a thousand particles, each as small as a snowflake. She turned, straining to hear a sound she couldn't quite decipher. Wind? Wolf? Or was it Victor calling her? Head down, she tried to hurry, but the snow was deep here. The sweat-damp wool chilled her shoulders and back. She shivered in large, jerky spasms.

She had to find him!

When Dorie stumbled and fell, her arms plunged into the deep, fresh powder. Had she wandered off the road into the ditch? The cold cut against her skin, but she resumed wading through the thigh-deep drifts. Like a dream, the pines suddenly appeared in front of her, dark, quiet, the boughs heavy with new snow, and there, at the base of a tree, rested Buzzy's car. The engine ticked and pinged. The front of the car wrapped itself around the gashed meat of the tree as if the metal had softened like fresh butter.

All that remained of the windshield was a few jagged pieces. Had he been thrown headlong into one of the trees? Her stomach lurched. She entered the first row of pines, out of the wind and snow, into a still, black hush. How would she ever find him in this dark? Maybe if she crawled on her hands and knees, she might bump into his battered body. Would she freeze to death before she found him?

She heard a moan.

It came from behind her, in the car.

The driver's door was shut but not latched. As she swung open the door, she saw Victor slumped over on his side, his head resting on Sal's prone body. She grabbed his coat and pulled him toward her. The collar of his coat was wet. She put her fingers to his face. It was slick and sticky with blood. She flinched when her index finger grazed a piece of glass embedded in his eyebrow.

His shoulders began to shake. *He's crying. He must be in unbearable pain.* It took a minute for her to realize he was laughing.

"Victor?" She didn't know what to think. Had his mind snapped?

He tilted his head back, opened his eyes, and looked at her. "I was going to roll out of the car just before it hit the tree. At the last second, I remembered I had tied the rope that held the door around my leg. Sal was trying to take me with him." He wheezed a chuckle. "I did a good job making it look like an accident, don't you think?"

What *did* she think? Relief, worry, and beyond that, her mind raced with questions. How many cuts did he have? How much blood had he lost? Was there something wrong with his head?

Dorie's numb fingers worked to untie the rope that was cinched around Victor's thigh. "I thought we were going to stop the car and put Sal behind the wheel, and then crash it into the tree."

"You never *said* that's how we'd do it. This has my name written all over it, if I do say so myself." He held out his hands, palms up, and looked around the car.

"Anyway, it's not the time to discuss the finer points of our plan—you're bleeding. I can't see well enough to tell how bad it is." She felt around the inside of his coat for a handkerchief. His body heat warmed her hands.

"Oh, Dorie, are you making advances? Oh, hell, I've waited long enough." His arms wrapped around her back. He laughed again, trailing off into a cough. Chunks of glass glittered and crunched with each movement.

"I'm looking for your handkerchief, you fool." She was both thrilled and scared by his words. My God, he was positively silly.

Dorie's numb fingers slid into the inner pocket of his overcoat.

"What's this?" She pulled out a small box.

"Just a ring, Dorie. Something I picked up the last time I was in Minneapolis. I've been hanging on to it for, what, three months now?"

"A ring?" She opened the lid and ran a cold fingertip over the stones.

"I saw it in a jewelry store window on Nicollet Avenue. It said, 'Take me home to Dorie.' You always talk about how much you love garnets. I thought you should have something nice. I don't know. Then I got back to Osseo, and it didn't seem so right anymore because you belong to Louie, so I've just kept it."

The ring slid easily over her knuckle.

"Now this seems like such a good time to give it to you. In fact, this is just how I pictured it. I'm bleeding, in a smashed car with a dead man next to me, giving the woman I love a ring. Isn't it a rich life?"

Was it possible to have everything all wrong and right at the same time? She had scoffed at silly fables of love, but this felt close to the blush of romance.

"Victor, I'd kiss you right now, but I'm worried you'll bleed to death." There was no place to touch that wasn't covered with bits of glass and blood. "Oh, thank you. The ring is wonderful... I think... I mean." The words rushed out of her confused thoughts.

"I'd kiss you back, but my lips are too numb to feel it properly. Anyhow, I suppose you need to view the ring in the daylight to see if it passes your approval."

"That's not what I meant at all," she started, but then she felt him laughing again, heard him wheezing, and she knew he was teasing her. She suddenly realized she couldn't feel her feet. She was still standing outside the car in the deep snow.

"Please, we've got to get out of the storm. I put your car in the ditch, so I'm afraid we'll have to walk to Buzzy's farmhouse. Can you tell if anything's broken?"

"The parts that matter are working fine," he answered.

"Be serious, now." While she had heard plenty of coarse talk with the regulars around her kitchen table, his reference to his body and her effect on him made her feel like a young, tender girl.

"I'm deadly serious."

"Maybe I can put some snow on your face to stop the bleeding." Her teeth clattered.

Grabbing his arm, she ordered, "Let's see if you can move out of the car now."

Dorie backed up a step, and Victor swung his legs out of the car. She scooped some snow with her mitt, but it was too light, too dry, to press against the cuts on Victor's face. She wondered if the cold air alone was enough to staunch the bleeding.

If they just kept moving and followed the fence line it would take them to Buzzy's door.

"Can you stand?"

He nodded.

As she started to put her arm around him, she remembered her plan. What if someone finds Sal in the passenger seat? "Wait. I have to move Sal's body."

She reached into the car and tugged at his arm, bracing one foot against the running boards. The wool overcoat was wet with Victor's blood.

The body wouldn't budge. Maybe it was the angle that prevented the proper leverage or enough time had passed for him to go stiff. Suddenly, the passenger door opened. Victor lifted Sal from the floor, heaving him into the driver's seat. "Should we put him out near the trees? Make it look like he went through the windshield?" Dorie asked.

"This'll do fine." Sal's head hung back over the seat, his eyes fixed on the roof. Dorie slammed her door, causing the powdery snow that had gathered on the jagged edge of the windshield to sift down into Sal's lap. She wrapped the muffler around her face so that just her eyes were exposed. Already her mind was spinning the stories they needed to tell when the body was found in Buzzy's car. There was the matter of Victor's car and the blood on Sal's coat. How was she going to get home? What would Louie think when he awoke and found her gone? Would he call the sheriff? It seemed just as she tried to bend her mind to circle one problem, her train of thought would snap into brittle pieces. It was Victor's voice, distracting her when she most needed her wits about her, saying, *I'm giving the woman I love a ring.*

Arms around each other, heads down, they trudged, shapeless twins of sorts, through the dark snow blindness. Her limbs were tired and heavy, numb with cold. The act of walking felt like pushing something dense and unyielding. Her right mitten glanced lightly along the wavy line of the barbed wire, the fence posts. Each numb-footed step forward meant they were closer to the house.

Snow gathered on Victor's eyebrows and hair and Dorie remembered the wheezy cough. Did he have a broken rib? Would he even reach old age if he stayed with her? Guilt, heavier than her damp woolen coat or her own fatigue, settled in her chest. He had asked her to wait until after the storm passed, and she refused to listen. How long would it take for his new love to fray and give way under her demands? If they could only get to safety, she promised to mend her ways. No more pushing. No crazy ideas. She could turn her energies toward thinking of a new business. He turned to look at her, smiled a mischievous grin, and winked.

Buzzy's house lurched out of the darkness at them. In the first pale streaks of dawn, it looked as bedraggled and worn as Dorie felt. The screen door sat at the crooked angle of a loose tooth. Someone had stuffed a bed pillow in the broken window.

Dorie flashed to the summer morning, her first year as a new bride, when Lois had invited her over for blueberry pie and fresh lemonade. Lois was as round and doughy as a dinner roll, and she and her house were starched and tidy. Dorie remembered savoring the buttery crust and the clean, warm smell of her kitchen, protesting with a full mouth as Lois filled a basket full of bread and preserves for Dorie to take home "to the old bachelor Dorie had finally rescued." Now, the house stood empty, forlorn, all its history coming apart nail by nail.

"Dorie, we're here," Victor said, squeezing her shoulder.

The steps were completely covered with snow. Dorie kicked at the drift, trying to clear a path to open the door. When she yanked at the door, it pulled free from the frame, sending her stumbling against Victor, who only managed to keep them both upright by hanging onto the metal handrail.

Once inside, Victor leaned against the frame, panting deep gulps. He reached into his pocket and retrieved some matches to light the kerosene lamp on the table. In the yellow circle of light, Dorie surveyed the kitchen. Mice had taken over, as well as some larger critters, most likely raccoons—the scat on the counters and floor told her as much. Had Geno and Sal stood in this room? She turned her attention to Victor and fought the urge to gasp. His face and neck were covered with pink, frozen blood. Shards of glass glistened in the oozing wounds. What could she do for him? She needed hot water and probably a needle and thread to stitch him up, but what would she use for firewood?

She began rummaging through the cupboards, clearing the shelves of tins of spices and Rumford Baking Powder and a pail of lard with a sweep of her hand. She removed the shelf, leaned it at an angle against the wall, and kicked it until it splintered into pieces. She shoved all of these wood shards into the stove and used Victor's matches to light the fire. She hoped there was some firewood left in the barn, but if the storm didn't ease, the kitchen chairs would be the next things to go.

Next, she located a chipped enamel bowl and the frayed remains of a flour sack, both of which had been littered with mouse droppings. Holding them at arm's length, she opened the front door and flung them out into the winds before she scooped up a pan full of snow.

"Dorie, rest a minute. Don't make a fuss."

"I can see your breath! I think a fire will do us both a world of good, and I need to tend to those cuts of yours." She didn't say she desperately needed him to be well, to make up for her error in judgment.

Elbows on the table, Victor gingerly touched his face, wincing at the painful discoveries. "I don't suppose there's anything left to drink." The table wobbled under his weight.

To Dorie, it looked as though some animal had chewed at one of the legs. "Knowing Lois, I doubt there was ever any hooch here while she was alive. Buzzy bought a flask or two from us, but that was a long time ago. I'm sure the gypsies got hold of that." Dorie looked over her shoulder. She could picture Lois coming through the parlor doors, adjusting her shawl around her shoulders as she eyed the mess.

"Course, if you're desperate enough, you can make your way out to the still, that is if Sal didn't blow up the last of our stash," she teased. She was relieved that he was talking, making sense again, sounding like Victor. Waves of painful needles and pins came alive in her thawing feet and hands. She didn't think she'd ever get warm enough to remove the coat.

The large pieces of wood began to catch and snap, throwing off some meager warmth to the frigid room, but as the temperature rose, a fetid, musty smell began to simmer. The snow in the bowl began to melt. The ravaged, rank kitchen made Dorie sad. After Buzzy and Lois died, the house had stood alone, subject to vandals, both animal and human, who trespassed through these lovely rooms, ruined, stole and sold what they saw fit. If Buzzy and Lois had surviving children, all this would have turned out differently. Shuddering, she suddenly had a vision of her own dear house abandoned, tumbling down in disrepair. She had the urge to wield an ax and chase all of these long-gone intruders out of this house.

The snow continued to melt in the pan. After Dorie stirred the slush with a wooden spoon, she went back to take stock of the pantry. Food items in tins had survived the onslaught of mice: oats, salt, two cups of flour, and three tea bags. Dorie dipped the edge of the towel in warm water and went to work on Victor's face. She tilted his chin upward and brought the lamp as close as she dared and began to dab all around the deepest cuts. There were dozens and dozens of tiny nicks that seemed to have stopped bleeding, but the deep gashes in his eyebrows and forehead, and the one next to the base of his nose, the cuts with chunks of glass sprouting out of them like an evil garden, those wounds oozed and welled dark blood. Would there still be a mending kit somewhere in the house?

"You're a born nurse," he said, eyes closed.

"Okay, tell me what a nurse would do in your case."

"No, I mean it. If there's ever another war, I'm going to sign up just so's you can be my nurse."

She pinched the largest shard and pulled.

"Ouch!" he yelled.

"Sorry." Blood began to gush from the wound. It reminded her of an open mouth. She pushed the wadded towel against it, but after a full minute it was still spilling a lot of blood.

"I'm sorry," she repeated.

"It doesn't hurt that bad."

"I mean about making us drive out in this blizzard tonight. You were right. We should have waited. Hold this," she instructed Victor.

"I could have said no, you know. I'm not completely powerless in your presence." She held her breath. "So, is it big enough?" he asked.

"The cut?"

"No, the ring."

"I'm not going to answer you right now." Her thoughts scurried around the items that had been left in the house. Should she try to make some bandages to press against the wounds? But it would be impossible to keep them in place. She paced in front of the pantry. A memory came to her, watching Obeline make gravy for the first time. She had added so much flour that the juices congealed to jelly.

Dorie retrieved the tin of flour and opened the lid. She scooped a bit with her palm and, tipping his head back as far as it would go, she emptied her palm over the cut.

"What are you doing?"

"Trying something—don't move a muscle."

The flour turned red, swelled, even bubbled slightly, and then the bleeding stopped. He unbuttoned the first three buttons of his coat.

"Hold still."

"I'm not moving my face!"

She repeated the process until all the bleeding was controlled. As she worked, the room warmed, and her own aches came alive—the bridge of her nose throbbed, and her shoulder stiffened. She held the mess of the towel and surveyed Victor's face. With most of the blood cleaned up, he looked somewhat better, but he was going to have some nasty scars on that handsome face. The room at once began to swell around her, and she grabbed his shoulder.

"You're exhausted—hell, we both are. We need to sleep." Victor's low voice hummed in her ears.

With one hand, Victor picked up the chair and smashed it against the stove until it was a pile of shattered chunks and spindles. As he fed it into the stove, Dorie sent a silent apology to Lois.

Victor held the lantern as they walked to the parlor. Dorie propped open the door to the kitchen to let in the meager heat. They curled up together on the settee. Sleep pulled her body into its dark current so quickly that she didn't even have time to enjoy the peace of drifting off in Victor's arms.

16

Keeping Warm

Dorie awoke under a pile of musty quilts with Victor's heavy arm draped across her shoulder. The windows rattled in their frames. She liked hovering on this sweet edge of sleep. What time was it? She sighed. Physical discomforts pulled her into the waking world. Her mouth was dry—she was sure she had never been so thirsty. Needing to relieve herself, she edged off the settee, not wanting to disturb his sleep. She almost laughed out loud when she discovered she had slept in her coat and boots. She was stiff all over, but at least the dreamless sleep had left her rested.

Gray light leaked through the moth-eaten draperies. Dorie pulled back a dusty panel to survey the falling snow. Branches of the giant red oak wore a coat of white. The wind had picked up again, sculpting drifts across the pasture in white, frozen waves. Only the stubby tops of bent and yellowed cattails were visible by the watering hole. She let the curtain fall.

The short hair around Victor's ears was stiff and tinged with dried blood. The cut running through his left eyebrow was swollen, making it look like he was enjoying a skeptical dream moment. Her hand reached out to caress the curve of his cheekbone even though he slept halfway across the room. The ache for him was larger than her body could hold.

The old house creaked and groaned as the north winds bore down. It would be a while before she could get home. Would Louie be up yet? What would he think when he found her gone?

Tiptoeing into the kitchen, she found a few embers still glowing in the stove. Another missing chair meant Victor must have gotten up sometime in the night to tend the fire. Dorie eyed the stained magnolia wallpaper and reached up and grabbed the curled edge and pulled the long sheet away from the wall. Bits of dried flour paste fell to the floor. She pulled out a drawer from the pantry, dumped its contents and brought it down with a hard crack against the counter. She stuffed the paper and the smaller pieces of wood into the stove. She was happy to see her mittens and muffler had dried. She bundled up again and grabbed the enamel pan from the stove. The pink-tinged water sloshed in the pan as she made her way to the door.

She turned the knob and pushed, but the door wouldn't budge. There must be a drift pinning the door shut. The need to empty her full bladder was overwhelming now. She was too embarrassed to have Victor wake and find her squatting over a slop pail, if she could find one that is, so she pushed her good shoulder against the door, again and again, until it began to move. Snow began to swirl about the kitchen in an icy blast. Finally, she cleared enough of an opening to slip out. Stepping into the deep drift, snow, fine as sand particles, batted at her face and eyes. She held her mitten up to ward off the assault. The screen door Victor had propped up next to the steps was nearly buried. Holding the rail, she eased herself into the deep drift that blanketed the steps.

The gray sky and white snow pulled all color from the sheds and barn and blurred their hard edges. She could barely make out the ghost-like hood of an old tractor parked at the far edge of the property, which looked as if it were about to dissolve like bouillon dropped into boiling water. Once past the drift, the snow wasn't nearly as deep. She leaned into the wind and made her way to the outhouse. The door swung open easily, revealing piles of snow on the warped floor. A ragged curtain was plastered against the screen. Pages from the tattered stacks of old Montgomery Wards catalogues fluttered as the wind whistled a low pitch through the cracks in the walls. After she wrestled the frozen lid free, she relieved herself as quickly as possible and made her way back to the house, stopping to scoop another pan of snow. She cupped a mitten full of snow and brought it to her mouth. It melted against her tongue, fresh and cold.

Back in the house, the kitchen had begun to warm. After she brushed off the snow that clung to her trousers and coat, she set the pan on the burner and went in search of cups to hold tea. A photograph fluttered out of one of the pantry cupboards, and Dorie bent to retrieve it, moving to the window for better light. It was a wedding portrait of Buzzy and Lois. The groom's bushy mustache hid his mouth as he stood behind his new bride, one hand holding the lapel of his morning coat, the other resting on her shoulder. Lois sat washboard straight, holding a bouquet of pale roses, her ankles crossed. Lois had told Dorie she had married at the age of fifteen, which was nearly half Dorie's age. Did she ever again get to wear a dress as lovely as that one? Was she nervous? Afraid? Did she love Buzzy? What kind of life did they have together? Dorie couldn't remember seeing them sharing a loving look or a dance at the pavilion. It seemed as though Buzzy was usually out in the fields or tending to chores in the barn. The most she saw of him was the back of his sunburned neck at church services or the tip of his hat as he passed her on the road. From what Dorie knew, Lois cared for the house and spent more time with her dog, the one she referred to as "you ol' sinner," than she did with Buzzy, yet Dorie knew they ran their farm like a sewing machine, topstitch thread and bobbin. What chore one didn't do, the other did. She ran a chapped finger over the torn edges, over their faces to reveal their story with a touch.

She slipped the portrait into the pocket of her coat and began to tend to the tea, making do with two battered tin measuring cups. She gathered the bloodstained towel to protect her fingers against the hot enamel pan and sloshed the steaming water into the two cups. There wasn't a grain of sugar left in any of the tins. Slipping out of her coat, she carried the cups into the parlor, enjoying the warmth of the tin against her hand.

Victor was sitting up, smiling. Dorie couldn't suppress a gasp at the sight of him.

"I am a handsome devil, aren't I?"

"Most days, yes."

His face was a mass of dried blood, swollen, angry cuts, and tender pink skin. She hoped the flour paste hadn't done him more harm than good. Now that it was light, she could search more easily for a needle and thread.

"I made you some tea."

He didn't answer, only stared at her, making her flush with embarrassment. She couldn't check her appearance, but knew she probably didn't look much better than he did. She had the urge to pull back the hair that had come loose from the braid and cover the bridge of her swollen nose with her hand, but she was holding the cups and couldn't move. She wanted to stand before him after a long soak in a hot bath, her hair rinsed with lavender scents, hands softened with lotions. She pictured a dark-blue velvet robe, one she had never owned or even glimpsed, with a wide sash at the waist. But here she was, wearing Louie's rumbled, rank clothing, and her face must be bruised. Then, nothing about her moments with Victor ever matched the way she thought it should be. She shivered.

"Come here," he said. "Are your feet wet?"

She shrugged, the tea lapping over the edge of the cup, trickling over her fingers.

"Here, hand me the cups. Take off those boots and stockings."

Wordlessly, she handed the cups over, sat down, and began to work the wet laces of the boots. She heard him take a noisy sip of tea.

"How is it?"

"Hmmmm, pretty good for virgin's piss," he said teasing.

Dorie peeled off her damp stockings. Hopefully, the musty smell of the room overpowered the smell of wet wool and feet.

"I'm going to go hang these by the stove."

"No wait. Here. Put your feet here." He motioned to his lap.

She waited, her toes curling inward in the cool air. She was taking only the tiniest of breaths.

"Come on."

He finally bent down and picked up her feet, forcing her to swing sideways on the settee. Victor held both feet delicately in the open palm of his hand, as if they were fragile pieces of china.

"They're no bigger than children's feet! How do you stand on these little things? First thing we do when we get out of here is buy you a new pair of feet." He continued to examine them from all angles.

"My mother had size three feet," Dorie offered as an explanation.

He rubbed one foot between his palms. The other he tucked under his leg. Dorie squirmed.

It tickled, well almost. She watched, fascinated by the rolling movements of his hands and the sensations they created. How could it be? They were just feet, after all. The most thought she'd ever given to them was the delight in a new pair of shoes, but that was how they looked, not how they felt.

His thumbs moved in long, hard strokes up the arch. It made her think of the day in the car in front of the bank when he had warmed her hands. Her fingers curled around the wooden frame of the settee.

"This one is getting pink. I don't think you have frostbite."

"Hmmmm," was all she could manage as a response. Now he was working a circular movement around the ball of her foot. Then he pulled and stroked each toe. Just when she thought she couldn't stand it any longer, he slipped that foot under his leg and retrieved the other one.

"Here, drink your tea before it gets cold." He handed her the cup.

She settled back into the quilts and sipped the bitter brew.

"You're right, this is vile."

"Look, this one here on the end—it's bruised. Do you suppose you broke it?" Victor held up the foot for inspection.

The toe felt stiff and ached slightly when she wriggled it, but she couldn't remember the exact moment it might have been battered in the previous night's struggles. In any case, she couldn't answer. Eyes closed, she tried to understand the odd mix of sensations running through her body. Her mind was quiet, her thoughts slow and thick, but her skin and muscles were wide awake, aware of the texture of each callous in his palm, the weight and pressure each finger could bring to bear.

After he had kneaded the second foot in much the same way, he took the cup from her hand, leaned in, and covered her mouth with his. She kissed him back, her lips parted as his thumb touched the hollow of her throat. Her arms came up, and her fingers grazed the line of his jaw, lightly so as not to disturb any wounds, before her palms settled on the back of his clean-shaven neck to pull him closer. She tasted the bitter tea on his tongue.

Victor shifted his weight. His hands moved to her waist, his mouth to her neck and throat.

"Does this mean if I would have warmed your feet months ago, you would have kissed me like that?" He murmured in her ear. His tongue followed her collarbone, and she moaned, wanting that mouth over hers again. How different from Louie's kiss! She recalled twisting her head away to escape her husband's mashing, wet lips. Too much spit! And that constant heavy pressure as if he was fastened to her mouth! *Leave me be, Louie. I deserve this,* she thought.

He peeled the flannel shirt from her arms, taking care with her shoulder. "Buttons. My God, so many buttons," Victor growled as he encountered the union suit.

"I wanted to be warm. That's why I wore it," Dorie said breathlessly.

"Are you warm now?" His lips followed each released button.

"Very." His warm breath pressed through the thin gauze of her chemise. Impatient to be rid of the scratchy wool, Dorie squirmed out of the sleeves. He pulled the end of the ribbon that cinched the bodice top. She shivered again.

"Wait," she said, sitting up. As she straddled his lap, he pulled the quilt around her shoulders, enveloping them. She was suddenly desperate to mimic his movements, desperate to feel his skin next to her own. She pulled the braces from his shoulders as she carefully kissed his lips, mindful of the cuts and bruises. Her tongue ran over his lower lip before it darted into his mouth, something she had never done before. His hands moved up under her chemise, to the skin of her bare back, and she arched forward against him, pinning him to the back of the settee.

This was all new.

Victor made a low noise in his throat. "Even in my best dreams, I never pictured this, Dorie."

Her hair was suddenly loose, tumbling over her shoulders, falling between them. One of his shirt buttons came off in her palm, and the ridiculous notion flashed in her head, *I'll have to sew this back on later when I locate some thread.* Why think about mending now? The buttons felt impossibly small. When she undid the last one, he shook his arms to be free from the shirt, forgetting the buttoned cuffs. She laughed as he gave a frustrated yell and then pulled the shirt over his head. Outside, the winds hammered like fists pounding against the doors and windows.

Her fingers flew to her lips when she saw the bruise on his chest, a perfect purple arch that matched, she realized, the steering wheel of the car.

"Are you okay?"

She touched his smooth chest, running her fingers over the warm, warm skin, fearful she would find a lump that would signal a broken rib, but all she found were the two scars from the bullet.

As an answer, he ran a hand up her back to her neck and pulled her toward him for another kiss. His hands moved across her shoulder, down her bare arms, his thumbs grazed the sides of her breasts, and then, to her wonder, they moved back and forth across her nipples, a whisper of a touch, and it was her turn to moan. This too, was new to her.

She not only wanted to kiss him, she wanted to have carnal relations with him! This was the passion she had heard about and never understood. She wanted to laugh out loud with the joy of it. His tongue flicked delicately between her lips, and she boldly caught the tip between her teeth and sucked. Suddenly there were just too many clothes, too many folds of blankets between them. She scooted off his lap, hastily unbuttoned the wool trousers, and peeled them off along with the rest of the union suit. The loose chemise flew over her head. When the air cooled her bare skin, she retrieved one of the quilts from the pile at her feet and pulled it over her shoulders as Victor shimmied out of his own pants.

"Dorie, I don't have any French letters with me." His voice sounded far away.

She squeezed her eyes shut tight, covering them with her forearm as she curled up at the edge of the settee.

"It's not important. Doc Pitzer says I'm not able to have children." Something pounded in her ears. He stroked her wrist and pulled her arm away from her eyes.

"Come, sit as you were before."

She straddled him again, watching his eyes, heavy, nearly closed, as the bare skin of their thighs touched.

"Wrap your legs behind me." He held her waist, pulled the blanket around them, and, as she maneuvered her legs around him, he slid into her, easily, deeply. No awful struggle, no awkward poking. One hand was pressed firmly into her lower back, the other hand rested at the nape of her neck. Her breasts touched that dreadful bruise. Her hands moved to match his own placement on his back and neck, a mirror image, she realized as they began to rock together. Could it really be this different? She thought of the times, flat on her back looking at the ceiling over Louie's heaving shoulder.

Then she realized this is exactly how he intended it to be, clever man. How did he know these things?

"I love you, Dorie," he said, holding her gaze with those blue eyes, and she knew he was showing her his heart.

She couldn't look away. "I love you so much," she gasped. Something was building inside of her, and she moved with him, chasing it, for fear of losing this feeling. This too was new to Dorie.

He smiled then, watching her, as if he were about to tell her a secret.

17

Waiting Out the Storm

Since they had no timepiece, Dorie marked the passage of the hours that day by how many pantry shelves they splintered and fed into the fire. The crystal of Victor's pocket watch, they discovered, had been shattered in the accident, the hands bent at crazy, useless angles. Outside, the storm raged on, blowing drifts against the north side of the house. The snow inched higher and higher until it covered the windows, muffled the noise, and wrapped the room in permanent nightfall and warmth. When they weren't scouring the cabinets for food, they kissed and touched in the huddle of old quilts on the floor. The sagging settee was too small to support their antics.

They dozed frequently, and Dorie not only lost track of night and day, but sometimes she was unsure whether or not she was dreaming as his tongue and fingers explored her body. In this half-dream world, she encouraged him with her moans. Always a fast learner, she boldly asked, "What do you like?"

"The flesh is weak," Father Caouette had intoned in almost every sermon, and she never paid much attention to these warnings because she believed the chastisement was, of course, directed toward the men sitting in the pews. When she read about the flappers, who were actively taking lovers outside of marriage, she wondered why anyone would ever want to do that. Now she knew what all the fuss was about. Once, when they had finished, Dorie had breathlessly cried out, "That was so much fun!" and Victor had laughed until tears streamed down his battered face. Then they dozed together once more.

Slamming and thumping noises emanated from the kitchen. When Dorie awoke, Victor wasn't beside her. "What are you doing out there?" she called. Dorie rested on her belly, her chin propped in one palm. She liked the feel of the quilts against her bare skin. She smiled as she touched Lois's perfect, tiny stitches running through the faded squares of calico fabric. A field mouse scurried into the parlor, rearing up on its hind legs to sniff the air and consider Dorie. She didn't care. She had no desire to pin him under a broom. Today, she was happy to share the warmth and shelter. Victor gave a muffled whoop.

"What's going on?" she called.

"Close your eyes."

Dorie didn't like that game. She always needed to know what was coming. Her mother had always accused her of possessing basic mistrust coupled with unladylike impatience. Whatever the reason, she put both hands over her eyes, spreading them just enough to view the entryway to the kitchen.

"You're peeking. I know it."

He carried two brown bottles and a canning jar. She pretended to squeeze her fingers tight.

"Am not."

He knelt and planted a noisy smack of a kiss on the top of her head and wiped the mouth of the bottle on his shirttail before he held it under her nose. "Root beer? Where did you find it?"

"There's a cellar the bums missed—hidden under the flooring the same as your kitchen. Look here, pickles too."

The thick layer of dust, crumbled limestone, and cobwebs dulled the shine of the canning cover. He peeled off his shirt and pants and scooted under the quilt. A blast of cool air followed him as he flopped on his belly next to her. She liked the feeling of his leg sliding against hers. He handed her one of the opened bottles.

"What else is in the cellar?"

"Well, if we're starving, there's a jar of pickled eggs—not one of my favorites. Ingeborg made me eat—"

"I mean, are there bags, or a tin chest of some kind that the money might be in?"

"What money?"

"Remember, Sal accused me of taking the money his brother came here to hide." Dorie rolled the cold bottle between her palms.

"You don't believe that. Do you?" Victor tipped the bottle and took a long drink. "This tastes good! Try some."

"Why would he say that if it wasn't true? Can you tell if the floor has been dug up recently?"

"No, not that I noticed. Then again I was using some rolled up wallpaper for a torch, so I didn't have much time to look around. Here, hold this." Victor passed his bottle to Dorie and twisted off the lid of the pickle jar with a noisy pop. He fished two fingers deep into the brine and retrieved a fat pickle. He held the dripping end over his mouth and took a bite. "Hey, these are still good—we're living like kings now!"

"I want to go look for myself." Dorie scanned the room for the last place she left her trousers and shirt.

"No. Don't get up, Dorie. The cellar's small—much smaller than yours. The floor was packed hard. There's no pirate treasure down there."

"We should turn this house upside down while we have the chance." Dorie made a list in her head of all the places she stored her tins of money: in the walls behind the floor molding, under the floor boards, the sheds... good Lord, there was the entire barn to consider.

"I can think of better things to do than take apart this ice-box of a house." He slid a finger, cool from holding the pickle jar, lightly up the middle of her spine and back down again.

Dorie shuddered, but she couldn't get the idea out of her head that there were bags and bags of money waiting for her.

"Aren't you even curious?" she asked as his tongue traced the pulse on her neck.

"I need more proof before I go off on a wild goose chase."

"What do you mean, proof?"

Victor turned her chin to better look her in the eye. Her skin, wet from his tongue, cooled in the air. "Sal was drunk when he accused you of stealing the money, right?"

Dorie nodded.

"We don't know if there was any money in the first place. Maybe he was talking nonsense."

"He said his brother came up here to hide money." Memory whispered in her ear. She closed her eyes, but could feel flecks of his saliva landing on her face as he threatened her life. Dorie shook her head to escape the phantom.

"See? There's so much we don't know about Geno. Just say there was money in the first place. Maybe he was robbed on his trip up here from Chicago. What if he was trying to double-cross his brother and keep the loot for himself? Sal had lots of time to snoop around this farm. Doesn't it say something if he couldn't find it?"

She sighed. What he said made sense, but she could still see her hands gripping the necks of heavy burlap sacks that swung against her thighs and pitched her off balance as she heaved them up on the table, sending fat stacks of bills tumbling over each other and spilling to the floor. She would never have to worry about money again.

"That dreamy look in your eye—you must be thinking about my kisses, eh?"

Dorie laughed and sipped the root beer. It was cold, sharp and delicious.

"This is wonderful! How many more bottles are left?"

"Oh, you're changing the subject. Maybe I can hope that you are thinking of my kisses as we roll on top of the bankroll then?"

"I like that idea very much. Let's pretend we've got the money right here." Their kiss was cold and long. She felt him stiffen against her thigh.

"Put that money out of your mind, Dorie. If it belongs to the D'Agostino brothers, you can bet that more family members will be coming here to claim it," he murmured as his empty bottle tipped and rolled across the wood floor. His kisses moved down her shoulders, across her breasts and belly.

"If I were to find the money, though, I could buy off Louie."

Victor froze. She wanted to gather up those words and hide them behind her back, but it was too late. At last she heard him exhale a long breath.

"That's what you plan to do with Louie? Throw him handfuls of cash?" Victor rolled over onto his back and stared blankly at the ceiling. "Louie has no more interest or want for money than say... um, a fish in Eagle Lake needs a pocket."

What about Louie? Tucked away safe from the snow and winds, alone with Victor's skin touching hers, there was no Louie. She was amazed how far she had been able to push him away.

"What I meant was that I could buy him a place—maybe in town. I could hire someone to look after him, cook meals and wash his clothes."

"Will you be making a weekly hooch delivery too?"

There was an edge to his voice she had never heard before. "Maybe not. It might be a good thing for him not to drink so much."

"I imagine he's not going to be too happy about getting kicked out of his home. Think about how he'll feel if he can't get any more moonshine."

"Should I let him stay at the farm?" The farm had been handed down to Louie, but she had always thought of the place as more her own than his because she had taken care of it. She hated to think of the house and buildings going to ruin if Louie were left to his own devices, but if she were to move, where would she go?

Victor rolled over and threw an arm over her shoulder. "Dorie, I think it's grand that you want to take care of Louie, but you have to think about how Louie is going to feel about all this. Sure, he's a harmless drunk most of the time, but my guess is that he's going to be hopping mad." He rubbed her back in a comforting way that said he wasn't mad at her. Louie would be deeply hurt, she wanted to tell him, but he wasn't going to get angry—he had never had a fit of temper in all the years she'd known him. Even when he cursed the broken-down tractor, he did it with a grin.

"I don't know what to do." Something thick caught and swelled at the back of her throat. Her vision blurred. Oh, God, was she about to cry in front of him? She had never cried in front of anyone before! Louie had cried so many times in their marriage that her tears always felt useless.

"Do you want to stay with Louie?"

"No!"

"Dorie, my whole life I've only been a bachelor. I don't know what it's like to have to take care of a horse, much less a woman... or a child. I don't know what to tell you to do. I can only say that I love you and I want to be with you."

"I want to stay here!" she blurted.

Victor chuckled. "Well, we might end up burning down the whole house for warmth before spring arrives, and I don't know if I can stomach those pickled eggs."

"No, I mean I want to buy this place. I could pay the back taxes and buy it from the D'Agostinos. I could fix it up—make it look like it did in the old days." She sat up, drawing her knees close, and pulled the quilts around her shoulders. She sniffed, staring around the old parlor with new excitement.

"Whoa. What would I do with a farm?"

"Well, nothing. We'd just live here."

"I don't think we should have anything to do with that D'Agostino family. We don't want them even to know we ever talked to Sal." Victor shook his head back and forth, his blond bangs swinging over his battered eyebrow. "Why don't you just pack a satchel, and we'll leave town as soon as the road's open?"

"Leave?" Her heart thudded in her ears. This town was all she knew. Leave the business? Abandon her house and all her hats and shoes and dresses? Where would they go? How long until her money would run out? She pictured them as hobos, jumping trains, sharing frigid cars with livestock, begging table scraps from farms just like hers.

"Yeah, sure, leave. Why not? If you think you have a hard time in town because you sell hooch, just wait until you leave your husband and take up with a two-bit guy like me." Victor inched over and nestled his head in her lap. "There's a world of things to see and do."

She looked down at him and traced the soft curve of his ear with her finger. He'd lived that wandering life before. She knew before he partnered up with her he'd been a salesman for Raleigh, going from town to town, selling liniments, nectars, and spices. Even with his charm and good looks there was not as much money to be made selling household items as there was selling moonshine.

"What about the business?" she whispered. His eyes were closed, and she wondered if he had drifted off to sleep.

Instead, he opened his eyes and moved to kneel in front of her. The rustling of the blankets stirred up the mingled musky scent of their bodies. "Maybe it's time to get out of the business. Look at what it's brought us—two dead brothers, and while neither death was entirely our fault I'll admit, we were involved in both." She stared at the crusty scabs on his battered face and the arch of bruises on his chest. The colors had already started to change, from a deep purple to the green of the sky just before it dropped a tornado. All of these truths made her head ache.

"Could we run our business in St. Paul? Get a house, bottle some moonshine, and meet some locals. It could be almost the same as it is now."

"Darling, that city would swallow up two country farmers like me and you. I've heard there are gangsters there that make the D'Agostino brothers look like spring lambs! There's no way we could muscle in on any of that business."

"What would we do then?" Panic scratched its way around in her chest.

Victor leaned over and kissed her… that wonderful mouth that made her throat swell and her legs go weak.

"We will figure out what to do. Don't worry." His tongue slid into her mouth. She smiled, as he tasted vaguely of root beer and pickles. He pulled her down on top of him. "Wait," he said breaking the kiss. "I forgot to tell you. When I got up last time and checked the weather, it felt like the winds were dying down. By morning, the storm should be over."

18

Steiner

She blinked in the darkness as Victor slept. He took slow, even breaths, and she forced herself to match each inhalation with her own, desperate to seize the rhythm, drift into dreams as if sleep were something they could catch and board together like a train. Curled against his back for warmth, her legs twitched with a crazy energy. She realized that the last time she had hours and hours to lie about without performing dozens of daily chores was when her mother had nursed her through the Spanish flu epidemic eleven years ago.

The other truth of the matter was that she didn't want to sleep through their last hours together.

She had kept him up talking and kissing as long as she could, wheedling hidden details of his life—his days working at the logging camps in Grand Marais, the year he spent on the iron ore freighter sailing Lake Superior. He even told her of the time when he was about twelve and a terrible earache had set in. For days, he lay twisting and moaning, refusing soup and sips of bourbon. The pain, he said, was like an ice auger burrowing its way through his skull, rending the tender flesh of his inner ear. A lump, hard and hot and the size of an egg, developed just under his earlobe. A mastoid, Ingeborg had told him as she attempted to ply hot compresses. When he started screaming, a frightened Ingeborg had tried to wrap him in blankets to transport him to the hospital. As the car jostled and Victor clutched his ear in pain, the mastoid burst, shooting a stream of yellow pus over the bedding. The infection had left him partially deaf in that ear, a fact Dorie had never known until that moment. It was the reason, he said, why he hadn't been able to serve in combat during the war.

"Tell me more," she begged. For the first time she wanted to be the one listening to all the stories. She liked how he ticked things off on each finger as he recited each event, or how he touched that poor battered brow whenever he tried to recall the lost name of a town or someone he worked with. Her heart swelled with love whenever he grabbed her hand in excitement. Finally, though, he drifted off to sleep in the middle of a sentence, like the last movements of a windup toy.

Tomorrow they would face the drifts of snow, the buried cars, and she would go back to the farm and to Louie. What would she say to him? She guessed she'd been gone two days now. What had he thought when he scoured the house, calling her name? She pictured him pacing back and forth in front of the window, lifting the curtains, rubbing his ear with worry. What would he think when he went to the cellar looking for more moonshine and found the splintered steps?

Her heart fluttered queerly. Something clutched at her, a hope, a wish, or a prayer that instantly made her ashamed. She pulled away from Victor and sat up, pushing her hot face into the quilts. *It would solve all her problems if he died,* she thought. No. No, she didn't want him dead. That was too harsh. But she could see it so clearly—Louie feeling his way down into the dark cellar, the way he had a hundred times before, his need for the drink so strong that even as his foot passed through the air where the step should be, he might not even have time to cry out in surprise as he pitched forward into the chilled, musty air, or register his confusion and shock before he slammed into the cellar floor. Would the fall kill him right away or would he feel the cold dirt leach into his sour bones as he bled inside his belly or head? *Stop it!* A whimpering noise escaped her tight throat. *But it would make things so easy.* At that moment, Victor exhaled a long whistling breath that ran shivers up her spine.

"Don't think about that," she whispered. All that came to her though were thoughts of the hidden money. It itched at her nerve endings like poison oak. If the last of the kerosene hadn't been burned earlier in the evening, she would get up now and begin rifling through all the likely hiding places. At the first light of day she was going to dress and begin her search in the frigid upstairs bedroom until Victor roused. Then after the roads were cleared—the spring thaw was certainly right around the corner—she could come back and take her time looking through the barn and storage sheds.

She heard the thump of collapsing wood from the stove in the kitchen. Yesterday Victor had kicked over a dilapidated shed near the outhouse. What would happen next? Before all this, before Victor, she hadn't given much thought to the next day, or the next week, much less the next year. It had seemed so predictable. She would cook and clean, continue the business, make money, and sock it away. What else was there? Now she didn't know where she was going to live. It was hard to picture a day-to-day life with Victor. How long would it take until he tired of her and the business and found some excuse to run off at the call of a new adventure?

All these questions banged around in her head, each new problem making more of a ruckus than the last. She shivered, climbed over Victor, and, as if she had made the request aloud, he curled his body around hers, and his arm slipped over her shoulders. She marveled at the perfect fit and the reassuring feeling of his breath on her neck.

Suddenly she was standing on the shoreline of Eagle Lake, confused because all the snow had melted, and it was so hot she could barely draw a breath. How did that happen? She waded into the green water wearing a white-linen long-sleeved blouse, a long skirt, and boots. How silly to have forgotten a bathing costume! The sun was a low orange globe against a pink-streaked sky. She looked over her shoulder to see her sisters standing on the shore, smiling and waving delicate white handkerchiefs. Deeper and deeper she walked, the mucky bottom sucking at her every step. She was looking for something, but she couldn't see it through the faceted waves that sparkled like her Czech glass earrings. The water numbed her legs and pulled on her heavy skirt. Why was the water so cold on a hot day? How odd not to see any boaters or swimmers! She realized, too late, that the water would ruin her delicate hat, but she couldn't turn back and hand it to someone on the shore for safekeeping—there just wasn't any time. The water lapped under her chin. She drew and held a deep breath, knowing her next step would take her under the surface. When she opened her eyes the underwater world shimmered a brilliant blue-green, and she began walking along the steep decline of the bottom as effortlessly as she moved down Main Street. There was no evidence of the usual lake life, no sunfish or walleyes, not even any weeds or rocks, just an expanse of green. Her lungs began to burn, but she didn't want to leave, not when she was so close to finding it! She opened her mouth expecting a flood of choking water. Instead, her lungs filled with a rush of cool air. It was possible to breathe underwater! She took breath after breath, laughing at the wonder of her discovery and the realization that she could stay on the sandy bottom as long as she pleased. A rowboat floated by overhead, and Dorie heard the sound of someone pounding on its bottom with an oar.

"Dorie, Dorie, wake up. Someone's at the door."

Was he in the boat? Why didn't he just jump in and join her at the bottom? The current jostled her back and forth.

"Look at me, Dorie. You have to get dressed."

"It's a miracle," she told him when she opened her eyes. "I can breathe underwater."

Victor squinted at her. "What? Listen, I'm getting the door."

The dream began to recede quickly in the gray light of the parlor. The disappointment and loss of that peaceful feeling was unbearable. It had been so real! She heard Victor struggling to open the kitchen door.

"Is anybody in there?" A muffled voice shouted from the front steps.

"Hold on!" Victor answered.

Panic seized Dorie. Who was it? Louie? She hastily pulled on the trousers while looking around the room for the wool shirt. She spotted the plaid collar in the tangle of quilts and hastily slid her arms through the sleeves. *Please stay in the kitchen,* she prayed. *Should I hide?*

She heard the stomp of boots in the kitchen. Was Victor even dressed? Where were her stockings?

"I'm Sheriff Larssen… Steiner, if you will." Dorie heard a rusty voice and tried to imagine his face. "Ah, Emmett Stubka and his team were clearing the country road out there, and he spotted a car there in the ditch—just the front end actually—nearly buried, it was. He also saw smoke coming from this chimney and hightailed it back to town because he knew this place had stood empty for a while now." His voice echoed in the empty kitchen.

"Victor Volk. Don't believe I've had the pleasure. Here, come by the fire and get warm."

"I just got down here from Anoka a month or so ago. Got called in after old Sheriff Irving stroked out."

When had that happened? Dorie wondered. Had Freddie DeMars mentioned that at one time? She couldn't remember. Her head felt heavy as if it were stuffed with mortar. She had never had any run-ins with Irving. Then again there hadn't been any trouble until Victor got shot.

"Anyway, Emmett found a car…"

Which car? Dorie wondered. Victor's car she had driven into the ditch or Buzzy's car that held Sal's body? She shivered in the cold air, but didn't dare move to give the floorboards a chance to creak.

"Yes," Victor said carefully. "There's been an accident."

"I'll say, by the looks of ya. You okay? Nothing broken?"

"I'm a bit banged up," Victor laughed. "I'll live. After the crash, I followed the fence to the house to wait out the storm."

"Seems like the best thing to do. I sent Emmett to get some help. We figured there might be someone needing medical attention. When he gets back, he'll be clearing the drive with his plow. It'll take him a while, but I'll give you a lift to wherever you call home." Dorie heard Victor cough. "I barely managed to walk in here. I had to shovel my way in through a few spots. Lord, the drifts are five feet high in some places! Quite a storm, but I guess you'd know that."

Dorie held her breath. *Tell him, tell him,* she urged. Steiner's going to find the second car sooner or later. What was the likelihood of two travelers crashing at the identical stretch of the road? She wished there was a way she could become a mouse so she could sneak into the kitchen and get a good look at Steiner Larssen.

"Well, Steiner, I appreciate all your hard work. I feel like I put you out." Dorie heard the sounds of Victor feeding the woodstove.

"Not a bother, really. Truth be told, I didn't exactly know what I'd find when I got here."

"How so?"

The blood pounded in her ears loud enough to nearly muffle their words. "The thing is, I found a second car across the way from the first one. I don't know how Emmett missed it, maybe he's got a case of snow blindness. He's been plowing since midnight when the winds died out. What was I saying? Oh, yeah, the front end was all scrunched up like an accordion against one of those pine trees at the end of the drive, and the front window was all broken out. You don't happen to know anything about that, would ya?"

"I might be able to clear up a question or two," Victor answered.

Dorie's feet were pale with cold, and she clenched her jaw to control her chattering teeth.

"Go on," Steiner said.

"I'm guessing you found a dead man in that car."

Dorie counted her own heartbeat in the silence that followed.

"That I did," Steiner said finally. "When Emmett and I stuck our heads in there, we found blood all over the inside of the car, and not a mark on the dead fellow, far as I can tell, outside of a busted neck that is."

Dorie LaValle

Dorie found herself staring at the dark squares on the wall where Lois's family photographs must have hung. Years of sunlight had bleached the wallpaper around the frames. Possible stories ran through her head and were rejected at a furious rate. Why would Victor have traveled with Sal? If he said Sal was giving him a ride back to town, then why is Victor's car in the other ditch? If Victor said he was driving Sal home for some reason, then how would he explain Sal's body in the driver's seat? She had hoped the car and the secret of Sal's whereabouts would have been buried for a few weeks, at least until Victor's face had time to heal.

Dorie bent to pick up a quilt and walked into the kitchen. She wished she'd had a bath, a good dress, and a chance to fix her hair. "If wishes grew on trees," she whispered and took a deep breath.

"Hello there! We've been rescued. You're the answer to our prayers!" She walked toward Steiner, adjusting the blanket over her shoulders as she extended her hand. "I'm Dorie LaValle."

They both turned to stare at her. Victor's scabby eyebrow shot up. Her hand hung out there for the longest moment before Steiner extended his.

"Nice to meet you, ma'am. Name's Steiner Larssen. I must say I'm a bit surprised to find anyone else out here."

The first thing she noticed about Steiner Larssen was his height. He was tall—well over six feet. Everything about him was long—legs, arms, even his fingers. She stared down at the pale freckled joints wrapped around her own hand and pictured God lengthening each section of finger like pulled taffy. His cleanshaven face was wind burnt, bright red against his gray eyes. He didn't blink much she noticed. Her bare toes curled as she encountered a puddle of melted snow.

"Call me Dorie. Do I have a story to tell you!" She tried to smooth her unruly hair. "Victor here has been a little confused since the accident," she whispered to Steiner. "For hours afterwards he talked mostly nonsense."

"Can you tell me what happened?"

"My husband and I were entertaining, the eve of the storm. I run a potato farm, just west of here. We had some of the neighbors over for cards and cake, when Sal D'Agostino showed up at our door—that's the dead man's name." She held Steiner's stare with her own. His face was thin, and the skin pulled tightly across his cheekbones like a hide stretched on a drying rack.

"Mr. D'Agostino is a neighbor then? Emmett didn't recognize him."

"No. He was from, let's see. What did he say, Victor? Ah, he was from Chicago." She realized she was babbling like a fool, but talking helped to keep her voice steady.

"And how did he find his way to your farm... from Chicago?" As if he suddenly remembered his manners, Steiner pulled off his fur-lined hat and ran his fingers through his pale red hair.

"I think my husband, Louie La Valle, met him in town and issued an invitation." She winced. That was the second time she said the word "husband" in the same conversation. It sounded odd to refer to Louie that way now. "Mr. D'Agostino was here because his wife had been willed this farm. Anyways, Louie's always bringing home stray travelers." *Don't babble*, she thought. "I don't want to speak ill of the dead, but he was dead drunk when he showed up at my door."

Victor gave her an amused glance.

"You didn't see him drink then? You weren't by chance serving any bathtub gin with your cake?" Steiner stretched his neck from one side to the other.

Dorie did her best to look horrified. "I should say not. In fact, the party broke up shortly after he arrived in that state." She moved closer to the stove for warmth. When Steiner didn't prod her on with another question, she continued. "I asked Victor here to please get Mr. D'Agostino out of my house. Victor had some business with him, so they left together." Dorie extended her hands, proud that they didn't shake in the least.

"Business?"

"Well, yes. You see Victor was thinking about buying this farm from Mr. D'Agostino. Sal told Victor he was taking the first train out in the morning, and if Victor wanted to take a look at the paperwork, he'd have to do it that night."

"Yes, some papers from the bank showing back tax amounts," Victor said evenly as he stared at Dorie.

"So, have you run across these papers?"

Dorie's heart thudded. Her mouth went completely dry.

"I burned them... along with the chairs, the shelves, and the drawers. Even the wallpaper had to go. We were trying to stay warm." She motioned around the room. "They were just papers with sums—not documents."

"If Victor left with this Mr. D'Agostino, how did you get out here?"

"A while after everyone left, I was tidying up in the kitchen, my hus—, Louie, had already gone to bed, and I found a money clip full of bills that belonged to Mr. D'Agostino. He'd said he was leaving in the morning, so I thought I'd take it out to him."

"In the storm."

"Well, it had only just started snowing. I didn't know a blizzard was coming."

"No, of course not."

"It was a lot of money," she added. "I didn't want to be accused of stealing. I told you, he was drunk. I wasn't sure what he might have to say when he sobered up in the morning and found his money gone." Dorie lifted her chin, pleased with herself. She wondered how Steiner could keep every muscle in his face so still. She had no idea if he believed any of this.

"I hit a slippery spot in the road and ended up in the ditch." What else was there? The story was perfect.

"Could I see the money clip then? We'll secure it with the body when we ship it."

"I, well, I think—" The clip was in Sal's pants. Did he know that already?

There was a loud commotion at the back steps. Steiner moved to open the door and Victor stepped toward Dorie, squeezing her shoulder briefly.

"You made it then, Emmett," Steiner said.

Emmett brushed the snow from his coat. "Watch your step! I didn't lose you in that last big drift, did I?" he called out to the white world beyond the kitchen door.

After him came Lenny Erickson, fresh faced and smiling, snowflakes settled on the brim of her hat, hoisting her medical bag.

19

Going Home

"Gentlemen, if you'll excuse us, I'd like to tend to Dorie's injuries in the other room," Lenny said as she led Dorie away from the men in the kitchen who stood snuffling, hats in hand, stomping snow from their boots.

"Injuries?" Dorie whispered.

"I didn't know I was coming to help you and Victor," Lenny said. "It was wonderful just to get away from the farm and all those noisy siblings. Just when I thought I couldn't stand being cooped up inside with them for another minute, Emmett showed up at the door saying there'd been an accident. I think it took us over two hours to get here!"

"What injuries?" Dorie repeated.

"Well, you have two black eyes for starters."

Dorie's hands flew up to her face. Why hadn't Victor said anything in all these hours?

Lenny raised her eyebrows briefly at the sight of the quilts and pillows on the floor but continued to prod the bones in Dorie's face.

"So you were in the car wreck?" Lenny smelled of fresh air and snow in contrast to Dorie's rank scent.

Dorie nodded. Lenny's delicate fingers undid the top button of Dorie's flannel shirt. She flushed as Lenny cocked her head from side to side while examining her collarbones and neck.

"Who did this to you?" Lenny asked quietly, looking quickly over her shoulder to make sure none of the men had entered the parlor. Dorie gasped and automatically clutched the shirt closed. Confused, she thought maybe Victor's ardent kisses had left marks on her skin, and then she remembered Sal's fingers crushing her windpipe.

Victor hadn't said anything about those bruises either.

Tears gathered, and Dorie could only shake her head.

"Surely it wasn't Victor. He's wearing that crazy-in-love look."

"You can tell?" Dorie asked.

"It about knocked me clear out of my boots the minute I walked into the kitchen. I think it's all very romantic. Who knows, maybe I was reading too many novels about true love during the blizzard, but my head is just full of love stories."

"Then you're not scandalized because I'm married to Louie?"

"Victor is a much better match for you. I could tell that even when he was unconscious, for gosh sakes." She tucked the length of her wavy bob behind her ear.

Dorie had never had a girlfriend. Women didn't seem to like her very much, and she knew it. It wasn't just the business she ran that turned the wives in town all sour-like. It started much earlier than that. By the end of her second school year, she had absorbed a roomful of knowledge by just listening to all the lessons of the older children. When Miss O'Dell discovered that Dorie could add large sums in her head as well as multiplication and division, she moved her up to the fifth grade. From then on, the girls her own age poked fun at her, and the older ones ignored her altogether. Other girls sang songs together as they swung lunch pails along the lane to school, skated arm in arm on Eagle Lake, and later, shared secrets at the dance pavilion, but never issued an invitation to Dorie. Her sisters always had each other. Since Dorie didn't share any female companionship, it seemed logical to become friends with the smartest boys in the class.

Sadly, all the longing for confession and commiseration had to be put on hold, as the men in the kitchen were anxious to leave. A reluctant Victor was briefly examined too, and Lenny pronounced him well enough to travel. They hurriedly put out the fire in the stove, bundled in their coats and headed out into the snow. Dorie craved a last kiss with Victor, quiet moments to speak of her love and make some plans, but it wasn't meant to be.

The sunlight stabbed her eyes. The whole world sparkled and glittered as Dorie made her way along the narrow trench of shoveled snow, and at times the wall of white extended over her head. She paused, reached a hand to the snow bank and shut her eyes tight against the dazzling, too-bright morning. Tears flowed down both cheeks, and she blamed the wind. She wondered if Lenny had any of those dark spectacles in her doctor's bag, the type given to blind people. When Dorie's legs wobbled, she felt Lenny's steadying hands, as if she were a patient just recovering from a long illness. Lenny must believe her to be some kind of weak ninny. Last time, she fainted in her own kitchen. Now here she was, a stumbling, bruised woman again in need of rescue.

As they climbed into the wagon, she didn't dare glance at anyone but Lenny. The men tended the horses as Lenny and Dorie settled themselves under blankets on the frozen bale of straw directly behind Emmett. Victor sat on a pile of feedbags in the back of the wagon, while Steiner jumped up on the seat next to Emmett. For now, it seemed the sheriff had no more questions for her, although she periodically sensed his stare. As the wagon began to jostle toward the main county road, Lenny shared a few wrapped sweets and asked safe questions about what they ate and drank during the storm. Meanwhile, Dorie tried to conjure a story that would persuade Steiner to bring her to town rather than home. She could argue that her driveway would surely be impassable because Louie was content to wait for the Johnson brothers to come by with their team.

She watched Buzzy's farmhouse get smaller and smaller as the wagon began to move and wondered when she and Victor could be alone again. She closed her eyes and slipped back to the parlor and the salty taste of Victor's kisses, the feel of his hands guiding her hips. She finally dared to glance at him where he sat across from her and saw that the brisk weather caused the cuts on his face to flare an angry purple. He raised one eyebrow, just slightly, and she took it as a signal he might be sharing her thoughts.

A whimper of sadness and frustration escaped the back of her throat, a noise no one could hear over the sounds of the horses, the wind, and the creaky wagon. She didn't want to go home, but going to town was out of the question because it would arouse too much suspicion. What woman wouldn't be anxious to return home to her husband after such a harrowing experience?

"I hope to go back to medical school in the fall," Lenny shouted over the wind and the scraping sound of the plow. My father's trying to arrange for my Aunt Eda to come and stay with us and look after my brothers and sisters." She rocked back and forth with excitement, or maybe she was just trying to stay warm. Her breath bloomed frosty clouds. "My father's counting on a good crop to pay tuition. He says he's due."

"Where will you go for schooling?" Victor shouted.

"The University of Minnesota, in Minneapolis." Lenny answered, pointing south as if the buildings were just across the farm field.

Dorie knew she should be keeping up the conversation, if nothing else than to quiet Steiner's suspicions, but the cold and the bumpy ride seemed to bother her shoulder again, and the straw poked through her woolen trousers. She was ravenous too. Her stomach clenched painfully at the thought of a platter full of roast chicken and grilled potatoes with steaming biscuits and gravy. Oh, she wanted to cook a decent meal for Victor—just the two of them, after a long soak in the washtub.

As the wagon approached the main road, Dorie looked over her shoulder and saw first Victor's car, and then Buzzy's car nearly covered with snow. Their shapes resembled strange, hulking animals. Was it really only two days ago they had set out in the storm?

"Maybe we'll come and see you next winter then," Victor shouted to Lenny. Dorie glared at Victor. She had no idea if Steiner could hear their conversation.

Lenny nodded vigorously. Victor was always brimming with plans, Dorie realized, not at all rooted in what was possible or prudent. Still, watching his excitement, his laugh, the way his arms and hands spread themselves in wide gestures, she almost believed him.

Dorie leaned back and tried to hear what Steiner was saying to Emmett, but his words were low and muffled. He gestured toward Buzzy's car, and Emmett nodded, pulling hard on the reins.

"What is it? What's wrong?" Dorie tapped Emmett on the elbow. They stopped close to the spot where Victor had driven off the road.

"I need to bring that fellow's body back to town, Mrs. LaValle." Steiner swiveled around to talk to her. "It's not right to leave him by the side of the road like he is. I don't want any animals getting at him. Besides, I have some work to do to prepare him for shipping back to his family."

"Back to town," she repeated numbly. The words felt dry on her tongue. Sitting this close to Steiner in the bright sunlight, she realized his sandy eyebrows were fine and delicate as a baby's. It was the mere suggestion of eyebrows really, as if they had been lightly sketched in.

"Yes, Mrs. LaValle, I do. I don't mean to offend your sensibilities."

A moment shimmered and hung there, as something shuddered through her. Maybe it was caused by the lack of food, or sleep, or the disarming arrival of the sheriff on the doorstep, but she wanted to giggle and tell Steiner that her sensibilities hadn't been offended one bit when she pushed Sal down the stairs or hauled his brother's body to the lake.

"I understand," she responded at last. The horses shifted and snorted as if impatient to be on their way. Emmett passed the reins to Lenny.

"Don't worry, I've seen bodies at medical school. It's not so bad. Look off to the horizon if you find it bothers you at all."

"Need a hand?" Victor called as Emmett followed Steiner along the path they had made during their earlier discovery.

Steiner waved him off, but Victor jumped out of the wagon anyway and waded through the drift after the two men. Dorie rubbed her mittens together to keep warm. Strands of hair escaped her cap and flew into her eyes and mouth.

"Can you stay on with me a bit at our farm, Lenny?" Dorie asked suddenly. "Just for a day or so?"

"Why, Dorie, there's really no call for that is there? What do you need me for?"

She could lie. Report some strange pain, or ailment—woman troubles. She could make something up that would force Lenny to stay, but suddenly she didn't want to do that.

"What is it, Dorie?"

"I need you to do something for me." And she whispered into Lenny's ear.

They both turned as the men approached the wagon. Steiner was shouting directions to Emmett who walked backward, grappling with Sal's legs. The black coat trailed along the snow, a stark contrast to all that white.

Sal's frozen body was curled up into a C-shape, stiff as winter laundry hung out on the clothesline. Steiner gripped the body under the shoulder and head. The top of Sal's head was coated with a cap of frozen snow and ice. Victor trailed behind them, calling out maneuvering directions.

She had the urge to complain to Victor, "My God, will we ever get rid of him?" Truth of the matter, it only bothered her if they got caught. Lenny seemed to be interpreting her fixed stare and stony silence for a deep disturbance.

"My mother always said that after death, a soul is already reunited with God so the body is just a body."

Dorie smiled and nodded then, sure that Sal D'Agostino's soul resided in a far different place than God's own kingdom.

"Would it make you feel better to say a few prayers, seeing how we don't have Father Caouette here? This man isn't from around here. How do you know him, Dorie?"

"The night of the storm he came 'round the farm," Dorie answered simply. Her eyes started to tear unexpectedly.

Lenny's green eyes narrowed for a moment and then widened. Her mittened hand flew to her mouth.

"On three then," Emmett called.

Lenny leaned closer and put her mouth near Dorie's ear. "This is the man who hurt you?" She heard the men count and give a grunt, and Sal's body landed squarely at their feet sounding, Dorie believed, exactly like a slab of salt-cured cod clattering on the kitchen counter.

Steiner and Victor jumped into the wagon and began to cover Sal's body with the empty feed bags, tucking the loose ends under him. Dorie could feel Steiner's gaze.

"We'll have you home in no time now, Mrs. LaValle." Steiner nodded to her before he climbed past her to join Emmett who was already slapping the reins and urging the horses on. Lenny slipped an arm through Dorie's and held on to the back of the seat for stability. The wagon turned slowly and headed west toward her farm.

Victor squinted at the body and then at Dorie and shook his head once. Dorie believed he must be thinking too, after all we've been through, Sal is heading right back to the farm.

The roar of Emmett's blade biting through the snow made conversation impossible. She hoped Louie wouldn't run from the porch yelling about the smashed cellar steps and babble to the sheriff in his helpful talk-too-much way. She stomped her feet to bring some warmth back to her numb toes. She would tell Louie the same story she told Steiner. Sal left with Victor to look over some paperwork about the farm. When she realized Sal had left his money clip on the table, she drove after them. It wasn't a problem that Louie wouldn't remember any talk of Victor purchasing Buzzy's farm. Dorie often filled in these details, either real or imagined, for him.

A gust of wind swept across the fields, blowing a fine powder of snow in their faces. Lenny and Dorie gasped in surprise. The wind also released the feedbags from around Sal's upper body. One side of his face, the cheek that had rested against the car seat, was a dusky purple color. His hand was frozen in such a way that he seemed to be offering something to her.

In the bright light she saw something sticking out the back of Sal's frost covered head. Something she hadn't noticed that night in her kitchen. She whispered to Lenny again and squeezed her hand. Lenny nodded.

"You're right, Lenny, we should say a prayer over the body," she shouted, grabbing her hand tightly. Lenny knelt next to Dorie, over Sal's body, and pressed her mittens together. Dorie moved her lips in a way that she hoped appeared convincing and placed a bare hand on Sal's head. She and Victor exchanged a worried glance. Steiner shifted in his seat behind her, and she knew he was watching too. Dorie held her position even though her knees ached from the cold and the hard wagon floor. Slowly she maneuvered her thumb and forefinger where she could grasp the wood splinter that stuck out of the back of Sal's head and pulled. The chunk broke off in her fingers. The embedded tip must be frozen in his head, she realized. Still, Steiner might not notice it now unless he ran his hand over the back of Sal's head. The wagon pitched then, throwing Lenny across Sal's body while Dorie managed to brace herself against his hard shoulder. Victor jumped up to help Lenny back to her seat.

The wagon slowed and Dorie saw they were at the end of her driveway. Home. She did miss it, after all. A drift of snow covered the north side like a layer of cake frosting. The barn and the pine trees near the buildings had served as a wind block. There was no sign of Louie. No smoke coming from the chimney.

Emmett guided the horses around the corner, the blade throwing up sparks as it struck rocks on the driveway. The sun beat on her face, and Dorie felt the first hint of warmth. Despite the drifts of snow, spring would soon follow.

She stood and allowed Steiner to help her from the wagon. How long would it be until she saw Victor again? Dorie turned to thank Steiner and Emmett for their troubles and contemplated asking them both to a meal to show them she had nothing to hide, when she saw the boot sticking out of the newly plowed drift.

It was Louie's old boot… the one he had knotted with a bit of twine to replace the broken buckle. The fat knots were crusted with snow and ice. Of course he would wear his old boots. She had taken his good pair the night of the storm.

20

Louie after the Blizzard

Dorie blinked hard, suddenly remembering the days immediately after her mother had passed away. "It's your turn to sit with Mother," Obeline had said as she pushed at her arm.

Dorie opened her eyes to see her sister standing over the bed, her thin fingers holding a handkerchief over her nose and mouth. Dorie couldn't tell whether it was to ward off contagion or protect her delicate nose from the sickbed smells of bedpans and poultices.

She turned over, wanting to burrow into her feather pillow, drift into the black, far away from this awful sickness.

"I'm too weak. I haven't been out of bed for..." How many days had it been?

Obeline's bony finger jabbed the tender area between her shoulder blades like a sharp stick.

"We've all taken turns tonight. Even Jeanette has sat with her twice, and it's nearly the time for her baby to be born. Go do your duty." Obeline yanked back the bedclothes, allowing the chill of the room to lick over Dorie's thin nightdress. She heard her sister's footsteps receding. "This is all your fault anyway," Obeline muttered as she went through the doorway.

Dorie swung her legs to the side of the bed, not so much obeying Obeline's order, as honoring Mother's wishes. She moved her hands over her thighs, belly, breasts, and arms, shocked at their thinness. My God, how unbelievably weak she felt! It was like her muscles and bone had been ground to fine, useless powder.

On the nightstand next to the bed was a serving of cold consumé and a glass of water. She looked at the skin of white fat that clung to the edge of the bowl as she drank the water. She drank every drop even though it was warm and tasted of metal. She slowly pulled the dressing gown over her aching shoulders and then reached for a quilt for added warmth. A coughing fit seized her then, deep wracking spasms that seemed to erupt from the bottom of her lungs. A sheen of sweat broke out over her upper lip as black spots danced in her eyes.

Though she was eighteen years old, nearly a married woman, she missed her mother's cool hand on her forehead as she applied compresses to her chest. Tonight there would be no mothering for Dorie. While tending the sickbed of her youngest daughter, Camille herself had fallen ill with the Spanish flu.

Dorie stood and wobbled toward the door, gripping the bedposts, dresser, and doorknob for support as she went. She floated down the hallway, rather than walked, and she wondered if maybe this was just another dream or perhaps she was a spirit now moving soundlessly through the house. Her feet were cold, and she realized she had forgotten slippers. Weren't spirits supposed to be cold?

As she passed the bedroom doors, she heard the sleeping sounds of her sisters, the creak of springs, a snore coming from Minnie although she always denied this habit. How strange to have them all back in the house again after so many years!

The front room of the house was lit by dozens of flickering candles, each forming trails of waxy tears down the tapers, across the base of silver candlesticks. Her mother would never have stood for the wax pooling on the linens. It would take hours and hours to clean up this mess. Oh, there was so much for her to do now, but she was so very tired. Even the candlelight hurt her eyes.

Janette sat in the rocking chair. Her head tipped forward, her chin resting on her breastbone. Dorie moved toward her and rubbed the back of her hand. Jeanette stirred, blinked rapidly and pushed herself awkwardly out of the chair. Jeanette was the thinnest of the sisters, and the pregnancy seemed to have invaded only the mid-section of her body. While her arms and legs still resembled chair spindles, the swell of her belly made Dorie think of a wood tick.

"I wasn't sleeping!" Jeanette protested. "I was only resting for a moment."

"I know," Dorie said. "Go to your bed now. I'm here to sit with Mother."

"Are you well enough to be up?"

"Our sister, Nurse Obeline, has ordered me fit for duty," she answered and smiled.

Jeanette placed her palm against Dorie's cheek and returned her smile. Dorie closed her eyes, grateful for her sister's touch.

They both turned then to look at their mother's waxy, pinched face in the cherry wood casket.

"It took her in only three days," Jeanette whispered. "So fast."

Dorie nodded. She recognized her mother's wedding dress—dyed black for the viewing, the thin fragile nose—a trait she and her sisters shared—and her wedding ring, looking large and lost on her folded bony finger, but this person in the casket didn't look like her mother at all.

"Those that can brave the cold will come to the viewing tomorrow. That's why we placed her in front of the window. No one will want to enter the house. They're afraid of contagion. The Devereaux family buried two of their children yesterday."

Dorie nodded again. "And are you afraid?" She placed her fingertips on the fabric that strained across Jeanette's belly.

"I'm not as fearless as you, Dorie, but I couldn't stay away."

Dorie eased herself into the rocking chair vacated by her sister. "Go rest now, Jeanette. If Obeline finds you still up, she'll skin us both alive!"

Jeanette smiled and pulled her shawl tight, kissing her two fingers before she held her hand up to say good night. As she moved toward the hallway, the candles flickered wildly after her, dripping more hot wax. Dorie knew she should replace the ones that had melted into fat stubs, but the effort seemed too great. Instead she pulled the chair closer to the casket and rested her face along the edge, near her mother's hands.

Dorie stared at Louie's boot, jolted back to the present. If God created all forms of calamities, illness, and blizzards in which people died, didn't He share some of the blame for this misery? Was it solely her fault Mother fell ill and died? Was she to blame for Louie venturing out, most likely drunk, into a blizzard? Dorie looked at the tattered bootlace and wondered who could answer her questions.

Steiner, Emmett, and Victor circled the boot as if witnessing the birth of a prized calf. They were all watching her, waiting for a reaction. What did they expect? Crying? Fainting? It seemed no one would move until she gave the go ahead, only she didn't know what to do. It seemed her heart was as numb and cold as her feet. Finally, Steiner gripped the heel and pulled harder than he needed to, spraying a boot full of snow over their faces. Dorie stole a quick look at Victor's face, not sure if it was pain or relief she saw ripple across his features. A flare of panic ran through her body. Now that they were away from Buzzy's farm, was he relieved she was married to someone else?

There was no white frozen foot, so, then, where was Louie? Dorie scanned the drifted snow between the steps and the barn, looking for a clue, a woolen cap, a glove, or a hand. She glanced up and saw that the guide rope, which was usually stretched from the porch to the barn, had been severed, leaving several yards of frayed rope twisting and coiling in the brisk breeze. He could be anywhere in the expanse of snow. He might have made it to the barn if his luck hadn't finally run out.

As if Steiner read her mind, he cupped his hands around his mouth and yelled, "Mr. LaValle... Louie... are you holed up in the barn?" The doors were shut tight against large drifts of undisturbed snow. It didn't appear as if anyone had been out to the barn since before she and Victor had left that night. The winds died down at that moment, and the sun shone on Dorie's face.

"When's the last time you saw your husband, Mrs. LaValle?" Steiner asked as he squinted to look at her.

"The night the storm started, he retired around nine o'clock." Her mouth went dry. *What did he think? She had something to do with his getting lost in the snow?* "I'm going into the house," Dorie announced, surprised when they all flocked behind her like chickens.

Energetic Emmett had already started to shovel a narrow path to the porch stairs, prompting Steiner and Victor to join in the work. Lenny stood silently beside her. Dorie was glad Lenny wasn't one to murmur platitudes about God's wishes or blind beliefs that everything would be fine when clearly all was not well. They could have gone to sit in the wagon, but the thought of looking at Sal's body only added to her discomfort. Besides, she might not be able to resist the urge to turn the horses around and head out away from there as fast as they could carry her.

Finally, when the steps were cleared, Dorie strode across the porch, entered the kitchen, and heard the clomping of boots as they followed behind her. She gasped, unable to move, as she surveyed the condition of her kitchen, the air so cold the room had a faintly bluish tint.

Everywhere she looked were plates with food, empty moonshine bottles, and overturned glasses, greasy with fingerprints. A trail of splattered coffee grounds led from the sink to the stove. The cast-iron pan was crusted with something black and unrecognizable. The air was sharp with a burnt tang. Above the sink, she saw the singed and tattered remnants of her red-checkered curtains. On the table sat three of Louie's half-painted birdhouses and an open paint can. Green splatters and drips covered the oilcloth. There was a crazy pattern of shiny green footprints around the table as if he had been dancing a waltz, and more prints, fainter now, leading to the parlor.

The others moved around her now. Lenny walked into the parlor. Footsteps thudded up the stairs to the bedroom. She saw Steiner pick up an empty bottle and sniff. There was nothing she could do about hiding the containers now. At least the cellar door hadn't been left open. She turned away before he could look at her. She was out of stories to explain this away.

"Well, Louie kept himself busy during the storm," was all she could manage. "Moonshine," Steiner said.

"Yes, and cooking and painting, too." There was an edge to her voice somewhere between hysteria and sadness.

"Where do you suppose he got it?"

"Louie, Louie," she heard Victor calling from upstairs. Something in her went weak at the thought of Victor standing in her bedroom. She clenched her teeth. Why couldn't they all just leave?

There was more noise now overhead. Footsteps thundered on the stairs. She heard muffled voices. Both she and Steiner looked up as if the ceiling would answer their questions. Then she heard, "My Dorie is back! Where is she?"

Lenny and Victor presented Louie to her then, one on each side, propping him up. He was crying, rubbing his bloodshot eyes. To her horror, he walked slowly to her, his arms outstretched.

However bad she smelled, it was nothing compared to Louie. He stank of urine, moonshine, stale sweat, and chewing tobacco. He was wearing the same tattered shirt and trousers he had on that night when Sal came to drink, now rumpled and stained with paint and grease, the buttons to his pants undone. "Gawd, Dorie, I thought you was gone." He blubbered more words she couldn't understand as he chewed on the cuff of his shirt.

Dorie stood ramrod straight, her arms hanging useless at her sides. She felt something shudder through her, a wave of bile and disgust so strong she bit down on the inside of her cheek to keep from crying out. She looked at Victor. His face was of full of sadness. She began to have an inkling of the layers of hell she would have to endure as punishment for sharing pleasure with Victor.

"I'm home," was all she could say.

"I was so worried... and... and then I was hungry, so I tried to make myself something to eat. You're always telling me I need to eat, but you weren't here, and then I spilled some of my drink when I was fryin' and..."

When the acrid smell of him became too much, she backed up a few steps. "Louie, the new sheriff is here. He and Emmett helped me get back home. Sheriff Steiner, this is Louie LaValle."

Louie squinted up at Steiner. Maybe something in the edge of Dorie's voice as she enunciated the word *sheriff* made some small part of his brain register that this was the law.

"Why bless your heart, Sheriff. Nice to meet you." There were strings of saliva stretching between Louie's lips and smears of green paint across his forehead. Honestly, the sight of him was enough to make her join the Sacred Thirst Total Abstinence Society.

"We found your boot out in the snow," Steiner said, though he didn't offer his hand.

Louie rubbed his face as if the stroking helped find and organize his thoughts. He snapped his fingers soundlessly together. "You know, I thought maybe Dorie had taken a notion to go out to the barn during the storm. I was going out after her, but I lost my balance and the rope broke, then my boot came off. That snow was pretty deep. You know, it was up to here…" Louie made a sweeping motion a foot above his head to indicate the depth of the snow. "So I crawled back to the porch door and decided to stay put."

"That was a pretty wise decision. Was that before or after you started drinking the moonshine?" Dorie held her breath. Steiner's face was impassive.

Louie looked around, first at Dorie, and then at Victor. He was not a good liar. She hoped he realized it was hopeless to deny drinking. She nodded.

"I was worried about Dorie, you see," he answered carefully.

"Where did you get the moonshine?"

"Oh, some guy at the train station. I don't know his name. Dorie doesn't like my drinking much, so I hide it around the house."

One pale eyebrow of Steiner's lifted as if an invisible fishhook had been run through the center.

At least half of what Louie said must be true, Dorie realized. Louie most likely had never gone to the cellar for more moonshine since he had his own stash. Helpful Emmett had banked the stove that Louie had let go cold, and the room began to warm enough for Dorie to feel uncomfortable in her coat. She began to sway with fatigue, hunger, and sadness. She closed her eyes.

"I may have more questions for you later," Steiner said. She wished it were Victor reassuring her that he'd visit her soon. Instead it meant that Steiner had suspicions. Maybe he would just come back here and raid her house and arrest her outright.

"We need to get Miss Erickson home, and check on some other folks."

"Thank you so much," Dorie babbled. The words felt awkward and queer rolling off her tongue as if she was thanking Steiner for a gift or a party invitation. She turned away to blink back some unbidden tears as the others began to button their coats and put on their gloves. Emmett soundlessly tipped his hat to her. Lenny gave her a little squeeze and pecked her cheek. Finally, Victor stood in front of her, while Steiner watched, leaning against the counter with his hat in his hands.

Of course, she and Victor should say good-bye to one another. How would it look if he just left? She hated Steiner for watching. She hated Louie more for moving closer.

"Rest up now. You've been through a lot," he said. Victor's three-day growth of reddish-blond beard sprouted all around the scabs on his face. Despite his bedraggled appearance, there were those blue, blue eyes that made her legs weak.

"You, too." She searched for some secret message, something she could say to him to express her love, her longing, but nothing came to her.

"Oh, by the way Mrs. LaValle," Steiner said, "I need Mr. D'Agostino's money clip—the one you went out into the storm to return to him."

She hoped for an interruption from someone, something that would allow her to stall for time.

"It's in your coat pocket, right?" Lenny asked from the doorway. "I thought I saw you put it there for safekeeping."

Dorie slid her fingers into the pocket and produced the silver clip, the metal cool against her fingers, and held it out to Steiner's open hand.

21

What Louie Knew

They all left.

Dorie, throat aching, watched from the window as Victor made his way back to the wagon and helped Lenny settle into her seat on the straw bale. From this vantage point, Sal's frozen body looked small and insignificant—like a few sacks of corn. Just as Emmett maneuvered the horses and the wagon around to head out toward the road, Victor looked back at the house and raised a hand. She knew he most likely couldn't see her face due to the glare off the panes, but he made that small, parting gesture just the same.

Dorie wanted to crawl up to her room and pull the quilts over her head, but Louie flickered silently around her, and she imagined him hovering over the bed even if she were to find her way to a fitful slumber. She realized if she slept now, it would mean facing the long night awake and alone. Besides, she felt unsettled and was far too famished and filthy to sleep. Work was a good diversion, and she planned accordingly—clean the kitchen, eat something, then she could bathe and collapse.

She surveyed the mess in the kitchen and began pumping water to heat on the stove.

"Where did you and Victor go in the storm?" he asked over the splashing sounds against the metal pan.

"We got stranded at Buzzy's place."

"You were gone a long time." A full glass of moonshine had mysteriously appeared in his hand. Where was his bottle?

"Have you been out to the barn at all to feed the chickens and goats?" She asked this even though she already knew the answer. "Go and check on them. They're probably half-starved or frozen to death by now. Oh, and while you're outside, look around for some wood in one of the sheds to repair two of the cellar steps." She tried to scrape the blackened mess on the bottom of the fry pan but only succeeded in bending the spoon.

"Why were you out at the still?"

"We didn't go to the still." Dorie repeated the story she had told Steiner about following Victor and Sal out to Buzzy's to return the money clip and the ensuing accident. The handle of the heavy pail dug into her hands as she lugged it to the stove. When he didn't comment, she added, "Get the saw and a handful of nails, too. We need to get those steps fixed sooner rather than later."

"That's not true," he said.

She pumped some water into the fry pan and went to the pantry for a box of baking soda. Of course he was going to argue about the repair job. "No, the stairs need to be fixed today, before Steiner takes a notion to come back." Louie didn't ask which stairs were in need of repair. Had he peeked in the cellar after all? How was she going to match the wood so that the stairs didn't look as if they had been recently repaired? If only it were warmer and she had the time to paint them! She mulled over the possibilities as she set the fry pan on the stove to soak.

"That's not what I meant," Louie stood over her shoulder, as close as if she were an angel and he was a pair of recently sprouted wings. He wiped his mouth on the sleeve of his shirt. "I saw you and Victor the night of the storm."

Dorie spun around. "What do you mean, you saw us?" The smell of him burnt her nostrils.

"I woke up when you came into the bedroom." He looked her up and down for a moment and added, "You took some of my clothes. Then a few minutes later, I heard voices. I came downstairs. I saw you and Victor standing over Sal—he was there…" he pointed, "…on the floor."

The lie slid easily into her thoughts. "Victor came over after you'd gone to bed that night. He found Sal passed out in the snow so he decided to give him a ride back to Buzzy's." Maybe she should have told Steiner that tale. She gathered the assortment of sticky glasses from the counter and table and placed them on the counter next to the sink.

"Sal wouldn't have left here without his coat."

Dorie's mouth went dry. "Where were you standing?" Dorie recalled her struggle to put the coat on Sal's lifeless body.

"Here," Louie replied, and he moved to the archway between the kitchen and the parlor and showed her how he leaned over just enough to reveal half his face.

"You were drunk," she countered. "Maybe you dreamt it." She shuffled the dirty plates together.

"I saw you fittin' on his shoe," Louie added.

"And you didn't say anything."

"No. I was scared. Then you went outside. I thought you'd be back. I waited for a long time."

Dorie looked around the shambles of her kitchen—the splattered paint, the dirty plates, the ruined curtains. With a sweep of her hand she cleared all the dishes and pans from the counter into the sink. Louie cringed at the sound of breaking china and glass.

"Fine. I'll tell you what happened. Sal came back here that night after you'd gone to bed and forced himself on me, and then he tried to choke me." Dorie pulled at the collar of the shirt to reveal the bruises. "Where were you when I needed you?" She clenched her jaw hard enough to send a pain up the side of her head. "Dead drunk in your bed as usual, that's where."

His hands fluttered around his open mouth. "Oh, my poor Dorie. Maybe you misunderstood. I didn't think Sal would ever..." Staring, she realized that at some point in the last three days, he had lost an eyetooth.

"Misunderstood?" Blood thundered in her head. "The only thing I ever misunderstood was what my life with you would be like." She was breathing hard. It felt so good to lash out at him.

She stomped into the pantry pushing at her tears with the palm of her hand and blindly grabbed a can and the opener. As she punctured the top, the cool juice slopped across her knuckles. She licked the peach syrup from her fingers. From the curtained area under the pantry counter, she slid out the large galvanized tub and pushed it across the floor in front of the stove. She set the can of peaches next to the tub, hung flour sacks on the open oven door and retrieved the folding screen from the frigid porch, which she positioned around her bathing area. All the while, Louie muttered and paced around the kitchen. Dorie purposely thumped and banged the kettles as she began to fill the tub, intending to drown out the sound of him. When the tub was filled with steaming water, she added a liberal dollop of lavender scent she kept on the shelf with the spices and gathered the sea sponge and her last precious bar of soap from George.

"I'm going to bathe now. You might think about cleaning yourself. You can use this water when I'm through." She hoped her announcement would prompt him to leave the kitchen.

The cool air raised gooseflesh across her arms and breasts as Dorie shed the filthy clothes she fully intended to send to the ragbag. She eased into the hot water a delicious inch at a time until her shoulders were covered even though this meant her knees were exposed to the air. She retrieved the can of peaches and carefully lifted the lid with the nail of her index finger and fished out a fat slice. Juices ran down her hand and arm and dripped from her elbow. She ate each section quickly, reveling in its sweetness and the power of her hunger until the can was empty. Then she tipped the can and drank the remaining nectar.

Afternoon sunlight streamed through the kitchen windows, and from her vantage point in the tub she could watch water run from the eaves. As many winters as she'd seen, the fast spring melts always surprised and delighted her. Squeezing the fat sponge, she trickled the scented water over her face and arms. Dorie undid her hair and let it float all around her in the tub before she rubbed the soap into her scalp. The splashing sounds of water, both in and out of the house, soothed her mind until she realized she was scrubbing away the last traces of Victor. She closed her eyes, wanting him there with her to rinse her hair and cook those wonderful eggs again. She pictured him sitting on the floor next to the tub, his shirtsleeves rolled up, cheeks pink from the steamy water. They would share a cup of strong coffee and make plans how to handle Steiner. She would hook the V of his shirtfront with her wet fingers, not caring that she soaked it entirely, to bring him closer for a kiss. Her mouth opened at the memory of his tongue sliding to meet her own. She tipped her head back imagining his hands gliding underwater over her shoulders and breasts and across her belly as he teased her with his fingers.

"Where did you get that ring?" Louie asked suddenly.

Startled, Dorie opened her eyes to see him peering over the top of the folding screen. She looked at her hand hanging off the side of the tub as if she hadn't seen it before. The dark garnets winked. Chuckling, she remembered the countless times she had modeled a remarkable hat or a new dress always waiting in vain for Louie to notice and comment.

"What's the joke?"

A lie here or there, which one to choose? The ring came from one of her sisters? Stolen from Sal's pocket? Maybe it was time for the truth. "Victor gave me the ring."

"Our friend is generous, or is he in love?"

The heat from the water and the stove along with Louie's questions made her head pound.

"He's both," she answered boldly. She hung her elbows over the side of the tub, making no effort to conceal her nakedness.

"And what did you give him?"

She brought the heavy sponge over her head and squeezed it slowly to rinse the soap from her hair. Water streamed over her face. How should she answer him?

She gasped and sputtered as he roughly grabbed her wrist. "Don't ignore me, Dorie. You're always doin' that—tellin' your stories, making plans as if I'm not here."

The skin on his fingers looked yellow against her white wrist. His grip was stronger than she expected. She yanked her arm free, splashing water against the hot stove in a steamy hiss. Something flashed in his bloodshot eyes that Dorie had never seen before—something hard and mean.

"Leave me be. I'm bathing." She tried to keep the tremor from her voice. She had expected weeping, but certainly not anger. She hated him standing over her like that.

"I'm not leaving until you tell me where Sal is. I want to talk to him. I want to ask him what you and Victor were up to during the storm."

Oh, God, he really doesn't know. The tub water suddenly felt cool. "Sal's dead," she said, and then saw the horror register on his face.

22

St. Vincent's

The March morning sun flared through the stained-glass windows at St. Vincent de Paul church, casting rivers of blues and greens over the heads and shoulders of the faithful gathered for mass. Dorie stepped through the main door as the opening chords of organ music brought the congregation to its feet. Her stomach churned fiercely, and she gripped the worn leather missal for courage. She was a sinner waiting for God to make a show of the power of His displeasure at her arrival. It would be a dramatic sign. Perhaps the statue of St. Francis would tip from its moorings and land in such a way as to point an accusatory finger at her. Or maybe the marble floor would simply open and swallow her. The faint clicks of rosary beads along with her mother's voice spinning these scenarios seemed as real as if Camille Bibeau had come from the grave to stand behind Dorie's shoulder and whisper in her ear. When the drone of the processional hymn ended, off-key and a full beat behind the organist, and there was no flash of lightning or clap of thunder, only then could Dorie relax her tense muscles and search for a place to sit.

Ordinarily she sat in the front pews, not from the desire to be closer to God, but because it gave her the opportunity to show off a new hat. Today, however, she slipped into one of the empty pews in the back on the right side, only a few feet away from the imposing oak confessional doors. When Father Caouette didn't turn around and order her to leave his church, the thought came to her that maybe she wasn't the only one here with heavy secrets and sins. She hoped God was too preoccupied hearing endless confessions or meaningless promises of a renewed spirit to be overly concerned with her small life, or maybe she was simply beyond redemption—a lost cause to God.

The first thing Dorie always noticed about Father Caouette was his slight build. The first time she saw him, she mistook him for a young boy. It was as if he was a scale model of a regular-sized man, like a picture in a catalogue. The second thing of note about the priest was his head of chestnut-colored wavy hair. What a crime to waste such wonderfully thick hair on a priest!

"*En nominee patris, et filii spritus sancti,*" Father intoned.

Dorie scanned the backs of heads looking for Victor. She hoped he was doing his duty, as the good nephew, escorting Ingeborg to church. It had been over two weeks since her arrival back home, and she didn't know his whereabouts. All she thought about was their time together on Buzzy's farm. When she closed her eyes, she could summon the feel of his hands or his mouth—a ghost touch. She blushed furiously as she shifted her weight, crossing and uncrossing her ankles, as if her thoughts had been broadcast to those around her. To Dorie, this evidence proved she didn't belong there. Certainly she was the only one thinking about such matters during a mass. Where was he? Maybe she could slip out and go to the boarding house and leave a message for him there. She was desperate to see him, to reassure herself of his feelings. Funny, when she was with him, she was at peace. He told her he loved her at all the right moments. When they were apart, she pictured him itching to leave and anxious to wash his hands of the mess of her marriage and their business.

Dorie stood for the reading of the gospel and looked toward the fresco on the ceiling, hoping to at least look pious, even if she had failed to produce one single holy thought. Teeth gritted, she tilted her chin upward and waited for stares. Someone was bound to turn around and spot her there, and then nudge the next person and whisper. Emmett must have told his wife, who would have told everyone in town by now that Dorie and Victor had spent the blizzard stranded together out at Buzzy's place. To Dorie, it felt as if she were visibly marked in a way that others could see, just as the bruises from Sal's fingers had stained her skin. On the ceiling, fat painted cherubs clutched banners that read: *To God, I belong. To God, I return.*

Dorie unbuttoned her coat and slipped her arms from the sleeves, allowing the coat to rest on her shoulders. Temperatures were well above freezing these last few days, and the heavy coat felt bulky and uncomfortable. At the sound of a side door creaking, Dorie looked over to her left and saw Ingeborg stalk past the statue of the Virgin Mary as she furiously crossed herself with holy water. Droplets flew over her shoulder, and the flames of the red votive candles waved in her wake. Victor strolled in a distance behind her, running the brim of his hat through his fingers. Dorie's heart turned over at the sight of him.

She smirked. Victor must have been late picking up Ingeborg. Dorie remembered the pocket watch broken in the accident and wanted to immediately make a trip to Minneapolis to buy him the finest timepiece she could find. How handsome he looked! From this distance, the cuts on his face looked to be healing. She wished she could wave or call attention, but he followed Ingeborg like a gosling to her regular seat in the second row. Why Ingeborg would want to sit in such a place of attention with that worn, homely hat, was beyond Dorie.

"*Dominus vobiscuim*," Father Caouette droned.

Now she would have to stay for the rest of the service and wait for her chance see him. Dorie could hear her question "Where's Mr. LaValle?" To which she would answer that he was under the weather. This wasn't a lie because Louie might be sick. The stash of moonshine from the cellar was completely depleted now. She had smashed all the empty bottles out behind one of the sheds in case Steiner came to poke around. It was possible that Louie had bottles hidden elsewhere, but at the rate he was drinking the last few days, she guessed they might be nearly gone too. Truth be told, she didn't know Louie's exact whereabouts. After the fight in the kitchen that day, she caught glimpses of him skulking about the yard or going in and out of the barn. Why, he even slept out there now. Yesterday she heard him sneak into the kitchen when she was upstairs. Later, she discovered a loaf of bread and some sausage missing. What was he doing with his days? Building more birdhouses or drinking? She didn't really care. For now, she felt pure relief to have him gone from her sight.

Dorie fidgeted in her pew and tried unsuccessfully to send her thoughts to Victor. She resorted to counting things to keep her mind occupied, the number of small babies under the age of one, the number of men in attendance today who had come to drink in her kitchen. When she started counting blond children, she was surprised to recognize Steiner's ramrod posture. He sat several pews ahead of her next to the aisle with a woman who must be his wife. Was Steiner deep in prayer or was he thinking about Dorie, Victor, and the dead man in the car?

As the throng bent to their knees, Dorie pulled out the kneeler and clasped her hands. Her mouth could mumble the words and follow the lines in the missal along with the congregation, but her heart prayed something entirely different. *If you have the inclination to hear and answer this prayer. Let us get out of this mess. Keep Victor safe from harm. Let me find that hidden stash of money.* That was as much of a prayer as she could muster. She crossed herself and eased back to relax her posture, realizing she had not said a word about Louie.

"Kyre, Kyre, elisian," Father sang.

Moments later, it was time for communion, and Dorie felt a cold sweat break out over her upper lip. What would happen if she tried to take communion with these sins on her soul? Camille had warned that the host would burn the lips and tongue of people with mortal sins on their soul. Suddenly, her coat was too warm, and it was hard to breathe. Tears stung her eyes, and she stumbled, catching her skirt on the edge of the kneeler, nearly sending her crashing to the floor. Dorie yanked on her skirt to free it, causing the kneeler to rise for a moment and then slam to the floor with a resounding thud. She sensed, but did not see, the congregation turn to watch her retreat, as she made her way to the back of the church.

Thankfully the organ groaned to life again, the opening strains of the hymn drowning out the hollow click of her heels. Had Victor seen her leave? If so, she half-hoped he'd follow her and then thought better of her wish. As usual with matters concerning Victor, there was no pure decision. As soon as she'd entered the narthex, she closed the heavy door behind her and leaned against the carved wood, panting as if she'd run a three-legged race at a picnic. She would go to the boarding house and leave word for Victor. Suddenly the solidness of the door behind her gave way, and she fell backward into Steiner's arms.

"Mrs. LaValle, are you feeling ill?" he whispered.

"Sheriff, I... well, I felt suddenly overheated. A dizzy spell is all. No need to trouble yourself."

He guided her back into the narthex and shut the door behind him. The cool air rushed around her in the dim light. It was a relief to be away from the bright, loud service.

"Maybe you are suffering some after effects from the accident?" She couldn't read his gray eyes, and it maddened her that she couldn't tell if his concern was genuine or not. Behind Steiner hung a painting of a white-robed Jesus, staff in hand, guiding a flock of lambs. Dorie had never seen such unnaturally white sheep before.

"I've had no breakfast this morning. I had to allow extra time in case I got stuck in the mud." There was a small scorch mark on the pocket of his crisp shirt.

"And if you were alone, mired in the mud, what would you have done?"

What was he getting at? Was he trying to figure out if Louie accompanied her or if she was with Victor?

"I imagine I would've caught a ride with another driver on his way to town." She tried to answer casually, but it seemed he was weighing each of her answers like a teacher giving an oral exam. Who indeed would pick her up stranded by the side of the road? Only the regulars, provided their wives were home sick in bed.

"Somehow I pictured you pushing the car out of the muck yourself." There was a slight trace of a smile, or rather, more a crinkling at the corners of his eyes than anything else. Was he teasing her?

She smiled back, a woman easily charmed without a care in the world. Is that what he wanted?

"I'm glad I saw you this morning. I was going to stop by your farm after the service today anyway." His arms were crossed, those long, thin fingers tucked away. He stood in front of her, unmoving, almost like a statue. She was accustomed to the nervous tics of men as they spoke to her. God knew Louie was a satchel full of twitchy movements, but Steiner didn't run his hands through his hair or smooth his tie or scratch his chin. He had no "tells," she realized. Her Grand-père Madore wouldn't have played cards with a man like Steiner.

Here it comes, she thought. Was he going to arrest her here in church for making moonshine or for having something to do with Sal's death?

"I was finally able to make contact with the D'Agostino family in Chicago. They're sending someone to claim the body."

Dorie tried her best to look polite, but unfazed.

"Oh?"

"Some business has come up that I must attend to at the end of the week, and I was wondering if you could meet the train. The family said they had some questions for the folks who last saw Mr. D'Agostino alive, so you would be meeting with them eventually."

"I see. There's no one else?"

"Is this an inconvenience? If you're unwell, I'll see what other arrangements I could make. Perhaps Louie could meet the train, instead?"

The blood pounded in her ears. Why was he asking her to do this? "What time does the train arrive?"

"At one o'clock on Friday. Then you'll do it?"

Dorie pictured pulling a sheet from Sal's gray, cold face as his father or perhaps another brother collapsed and sobbed over the body.

"The body," she began. "I'm not sure how..."

"No, Mrs. LaValle, you've misunderstood my request! If you could just meet the train and get him settled at Mrs. Hamm's boarding house." The muffled organ music seemed to vibrate through the door.

"I'm a good hostess," Dorie breathed out. She could do that—meet the train, show the visitor around town.

"That's exactly what I was counting on," Steiner nodded. "Now, if you'll excuse me, I'm going to return for communion. Are you coming back in?" He uncrossed his arms and grabbed the heavy brass door handle.

"I believe I'll collect myself for a moment here." She couldn't go back in there now. It was enough to have them all talk about her and Victor, but now they probably all saw the sheriff leave the service to have words with her. She'd have to find another way to speak to Victor. She imagined they were all itching to press their ears against the door to eavesdrop on their conversation.

"Still feeling faint?"

Her legs trembled. "No, I'm fine."

"If you're sure then. Thank you for your help, Mrs. LaValle." He nodded. In this light, his eyes had more of a bluish cast to them.

"Oh, Sheriff, what is the name of the relative I'm to meet?"

"The telegram didn't say for sure. I assume it'll be the senior Mr. D'Agostino. He's the one who sent the telegram."

23

At the Boarding House

The shelves in Mrs. Ruth Hamm's parlor were filled with books. Some that wouldn't fit on the shelves rested in teetering stacks on every delicate end table and atop the player piano. They were mostly poetry volumes or adventure stories. Dorie knew this because Victor had told her Mrs. Hamm required the boarders to read every day. Some books had their spines splayed open, and others trailed tasseled markers. It looked as if a roomful of readers had been suddenly called away. Dorie rang the small silver bell at the desk and stood, hands clasped behind her back, feeling again like a ten-year-old school girl confident of answers to all the questions, but one who often got the hairy eyeball for her behaviors. Mrs. Hamm had been, in fact, her primary school teacher for eight years. After Dorie graduated from high school, Mrs. Hamm and her husband built this house in town in 1920 and retired together from farming and teaching. However, when Thomas Hamm died two years later, a childless Ruth was obliged to take in lodgers in order to support herself. Dorie looked down and recognized the dark cherry wood desk, now used to register the lodgers, as the same one positioned in the front of the Eagle Lake School room for all those years.

Dorie had left her coat in the car. Warmth of the nearly spring day made her feel as if she never wanted to wear the heavy wool again. Mrs. Hamm embraced the change in weather in a similar way. Two of the narrow windows were propped wide open, and Dorie remembered how, when Mrs. Hamm perceived her students to be sluggish in their responses, she would wake them even on the coldest days by letting in the winter air.

Mrs. Hamm pushed through the swinging doors, wiping her hands on a dish towel. A fat yellow dog with milky white eyes followed closely at her heels.

"Yes. Who's there?" Mrs. Hamm pushed her spectacles up the bridge of her thin nose. "Is that Dorie Bibeau? What brings you here?"

Dorie stood speechless. It had been quite a few years since she had last spoken at length with her former teacher. When Dorie was her student, Mrs. Hamm stood not quite five feet tall. She always said she liked being close to the size of her students.

Today she stood before Dorie at barely four-foot-nine. Her wispy hair was snow white but still parted precisely down the middle of her head. As Mrs. Hamm waited expectantly in front of her, Dorie remembered her teacher's habit of pursing her thin lips to cover her crooked teeth and sour breath.

"I've never known you to be at a loss for words, Dorie Bibeau." Mrs. Hamm leaned two palms against the desk and narrowed her pale-blue eyes. The dog suddenly poked its nose under the hem of Dorie's dress, causing her to back into the hat rack. "That's Emily Dickinson. I brought her with me from the farm."

"There are two things I need your help with," Dorie began as she patted the dog's soft fur. Even with fresh air circulating in the room, she caught a whiff off Mrs. Hamm of fry grease and sour milk. "I'd like to see if you have a room for a traveler arriving by train at the end of the week. I think the stay will be two to three days. The last name is D'Agostino. I'm afraid I don't know the first name."

"A stranger. You expect me to take in a stranger?"

Dorie was surprised. She guessed at least a portion of Mrs. Hamm's business involved taking in travelers.

"Well, yes, a stranger."

"I don't know if I have a room." The dog leaned its ample weight on Dorie's foot.

"Is anyone else in town taking boarders at this time?"

"Do you know how my husband died?"

Dorie searched her memory for details of Mr. Hamm's death. An accident of some kind? Before she could answer, Mrs. Hamm supplied the response.

"The drink got him."

Dorie wrinkled her brow in confusion. Mr. Hamm died before she had started selling moonshine. "I'm sorry."

"The drink grabbed hold of him like a rabid dog and shook him until he was dead."

"I hadn't heard," Dorie answered, but now something flickered in her memory far different from Mrs. Hamm's explanation.

"Smart girl like you, didn't I tell you to become a nurse? Now nursing, that's a respectable profession." Mrs. Hamm straightened the already immaculate desk as she spoke and began running a dust rag she had pulled from her apron pocket over the dark wood.

Dorie remembered Mrs. Hamm counseling her female students to "get some training in case the farm fails." She strongly recommended three lines of work for all the girls: nun, teacher, or nurse. At the age of fourteen, Dorie had dismissed these suggestions with disdain. Then she recalled Victor arriving at her door with the bullet wound and the battle she had waged against the infection. Dorie smiled ruefully. Yes, maybe she should have become a nurse after all.

"If you don't have a room, I'll have to ask the sheriff what other arrangements might be made. Is it possible to leave a note for Victor Volk?"

"What do you want with Victor? You're not trying to make that poor man drink your evil brew, are you?"

Why did everyone think Victor was an innocent? It wasn't fair.

"I just want to leave him a note," Dorie said. The dog's weight numbed her foot.

Mrs. Hamm blinked slowly.

"May I use a piece of paper?" Dorie asked.

"You didn't bring your own?"

Dorie bit her lip in frustration. She should just leave.

"What does the sheriff have to do with this?"

"Sheriff Steiner asked me if you'd hold a room for the out-of-town visitor."

"Why did the sheriff ask you to do that? What business does he have with you? Oh, I suppose he comes out to your place to drink too." Dorie noticed the brooch at Mrs. Hamm's throat held a lock of hair that probably belonged to her dead husband.

"I saw him at morning mass, and he knew I was coming over here. He asked me to do him a favor… that's all."

Mrs. Hamm opened up the leather ledger on the desk. "In that case, I'll rent a room if the sheriff deems it. This guest's a reader then?" She dipped the pen in the inkwell.

Dorie clenched her teeth. "I really couldn't say."

"Spelling?"

"I don't know if he knows how to spell. I don't even know if he speaks English!" Dorie stamped her foot, and the old dog moved with a whimper. Dorie couldn't wait to get away. How did Victor stand living here?

"Emily, come here. No, I mean, how do you *spell* the lodger's name?"

After Dorie obliged, she asked again for a piece of paper and an envelope.

"No envelope," Mrs. Hamm said shaking her head. "It's wasteful." She pulled a sheet of paper from the blotter, creased it and tore a quarter of it off and offered it to Dorie.

She'd have to be careful what she wrote, although even if she had been provided an envelope, Mrs. Hamm would most likely peel it open before the glue had set as soon as Dorie's boots hit the porch. Hell's bells, she'd probably correct her grammar and spelling errors too. What would she say in a note to him even if she believed it would never be seen by any prying eyes? *I love you. I miss you. I can't wait to kiss you.* She had no words for what was in her heart.

Mrs. Hamm didn't turn to give her any privacy as she handed her the pen. Dorie paused for a moment and began to write. *Sheriff Steiner has requested that I meet the train at the end of the week to escort Mr. D'Agostino, who is arriving here on business. Can you meet us at the station in case he has any questions for you regarding the sale of Buzzy's farm?*

Mrs. Hamm pressed two fingers over her lips. "I expected more of you Dorie. You were the smartest little thing ever to come through Eagle Lake School. It's a crime what you do, selling that stuff to the men around here."

Dorie flushed, expecting Mrs. Hamm to pull out a ruler any moment and rap her knuckles or make her kneel on the broom handle for the afternoon. "I don't know what you're talking about Mrs. Hamm. I'm sorry about your husband, but I never sold him a drink. I had nothing to do with his death!"

"Prohibition was meant to stop that sin-juice from getting to the men."

"Your husband didn't die from whiskey. I remember now. He fell, didn't he, from the barn loft or a roof." Dorie was breathing hard now and wondering why she was bothering to argue. Did she think she could sway Mrs. Hamm's opinion?

"Thomas was a decent man who treated me right and honored all of our wedding vows until he started drinking. Then everything turned ugly." She fingered the brooch at her neck as she spoke. "It just got worse and worse. I tried to dump the stuff down the drain, but he always managed to get more even if it meant using the money set aside for food." The dog began to snore at Mrs. Hamm's feet, and she bent to scratch her back.

"That day he came home in the afternoon with a snootful and started chasing me around the house with his Colt pistol. I was so scared I didn't know what to do so I ran clear across our south field to a neighbor's place. Olivia took one look at me and locked all the doors to keep him out. I ran upstairs to her bedroom and hid there. Thomas walked around the house, hollering my name, peering in all the windows even though Olivia shouted for him to go home and sleep it off." Mrs. Hamm stood and wiped her hands on her apron. Her magnified eyes were red-rimmed behind her spectacles.

Dorie shifted uncomfortably.

"Finally, Thomas propped a ladder against the house and climbed up to look into the second-story bedroom window. When he saw me, he put the muzzle of the Colt to the window and fired. When the glass shattered, I screamed and fell to the floor. I didn't move a muscle. I was so scared I just froze up. I figured he'd climb in the window and come after me, or worse, after Olivia or her babies if I took off running again."

Mrs. Hamm grabbed Dorie's hand in her own hot one and squeezed hard. "There came a moaning noise from him then, no sound I'd ever heard him make before, but I kept my eyes squeezed shut—waiting—just waiting for what felt like forever for the bullet that was meant for me."

Dorie thought the bones in her hand might shatter. Mrs. Hamm's eyes were pinched shut as if she were still lying on Olivia's bedroom floor.

"Then the gun fired again, but he didn't aim at me. He must have thought I was dead, and so he had put the gun under his own chin and pulled the trigger. And then I heard that terrible thud when he hit the ground."

Mrs. Hamm opened her eyes and pulled Dorie closer. "None of that was Thomas's fault. It was the drink, you see."

24

The Train Station

Dorie stood alone on the train platform. She had arrived forty-five minutes early to meet Mr. D'Agostino's train. The spring-like warming sun of the previous day had vanished, forcing Dorie to again don her tired woolen coat. The sky was the discouraging color of a galvanized bucket. Slushy ruts had frozen overnight, making the drive into town a bumpy one. But at noon now, despite the absence of sun, the temperatures hovered just above freezing, causing the snow banks and icy walkways to soften like ice cream that had set out too long. She shivered in the chilly, damp air.

Dorie changed her dress three times before deciding on the dark-blue wool dress with the tiny emerald-green glass buttons. She finally settled on this dress because the high neck managed to cover the last yellowish traces of the bruises on her neck. A nervous stomach prevented her from eating her usual breakfast, and she could only manage some dry toast and weak tea. What would Mr. D'Agostino be like? Would he be an older version of Geno and Sal? Old and doddering she hoped—that type of man was her specialty.

Did Victor ever get her message? A slab of snow let loose and slid down the steep roof that angled over the tracks, splashing mud near the platform. The eaves dripped too, a quick beat that matched her pulse. Mrs. Philodeaux opened the door, and three noisy children burst past her, making their way directly to the pools of muddy slush. Despite her feeble protests, the boys jumped in the puddles. Dorie stepped aside as Mrs. Philodeaux backed away, whether to distance herself from her ill-behaved children or from the woman who supplied her husband with moonshine, Dorie couldn't guess. What she did know was that she had the urge to push those scrawny, pale boys face first into the mud or better yet in front of the soon-to-arrive train.

Her own children would be so very different! She pictured them clearly, as if they were real flesh and blood. A blond girl so like Victor, healthy and tall with good posture and deep-blue eyes. Dorie would dress her in only the finest apparel. One day she would stand with her daughter, waiting to board a train that would take her away to college. Like Lenny, maybe she would become a doctor or a teacher. The boy, younger than her daughter, would have her auburn hair and Victor's solid build. The boy would miss his sister so much they would have been inseparable since the day of his birth, but he would bear his grief stoically. What would their names be? She had always favored Eloise for a girl's name. The boy might be named after someone in Victor's family. Dear God, what was she thinking? Children with Victor? She spun around when a hand touched on her shoulder.

"Victor!" she said. Her heart felt as if it were trying to escape her body by squeezing itself out of her rib cage. It had been over four weeks since the day Steiner had delivered her back to the farm after the blizzard! She smiled to see his face had healed remarkably well. The scabs were nearly gone, and the worst of the wounds, the one through his eyebrow, was now a pink shiny scar. His hat was pushed back at a boyish angle on his head.

"Love, you look like you've seen a ghost." He smiled.

Just the ghosts of your children, she longed to tell him.

Sensing Mrs. Philodeaux's gaze, Dorie turned, pretending to concentrate on the spot on the horizon where the train was due to appear rather than look at Victor. A few more people had wandered out to the platform by this time. Oh, he was here and he called her love!

"I'm wondering if you are a ghost. It's been so long since I've seen you, I don't know if you're real or not." She kept her voice low as she spoke.

"I thought I should stay away." There was a long pause, and she wondered if he was going to offer any other explanation. She bit the inside of her cheek waiting for him to form his thoughts. Finally he looked over his shoulder and said, "When I saw Louie that morning after the blizzard ended, that poor pitiful bastard, I couldn't face him again. But believe this, I wanted to come and haunt your bedroom. Does that make me a ghost?"

Dorie's knees weakened at his words. Hadn't she pictured just the same visitation every night since the blizzard?

"Hmmm," she managed to answer.

"If I'm a ghost, then I can kiss you properly right here and now. No one will see! Not one of those silly pecks on the cheek either. I mean a long and slow one."

Dorie shivered with the excitement of having him talk to her like that. Where could they go to touch and kiss without being noticed?

"So you got my message after all? I didn't think Mrs. Hamm would give you my note."

"Are you kidding? She nearly knocked me over when I came in the door. So many questions, Ye Gads! She seemed to believe you were going to put me in the middle of some kind of wrongdoing. Can you imagine?"

"Yes, I can." He smelled spicy clean. She wanted to bury her nose in the front of his starched shirt. "All the women in this town think that." Dorie glanced over her shoulder. Mrs. Philodeaux's stare was hot enough to melt the remaining snow.

"So another D'Agostino is coming to town," he said. Dorie watched him feel for the pocket watch that no longer hung from the chain. "Why do you think Steiner asked you to meet the train?"

"I don't know. He said he had some business that prevented him from being here this morning."

"Is that the truth? Maybe he wanted to see how you'd react to that suggestion. Or else he's someplace close watching your every move—and mine too for that matter." Victor looked down as if he was intensely interested in his shoes.

She couldn't imagine Steiner in an outright lie. She knew liars, and he wasn't one. Still, Victor's suggestion confused her.

"He said the family had questions for the last people to see Sal alive. Steiner wanted us to talk to him."

"To rattle you?"

Dorie searched the faces of the crowd that had begun to gather and had the urge to dash about on foot and check behind the pine trees that grew to the right of the platform and then inside the building near the ticket window. What if he were farther away peering at them through a set of binoculars?

Victor firmly squeezed her elbow. "Easy. I'm just trying to figure out what's going on here. Here's what I think. Steiner thinks we're responsible for Sal's death, but he can't prove it because there are no witnesses. All he has to do is point the D'Agostino family in our direction and, in his mind, justice will be delivered."

Dorie felt a feathery chill skitter across her neck like a centipede dropped from the ceiling of the cellar. Mrs. Watson moved next to her, clutching a satchel close to her body as if it were a prize.

"You were the one who never believed that family was actually in the grocery business. Those fancy suits Sal wore and the money clip he carried—you told me some story about the still heists. Maybe it's true!"

Mrs. Philodeaux's youngest boy pointed and shouted the arrival of the train. Dorie watched the approach of the black engine moving across the landscape. Pale gray smoke blew into the darker sky. She could hear the engine now as it chugged past the barren scrub trees and stubborn banks of snow. The passenger cars followed the wide bend around Eagle Lake. Dorie wondered if, at this minute, Mr. D'Agostino was looking out the train window across the expanse of frozen land.

"Steiner might be leading us to the hungry lion's den then, is that what you think?" Dorie pictured the mobsters she had read stories about leaping from the moving train, hats low over their eyes with machine guns poised in both hands. In a shower of gunfire, they would spray bullets at everyone standing on the platform and escape to a running car. Dorie sniffed, her nose running in the cold wind. Victor pressed a handkerchief into the palm of her hand.

The train whistle blew one long burst followed by two short ones. The small crowd began to talk loudly and shuffle forward. Others waved scarves or stood protectively near their trunks and belongings.

"I told Louie we are in love," Dorie said suddenly, keeping her eyes fixed on the motion of the wheels. The words spun away from her mouth as if she had no control over them. She felt Victor startle. He swung around and turned to look her in the eyes for the first time.

"Dorie, I didn't want that. Why? What happened?" His jaw clenched as he spoke, and his eyes darted over her shoulder, wondering who might be watching them. Dorie wondered if they would both be doomed to a life of looking over their shoulders.

"He saw the ring." Dorie held up her hand to display his gift. "He seemed to know already." It was hard to talk quietly over the sound of the approaching engines.

"When did you tell him?"

"The day we returned from Buzzy's."

"You should have told me sooner. What if he comes after me?"

Dorie snorted. "This is Louie we're talking about here."

"Yes, but Louie is also a man and your husband. I can't believe he'd fancy sharing you."

"No."

"So how did you leave things?"

"I haven't seen much of him. He's taken to living in the barn."

"The barn? You're not telling me the truth. The barn," he repeated.

"He comes into the house and gets food and clothes when I'm out."

"This can't go on," he hissed.

"Well, the worst of the winter is over now. He's dry." Victor's eyes went wide at her words. Dorie couldn't believe he seemed so horrified at what she believed was a good solution to her problem.

"Dorie, your husband is living in a barn like an animal. Is he drunk most of the time, do you suppose?"

Dorie shrugged. "The cellar's empty. In the last three weeks, I've sold off the last of the final batch you brought that day. It's just as well in case Steiner comes to snoop around. Anyway, Louie might have hidden some on his own."

"Do you think he's been out to the still? I'd left a few cases out there before all the trouble started."

Dorie remembered that day when he showed up with the last delivery, bleeding from the gunshot wound. It seemed like a lifetime ago.

"I don't want him out at Buzzy's! It'd be just my luck that he'd stumble across the money before I have a chance to find it! It's my money. They owe me."

Victor laughed. "Your money? If there is any truth to what Sal said, then the money's probably stolen. What makes you think you have any claim on it?"

"Geno and his scoundrel brother ruined my business. If they'd stayed away things would have gone on as before, and I would still be making money."

It came to her then, a question she should ask him. "Victor how are you getting by? Do you have any money left?" She knew he spent his earnings before the bills had time to warm in his hands. It had been a week or two before the shooting, since she'd given him a share of their profits. She had twenty-five dollars rolled into the sleeve of her dress—maybe that would be enough for now. "Here, let me give you some now."

His furious blush provided her answer. "Now, Dorie, I don't want to talk about that now," he whispered.

He shoved his hands deep into his pockets and worked a shoulder muscle as if it were stiff. Suddenly everything felt wrong. She had upset him by telling him about Louie, and now she had offended him by offering money. All of these missteps were due to the fact that she couldn't be alone with him. She needed to explain herself properly and squelch all these bad feelings with a kiss.

Passengers began to step from the train. Mrs. LaFranier hugged a red-faced woman who must certainly be her sister. Dorie searched each man's face for any likeness to Sal and Eugene. The conductor stepped down to help an elderly man, taking him by the elbow. Another passenger guided him from behind as he slowly maneuvered the steep stairs. In his hand he held a cane with an ivory handle. It was hard to see his face because he looked down, deliberately placing each shaking foot in front of the last. He had snow-white hair that escaped from underneath his hat and wore an overcoat that was several sizes too large.

Dorie smiled. A palsied old man would be no problem. Why, he didn't look as though he could survive the trip home. She would be able to tell him stories to confuse him and deflect suspicion. She nudged Victor and nodded in the direction of the old man. When he didn't respond, she turned to look at him.

Victor wasn't watching the old man, who was enveloped in the embrace of Mrs. Philodeaux. Instead, she heard Victor give a small gasp as he stared at a dark-haired woman who stepped from the train. Her rich black hair was swept back from her oval face in a complicated bun. She looked fresh and rested from her trip. It was the woman's eyes that caused Dorie to stare—large and deep set, and, from where Dorie stood, they appeared black against her olive skin, framed by sweeping, graceful brows.

She looked like she owned the world.

"Hello!" she called. "Are you Mr. Steiner Larssen?"

Victor shook his head but didn't say anything.

"Do you know him? Could you take me to him, then?" The conductor helped her from the last step. "I'm sorry. You don't know my name. I'm Francesca D'Agostino." She smiled, flashing her white, even teeth.

There had to be a mistake. Steiner said they were to meet Mr. D'Agostino—a father or another brother, but most definitely not a woman.

The wind kicked up at that moment, parting the woman's brown fur coat, and Dorie saw that she was expecting a child.

25

Francesca

Francesca shivered, pulled the mink collar closer, and stared out the train window at the flat expanse of snow-covered fields. Off in the distance, red barns passed in and out of view, and closer to the tracks, splintered stalks, bleached pale as a Swede's head of hair, poked through the white blanket. She had never stepped foot on a real farm, so it was ironic that she now owned one, courtesy of Uncle Buzzy's will. The idea of owning property made her smile for she had always lived in someone else's mansion.

Thoughts of a farm made her remember when Mrs. Harrington would return from the market lugging heaping baskets of corn. Her two oldest boys, Joseph and Geno Junior, loved to peel the papery covering from each ear, sampling the crunchy rows of yellow pearls before Margaret was able to toss the corn into the pot of boiling water. Francesca avoided this messy process since the time she had spotted a weevil rearing and twisting its body, and then it fell into the folds of her dress. Oh, how her boys laughed at her screams. She smiled to remember how Geno would gather the fine corn silk to form a shank and then chase little Joe around the house pinning it to the back of his head and taunting, "Can I have a smooch, bella?"

The memory of the corn set her mouth to watering. Her stomach cramped like a clenched fist. It had been an error, she realized, to eat as soon as the train had pulled out of the Chicago station, but her departure felt like such a celebration! Every minute on the train meant she was farther away from Giovanna's glare and the constant sobbing that had filled the large hallways since the arrival of the telegram announcing Sal's death. Even constant prayers to Elizabeth Ann Seton, the patron saint of in-law troubles, did nothing to ease their tensions.

The old man sitting across from her stirred and gestured toward the window. "There's Eagle Lake! We're almost to Osseo," he called in a loud voice even though they were the only two left in the car. "It's flat land, isn't it? If you stand on a chair, you can see the back of your own head." He laughed and snorted.

Francesca startled because he had been so quiet, mostly dozing upright for the last several hours, she had nearly forgotten about him.

"I'm home. I've been to bury my last sister, and now it's time to wait my turn."

Francesca waited for him to complain the way her father-in-law would rally loudly against the passage of time, if the recent massive stroke had not silenced his salty tongue. Instead, the old man merely smiled, more teeth missing than present, and patted her hand with his own dry one.

"Dear, don't be sad. I've had the best life you could imagine." His unruly eyebrows wiggled over his sharp green eyes. "Look at me. I'm eighty, and I'm with the most beautiful woman on the whole train. Just wait until my son sees me! I'm going to tell him you're his new mother. 'Met you at Bess's funeral,' I'll say." He made a noisy sound somewhere between a cough and a laugh. "I'm Guy Philodeaux." When he tipped his hat, he released a halo of wispy curls.

"Pleased to make your acquaintance. I'm Francesca D'Agostino," she answered.

"And how is it you find yourself on this train going to the frozen northern parts?" he asked.

Same as you, death, she wanted to say to him. She had been sent to escort the body of her brother-in-law back to Chicago for burial. And her husband had been missing for months now. If Sal was dead, what did that mean for Geno?

There had been no word from her Geno, and in the beginning she hadn't worried too much because he always made it home. Yes, he had been in some scrapes. Once he had received two black eyes, another time a few broken ribs, but nothing a lot of complaining, bragging and drinking wouldn't cure. Now that they had received word of Sal's death, she began to wonder if her husband's luck had finally run out too.

"Miss?" Mr. Philodeaux cupped a hand around the pale skin of his large ear and bent it in her direction. "What brings you to Osseo?"

"I'm here on family business," she said, borrowing one of Sal's favorite lines. She looked out the window at the expanse the old man had identified as Eagle Lake. She saw dozens of impossibly tiny houses across the snow. Why, they were only large enough for one person to turn around in! Did poor people live here all winter? This must be a cruel place of great poverty. Back home, at least Mrs. Harrington had a two-bedroom apartment for her family.

"Family business," Guy repeated and began to chuckle. He clutched one hand to his heart. She wondered if it meant he was coming home to die right now, this minute in the train car. "Is that what they're calling bearing children now?"

He gestured toward her open coat.

As if responding to a greeting, the baby in her belly moved in a fluttery wave, and Francesca flushed. If her in-laws knew about this baby, they would have never allowed her to step out of the house, let alone venture to Minnesota.

Her condition had been easy enough to hide. She had ignored her symptoms as long as possible, and then when her dresses strained at their seams, she stayed in her room or with the boys in their nursery as much as possible. In the last few weeks, she had kept a bulky shawl around her shoulders, claiming the need to ward off the winter chill. A rush of annoyance flickered through her. Was this old man making fun of her? Then he smiled so broadly, so innocently at her, that she had to let her feelings pass.

Before she had a chance to respond, the train car door slid open, and the porter announced the Osseo stop. Francesca stood and gathered her hat and gloves and gripped the handle of her satchel. Suddenly the thrill of the adventure and newfound freedom drained away. She had never been alone before. Where would she stay? She was sure the meager funds tucked into her bag by Giovanna wouldn't be enough to cover very many expenses. Her orders were clear: come home as soon as the sheriff releases the body.

A wave of dizziness surged upward from her toes, and she groped for the seat. She felt a hand at her elbow, but she tipped backward too quickly and pulled him on top of her. His head bumped against her mouth.

"I've saved you!" Guy announced. "In my day, I was strong as an ox. Of course, my day was years ago."

Her tongue throbbed. As Guy struggled to right himself, she caught the smell of fried eggs and menthol. She flushed, embarrassed by the dizzy spell, and more so by the proximity of the old man.

"I'm just hungry," she said by way of explanation. She touched the tip of her tongue with her fingertip, but didn't see any blood.

Guy sat back against the seat, breathing hard. "Why didn't you say sumpin'?" His hand fished deep into the pocket of his trousers.

"Here," he announced triumphantly as he placed a twisted sweet into her hand. "My sister was famous for her caramel recipe." Francesca examined the caramel, trying to ignore the fact that it was still warm from the heat of his legs. If the cook was dead, how old was this confection? Her hunger won out over her objections, and she unwrapped the dark caramel and let its sweetness melt in her mouth a moment before she sank her back teeth into the chewy mass. The cut on her tongue stung.

The train lurched forward as the brakes locked. The screech of metal on metal filled her head. Francesca nodded her thanks to Guy.

"Come on, my bride," he said offering her his arm. "What names have we picked out for my new heir?"

Francesca worked the caramel that had stuck to her back teeth. Why, she wasn't even offended by his improper jokes at all! How different this was from the way even a look from Sal could make her feel—sick like she'd eaten a pound of bad mortadella. Maybe this is the way of this northern land. Tiny houses, old men who made nearly indecent proposals. What next? She took his arm, grateful to know at least one person in this strange part of the country.

Guy Philodeaux might be the first friend she had made outside of the D'Agostino family.

As she waited to depart the train, Francesca braced herself for the cold Minnesota weather. Mrs. Harrington had told her of air so frigid that exposed fingers snapped and dropped off like twigs on trees. She could almost hear the noise! She also said that if you threw a cup of water in the air, it would fall to the ground as chunks of ice. She prepared herself to breathe in a shallow manner to protect her lungs.

A man named Sheriff Larssen was to meet her train. What did he look like? Her only familiarity with police was the stocky, black Irish duo that came sometimes to the business meetings at the house. Brothers or cousins she guessed by the looks of their jet-black hair, white skin and dark-blue eyes, both prone to frequent fits of laughter. They always slapped him on the back as they slid the fat envelopes from Sal into their coats.

The picture she had in her mind of what a northern lawman might look like came from a drawing and a description from one of her son's western storybooks. Steiner would look exactly like a cowboy named Shane who dressed all in black and pulled a cowboy hat low over his eyes before he spun his six-shooters out of his holster to gun down the bank robbers.

As she was about to descend the stairs, she was overcome with the awful, horrible pressure of having to relieve herself. She squeezed her legs together, bent forward, and tried to bear against the urge. Sweat broke out on her upper lip.

Guy, despite his additional sixty years, scooted down the stairs to the platform where he was swarmed by a woman and three stick-thin boys. "Grandpère," they called as they danced around him, pulling his coat and nearly knocking him to the ground. Sallow colored, with hair in need of barbering, these boys weren't nearly as handsome as Francesca's own. An ache of love and homesickness for her boys clenched at her heart. The smallest boy, who wore a coat that was several sizes too small, turned and stuck out his tongue at a woman on the platform.

What was she doing so far from home? This was craziness.

There was no cowboy dressed in black waiting as an escort. The porter jumped down the stairs and offered a gloved hand. The Minnesota air was chilly and wet, much like the temperature back home… certainly not the frightening cold she had been warned about.

Francesca gazed at the last two people left waiting. They stared back at her. There were no other arrivals off the train. As his family swept Guy along, he turned and raised a finger in her direction. She nodded. Her new groom was already leaving her behind.

Francesca called out to the man on the platform, "Hello. Are you Mr. Steiner Larssen?" Where was the telegram? "I'm sorry. You don't know my name. I'm Francesca D'Agostino."

The big German stepped forward. He looked to be in his thirties. *O, il mio dio*, so many white teeth in that crooked smile. His eyes were the same blue as a Maxfield Parrish painting.

"Excuse our poor manners," he started, without any trace of German accent. "I'm Victor Volk. We were told to meet *Mister* D'Agostino." He offered her his hand.

"Then they have sheriff-gals in this northland?" Maybe Steiner was a woman's name. Francesca nodded toward the woman who stepped in close enough so that her shoulder brushed Victor's arm. Francesca was surprised to see that the woman's hair was hennaed red.

The man laughed, revealing a deep dimple. She wondered if he could do parlor tricks where he held coins in that crevice. "Let me start again.

This is Dorie LaValle. Sheriff Steiner was called away on another matter and asked us to meet your train." The woman he called Dorie still hadn't said a word. She was fine featured with small dark eyes. She wore an attractive hat adorned with dyed feathers. She looked French, that one. She saw Dorie's eyebrow arch as her gaze fell to Francesca's open coat.

"I'm sorry to confuse you. My father-in-law suffered a stroke at the news of his son's death. My mother-in-law has not left his side. It was under these circumstances I was allowed to make the trip. If the body is indeed Salvatore's, then I am to escort him home for burial."

There was a long silence. The woman glanced at Victor, but he stared somewhere off in the distance. Finally, he spoke. "We're very sorry for your family's troubles. Let me take your satchel." A muscle clenched in his jaw. Francesca noted fresh scars on his jaw line.

"If you would point me in the direction of the nearest hotel and also where I could get a hot meal. I haven't eaten in many hours, and I fear I might faint."

"Dorie, let's take our guest to Schieffer's. I could eat a bear myself. I'll pick up your trunk when we get you settled at Mrs. Hamm's."

"Yes, that would be good," Dorie finally spoke. Her voice was clear and strong.

When the woman slid her hands into her fur muff—not as fine as her own of course—Francesca caught sight of a thin gold band. Then they were married, but why did she have a different last name and why didn't he introduce her as his wife?

Victor offered Francesca his arm, which she took gratefully. It had been a long time since an attractive man had dared to smile and offer himself as an escort. He looked strong enough to pick her up and carry her to the restaurant, and the powerful hunger that left her weak in the legs made her wish that he would do just that. Did Victor say boarding house? Didn't they have a hotel in this town? The woman trailed behind them, and as Francesca looked over her shoulder, Dorie's stare felt like a shove.

26

Francesca Goes to Schieffer's

What a tiny place, this Osseo! How could a whole town be only a matter of a few blocks? The muddy main street, divided into two rows of squat brown buildings, lined up like dry goods boxes on a shelf. The tallest part of town was the steeple of the white church. They drove from the train station to a diner, even though it was only a matter of blocks, but Francesca was grateful for this luxury.

Francesca waited on the walkway as Victor opened the door for Dorie. She listened to the muffled din of voices and wondered about the women in shabby coats she saw walking on the sidewalks. Did they live in those little houses on the lake?

When they passed through the crowded entryway, the sound became deafening. Two waitresses shouted out orders, and the cooks hollered back. Patrons called out news and greetings. Silverware and dishes were on a collision course with each other and the floor. Sunlight broke through the gray cloud cover and blazed through the front windows, steamy from the heat of cooking and bodies.

Diners turned their heads when she walked past their booths, and she gave them a little smile in return. It was so different from back home where the men in the family commanded the attention, the smiles, the best wines, and special food from the chefs.

Francesca felt like a decoration most of the time, no different from the chandelier that hung from the ceiling. Why, it could have been any woman at their side. Well not Maria Iaquinto, because her mustache was nearly as thick as her father-in-law's, but any number of dark, pretty girls to make the

D'Agostino men look good. It didn't matter if her head was full of fierce business ideas—no one ever asked.

They found the last open table, and Francesca made excuses to freshen up. The baby shifted again, and she was worried she would either soil her dress on the way to the washroom or walk crouched over like an old woman. Oh, the glorious smells of this place—baked goods, coffee, grilled onions. Her mouth watered. After she had washed up, she hurried back to the table, and Victor pulled out the chair for her.

"What is the house dish, then?"

"You won't be disappointed by the Blue Plate Special—sliced turkey, mashed potatoes, and gravy. Edwina makes biscuits as big as my hand!" Victor waived a fist. "You can use them to mop up the gravy or slather them with honey and butter. Edwina's a beekeeper. She makes the best honey around."

Francesca smiled to hear him talk. He seemed so full of joy for such simple things.

"Dorie?" he said as a question. She nodded but didn't look enthused. Victor signaled the woman who brought them coffee by holding up three fingers. She waved to Victor as she counted back change to a customer.

"It's busy here," Francesca commented.

"It's the only place in town to get a hot midday meal. The men can't get into the fields for another month or until things dry out. I think they get antsy waiting for spring," Victor said before he took a sip of coffee.

Francesca looked over Victor's starched shirt. He was the only one in the diner wearing a tie. "You're not a farmer then, are you? What do you do?"

He shifted in his seat. "Most recently I've been selling this and that, but I might have to look for another job." When he gripped the mug, all the color left his thumbnail.

"Hmm, I was hoping someone could tell me about running a farm. My uncle deeded me his farm in this area." The baby pressed a foot hard against her side. As Francesca rubbed the taut spot with the heel of her hand, she sensed Dorie's stare.

"We knew your Aunt Lois and Uncle Buzzy," Victor and Dorie said at the same time.

Francesca looked back and forth between them. Dorie's expression had softened for the first time that day, and her eyes were bright with tears. Francesca recognized that look immediately as that of a wistful, barren woman.

"How many children do you have?"

"I have three sons back in Chicago—Geno, Joseph, and little Biaggio. They are my blessings." She said a quick prayer to Saint Dominic Savio to watch over them in her absence. The love for her sons, this baby she was carrying, and the lost look on Dorie's face made Francesca reach across the table to touch Dorie's hand. "Those blessings will come to you too, you'll see. You must pray to Andrew the Apostle. He's the patron saint for women who wish to become mothers." Francesca witnessed a single tear follow the curve of Dorie's lovely cheekbone. Victor sat motionless.

"I predict this husband of yours will give you a child before the year is out." She winced when she realized she sounded like Geno's grandmother who read each day's fortune in the coffee grounds.

"Oh, Victor isn't my husband." Dorie yanked her hand from Francesca's grip and proceeded to blush furiously as she adjusted the napkin in her lap.

Ah, but you're in love with him, Francesca thought.

"My husband is Louie LaValle. We have a farm just outside of town. We raise potatoes."

"Oh, my mistake. When I'm hungry, I don't think clearly."

No one said anything else until the waitress arrived with the steaming oval plates balanced on her arms. "Vic, Dorie, anything else you'd be needin'?"

Francesca looked at the gray-haired waitress and was reminded of the steel girders they used to erect buildings back home. She plunked the heavy plates down in front of each of them.

"We're fine, Edwina. Thanks," Victor said. He smiled that crooked smile again.

Francesca scooped a large forkful of mashed potatoes, butter, and gravy. She groaned as the flavors melted in her mouth. Victor followed suit and tore open a steaming, golden biscuit, coated it with butter and drizzled it with honey before he popped it into his mouth. "I love biscuits!" he declared.

Dorie picked up her fork and poked at the potatoes. So Dorie was Victor's mistress. She wasn't shocked as other women might be. The men in the D'Agostino family routinely kept mistresses, oftentimes treating them better than the wives who bore their children. Even Francesca herself had had offers from potential lovers. She had turned them down partly because of the family's murderous fury and partly because she just didn't see the point of having two men demanding service. She had beautiful clothes and some jewelry. Her children were fed and housed. What else could a man offer? It was all just nonsense as far as she was concerned. What Francesca longed for was someone to share ideas with and most men made it clear they were interested in more than an intellectual exchange.

"So you knew my aunt and uncle? Tell me about them. I'm afraid I don't know very much about my mother's brother and his wife. My mother died when I was born. My father died shortly after that." Francesca cut the turkey and dipped it in the gravy. She was eating in a very unladylike fashion, but her hunger made her forget her manners. "Have you seen the farm? Is it beautiful?"

This question caused the pair to exchange a long glance. "Yes, it's a good farm," Victor started. "The house and the other buildings are in need of work—some fixing up, painting, along with a good cleaning and a dose of elbow grease." Victor wiped his mouth with his napkin and replaced it in his lap. "We could take you there if the roads aren't too muddy."

Francesca studied Dorie. Her cheeks had pinked up again. This time it wasn't from embarrassment, but rather passion. Francesca had had her own leg stroked under the table often enough to recognize the look. But Victor didn't seem like the same kind of wolf she was used to dealing with in secluded hallways or cloakrooms. Ah, that look that he had for Dorie—that was a package of love and lust tied up with a big, red bow.

Their passion came across the table in waves now. Francesca shifted uncomfortably on the wooden bench and struggled for something to say. Sadness too washed over her. It seemed she had missed the chance to love someone so fiercely.

"I was telling you I didn't know my aunt and uncle very well. I only met them once when they traveled to Chicago for a wedding. They took me with them to the ceremony, and I was jealous of the bride's beautiful dress, so I cried and cried. Lois tatted a white dress for my doll to make me feel better." Francesca stopped when she realized she was babbling. Victor's right hand was under the table. He looked slyly at Dorie and picked up his coffee cup with his left hand.

Were they even listening to her?

"Lois knew her way around a kitchen," Victor said still gazing at Dorie. "Every year she won a blue ribbon for her pies—peach, rhubarb, blueberry. When I was a boy I'd volunteer chores with Buzzy just to get a slice of pie with homemade ice cream. You know, her right arm had muscles like a man's from cranking that—"

"I don't think she baked a pie again after her son was killed in the war," Dorie interrupted. "Pie was William's favorite too."

Francesca stared at her nearly empty plate and wondered where all the food had gone. "I know William's death is the reason the farm was left to me. Do you know my husband didn't allow me to come to either of their funerals? In fact, Geno didn't tell me until very recently that I had been deeded this farm at all! I owned property and I didn't even know it!" She remembered their fight on that morning before he left town. She was so mad she didn't even pray to Edward the Confessor to heal their marriage troubles.

Edwina refilled their coffee cups and balanced Francesca's empty plate on the stack of four others. Her hands were the color of raw meat.

"Well, anyway, this might be the end to all those secrets. I think this will be my last baby too. My Geno has gone missing for weeks now, and not a word from him." Francesca gripped her napkin tightly. God in Heaven, she was suddenly so mad at him! Mad at him for going off on one of his schemes, mad for trying to sell her farm, mad for leaving her all alone. She knew then that he had run off to live with another woman and had left her to suffer with his bitter mother and father. Her jaw quivered.

She forgot for that moment all about Dorie and Victor.

They were staring at her with nearly identical expressions of shock. Victor pushed his blond hair back from his forehead with both hands. Dorie, pale and silent, pressed her back straight against the back of the booth.

"I can see how upsetting it is for you to have your husband gone," Victor said. He cleared his throat. "I'm so sorry."

The gravy had gone dull and thick on Dorie's full plate. *They think I'm sad*, Francesca thought. Was she sad? What was it she was feeling besides anger? Loneliness? Relief?

The door of the diner crashed open behind her. The din of voices quieted. Francesca turned and saw a man shaking a finger at her. His shirt was tattered and unbuttoned despite the weather, his long johns stained.

"There she is, all high and mighty, taking a noonday meal with him as if there's nothin' wrong with it." Spittle flew from his cracked lips. Even from this distance, Francesca caught a whiff of him and wrinkled her nose.

"Oh, good Lord," Victor muttered.

Francesca saw then that the crazy man was missing a boot, his foot poked through the wet stocking.

"Have you no shame?"

Victor slid out of the booth and attempted to guide the man out the diner door.

"Oh, I won't be needin' any of your help, Victor. I'd say you've given enough help." His face, Francesca noted, had a yellowish cast of mildewed books.

"You were my friend, Victor. You took meals in my kitchen." The man began to cry, great gut-wrenching sobs, and then he collapsed against Victor's immaculate shirt.

Francesca turned to Dorie. Her face was stained red, but she stared straight ahead against all the glances of the other diners.

"And that's my husband, Louie LaValle," she whispered.

For Francesca, it felt like sitting in the Avalon Theater watching the flickering picture show. This wasn't real. Head held high, Dorie slid out of the booth and moved to the coat tree. Only Francesca noticed the slight tremble of Dorie's hands as she slid her arms into her sleeves. Edwina stood still, holding plates of pie and ice cream. Other patrons sat silently, the men shifted in their seats. Some threw worried looks in Louie's direction. The women stared boldly at Dorie. One woman pressed a napkin to her lips; another leaned closer to her male companion and whispered.

Louie crumbled, sat on the wet floor, a spindle of snot hung from his nose. Victor squatted down next to him. He absently rubbed that fresh scar that sliced through his brow, but his eyes were locked on Dorie as she made her way to the door.

Francesca held her breath, That feeling that something bad was about to happen prickled at the back of her neck. *Go out the back way*, she wanted to call to Dorie. She and Geno had slipped out through the kitchens of plenty of restaurants at the first sign of trouble. Her words of warning were trapped in her own head.

Louie's bony hand pulled a gun out of his pocket. His other hand snaked out and caught Dorie's ankle as she tried to pass him to go out the door. He pressed the black muzzle to her thigh.

"If I maim you Dorie, do you think he'll still want you?"

A woman screamed. His eyes darted wildly around the room. Victor reared back on his haunches as if he'd been shoved.

"Whoa, Louie, put down the gun," Victor croaked.

Dorie's face contorted, and she tried to wrench her leg away from his grip.

Louie wrapped his arms around her leg in a fierce embrace, the gun still touching her dress.

"You're my wife," he crooned. His lips brushed her thigh.

Francesca struggled to her feet. She grabbed one of the glasses of water on the table and poured it down the front of her skirt.

"Oh, my dear Lord in Heaven," she called out, thankful that her voice had returned. "I'm going to have this baby right now!" She bent forward and held out her dripping skirt and howled.

All eyes turned to her, but Victor took advantage of the distraction. He slammed his shoulder into Louie's concave chest and sent him backward, and then pounced on him, pinning Louie's wrist with his knee. The gun sprang from Louie's hand and spun in circles near Dorie's feet.

No one spoke. One of the men stooped to pick up the gun and slapped Victor on the back. His blond hair had fallen over his eyes, and his shirt had pulled free from his trousers.

Two women appeared on either side of Francesca, each taking her by an arm. One woman had thin, colorless hair pulled back from her high forehead. Her skin, lined and chapped, made it difficult for Francesca to guess her age. Her companion wore a light brown dress, the fabric so thin in places she could see the woman's undergarments. Even so, she wore a lovely cameo broach at her throat. Edwina pulled up a chair and pressed Francesca's shoulders downward.

"Sit, dear," said the woman wearing the broach. "I'm Sophie, by way of strange introductions."

"Is this your first, dear?" the other woman asked. "My name is Hazel."

Francesca flushed with pleasure. She liked being fussed over. An only child, she had been without her own mother since birth. When she was young, she had always longed for someone to repeat the stories of her birth while brushing her hair one hundred strokes or to embroider her dresses or buy her fine things. Now, grown and married, she still felt alone. When she had labored with the other three boys, only the maid stayed with her until Giovanna deemed it was time to call the doctor. Edwina patted her back in a reassuring rhythm.

More people flooded into the diner now. The commotion attracted them the same as in Chicago—they just had to see what was going on. Two men, brothers Francesca guessed by the looks of them, both pink-faced and nearly hairless like new babies, had Louie by an arm in the same fashion of Francesca's ministering.

"Dorie, we'll be takin' him home for ya," they called out.

"Is the pain bad, dearie?" Hazel whispered in her ear. Francesca flushed, embarrassed at the scene she had caused. Her clammy skirt clung to her legs.

Dorie nodded at the men who spoke, but she turned away from Louie who was crying quietly as they herded him out the door. She walked toward

Francesca as if she hadn't a care in the world. Haughty French is how their maid Bridgid would describe her.

"Let's get you over to Doc Pitzer," Dorie said. Francesca watched to see if Dorie exhibited any sign of nerves.

"You know Mrs. LaValle then?" Sophie asked.

"I just arrived on the noon train," Francesca answered. "I'm here in town for some family business." She repeated the line she had told to Guy earlier. Someone slipped a shawl around her shoulders.

"What do you know about a woman's time to have a baby, anyway, Dorie?" Hazel's voice sounded sweet, but Francesca saw a muscle in Dorie's jaw tighten in response.

"Hazel, I know enough to get her to a doctor, and at least I know how to drive something more modern and comfortable than a tractor."

"You poor thing," Sophie whispered. "The first person you meet when you arrive is Dorie."

Francesca realized the women were flanked protectively around her in the same manner as the men who worked for Sal, Geno, and her father-inlaw. They all hate Dorie, she realized. *What was this all about?*

"That's odd, Sophie. Your husband didn't mention that your temperament had soured so when he picked up two quarts from me last month, but then again, maybe it explains why he wanted to double his order."

Francesca heard the gasps behind her. They weren't talking about milk orders here. Dorie must be a gin-runner! Ah, this was something she understood. Dorie had probably spent more on her fine hat than the yearly clothing allowances of all these women put together. She served their husbands liquor and gladly took their money. She heard Sophie, Edwina, and Hazel whispering. She couldn't make out all of what they were saying, but she heard "Something to do with that Italian fella they found dead in Buzzy's car."

Francesca sat very still. She felt heavy, sodden and suddenly tired. Her mind jumped to the telegram Giovanna had held to her breast. Salvatore D'Agostino dead. Automobile accident. Condolences. She thought of the pink wounds on Victor's face. Had Victor been in the car with Sal? The baby shifted, settling its bottom low in her belly, and then began a series of staccato hiccups. *Was it dangerous to bring this up with Victor?*

The wet skirt gave her a chill. The long trip, the big meal, and all this excitement took its toll. "I should like to go see that doctor of yours, Dorie."

"Are you having more pains?" Hazel asked.

"I don't think she should be moved," Edwina said.

"You're not going to leave her with that woman, are you?" Sophie whispered.

Francesca turned to them and smiled. "The pains have eased for now. I think I should like the advice of the doctor since I'm so far from home. I have some delicate questions I'd like to ask." She pulled the shawl from her shoulders, folding it before she handed it back. "I thank you all for such kindness. You have made a stranger feel very welcome." Francesca suddenly had a lump in her throat. She had just met these women. In fact, they didn't even know her name, yet they had shown her concern as if she were family.

Their heads turned and observed Dorie as she pulled a roll of bills from the sleeve of her dress. She peeled off two dollars and placed them under a drinking glass on the table. *Don't flaunt your money*, she wanted to tell Dorie. *Don't make it worse*. Like a chorus, she heard their clucks of disapproval. Then Francesca understood. Dorie would never be able to sway their opinions even if the Church declared her a saint tomorrow, so she rubbed their faces in the fact that she was a woman with money of her own.

"After you've recovered, come back and have some pie," Edwina called.

Francesca stared at her for a moment before she remembered she was supposed to be nearing the time to have the baby. She grimaced, she hoped dramatically, as the women helped her on with her coat.

"Get word to Edwina here, once the baby comes. We want to know how you're making out."

As Dorie took her arm, leading her toward the door, they called out after her, "But where will you stay?"

Francesca looked at Dorie. Where would she stay?

Dorie didn't turn to address them, but simply called out, "It's been taken care of," as she pushed open the door, pulling Francesca behind her.

27

Back in Chicago Last Summer

Francesca sat at the far end of the dining room table with Geno and Sal, surrounded by the blue air of their cigars. She longed to open the windows to release the hot, staleness of the room, but in the last few months, Geno and Sal declared that the front room windows that faced the street should remain latched with the heavy drapes always closed. The children were confined to the nursery and playrooms at the rear of the house.

Geno pointed to the haphazard stack of dirty plates, smeared with congealed ossobucco and dried risotto, and empty wine bottles with his lit cigar and made a movement for her to remove them. She stared at the red wine stains on the front of his shirt. When she didn't respond immediately to his request, twin furrows appeared between his dark brows.

"Hey, what are ya dreamin' about? We're havin' a meetin' here." Geno leaned both elbows on the table and squinted through the smoke. He stubbed the cigar out on a piece of veal.

"But Bridgid has gone home for the evening," Francesca said.

"And what, your legs are broken?"

It wasn't that she was so offended by his request, but she longed for him to pull out a chair and bring her into the discussion of their latest scheme.

Sal poured himself a shot of grappa and refilled his brother's glass. Now they both stared at her. They moved like mirror images of each other, eating, drinking and smoking at the same time. Once she had a dream that they both climbed into her marital bed, identical pairs of hands and lips moving over her body, their thick rusty voices murmuring in her ear. She woke up sweaty and sick at the thought, too ashamed to bring that sin to the confessional.

Their intense stares reminded her of that dream. She blushed and lifted the stack of plates and held them as far away from her as possible to avoid getting stains across her cream pleated blouse. She felt a bit guilty leaving the plates on the sideboard for Bridgid in the morning, but there was nothing she could do about it now.

Francesca spied some small dessert dishes sitting on a tray. Ah, figs in red wine and sugar. Bridgid must have prepared them before she went home to feed her own family. Francesca had a mind to gobble them all to spite Geno's efforts to turn her into a maid, but that would only make her as heavy as Giovanna. At twenty-two she was still too young to let her looks go. As a compromise, she popped one of the figs into her mouth and sucked the softened skin, enjoying the mingled sweetness of the fig and the tart wine. As she walked through the dim hallway back to the dining room, she heard Sal's terse voice.

"The problem here, is we already hit all the joints for twenty miles. Word might be out by now that we are running the fed scam." Sal chewed his wet cigar. "Remember when we hit that place on Eighteenth, the one in the basement of the meatpacking joint? The guy there, ah… what's his name, Banda? He recognized ya."

"The guys that run those places, they keep to themselves. Whadda ya think they have regular meetin's or somethin'?" Geno licked his lips and nodded as if he'd answered the question.

"Oh, Christ on a bike, Geno."

"Hey, watch that mouth. Francesca's here. She'll have to go pray to the saint of swearing or something now, right Frannie?" His hand squeezed her wrist as she lowered the tray.

"Got any *pizelles*? I've been thinkin' about eatin' them all day," Sal said.

"I've got figs in wine, and I know better than to waste time praying for your brother's immortal soul because your mother's already worn out two rosaries and her knees for that cause. You can see what she's got for her efforts."

"Hey, Frannie, watch your mouth now." He snickered as he said this, and Francesca was relieved he wasn't going to turn on her for her comments. "What's the matter if they know we're not feds? We got the same guns."

"The phony badges are probably the only thing saving us from them shootin' back, is what." Sal rubbed his hands over his chest. "A second hit on those places is too risky."

"Not if we take 'em by surprise."

"And won't you be surprised when they put a hole in you?"

"So you're sayin' we need a new business venture. How 'bout we get the family in Calabria to send us more grappa and wine to sell?"

Sal shook his head. "Naw, that's bad for lots of reasons—too much risk at the docks and not enough money. These guys at these joints, they don't have all kinds of cash to spend. They just want to get drunk fast and cheap."

Both Geno and Sal's faces were shiny with drink. Sal's jaw waggled around like it had a loose hinge. Francesca pulled out the chair and sat down. The warmth of the room and their bodies, along with the stink of cigars made her want to plug her nose.

"Then how 'bout we take over somebody else's operation. We make the stuff ourselves," Geno said, scratching his head as he thought this over.

"Too much work. You don't want to be measurin' and stirrin' and cookin' the stuff. Ya might as well run a restaurant."

They both chomped noisily on the figs. Geno picked up the small bowl and slurped.

"Okay, we do the same thing we've been doin' all along. All's different is we just move northward. We go to all these little towns and find out who's runnin' the hooch, and we give them the fed routine." Sal pursed his lips and pushed aside his dish.

"Travelin'? I don't know, Sal. I don't like goin' too far from home."

"Why, brother, are you worried about what would go on under your own roof if you left town?" Sal's lip curled into that smirk she hated so much.

Francesca's heart fluttered. She had to say something before Geno reacted. She tried to keep her voice low and casual. "Why don't you hook up with the people making the gin-juice in the city and offer to distribute it to the people who live out in the country?" She watched as their mouths fell open. Sal snorted and shoved his chair back from the table. Francesca put her fingertips to her throat, feeling nervously for her necklace.

They all turned as they heard a wailing voice coming closer. Just then, little Biaggio ran into the room, tears flowing down his face. He rubbed his eyes and stumbled toward her. Francesca knelt and opened her arms. One of the maids, Anne, appeared behind him, her ample chest heaving with the effort of the chase.

"I'm sorry, ma'am," she panted.

Biaggio threw himself against Francesca, pressing his flushed, sticky face into her neck. She put her lips to his forehead to check for a fever.

"That's what you should do. Take care of these children so they're not running around all night long. This here is business. It's not for the ladies. Go now," Geno ordered.

Francesca scooped up Biaggio, pressing his small body to her. His sobs quieted to sniffles.

"Yes, Geno."

Over the baby's head, she looked up to see Sal's satisfied smile.

28

Going to Mrs. Hamm's

An automobile chugged past Dorie as she stood on Main Street and when the wheels threw a spray of slush across her ankles, Francesca heard her utter a curse word. Dorie pushed the cuff of her coat up to her elbow, clenched her jaw, and grabbed hold of the crank as if she meant business. Francesca watched, amazed. Geno had never taught her to drive, and she wasn't acquainted with any women who had the chance to operate their own vehicles. "Pull the choke out, will you?" Dorie yelled.

Choke? Was that some farm saying?

"Get in the car before you have that baby on the walkway."

Francesca walked to the passenger side door and climbed obediently into the cold seat. She pulled a woolen blanket draped across the seat over her lap and watched the sky as it seemed to sag under the weight of the dark-gray clouds. The wind had gathered strength, and she watched people put their heads down, trudging against the damp gusts.

Dorie opened the door. "Didn't you hear me? I need you to pull out the choke!"

Francesca shrugged. "What's that?"

"Here." Dorie pointed to a black knob on the dash. "Pull this out, and when the engine catches, ease it back in." Francesca pulled the cold knob and watched as Dorie clenched her jaw and began to turn the crank. The car shuddered and roared to life. Francesca pushed the knob back in, and the car engine wheezed and stopped.

Dorie hollered, "Pull it out again!"

Francesca sighed. Why did Dorie seem so annoyed? She was only doing what she asked! This time, when the car started, Dorie scooted around, jumped in, and eased the knob back in until the engine sounded less frantic.

"You can't operate an automobile, can you?" Dorie settled herself in the seat and examined her boots.

"Well, not really."

"Either you drive or you don't."

"Fine, I don't drive. Someone drives me wherever I need to go."

"Everyone should know how to drive." She warmed her hands in her muff. "I wished the damn snow would just melt off and be done! My boots are soaked through. Say, do you really want to see the doc?"

"No, it was just something to say to them." Francesca motioned with her head toward the diner.

"I thought as much. That little act back there—not bad." Dorie pulled hard on the wheel, and the car jerked as it slid onto the road. A wind whipped through the side canvas flaps.

"It just came to me. You seemed to need help." She stared at Dorie's profile, the delicate curve of her nose, the way the curled tendrils of red hair escaped their pins and danced with the wind across her pale cheekbone. "Dorie, where are we going?" It felt like her words were blown and scattered so that they lost their connection to each other.

"I'm taking you to the other end of town. Mrs. Hamm runs a boarding house there. I made arrangements for your stay. I'll warn you, she doesn't think much of me, but she'll probably love you." Dorie sniffed and brought a handkerchief to her pink-tipped nose.

Does everyone hate you? She wanted to ask. Instead, she said, "Where's Victor gone? Where are my things?"

"Victor has a habit of disappearing whenever Louie shows up these days." Dorie pursed her lips as if she were going to say more, but then decided against it. She dabbed the corners of her eyes. Even in the frosty car, Francesca detected a lavender scent. Was Dorie crying?

The car chugged down the road. Francesca took in all the smallness of this place—the mill, a dry goods store, a seamstress, a photography studio. It reminded her of a pretend town game little Joseph would play, lining up two lengths of stacked blocks on the floor of the nursery. His dear little voice rang in her ears, "Here's the restaurant that serves only meatballs. Here's the sweets store. This is Nona's church next to the bank that makes all the money."

It was then that she spotted Evan's Furniture Store and Mortuary. Was that where Sal's body lay in wait for her to claim it? Suddenly the whole reason for this trip flooded back to her—Sal. His body was here in this toy-block of a town, and she had to bring it home. She pictured keeping a vigil in the cold rail car as they lurched back home toward St. Mary of Perpetual Help, his ghost streaking above the train, anxious to return to his weeping mother and mute father. Maybe his mysterious death had endowed him with the same powers of earthly visitation as his grandmother possessed. Francesca could feel those cold lips pressed to the back of her neck as he lifted her heavy hair, promising to take the place of her missing husband. The back end of Dorie's automobile shimmied and slid, and Francesca screeched a strange sound she didn't know she could make.

"Oh, Lord, what is it now?" Dorie peered in both directions down the crosswalk.

"Excuse me." Francesca scraped a fingernail against the frosty window. She wanted to ask more questions about Louie. Where was he now? Would he try to harm Dorie again?

Dorie pulled hard on the steering wheel, and the car veered to the right off the main road onto a side street.

"This isn't a proper a hotel, then?" She knew the answer to that question before the words left her mouth. They pulled up in front of a white clapboard house with a narrow porch. A lamp in the front room window glowed against the graying afternoon light.

"Osseo doesn't have a hotel. Mrs. Hamm takes in boarders. Some stay there a long time. Others just for the night."

Francesca could feel sweat gather under her arms and between her breasts despite the damp and the cold. Dorie planned on leaving her here. Alone. She was used to having a maid, her children, and her husband. Her tongue felt like a stiff piece of leather. On the train, this seemed like an exciting lark, a chance to try on the lives she had read about, explorers or missionaries who ventured into wild lands, but now she had lost her nerve. When the car shuddered to a stop, Francesca imagined her heart doing the same.

Dorie was already out of the car, anxious to be rid of her, she was sure. Ashamed of her fears, she felt like her little Joseph, sobbing in the dark about the monsters with knives that lurked under his bed.

"Francesca?"

"Coming," she answered. She never got used to this clumsy, awkward feeling during this stage of pregnancy. She would rotate her puffy ankles, wave her fat fingers, and wonder how these strange appendages became attached to her body. She saw the disgust for her altered shape in Geno's eyes too. The real reason Geno traveled north was not in search of new business, but to escape the sight of a wife who resembled cooked sausages.

Her boots crunched against the snow. When she looked up, Dorie stood next to her, offering her an arm of support.

"I may pull both of us down," she warned Dorie. Francesca smiled, pleased that Dorie hadn't left her behind.

Dorie stomped her boots on the porch and reached for the doorknob.

Francesca slipped inside, grateful to escape the damp air. Oh, the smells inside this house! Burning wood, beeswax, cinnamon, and tobacco. She moved to the hearth to warm her skirt. A man with spectacles closed his book and stood to greet her. "Ma'am," he dipped curtly.

Dorie walked to a wide oak desk and rang the brass bell.

Francesca nodded her acknowledgement as the man made a gesture to give her his seat.

"I've caught a chill," she said. "I think I'll stay by the fire."

The pomade from his dark hair left a stain on the oval doily on the back of the chair. Francesca listened to the comforting tick-tock of the mantel clock and studied the shelves of books all labeled on white cards in precise penmanship: BOOKS ABOUT FOREIGN LANDS, BOOKS ABOUT PLANETS, BOOKS ABOUT PRESIDENTS.

A tiny old woman burst out of the swinging doors, wiping her hands on a towel. Her lips resembled slivers of anchovies. "Oh, it's you again," she addressed Dorie.

"I'm here to deliver your boarder," Dorie answered.

The woman stared at Dorie, head cocked at an angle. She didn't blink for a long moment. Round lenses magnified her bright-blue eyes. Finally, she opened the ledger on the desk and ran a crooked finger down the page. "Where is he then?"

"The room is for me," Francesca said. She reluctantly left the warmth of the fire to join Dorie near the desk.

"But you're not..." she paused and examined the name written in the column, "Mr. D'Agostino."

"No, I'm Mrs. D'Agostino."

The tiny woman's face was frozen. Was this a fit of some kind?

"You're a woman."

"Clearly, she is," Dorie snapped.

"She can't stay here." She closed the book.

"I know you have a room open because I made the reservation."

"No. I have men sleeping upstairs. It wouldn't be proper."

"But you're here. You're a woman," Dorie argued. "She wouldn't be the only woman under this roof. Besides, she's married."

"Where's her husband then?" Her tongue made strange clicking noises against the roof of her mouth.

Francesca looked at Dorie who dropped her head. Even in the golden dim light of the parlor, Francesca detected a blotchy stain working its way up Dorie's neck, into her cheeks. Was Dorie embarrassed for her? After all, it wasn't wartime—she should know the whereabouts of her own husband.

"Well?" Mrs. Hamm buffed the already gleaming surface of the desk in furious circles. The skin stretched tight across her knucklebones reminded Francesca of a row of large stones. "Huh, I thought as much. The only lady who travels in that condition is the Blessed Virgin when she carried our Lord, and she had Joseph with her at the—"

Francesca watched the exchange. She had never dealt with hotel clerks before—Geno took care of things like that. She cringed to think of her husband's reaction if he was refused a room.

"She'll follow the rules. She reads." Dorie raised a hand over her mouth and muttered to Francesca. "You can read, can't you?"

Confused, she nodded. What did literacy have to do with securing a room?

"Listen, Mrs. Hamm, Sheriff Steiner asked that I make arrangements for this traveler. I'm only following his orders. You wouldn't want to go against an officer of the law, would you?" Dorie leaned across the desk at Mrs. Hamm.

"I've no reason to fear the sheriff. Unlike some people, I'm a law-abiding citizen. I've made up my mind. She's not welcome. Now, I have biscuits baking and I need—"

Dorie cut her off again. "Look, if it's a matter of money…" For the second time that day, Dorie snaked the roll of bills out from inside her sleeve. "I'll pay you double."

Now it was Francesca's turn to blush as she watched the look of horror on Mrs. Hamm's face. She most likely had a long list of what wasn't proper, and a woman possessing anything more than pin money ranked right up there with flappers who drank, smoked, and refused to wear proper undergarments.

"No, no." She raised both hands in front of her face as if she were warding off blows. "I don't want your gin-juice-sin money." For a tiny woman, her voice grew louder and lost all traces of elderly quaver. "Get out of here right now."

The lodger kept his head down but looked over his spectacles at the scene. He pressed himself against the back of the chair. Mrs. Hamm scuttled out from behind the desk swinging the towel at Dorie.

"Scoot now, both of you."

To Francesca's surprise, Dorie started to laugh. The towel snapped wetly near Dorie's head, nearly taking off her hat. When she grabbed Francesca's hand, her delicate fingers were surprisingly strong. "Let's go! Run now!"

Francesca's bladder ached again, and she stumbled after Dorie's peals of laughter. Even the boarder snickered behind his book. The towel flickered again. They burst out to the porch. Seconds later they heard the main door slam hard enough to rattle the glass.

Dorie leaned against the porch supports and hooted. Francesca doubled over, hoping to catch a breath as she leaned on Dorie's arm and gave in to her own laughter. One by one, the parlor shades snapped down, and the light next to the door winked out. This only served to send Dorie into another round of giggles.

"Now what?" Francesca panted. For the first time in hours, she felt warm. Dorie wiped the tears from her face. "I guess you're coming home with me."

29

A Night in the Narrow Bed at Dorie's House

The pain twisted through her, familiar and awful. It pounded in waves. She closed her eyes against it, feeling the rough hands move over her thighs and belly as if she was nothing more than a lump of dough. It devoured her—this hard edge of pain, chewing its way into her back, splitting and shattering bone. It hurt too much to cry out. Then suddenly, it was gone, and when she tried to open her eyes, there were coins, cold and heavy, positioned on her lids. Am I dead? Where is the baby? There were no mewing cries. She was frantic to feel the tiny, wet body, but her arms were leaden, folded across her chest. It's a mistake! I'm alive! If they would only take the time to hear her heart beating! Whispering voices floated around the room.

"It's a worthless girl. Sal won't want that."

"What should we do?" The baby made a quavering wail.

"Put her in the sack with the kittens. I'll take it down and give it a good toss in the lake."

She tried to scream as they pulled the blanket over her head.

Francesca reared up in the narrow bed and clawed at her eyes. Her heart thundered in her ears. She clutched at her belly, relieved to feel the weight and bulk of the baby still inside her. A dream. She was safe in the tiny room at Dorie's house, in the narrowest bed she had slept in since childhood. She collapsed on the damp pillow and waited for her breathing to quiet. Usually the birthing dreams didn't start until she was much closer to her time. And why did the mysterious dream-midwives think Sal was the father? How strange!

Before Geno disappeared, Francesca put her children to bed every night with the same routine. She pushed her cupped hands under each of their pillows and said, "Hurry, hurry, put your heads down so the happy dreams don't escape." She wondered which of the servants put her children to bed last night. She prayed it wasn't Colleen, who mumbled criticisms and smelled of whiskey. She longed to sack Colleen, but she was Bridget's daughter, and she risked losing them both if she fired Colleen. As punishment, her mother-in-law would probably make her cook all the food or scrub the floors on her hands and knees.

Ever since Geno had gone missing, she had allowed the three boys to stay all night in her broad bed. The comfort was just as much her own as theirs. She stroked their smooth heads, listening as, one by one, their breathing signaled descent into sleep. If she didn't mind their little knees burrowing into her back or the smells of their sour morning breath, why should Colleen be bothered? She wanted to slap that chapped ugly face and yank at her thick bun, but of course she never did.

She freed her sweaty braid from the tangle of sheets and Dorie's borrowed nightdress. Oh, she missed her sons so much! She longed to stroke each plump cheek and nuzzle their necks. Why had she been so eager to leave them? Her mother-in-law had always accused her of not being content in the moment. "Always wanting the next exciting thing, you are," Giovanna's voice rang in her head. "You're like a cat missing half its tail and still seeking out more trouble." The air in this room was stale and old, like the odor from an old trunk. It was her own fault for jamming a chair under the doorknob in case Dorie's crazy husband made a middle-of-the-night appearance. She plumped the pillows and tried to get comfortable. What time was it? There wasn't a clock to help her judge time. The sky outside the window was black. She would get out of bed, but there was no morning maid and no fireplace. How could Dorie stand to live in a place like this? As they were getting ready to retire last night, Dorie had proudly shown her the water closet room, a recent addition to the farmhouse. A hopeless drunk of a husband, a primitive bathroom… Francesca would have run screaming for an annulment to the first priest she could find.

She heard noises coming from the back of the house and realized she needed to use that water closet, no matter its condition. Francesca struggled to a sitting position and slipped on Dorie's dressing gown. The sleeves touched her fingertips, and when she stood, the length swept the floor. She felt like a child playing dress up as she pulled the narrow woolen slippers over the plump feet. She put her nose to the sleeve and smelled Dorie's signature lavender scent. Dorie's life seemed like a book filed on the wrong shelf. She was not someone who should have to endure this harsh weather and outhouses, surrounded by endless flat stretches of land.

Francesca returned the chair to the corner, eased open the door, and followed the golden light through the dim parlor to the kitchen. The square kitchen was brightly lit, tidy, and smelled of soap and something baking. Checkered curtains hung over the window over the sink, each side tied back with a length of ribbon. In the center of the room sat a table and four white painted chairs. She shuffled across the speckled floor in her ill-fitting slippers. She spent no more time than necessary in the drafty, frigid water closet and went to the sink to wash her hands. She looked out the window to what seemed like the edge of the world where the dark sky warmed a mother-of-pearl color. Where was Dorie? Just then, the back door flew open, and a wicked draft licked at her ankles. Dorie stomped up the stairs and across the porch into the kitchen carrying an armful of wood. She then dumped the load into a crate by the stove. She brushed her hands together and picked at a few scraps of bark that clung to the plaid wool coat.

"Morning," Dorie said curtly. The bright color of her cheeks contrasted with the dark circles under her eyes.

"Have you been chopping wood?" Francesca asked. As soon as the words formed in her mouth, she wanted to chew them up and swallow hard.

"Yes, of course. Do you see anyone else around who has an interest in feeding the stove?" Dorie wore a pair of men's flannel trousers and a large gray sweater with silver buttons. The buckles on the ugly galoshes clanked as she moved to feed the wood into the stove.

Francesca glanced around the kitchen and the parlor and out the window into the yard. "I'm sorry. It's just that I've never chopped wood before." While this had never been a fact she considered a shortfall, it felt like one now.

"Don't worry," Dorie said. "If it's Louie you're looking for, he isn't anywhere to be found. I was out to the barn to get some goat's milk, and I didn't see him sleeping on the cot. I think the Johnson brothers took him to their place yesterday. In any case, you needn't be afraid of him. He's really quite harmless and rather ill from the drink." She unwound the red scarf from her neck.

"Your husband sleeps in the barn?" Francesca felt like she was in a foreign country with different rules.

"Yes, doesn't everyone's?" she answered and laughed momentarily at her own joke before she sobered and said, "Oh, I'm sorry. I wasn't trying to be cruel."

"Yes, well," Francesca mumbled when she realized Dorie was making another reference to her missing Geno.

Francesca shivered and rubbed her arms for warmth and watched Dorie move about the kitchen. When she was dressed in men's clothing, she swung her arms and walked in long strides, just like a man. Dorie latched the porch screen door and then slammed the kitchen door.

"I'll put on some water for washing up and coffee."

"He did point a gun at you, Dorie." The wood joints of the kitchen chair creaked as Francesca sat down.

"He has no quarrel with a stranger. It's me he's furious with."

"It's because of Victor, isn't it? You love him, and he returns your feelings," Francesca blurted out.

Dorie moved the full kettle too quickly. Water slurped from the spout of the enamel kettle dousing the flame with a loud hiss. Her shoulders hunched for a moment, and then she turned around to face Francesca.

"Good Lord, are we that obvious?" She looked down and spun the gemstone ring around and around on her finger.

"When I met you, I thought you two were married." She shivered again, and Dorie removed the sweater and held it out to her. When she held up her hand to protest the offer, Dorie pushed it at her.

"I'm sweating. You take it," she sighed and fed some small chunks of wood in the burner before she struck another match to relight the fire. "How long before tongues start wagging around town?"

Francesca wasn't sure whether she was supposed to answer that question. If the locals found out that Louie had been living in the barn, it would make for terrible gossip. Then Francesca remembered the disapproving looks from the women in the diner. Would it really be any worse for Dorie if she moved a troupe of gypsies into her house and bore a wagonload of babies?

"Hungry? I've made some buttermilk biscuits."

Francesca's mouth watered. It wasn't light yet, and Dorie had already milked a goat, chopped a load of wood, and baked. "Umm, yes actually."

Dorie set a bowl on the table and unwrapped a towel to reveal a mound of warm golden biscuits. Next, she placed a jar of jam and a crock of butter with plates and knives in front of Francesca. "Do you want a glass of goat's milk too, or do you prefer tea?"

"I've only had goat's cheese before—never just the milk."

"Then you should have your first glass now. It'll be good for the baby."

Francesca blushed and rubbed the side of her belly. "How long have you been up?"

Dorie shrugged. "Can't sleep much these days. I figure, if I'm not sleeping, I might as well be working." She lifted the cheesecloth from the pail on the counter and poured the creamy froth into a small glass. "There's always so much to do around here—mending, cooking, laundry, making—"

"Making bathtub-gin," Francesca finished.

Dorie looked at her, eyebrows raised, and set the glass next to Francesca's plate. "I was going to say making soap."

"I may not know how to operate a vehicle or chop wood, but I am observant." She liked having Dorie's full attention. This was better than being scolded because she didn't know what a choke was. "And I understand how money is made."

"Who told you about my business? Did one of those biddies at the diner fill your ears with stories?"

"You have more pin money than anyone around this town. You told one of those women how her husband 'doubled his monthly order.' I'm guessing Victor is your partner. He doesn't look like the rest of the farm-folk around here."

"Well, you're in our little town for less than a day and you know all our secrets." Dorie sat down across from her and buttered a biscuit.

Francesca followed her lead. Was Dorie angry? Her expression gave away nothing.

"Lingonberries?"

"What's that?"

She pushed the jam closer to Francesca. "The Johnson brothers bring me jars of this every Christmas. It's good, but I can't bear to eat any more of it." The water kettle on the stove began to rumble. "So, what do you know about making money?"

"My mother died giving birth to me. My father worked for Johnny Torrio at the Four Deuces—that was a bordello Johnny managed for his uncle. Maybe you've heard of him, Diamond Jim Colosimo? When my father was killed in a shootout, Johnny brought me to live with him. I was a baby at the time."

"I don't know who he is." Dorie nibbled at her biscuit.

"Johnny gave Al Capone a job ten years ago."

"Ah, I've read stories about Al Capone. Do you know him?"

"I danced with him at my wedding."

"So you've waltzed with mobsters. What do you know about bootlegging?" The clock in the parlor chimed six times.

"Johnny told me everything. Even his wife didn't know the true nature of his business. I know that when his uncle refused to get into the bootlegging racket, Johnny took out a contract on him. That was about eight years ago. The police have never been able to prove anything. After that, Johnny made a fortune bootlegging."

What she didn't reveal was that she was largely ignored by Anna Torrio and raised mostly by servants and tutors. She spent her days with Johnny's bodyguards who taught her how to play cards and place wise bets. While it was true that Johnny took her into his confidences, those tutorial lessons were infrequent as he was either traveling or busy with the various aspects of his business. Often bored and lonely, she became a stealthy eavesdropper. By the time she was sixteen and engaged to Geno, she had gleaned enough to run her own racket.

"All anyone ever reads about is Capone this, Capone that. What happened to Johnny?" Dorie blew into her teacup.

Francesca swallowed the buttery biscuit. "Mmm, this is wonderful. Well, Johnny handed the business over to Al about three years ago after Bugs Moran and Hymie Weiss tried to kill him. They shot him so many times we didn't think he would survive, but he did." Francesca slathered another biscuit with the jelly, this time licking her knuckles as a glob slid over the back of her hand.

Dorie sat very still, her eyebrows raised slightly.

Francesca took a tiny sip of the goat's milk, which was both smooth and sweet. "Anyway, he retired and lives in Florida now. When Geno Junior was a baby, he sent for us to stay with him over Christmas. It was so odd to go to midnight mass with nothing but a shawl over my shoulders—"

Dorie jerked to her feet, and the chair hit the floor with a sharp crack. Then she ran over to the sink and vomited.

Francesca stood and righted the chair. She hesitated for a moment, but then began to rub Dorie's back between her thin shoulder blades as another wave clutched her. With her free hand, Francesca wet a cloth that was hanging on the spigot and pressed it to Dorie's forehead. This reminded her of tending her own boys when they were ill, and she ached for them.

After a while, Dorie took the cloth from Francesca but rested her head against her forearm. Francesca poured some hot water to rinse the sink. The sky was a bright blue now with wispy clouds feathering out over the barn and muddy fields.

"When you said I knew your secrets, you may have been right," Francesca said in a low voice.

When Dorie didn't answer, she continued. "Have you considered you might be having a baby?"

Dorie reared up, blinking droplets of water that clung to her dark lashes. The sun blazed through the window, causing her to squint. The violet shadows under her eyes made her skin ghostly white.

"What? No! The doctor said it would be impossible for me to ever—"

"Everything is possible."

They both turned when they heard the rumble of the engine in the driveway.

"I'll bet that's Victor bringing your trunks! What will I say to him? Good Lord, I must look dreadful." Dorie began to pinch her cheeks. "I should go and change." There was the thud of the automobile door closing.

Francesca tried to look out the window, hoping it wasn't someone delivering Louie back home, but couldn't see who had arrived.

Boots stomped across the porch. There was a rap on the door, but it wasn't Victor's face in the window. The man was fair and tall like Victor, but despite the heavy coat, Francesca could tell he had a thin frame. Deep creases radiated from his eyes and framed his mouth like two exaggerated dimples. He raised a knuckle and rapped again.

Dorie opened the door. The crisp air swirled around them. Francesca caught the scent of tobacco and the musky odor of horses. She was suddenly embarrassed to be caught in this state of dress and vainly tried to cinch the dressing gown sash, which barely closed over her belly.

"Morning, Dorie." He nodded and pulled his hat from his head. His thin colorless hair remained pressed in sweaty waves to his forehead. "I'm Sheriff Steiner, Mrs. D'Agostino. I apologize for not being able to meet your train yesterday. I was called north on a cattle-poaching complaint. These things always take longer than I bargain for." His eyes were a queer light-gray color, nearly the same color as Dorie's sweater. She had never been with so many pale people before.

Francesca held out her hand. "Call me Francesca." His cold fingers felt as rough as a piece of old wood. She wondered if there was such a thing as getting splinters from human skin.

“Mrs. Hamm said there was a mix-up of sorts. We were expecting your father, I believe.” Steiner reached into his pocket and blew his nose on a rumpled handkerchief.

“Actually, it was my father-in-law you were expecting, but he was suddenly taken ill, so I made the trip.”

“You have my sympathies. I know the hour is early, but I’ve come to collect you to identify the body. Excuse me for asking, Mrs. D’Agostino, but is the deceased your spouse?” He rubbed at the stubble on his chin with his thumb. There was a smudge of dirt across one cheekbone.

“No, sir, he was my husband’s brother.”

Steiner frowned, his blunt eyebrows clamped down over his eyes. Just when it looked as if he were preparing to ask a question, Francesca and Sheriff Steiner both turned their attention to Dorie, who vomited in the sink.

30

Viewing Sal

Just after Dorie bolted from the kitchen, Victor showed up in a battered car with the trunks. When Francesca pleaded that she needed time to get dressed, Victor offered to drive her to meet Sheriff Steiner at Evan's Furniture and Mortuary. This plan seemed to agree with Steiner, who said he needed time to clean up and get breakfast at Schieffer's. Francesca was pleased too as she hoped this would give Dorie and Victor some time alone. Victor deposited the trunks in the tiny room and told her not to rush.

Oh, she was so happy to see her things! Francesca hugged her comb and brush before unbraiding her hair. She was even happy to see the undergarments and dresses that had been let out to accommodate her thickening waistline. Just a few days before she had packed these things in disgust, longing for summer when she would have new dresses and her old figure back. She plunged her fingers into the layers and folds searching for the photograph.

Buried under the silk stockings was the portrait taken just before the start of the Christmas season. Francesca sat on the bed and examined their faces. Geno stood behind her, one hand holding his lapel, the other on her shoulder. Geno Junior and Joseph handsomely flanked her. She remembered how, when little Biaggio had begun to squirm and fuss on her lap, Geno had dug his fingers into the flesh under her collarbone as if her pain would somehow control the baby. She pushed those thoughts from her mind now because it was such a pleasure to admire the beauty of her own children. She looked at them in awe as if they were great works of art created by Caravaggio or Michelangelo. Why, her darling baby resembled the *putti* with his chubby face framed by curls. All he needed was a pair of wings! Was it a sin of vanity to be in love with their beauty? Geno Junior looked every bit the D'Agostino, but the other two were little masculine versions of her own face. They both had her dimples and wide-set dark eyes. Even their hair grew in the same widow's peak! Since their births, she would marvel to herself that she had made these splendid creatures. As if to answer her thoughts, this new baby prodded her as if to say, *What about me? I will be the most handsome one yet. Just you wait and see!*

When she heard noises in the kitchen, she remembered that she was supposed to be getting ready to go to town. She was at a loss how to start. There was no maid to bring her warm wash water or to help arrange her hair. If she were to go into the kitchen in her dressing gown, Victor would see that she hadn't made any progress. Besides, she didn't want to interrupt any conversation Dorie and Victor might be having. With that, she shed Dorie's dressing gown and nightdress as she slipped shivering into a dark-green wool skirt and pleated blouse. She soaked the towel with cold water from the pitcher and washed up as best she could. Dorie's wedding portrait hung over the wash bureau. As she twisted her heavy hair into a bun high on the back of her head, she realized Dorie certainly didn't resemble the traditional demure bride gazing modestly at her bouquet or the one who looked frightened and unsure of her new life. No, Dorie challenged the photographer with her chin up and her shoulders thrown back. But like most brides, there was a softness of face that was absent now, the harder edges carved by worry and disappointment.

What time was it? Geno accused her of being deliberately slow to make him late, but how could she tell him that at times she went somewhere else in her own mind, like traveling down a long road where she would visit with her own dead mother, a faceless woman with long hair who stroked her temples and read her poetry. Why, if she told Geno that he would certainly have her locked up in the loony bin, never able to see any of her children again. Geno made it clear he had no time for the weak-minded.

Francesca sat on the bed with a buttonhook in one hand and boots in the other. After she struggled to slip on the boots, she leaned over to hook the tiny buttons, but her belly might just as well have been a giant boulder she couldn't climb over.

Boots flapping around her ankles, she walked to the kitchen to find Victor seated on a kitchen chair, leaning forward so that his elbows rested on his thighs. He spun his fedora on his index finger. His blond hair was dark with pomade and neatly combed with a part precise enough to have been made with a knife. He looked up and smiled.

"You look lovely, ready to go?" he asked.

"I'm sorry if you've been waiting long." She held up the buttonhook. "I'm afraid I need some help. Dorie doesn't have a suitable low bench for me." She didn't want to mention that her maid usually performed this duty for her.

"Allow me," he replied, offering her his chair as he knelt in front of her. She sat, and he held her heel in his left hand while his right deftly hooked the loops and slipped them over the buttons. Across each knuckle was a collection of fine blond hair. Like her husband's, Victor's nails were polished to a glossy sheen. He guided her foot gently to the floor and started working on the second boot. Clearly, he had experience with this sort of thing. She pictured Geno's response, providing she could get him even to perform this task. His dark brow would crease as he swore and muttered. His thick fingers would bumble the hook, or tear the loops from their moorings.

"Done," Victor said, handing her the hook. "Anything else?"

"Did you speak with Dorie?"

"She didn't come downstairs. Steiner makes her uncomfortable," he frowned and she knew they were both thinking that Steiner had been gone for some time now. "Or maybe she doesn't want to see me."

"I think she's ill," Francesca rushed.

"Nothing serious I hope?" Concern creased his face. God, his love for Dorie was better than anything she had read in *True Story*.

"Nothing a dose of Lydia Pinkham's Compound won't cure. You know, female troubles," she whispered. This wasn't exactly a lie. She longed to tell him Dorie's news, but this should not come from a near stranger. Besides, he would know soon enough.

She watched him stride a few steps toward the parlor and then pivot back around. Victor absently rubbed the scar on his eyebrow.

"We should be going anyway. I'll help you with your wrap."

The ride to town was warmer than yesterday's journey but more harrowing. The sun gleamed high in the bluest sky, turning the road into a muddy mess. The wheels spun, and the back end of the car wobbled and shimmied whenever Victor eased up on the gas. The gears growled as he fought to control the steering wheel.

"I guess it's best to go full out or we'll get stuck," he called over the wind. Francesca ended up bracing herself between Victor's arm and the door. In his concentration, he flashed those white teeth, and she pictured Dorie in her seat, throwing back her head and laughing as they roared toward town.

"Tell me, are we very near the place where Lindberg grew up?" she asked.

"Ah, Little Falls, no—that's north of here about a hundred miles. Why?"

"It's exciting to be so close to him. He's just so brave. Did you know he flew with no windshield? He only had five sandwiches with him. I mean, why didn't his wife send him with something that would stick to his ribs?"

"Lucky Lindy."

"It was more than luck, don't you see? Think of it. He had no radio, no parachute. I heard him tell later that it made him a little crazy. He started seeing things that weren't there."

"You sound sweet on him," Victor teased.

"No, he's our country's hero," she corrected. "I'd never want him for a fella, but it would be such a thrill to fly with Charles someday." She didn't tell Victor about how her outfit would match her hero- aviator's, right down to the cap and goggles. Their silk scarves would trail behind them as the plane went airborne. It was there in the clouds that she could admit to him how she had prayed the rosary non-stop until he landed. Well, she did sleep a bit here and there, but she had prayed harder than she ever had before.

"Francesca, maybe you should be the first woman to fly across the ocean."

"No, it should be Dorie. Easily Dorie. I haven't the nerve for real-life things. More exciting things in life take place here." She tapped her temple.

Victor smiled and nodded, and they drove in silence for a few miles.

She pushed away a strand of hair that had escaped her clumsy bun and caught against her lip. "You were with Sal when he died, weren't you?"

"Did Dorie tell you that?" Even in the brisk breeze of the car, she saw him color.

"No, we haven't talked about Sal's death. There's the matter of the scars on your face."

He touched that eyebrow again and squinted at something farther down the road.

"Sal was in my car, yes. We were driving out to your uncle's farm in a snowstorm. We crashed."

She watched the muscle in his jaw line flex and beat like a tiny heart. Some of this was the truth, but it seemed more like the real story was a small box nesting in a larger one.

"Why?"

"It was a blizzard—too dangerous for driving."

"No, I mean, why were you going out to the farm, my farm?"

"Sal had some papers pertaining to the sale. I wanted to look them over."

"Sal was staying at my farm?" She startled at the sharp bark of a dog. When she turned, she saw a small black-and-white dog yelping and running at a pace that kept him even with the rear wheels of the car.

"Yes."

"He was trying to sell you my farm?" She realized she was speaking about him as if he were still alive, as if she wasn't about to identify his dead body and send it back on the train to the place of his birth. She found herself clenching her fists, nails biting into her palms, in that familiar way whenever she thought of Sal.

"He told us the woman who had been deeded the farm was his wife." Victor swung the wheel into a wide turn to avoid a large muddy hole. Francesca braced herself to keep from bumping against the door.

"He was pretending to be Geno?"

"No… and yes. The story he was shopping around town was that his wife owned the farm and now that Buzzy and Lois had passed, he was interested in selling it."

Why would Sal pretend to be Geno? Had Geno made it this far north? The baby turned, stealing the last bit of air from her lungs. Could Geno be in hiding at the farm? She realized she dreaded the idea of seeing him again. But why? He was her husband. Still, if he could run out on her and the children all these months without a word, he must not love her. What if he had taken up with another woman? They passed two white horses standing in a muddy pasture, heads bent as they nibbled a bale of hay, their long necks brushing against one another. She felt uneasy. Maybe it was thinking of Geno and Sal or maybe it was all this open space, this flatness, that made her feel as if she were near the edge of the world.

"Victor, I need to go out to see my farm. Will you take me there?"

"Now?"

"No, after I meet Steiner at Evan's Mortuary."

"Will this be hard for you, Francesca? To meet with Steiner, to see your brother-in-law laid out? Were you close to him?"

Close to him? She nearly laughed out loud. How could she explain it was like having two husbands instead of one? Sal seemed to always be there, lurking behind doors, constantly appearing to offer his opinion or his way of doing things. He sat across from her at every meal, attended mass with them as if he were the most faithful of God's followers. Why, he would even creep into their room after he had returned from a night of gambling and slump drunkenly across the foot of their bed and proceed to tell Geno of his lurid exploits at the prostitution houses. At first she was insulted because she thought he talked as if she wasn't there. Then she came to understand that the stories Sal chose to share with his brother were told in a way to get her ire. The only way she could find any peace from Sal was when she went to be with the children in the nursery or in their rooms. Sal was not fond of his nephews, nor did they hold any affection for his dismissive ways.

"We shared a home. He was my husband's brother," she replied.

Victor frowned slightly as they eased onto the muddy main street. The warmth of the morning had encouraged people to be out and about with coats unbuttoned. She realized how much she missed being in the city. Victor eased off the accelerator, and Francesca looked for the storefront she had seen the day before. People on the walkway smiled broadly, shifted wrapped packages under their arms, and waved when they saw the car. Victor tipped his hat to several groups of people.

"Maybe you should run for mayor," Francesca suggested. "You seem to be a popular fellow around town."

"Hmm."

"My maid has a saying that would describe you."

"What's that?"

"She would say this about you—'He is the type of fellow who would pack his troubles in his trunk, then sit on the lid and laugh.'"

Victor pulled into Evan's Furniture and Mortuary and killed the engine.

"That may have been true at one time." Victor unbuttoned his coat and rested his hand on the door. He exhaled a long breath, and a dark sadness rolled from him like it was something a person could touch. Francesca saw another of those new scars across his knuckle. This one resembled a teardrop. Just when she was about to open the door, thinking he had no more to say, she heard him mumble, "I'm afraid those days are long gone."

31

Evan's Mortuary and Furniture Store

As Francesca pushed open the door to Evan's Mortuary and Furniture Store, the shop bell jangled. She breathed in the sharp smells of fresh cut wood, beeswax, and linseed oil. Sunlight burned through windows so clean that, if it weren't for the backward letters hanging in the air, she would swear there wasn't any glass at all. It was warm in the shop. She unbuttoned her cloak, slipped it from her shoulders, and laid it across the back of a rocking chair.

"Hello?" she called. "Is anyone here?"

Francesca walked, trailing her fingers across tables, buffets, and bookcases, following the streams of wood grain under the gleaming polished surfaces. She amused herself by pretending her finger was an aerial artist named Antonia the Great. Even though Antonia was less than three inches tall, she performed fearless acrobatic jumps from one piece of furniture to another. Antonia was getting ready to execute her most difficult trick to date when she came face to face with the row of coffins along the back wall.

This was certainly different than any of the shops back in Chicago.

Stacked upright, she counted seven coffins, ranging from the plainest pine to a rich mahogany with ornate carvings. She stepped closer. The carvings were clusters of roses, some in buds, others fully opened, each petal carved so lovingly, in such careful detail, they looked as if they might be supple to the touch. Was it intentional that the stain and selection of the wood made the blooms appear black and rotted? She spied a yellow tag tied to the latch. Francesca first looked over her shoulder and then flipped it over. In blocky, firm letters was written: MRS. ALVINA BEIL.

Was she supposed to pick out a casket for Sal? If so, how was she to pay for it? There were so many questions she should have asked before she fled Chicago. Suddenly, she felt a hand on her shoulder. She gasped, swung around, and her belly bumped into a man.

"Excuse me," he said, blushing. He stepped backward and knocked into a side table. The drawer pull rattled, and he moved to steady it.

"You gave me a fright. I didn't hear you."

Francesca stepped back too, embarrassed again that her body felt like an awkward satchel she was forced to carry around. If she guessed right, he appeared to be about her age.

"I'm sorry. I did call out to you, but you didn't hear me. I'm David Evan. This is my father's business." He had curly, brown-blond hair that escaped from where he tried to tuck it behind his ears and brown eyes too. Maybe it was the surroundings and the smells, but his coloring made her think of red oak. In fact, David Evan had such perfect posture Francesca wondered for a moment if his spine was made of wood too.

"My name is Francesca D'Agostino. I'm to meet Sheriff Steiner here this morning." She held out her hand. He looked nervously at it as if she had offered up something dangerous, like a knife, but then finally he reached out and gave only the very tips of her fingers a brief squeeze.

"Oh, then you're here about the..." He didn't finish his sentence.

He glanced all around the room, anywhere it seemed, but at her.

"Yes, my brother-in-law, Salvatore D'Agostino."

He stroked his too-thin mustache. Francesca was accustomed to men who could grow a better-looking mustache by the day's end. What was he saying? Why couldn't she pay attention to him?

"…so my father and my older brother are retrieving, um, they have gone to bring a customer here." He looked so miserable she felt sorry for him.

"Maybe I should go?" She didn't want to view Sal's body. Why, there had been so many distracting things happening since her arrival, she had pushed this task from her mind even though this was the sole purpose of her visit.

"Ah, well, I'm not sure," he answered. He locked his long arms behind him and began to slightly lift up on his toes. He was a nice-looking man—regular ears that didn't stick out too much, even teeth, and a nose that went with all the rest of the features. He examined the ceiling as if he expected it to fall on their heads at any minute. Maybe it was her condition that made him uncomfortable or perhaps he was more at ease with the dead, she reasoned.

No one said anything.

"So, you like your line of work?" Francesca finally blurted out. She liked to ask this question of people who had honest jobs. She didn't know very many, but she wanted to find out as much as possible about respectable professions so when her boys reached manhood she could advise them as to which professions to pursue.

"Um, well, yes. My father's happy to have this business to hand down to his sons. I'm afraid we aren't suited to farming." She thought of Victor who had expressed a nearly identical sentiment, but she guessed he wasn't suited to David's line of work either.

"What's it like, then?"

"Like?" The tip of is tongue darted out to wet his upper lip.

"You know, touching dead bodies. I've never done it myself." His discomfort made her babble.

"Why no one has ever asked me that before—not even my father. Truth be told, I love working with wood. The other, well, it's my duty."

"Then you must pray to Stephen the Martyr, the patron saint of casket makers, for guidance. He was stoned to death, you see—"

Francesca felt a tightening across her belly, as if it had begun to petrify like wood. She breathed shallowly and placed her hands on her sides to wait out the spasm.

David looked stricken. "Oh, my word, Mrs. D'Agostino. Are you all right? What do you require?"

"A chair please, and maybe a glass of water."

David spun around as if he didn't realize he was in a furniture store. Finally, he went by the window where dozens of chairs hung on overhead pegs. He grabbed the leg of an oak spindle-back and swung it down, knocking over a plant stand in the process. Francesca leaned against a buffet as the spasm eased. David righted the plant stand and placed the chair in front of her. He stepped back and stuffed his hands into his trouser pockets.

"Water?" She reminded him.

"What? Oh, yes."

David scooted behind a curtained area. Francesca sat and rested, unable to believe how tired she felt. She stared at her arms and legs, expecting to see boat anchors attached. The bell jangled again. Francesca turned to see Sheriff Steiner stride into the shop.

"Mrs. D'Agostino, have you been waiting long?"

"Only a few minutes, I assure you."

David reappeared from behind the curtain. He had overfilled a glass so that, with each step, water sloshed over his hand and dribbled to the floor.

"Ah, you must be Mr. Evan's son. You bear a close resemblance to your father. I'm Sheriff Steiner." He shook David's hand before they both realized it was wet.

"Uh, pleased to meet you, sir. My father is out with my older brother."

Steiner nodded.

When David passed the glass to Francesca, the glass was only half full.

"Are you unwell, Francesca?" The sheriff 's face was pink and shiny from a fresh shave, but his eyes looked sunken and tired. In this bright light, he looked much older.

"I'm fine, really."

"Edwina, from the diner, was under the assumption that you had that baby yesterday." His gray eyes held hers. "When I told her I was meeting you this morning, she was alarmed you'd be out of bed so soon."

"I'm afraid it wasn't time for the baby after all. The trip, all the excitement at the diner—it was just too much for me." She was sure he had been told about Louie's appearance and the gun.

"Then you're not thinking the baby will come today? I've had experience helping cattle at their time, but I can't claim to know how to help a woman give birth."

She waved him off, blushing at the thought of him kneeling between her legs. When she glanced over at David, he was scarlet too.

"I'd also like to apologize to you for how you've been treated since you came to town." He scratched at his smooth cheek with his thumb. "I didn't intend for you to have to stay with Dorie LaValle. In fact, I had a talk with Mrs. Hamm, and she's willing to overlook, to ah, change her rules to accommodate you this evening."

"You spent the night at Mrs. LaValle's farm?" David asked. He leaned in closer to look at her as if she were an exotic creature.

"Dorie's been most kind to me." She looked back and forth at their faces. "Is there some problem?"

David began to pace and mutter to himself. "Only drinking and card playing."

She thought back to the poker games with her uncle's bodyguards. How old had she been? Nine perhaps? Her face wouldn't show any emotion when she looked at the cards dealt to her. She won money from the best of them with this trick. Even when they poured champagne for her, she kept her mind on the cards. She remembered the sweet, bubbly taste and that feeling of falling off the edge of the world.

Francesca did her best to look stricken by David's accusations. "I assure you there was none of that going on while I was there. In fact, Dorie seemed busy enough doing, uh, farm things. You know, she was chopping, and she got milk out of a goat." She paused, unable to adequately name all of Dorie's duties. "She did what needs to be done to run a farm."

"Right then." Steiner crossed his arms and turned. "Let's get this formality settled then. Of course, there are some papers to sign as well."

For a moment, Francesca had no idea what he was talking about.

"I'm worried this might be too upsetting for you."

Oh, yes, Sal's body. Her heart thrashed around inside her chest.

"There is an irregularity I need to talk about."

Irregularity? Did he know about Geno's disappearance? Did Steiner have some reason to suspect this wasn't Sal's body? Her tongue felt large and dry in her mouth. She remembered the water glass and took a tepid sip.

"David, if you would be so kind to assist us."

Steiner held her elbow and guided her toward the curtained area. David parted the curtains with one hand and allowed Francesca to pass in front of him before he let the curtain fall. Next, he lifted the hurricane globe of the kerosene lantern and struck a match on the side of the counter. When he brought the flame to the wick, his fingers shook. As he adjusted the height of the wick and replaced the globe, she saw twin flames burn in his brown eyes.

"This way then," David said, clearing his throat. He swung open a door and headed down a set of stairs. Steiner went ahead of her, turned and went backward so he could hold her hand as they both followed David. His large palm was cool and dry. The shadows from the lamp jumped and arched all around her. Francesca descended into a rush of chilly air, and she wished for the coat she had left upstairs.

"Two more stairs now," Steiner called. The room smelled of dirt and something sweet. The cramped quarters made it necessary to stand close to each other. The floor was cold under her feet.

"I'll give you a hand there, David," Steiner said.

"Would you mind?" David handed her the lamp. The yellow light licked up the wall, and she saw the end of a coffin with a rope handle nestled in hewn-out space.

"Storage," David said. "My father hollowed the space to store four coffins and then lined each space with timbers to prevent the walls from collapsing."

David braced his foot against the wall and tugged at the rope. Loud rasping noises echoed as the coffin scraped across the rough timbers. When it was nearly out of the wall pocket, Steiner crouched and supported the other end with his shoulder.

Francesca gripped the lamp as David grunted with the effort. She pictured David's thin arms and legs snapping like matchsticks under the strain. They settled the coffin on a low table against the wall with a thump. Wouldn't it be just like Sal to sit up complaining, "*Whadda ya doin'? A little courtesy here!*"

David dusted off the front of his suit with a handkerchief. "Here, I'll hold that now," he said taking the lamp from her hands. A draft swirled around her, and then she felt a sensation of icy fingers caressing the back of her neck. She looked at Steiner and David. There were no footsteps on the stairs. No arrivals of fathers or brothers. No one stood behind her.

Sal's here.

It was the same feeling she always had when she realized he had slunk quietly into a room to watch her. She bit down hard to keep her teeth from clattering together and rubbed her arms for warmth. She realized the baby hadn't moved. Was he waiting and watching too?

"You're cold," Steiner said. He shrugged off his coat and slung it over her shoulders. Francesca swayed under the weight of the garment but felt comforted by the smells of tobacco and smoke. The coat radiated warmth as if it were a live thing.

David lifted the lid from the coffin and leaned it against the dirt wall.

How many days had he been dead? What would he look like? Would there be a smell? Her panic became a watery roar in her ears. She had never seen a dead body close up before, but she had heard stories. Once when she was around eleven, she overheard her uncle talk about Leggie Gremelli, who double-crossed him in a business deal. Leggie was discovered months later stuffed into an oak barrel, his bloated remains smelling worse than the fish market on a summer day. Maybe it was because she knew Leggie, or maybe it was her uncle's vivid description, but, in any case, those pictures had stayed in her mind and visited her dreams for months.

What if it was Geno? What would she do? Giovanna would see that the children would be cared for, but would she be so generous with a daughter-in-law she barely tolerated?

Would she really miss him? He was her husband, wasn't he? She realized that in the last few years, her love for Geno was more an obligation than a passion. It was like her charity visits to the poor—she knew she was supposed to do it, and she couldn't speak of her reluctance. Then she recalled the first time he had spoken to her, asking to escort her to a picture show. He had mopped his brow and stammered his way through his invitation. Oh, such strange, odd feelings mixing around inside her head! David's wheezy breathing brought her back to the present.

Steiner placed his hand on her back to urge her forward. Her toes were numb, and she pressed her hands together.

"I'm afraid he'll be too gruesome to..."

"The damage from the accident was minimal. It was his neck that broke, you see," David said. "When we embalmed him he—"

Steiner cut David off. "This viewing can be as brief or as long as you wish, Mrs. D'Agostino. I don't wish for you to be uncomfortable."

Embalmed. Ah, of course he'd been embalmed. What was she thinking? Francesca moved forward. In the golden, waxy light she looked down into the coffin. She let out a breath she didn't realize she'd been holding. It was Sal all right. They had gotten that right. He looked mad. Of course, now he had more to be grim about. What an absurd thought! She jammed a knuckle to her mouth to keep from laughing. His mouth didn't look quite right because his lips were pressed together. In life, he held his mouth slightly open, lips pouted as if she'd said something to displease him.

He wore one of his own suits, the shirt freshly starched as if he were going to a meeting or out to pick up a prostitute. Was this the suit he died in? If so, who took such care with his clothes? His thick hair was neatly parted and combed, though he clearly needed a haircut. How strange to see him so still! Sal moved constantly, stretching his neck, stroking his chest, always pacing and prowling about a room.

Steiner's hand squeezed her shoulder. They were waiting for her to give an answer, but a wish bled into her thoughts. If he had been disfigured in the accident she could say it was Geno and not Sal lying here in this pauper's coffin! Oh, she will be struck down for her evil thoughts. She made the sign of the cross.

"Yes, that's my brother-in-law, Salvatore D'Agostino." It came as a whisper.

"Please take as long as you need for your prayers," Steiner said softly.

Ah, they think I'm praying for Sal's soul. She abruptly turned and stumbled toward the dark stairs. She had to get out of there, out of the dark, chilled grave. Her shin smacked hard against the step. Tears welled in her eyes.

"Let me assist you, Mrs. D'Agostino. The stairs are steep and not well lit." This time it was David who shuffled after her. He held the oil lamp over her shoulder, but didn't try to hold her elbow. She tore up the stairs, through the storeroom, and headed into the bright light of the front of the store. Steiner's coat fell from her shoulders. She gulped great breaths and leaned against a table, not trusting her shaking legs. The baby stirred again as if he too felt the relief of her escape. David stopped short behind her, still holding the lamp.

She waved him off. "I'm fine. I just needed some air."

He looked stricken, spun on his heel, and headed back through the curtained area. What now? Were they going to wrap Sal up in brown shop paper and string like a package for her to take? She pictured walking out the door with him under her arm as if she had purchased bread or a bolt of fabric. She would giggle if it weren't so hard to breathe. This always happened to her at this time of her pregnancy. Breathing felt like a case of pleurisy. She let the sun warm her face. Well, now her task in Osseo was completed. She was free to catch the next train home to her beloved boys.

When she opened her eyes, Steiner stood before her. He had retrieved his coat from where she had let it fall to the floor and folded it over his arm. His head cocked to one side as he studied her. "It was my fear all along that this was no job for a woman, especially one in your condition. I regret we couldn't have made some other arrangements in this matter."

Francesca felt annoyed. Her reaction wasn't due to her pregnancy or womanhood! She looked at his concerned face but knew she could never argue this point to her benefit.

"You mentioned there was some irregularity you needed to discuss?" She would prove to him she was just as strong as Dorie.

She could see him weighing whether or not she was going to collapse on the maple table in a dead faint or perhaps birth the baby in the store.

"I've changed my mind, I should better discuss this with Mr. D'Agostino."

"Would that be my husband, who is missing, or my father-in-law who is mute from a stroke? As we have just verified, my brother-in-law is quite dead." Oh, it felt so good to have said all that.

David appeared at Steiner's elbow as if he'd been summoned. He tried again to tuck those curls behind his ear.

"Very well then." Steiner cleared his throat. "When David Evan senior was preparing the body after we retrieved it from the car, he found wood splinters imbedded here." Steiner touched the back of his own head for demonstration.

"Wood splinters?" What was he trying to say?

"You understand, we don't see how the automobile accident could have caused this. Not the way Victor claimed."

"I see..." But she didn't really. Two women walking outside the shop turned and stared at her through the window. Francesca stared back at them.

"Mr. Evan thinks your brother-in-law was hit with something, a wooden club perhaps. The blow most likely broke his neck."

"But I was told of an automobile accident. That's what the telegram said."

"When I sent word to your family, I didn't know of this development."

She couldn't see Victor swinging a length of wood aimed at the back of Sal's head—not that man who held her foot tenderly in his hand while he buttoned her boots.

"But, Victor has these fresh scars. I've seen them." She stared out the window at a skinny, spotted dog that walked down the middle of the street, head turning from side to side, his tongue spilling out as automobiles honked.

"I pulled Buzzy's Model T from the edge of the woods myself."

"But you think he died elsewhere."

David made a high-pitched sound in the back of his throat. Steiner turned and threw him a puzzled glance, but then turned his attention back to Francesca.

"You see why I have concern for your safety?" Steiner took her hand in his.

"The two of them, Victor and Dorie, they've cooked up quite a story. I need to find out what really happened."

32

What Steiner Thinks

Francesca remembered the day of her sixteenth birthday.

The satin dress had moved over her skin like a caress. Soft and luminous, it clung and slid over her body in a way that made tiny hairs on the back of her neck stand on end. The dress matched the blue sky on that June day, a color she would never have considered for herself, but Uncle Johnny had it made for her gift. When she sauntered along the street in the middle of the day, it felt like she had slipped into a new skin. Women who wore dresses like this didn't have to endure long lessons about the Etruscan Wars or learn needlepoint stitches. She listened to the sounds of the steady *click, click, click* of her shoes, people shouting, and horns beeping, without a real destination in mind. Maybe she would stop for a sweet or to get a pair of stockings. Even though the sun shone high in the sky, she felt the cool wash of shade from the tall buildings. Goosebumps rose over her arms.

She glanced over her shoulder. A man stared at her as he walked. Hands in his pockets, he swaggered in a way she had never considered a man could move. She didn't increase her pace, but watched his reflection in the windows. The hem of the dress flipped and danced with the breeze that matched the fluttery feeling in her belly. When she looked again, he was still there. He had pushed his hat low over his eyes. Should she know him? Did he work for Johnny? He dodged dawdlers and children playing a stick game, but didn't take his eyes from her. Farther and farther she walked, until her legs tingled with exhaustion. Should she run into the Chicago First Trust and Fidelity and announce that a man was following her? Might he just give up? Another thought hit her—what if he was sent to kidnap her? It would be in all the papers. She would be famous. Years later, at a club someone would say, "Aren't you the girl Johnny Torrio paid thousands of dollars to rescue?" She'd smile and show them how she had been bound at the wrist and blindfolded with silk scarves. They were smart you see, she would tell them. They knew if they harmed her, even so much as a single scratch on that tender, olive skin, Johnny would hunt them down and kill them.

She stopped and looked behind her, but he was gone. She was breathing hard, sweating now in her lovely dress. It clung to her breasts and back. She wondered if her maid would be able to clean the stains from the fabric or how she would explain the ruined dress to Johnny. She felt relief that the stranger had gone, but disappointed too, in some strange way she couldn't name. She leaned against the cool marble of the building, closed her eyes, shifting from one swollen foot to the other as she counted the number of blocks she would have to walk to get back home.

Then he was there, directly in front of her. He placed his palm against the marble over her head and leaned in closer. His eyes were large, so dark they appeared black. She could smell pomade on his glossy, thick hair. Her heart felt like fluttering bird wings trapped under a magician's scarf. He licked his lower lip and bit down.

"I can't take my eyes off you in that dress," he said. He picked up her hand where it hung uselessly at her side and kissed her palm. "I'm Salvatore D'Agostino."

With her eyes closed, Francesca sat in the front window of Evan's, a red brilliance blooming through her lids and thought about that summer day so many years ago. Funny, how if Johnny had picked a different gift for her, perhaps a piece of jewelry, or a fur for the winter months, she wouldn't be sitting here in this place today at all. Everything that happened in her life started because of that dress. Peaceful and warm, she thought this was what it must be like to live on the sun where there were no blue dresses or dead men in coffins.

Steiner wanted to talk. There was an urgency about him that reminded Francesca of how Geno Junior would shove Joseph out of the way to possess her attention. Steiner pulled a chair close to hers, his voice low and rough like the skin on his face and hands.

Words flew from his mouth, scattering like ash in the draft. She knew she should concentrate on what he said, but all she could see was Dorie and Victor as they sat in the booth at the diner, careful, tense, and full of feeling.

He had passed Dorie the creamer, taking the opportunity to stroke her index finger with his own when he thought no one would notice. As Francesca had watched them, her own finger tingled in response. The small, secret poignancy of this act, much larger than if he had gone down on one knee to proclaim his love aloud for all to hear, made Francesca ache even now. And still Steiner continued to speak to her! She wanted to scream she was thinking of true love and would he quit interrupting her thoughts. When it was clear David intended on scavenging for bits of gossip, Steiner had suggested going to the diner. Although she was hungry, Francesca felt reluctant to face Edwina or any of the women who might be there. In the end, they made their way to his office to sign the necessary papers to release the body.

They moved down the muddy street together, her arm linked through his, past the photographer's studio, a dress shop, and a general store. Ordinarily she would have loved to stop to peruse the wares, but this morning she was just too tired. Her lower back throbbed with a low ache, and she concentrated on moving more gracefully than her body would allow. Steiner had to stoop a bit to accommodate her height, his long legs bent as if he were arthritic.

Planks of wood, set out by thoughtful shop owners to cover the largest puddles, flexed under their combined weight. Francesca gripped Steiner's arm to avoid losing her balance. Steiner appeared not to notice the glances and furtive looks of the people they passed on their walk.

"When we were back at Evan's, you said your husband was missing. Can you tell me what happened?" She held her skirt with one hand, wondering who would attend to the splatters of mud.

"I can't think of that right now. Can we speak of something else?" Steiner looked startled. "Something else?" he repeated. She knew there was nothing else in his head but figuring out how Sal died.

"Those birds for example. They are so noisy! What are they?" She pointed to the small blur of motion darting from under the eaves of buildings.

"Oh, chickadees, house finches. Robins come back this time of year too. Spring." If there was more information on birds, he wasn't forthcoming about it, and she wasn't that interested anyway. Bells from the steeple began to *bong, bong, bong*, a sound that gripped her chest for the twelve count. "That church," she began again, "were you married there?"

"St. Vincent's? No, I wasn't born here. I lived in Fargo, North Dakota most of my life. My wife and I moved here only recently."

"And your children? Are they grown now?"

"Both of my sons died in the war. One was shot down. He was a pilot with the *Lafayette Espirit*. My younger boy died of dysentery."

"I'm so sorry." Francesca put her hand over her heart that ached for her own boys. Thankfully, there would be no more wars and telegrams.

"It was ten years ago," he commented, and his face went smooth. She didn't know if he meant his grief had eased in these years or if it seemed like only yesterday they had all sat together at the dinner table.

"Here's the office." He unlocked the door and pushed it open for her.

She expected the town jail would have stone walls stained with sweat and mold. There would be chains and iron cuffs that held skeletal prisoners as the rats scuttled across the damp floors. Admittedly her only reference to prison came from *The Tale of Two Cities*.

Instead, Steiner's office was a homey sitting room with a fireplace, a braided rug, and a comfortable sitting chair with a footstool across from a rocking chair. In the corner sat a cherry wood desk adorned with a rack holding six ornate pipes. A glass case behind the desk held three rifles. The neatly whitewashed jail cell had bars, just as she had envisioned, but also a cot with a neatly folded quilt made from tiny, bright squares, a sink, and a toilet. Across the window hung a checkered curtain with eyelet lace. Steiner took her coat and hung it on a peg on the wall near the door. She raised her eyebrows in question. "This jail, it doesn't seem..."

"My wife," Steiner said by way of explanation. "She feels this should be a comfortable place for both myself and the prisoners. Tea?"

Francesca sank gratefully into the chair and propped her tired feet on the cross-stitched footstool. On the small table, next to the chair, lay a book, *The Sun Also Rises*. Ah, a Hemingway man. She picked up the book and ran her fingers over the gilded pages. "Have you finished?" She waved the book at him.

"Many times over," Steiner answered. "I think Jake Barnes is one of the finest characters ever written."

"You?" he asked.

"Scott Fitzgerald," she answered. "Say, are you ever afraid they might just want to stay?"

"Stay?" He frowned.

"The prisoners... aren't you worried they might want to stay?"

Steiner chuckled. "No. I don't think they care much for my company. Since I took over, most of them just need to sleep off the effects of a night of imbibing. After they've endured a visit from one of the ladies of the Temperance Union, they're more than ready to go."

When he looked across the room at her as he placed the kettle on the hotplate, she sensed him waiting for just the right moment to pummel her with questions. An oil painting of *The Last Supper* leaned against the mantel.

"Could we speak again of your husband? How long has he been missing?"

Something about staring at the painting made her answer truthfully. "He left Chicago in the middle of January."

"And you've had no word at all? Where did he say he was going?"

"He intended on coming north, here. He wanted to check out some business ventures up here and find a buyer for the farm my uncle deeded to me."

"His name?"

"Eugene, but everyone calls him Geno."

"Hungry?"

"What?"

"Are you hungry?" he asked. He pulled out the chair to the desk and revealed a basket on the seat.

"My wife brings a lunch by for me at the noon hour."

He set the basket on the table next to her chair and unbundled a white towel to reveal several hardboiled eggs with light brown shells, a chunk of cheese wrapped in gauze, and a small, round loaf of pumpernickel bread. Francesca nodded.

Steiner sat in the chair and began to roll the egg between his palms. "So, in light of Sal's untimely death, what do you think happened to your husband?"

She could hear the shell crackling. Oh, so many choices! Run off with another woman. Jailed in some other city. Dead like his brother? "I don't know what happened to him." That was honest.

"This business that brought him here, is it fair to say it's similar in kind to the one Dorie and Victor run?" Her stomach growled loudly. He didn't wait for her to answer, but continued, "I believe the hootch business is the reason Sal ended up with Victor that night."

"No, it was to sell my farm. He came here to see what it was worth so he could negotiate the best price."

"Why was your brother-in-law trying to sell your farm? Shouldn't that have been your husband's doing?" He set the first egg down and repeated the rolling process with the next.

Francesca hated to admit she wasn't exactly clear about that, but how could she explain how the brothers often moved as one, dressing alike, finishing each other's sentences? The fact that Sal was selling her farm didn't seem that odd, or did it? All these questions made her head ache as much as her lower back.

"And you think Victor, a man who has never earned a cent by working with his back and his hands, would be that buyer."

"Victor spoke with genuine affection for the place."

Steiner's cheeks burned red. He stood and began to make a big production of making tea. He cleared his throat and continued. "I found the two of them, Dorie and Victor out at your farm. Weeks ago, they were stranded there after the last big blizzard… same day as I found your brother-in-law's body in your uncle's car." He carried the two cups back and handed her one, but the fact that he was speaking of infidelity seemed to prevent him from looking her in the eye. The cup warmed her fingers, and she rested it on her belly.

"I don't have the answers you want. I'm not allowed to participate in any of the D'Agostino business. My children occupy my time." She blew into the amber liquid.

"I want you to bring back a message to your family from me." Steiner paused and slipped the egg from the shell in one movement. She watched as he pulled a bone-handled knife from the basket and pressed the blade against the side of the egg. The pearly white skin dimpled for a second before the blade sliced neatly through the egg. Steiner presented half to her along with a salt shaker the size of her thumb. She doused her egg and handed the shaker back to Steiner before she sank her teeth into the golden yolk.

"Speaking of my family, I'd hope you could tell me when the next train back to Chicago is due to arrive. After I sign your papers, I'm anxious to return home as soon as possible." She munched happily on the egg and eyed the loaf of bread. It was true. Her mission here was completed. Now she could return home to her boys.

Steiner popped his half of egg into his mouth. Before he started to chew, it looked like a protruding tumor. "I want you to tell your father-in-law that I intend to arrest the person responsible for Sal's murder very soon."

"Arrest?" The egg became an impossible mass threatening to choke her.

Steiner calmly shaved piece after piece of cheese as he chewed the mouthful of egg, stacking one next to another on the towel. He gestured at the curls with the tip of the knife. "Pull off some of the bread. It's still warm."

Francesca took a mouthful of the tea, forgetting its temperature. She sputtered, “Who do you mean to arrest?”

“Why Victor, of course.”

“You don’t have any proof of that beyond the fact that Sal was with Victor in the car.”

“What more do I need? Those two were involved somehow, and I need to show these people I’m the kind of sheriff who will protect this town. I know where to draw the line.”

“The line,” Francesca repeated. Her appetite dulled. The salt and the egg left a queer metallic taste in her mouth.

Steiner pulled a chunk from the loaf of bread and pressed two slices of cheese into the soft center. He handed it to her, and she took it but knew she could never swallow it. “You see,” Steiner started. “When I was first appointed sheriff, I learned all about Dorie’s moonshine business. It was my feeling that, as long as no one was getting hurt I’d leave well enough alone. I don’t think one person could ever stop anyone from making the stuff anymore than I think I could stop someone from drinking that poison, if that’s what they had their heart set on.”

Francesca nodded, unable to speak. She thought of Victor in handcuffs, and Dorie, pregnant and alone.

“Look what’s happened. Your brother-in-law is dead. Dorie’s husband tried to shoot his wife in the diner. I think it’s more than a coincidence that one brother is dead and the other is missing.”

The only sound was the faint creak of Steiner’s rocking chair. Her heart seemed to tremble rather than beat. “Victor couldn’t have had anything to do with that.” Francesca found it hard to catch her breath. “He’s just too... nice,” she finished lamely.

Steiner sat forward in the rocking chair and looked at the egg as if the answers to his questions were written across the oval. “So, you’re an expert on Victor Volk in your first few days here in town? Do you know he hasn’t held a real job in town that anyone can name? You do know that Dorie is married to Louie, but Victor parades her around town like he’s her fella.”

How could she explain to Steiner that Victor had a genuine goodness that a cold-blooded killer would never own? But then how did she explain how Johnny Torrio, who took care of her when no one else would, could also shoot a man in the back over a gambling debt?

“It’s his looks that got you confused. A man with a face like that always pulls the wool over all the gal’s eyes.” He chewed the bread and cheese and stared at her. It was Francesca's turn to seethe. Why did he think a man's looks would cloud her judgment?

"It's not fair," she said, "to arrest Victor for any of those reasons."

The clock on the mantel chimed twice. Francesca jumped at the sound and some of the tea sloshed over on her skirt.

"I'm interested in fairness," Steiner said evenly, "but I'm more interested in carrying out justice here so that members of your family don't come to my little town and think they will enact their own vengeance."

In the end, it always comes back to the D'Agostino family, she thought. Steiner salted another egg and held it out to her, but Francesca shook her head.

"I'd say if you're so interested in the truth, why don't you stick around here for a few days and find out what really happened." He winked at her before he popped the egg into his mouth.

33

Francesca Extends Her Visit

Francesca stole a look at Steiner as he squinted out the window of the car at a mysterious place off on the horizon. What was there to look at? Barns, houses, and bare trees that looked like the miniatures from Geno Junior's train set. How did someone ever get used to all this sky and flat colorless land? It made her feel like a lost soul.

Steiner hadn't uttered one word to her during the ride back from town. Sweet, wet air filled the interior of the automobile. She longed to pull deep gulps, but the baby seemed to push the air out of her lungs. She challenged herself to wait out his silence as he pressed his fingertips to the twin lines on his forehead hard enough to make the nail beds whiten. She wondered if he was one of those poor souls tortured by severe headaches, like Arturo, one of the bodyguards, who was often relegated to suffer alone for hours on end in a dark room.

"Ah, now you're mad at me just when we had become friends." Francesca couldn't stand his quiet calm another second. She saw the kitchen curtain part for an instant and then fall back into place as they pulled into Dorie's driveway.

He frowned. "As I said before, I'd rather you stayed at Mrs. Hamm's."

"Last time I saw her, she chased me out of there with a knife!"

"What?" He turned to her, and the creases he had tried to smooth out instantly deepened.

Francesca, embarrassed by her fib, imagined Mrs. Hamm clutching the bars of Steiner's cozy jail cell. "Well, then, maybe it wasn't a knife. Perhaps it was only a towel, but it just as well could have been a knife."

He made a small movement that looked like he was trying to clear his head. "Fine, if you don't want to stay in the boarding house, please come to my home. We have an empty room. It would give my wife pleasure to have someone to fuss over."

Francesca pictured trying to sleep in the room his dead sons had shared. Their military portraits would stand side-by-side on the bureau. No, she couldn't stay in that room where, on the last night before shipping out, they had whispered in the dark just as they had when they were children of their pact to return home to this town, to their girlfriends and to their parents.

"I'm comfortable here. Besides, it's only for a day or so."

A movement near the side of the barn caught her eye. What was that? Her mouth went dry. Could Louie be back? She clutched the package in her lap, causing the paper to crinkle.

She quickly looked away from the barn and smiled at Steiner. "Anyway, I've promised Dorie I'd help her with, ah, some of her duties."

"Farm chores. You're going to help Dorie. What will you be doing exactly?"

Francesca searched her memories for a task done by one of the maids. Washing linens? Baking bread? "I'll be helping Dorie polish the silver settings. I can sit at the table so it won't be too hard for me, you see."

"Dorie has a large silver service then?" He smiled and nodded his head.

"Of course, many fine pieces," she bluffed. Didn't every woman?

Steiner pressed his lips together. She couldn't tell if he intended on laughing or scolding her. Francesca decided he would make a very good poker player. She stared at the shirts pinned to the line, arms outstretched, touching as if they were dancers waiting for the curtain to open. The wind scuttled in causing the line to rise and fall in waves. She smiled at the thought of farmer-dancers putting on a show until she realized the shirts must belong to Louie.

Why hadn't Steiner considered Louie as a suspect? He must have been here the night of the blizzard. She wanted to ask Steiner why he didn't think anyone else might have had something to do with Sal's death. Just as she was about to blurt this out, she recalled Johnny's voice barking at his men, "I'm not interested in your fancy ideas. Just tell me what happened."

"Hmmm," he answered.

"Don't worry about me. Dorie is really most kind. You have the wrong idea about Dorie and Victor. They're not like that at all. Besides, you know I'm here. What kind of horrible fate could they have in store for me when the sheriff is a daily visitor?"

She couldn't wait to go to him and reveal that Louie was the man who had murdered Sal. She would march into his office as he sat behind his polished desk and lean on her fingertips the way she had seen one of Johnny's men do, and prove Victor's innocence. A few clouds edged in, swallowing the sun.

"I can't persuade you to stay with us, can I?"

She shook her head. A striped cat with a twitching tail shot across the brown grass and disappeared through a hole in a tiny building.

Steiner shook his head, opened his door, and walked around the front of the automobile. The wind picked up again, and Steiner put his head down, holding his hat with one hand. Francesca stared at what looked like a wooden toy mounted on a stick near the porch steps. It was an Indian sitting in a slim yellow boat holding a paddle. He wore a headdress of feathers. His red body bobbed frantically in the breeze. Steiner opened the door and held out his hand to help her.

"I'll be by later to check on you."

Her belly went hard again as she took his hand. She glanced around the yard as the afternoon shadows deepened like dark spirits. Was she being watched? Gooseflesh raised on her forearms. She nodded back at Steiner.

When Francesca entered the kitchen, Dorie was stirring something in a copper pot on the stove. She bent to wipe her forehead on the sleeve of her dress. The kitchen smelled of bacon. When the door closed, she turned, tapped the spoon against the lip of the kettle, and rested it on a plate.

"You're back," Dorie said wiping her hands on a towel. She didn't look directly at Francesca.

"Yes." Francesca was suddenly shy. It seemed like such a long time since this morning in the kitchen. There was so much to talk about—Dorie's pregnancy, Sal at Evan's, what Steiner suspected. She wanted to confess to Dorie how she hoped the body might actually be Geno's or how she could feel Sal's spirit watching her as she stood in the cellar with the men. Dorie bustled around the kitchen, retrieving flour sacks, an empty cheese crate, and a tin.

"Are you well? Is the matter with Steiner settled?" There was color in Dorie's face again. She looked healthier than the pale woman who had vomited at the sink.

"Yes, I've signed the proper papers."

Dorie had her back to Francesca. In a low voice she said, "I regret not going with you this morning. It was wrong for you to go alone. I should have been there to help you—"

"It's finished now." Ah, so that's the reason for her coolness.

"Then you'll be leaving soon."

"Yes, but first I'd like to see my farm. I've asked Victor to take me. Then I'll go back home to my boys and wait for this baby and Geno too."

Dorie didn't say anything for what seemed like many minutes. Francesca wondered if Dorie hadn't heard her or if she was upset about something else. Maybe she was about to be sick again. Francesca peered into the pot and pretended to be interested in the bubbling mixture.

"Sit, please," Dorie said finally and started to fuss with the water kettle. "Let me get you some tea. You must be starving. I've got some cold beef and potatoes I could warm." Her delicate fingers scurried over the kettle, a cup and saucer, a plate, a sugar bowl.

"This is for you." Francesca thrust the package out to Dorie. "I don't need anything to eat, really. Steiner and I had the noon meal together."

Dorie froze and then put her hand to her throat. "You bought something for me?"

She smiled for the first time, and Francesca sensed her pleasure. She had talked Steiner into escorting her to the dry goods store after she had signed the papers releasing the body. She felt giddy spending money, and why not? She hadn't spent anything on lodging, and she would be going home soon. She had never before bought a gift for anyone other than family.

Dorie pulled the string and unfolded the wrapping paper. She held the brown leather baby shoes in the palm of her hand and peered at them. Her fingertip traced the tiny eyelets. She sat down absently, a miracle she landed squarely on the chair.

"Oh, is the baby real?"

Francesca remembered her own wonderment with her first baby. She had loved holding the secret, waiting for the fluttery first movements that only belonged to her. These stirrings were the first language her son spoke to her, and she answered him back in kind with a stroke of her own fingertips.

"Have you missed your monthly?"

"I'm not sure. Well, maybe. I haven't paid attention for so long." She slipped two fingers into the shoes and marched them in place on the table.

"Any other symptoms?"

Dorie sighed deeply. "I'm not even sure what to expect, but after you left for town, I went back to bed and I slept." Her eyes grew large as she pulled her fingers out of the shoes and arranged them neatly in front of her. "I've never, ever before been such a lazy bones." Francesca watched as Dorie's hands moved to stroke her flat belly.

"Once, when I was in the early time with Joseph, I fell asleep during the Sunday dinner with Geno's parents! Right there at the table! Everyone thought I had fainted, so all was forgiven when I announced I was with child, but really I had just fallen asleep!" Francesca giggled. "I loved it. Everyone treated me like I was a queen! You'll see what I mean."

Dorie moved to the stove, frowned, and stirred the mixture again. "The only royal treatment I can expect is to be beheaded. Edwina and those biddies at the diner—can you see them when I push a pram around town with my big, blond baby? My Lord, my own sisters barely speak to me now as it is."

"I've prayed to St. Anne for you. She's the patron saint of pregnancy."

"You have an unusual affection for the saints. Why is that?"

"When I was a little girl, one of the maids in charge of my care told me bedtime stories of the saints. She said because they were real people, they were more likely to listen to our problems."

"And you believe this to be true?" Dorie asked, tapping the spoon against the kettle.

Francesca decided to change the subject before Dorie openly scoffed at her beliefs. "Is that soup?"

Dorie raised an eyebrow. "No, I'm melting down all the grease I've collected to make soap." Dorie gestured to the empty crocks on the counter. She put a handkerchief over her nose and shook a powder from a tin into the kettle. "Get back. This is lye. It'll burn your skin." A plume of white powder rose over the kettle.

"You make your own soap?" Francesca had never thought of soap as something someone made. It always just appeared on the shelves at the store or in the dish on her washstand.

"Lye soap, yes. It's not for me. It's for the hired hands to use. I imagine I'll have to bring on two this year. Louie won't be up to working the fields or putting the crop in anytime soon. I suppose it's back to farming now that Steiner seems intent on shutting down my business." A muscle in her jaw tightened, and Francesca could see Dorie's temper beginning to bubble like the mixture on the stove.

"Where is he... Louie?" Francesca looked out the window toward the barn.

Dorie put an empty wooden box on the counter. She bunched two flour sacks around the handles of the kettle. "Spread that cheesecloth across the box will you?"

"Like this?" Francesca arranged the cloth in the bottom of the box.

"No, over the top edges." Dorie lifted the kettle, gritting her teeth with the strain. The skin on her knuckles pulled tight and shiny. "I put a pail of food out by the back door, and it disappeared not much later. Louie's around somewhere." She tipped the kettle and began to pour the grease over the cheesecloth. "Hold it tight across the top, will you please? I need to strain out the bits of meat."

Francesca pulled the cheesecloth taut as the hot grease spilled into the box. "Dorie, was Louie here the night Sal and Victor were drinking, before they left in the storm?"

Dorie bit her lower lip and chuckled. "Yes. He drank himself to sleep that night. That's the usual for him." She used the spoon to guide the last of the rivulets of grease. She then set the spoon in the sink along with the empty grease crocks and the kettle.

"Now what?" Francesca flushed with pride for her part in the chore. The cheesecloth glistened wetly, and in the center was a collection of black bits.

"Hmmm?"

"I want to help you make soap. What do I do next?" It must be a mysterious process. All she had now was a cheese box full of hot grease.

"Ah, now that you own a farm you want to learn the ways of the farm wife?"

Dorie's comment felt like a mean kick. Why couldn't she? It was her rightful property, after all. She pictured herself sitting on the porch in a rocking chair, calling for the boys to stay close. They would wear overalls and go shoeless all summer. They would eat apples from a tree that grew in her yard. Their olive skin would darken from the days in the sun. They would wash their hands with soap she had made. It could be that easy.

"I know, let's grow mealy potatoes together in that impossible soil! Did your uncle tell you? All the farms around here are nothing but sand and rock. We are crazy in the head for trying to grow anything here! But think, we could drive together into Minneapolis at three in the morning each Saturday to go to market. I bet we could split, let's see, two dollars and two bits every week! Imagine that!"

Francesca sat down at the table. She had thought Dorie was the last person to make fun of another woman for wanting to make her own living on her own terms. She felt tears, hot as the grease burning behind her eyes. Oh, and so tired. She suddenly wanted to slump over the table and rest her head on her arms, but her skirt was too tight, her belly too large. There was no maid to let out her skirts for the final weeks.

Tears spilled down Dorie's face too, and she used the towel to roughly wipe her cheeks. "What's wrong with me? I'm crying like an idiot! I feel like a nasty snake today. I don't know how to tell you how hard this life is. And it's nearly impossible alone."

Francesca smiled as she pictured the snail-sized baby running on its tiny legs up into her head sprinkling a magic potion that would make her cry one minute and then laugh like a lunatic the next. This potion would make her sleep like the dead or forget words that were about to come out of her mouth.

"What about Victor?"

The towel twisted in Dorie's hands. "I've never loved anyone like I love that man," she whispered, "but Victor isn't a farmer. He's a businessman. He looks for opportunity—the newest and best deal."

"If you asked him to run this farm, I know he would. He loves you so."

"Oh, he might be willing to try, but he'd be miserable soon. Victor likes the easy money. No, he wouldn't stay around to eke out a living here."

Was Victor more like Geno than she thought? Her husband would never soil a shirt or mar his buffed nails in the act of labor.

"But what about the baby? Tell him! He'll be so happy."

Dorie gathered the tiny shoes and held them close. "How are you so sure? My drunk of a husband lives in my barn. My business is in ruins. Half the town thinks I'm no better than a gypsy." Dorie set the shoes down on the rumpled paper when she heard a knock on the door. "I didn't hear an engine, did you?" Dorie frowned and went to the kitchen window. She lifted the curtain, then moved to the back door and out into the porch. Would Steiner be back so soon to check on her? Could it be Victor? Louie?

Francesca stepped into the porch and looked over Dorie's shoulder.

Dorie shook her head at the man standing on the stoop. "No, Willie, I haven't got any to sell. I'm sorry."

"I'm good for the money, lookie here." His thick, stubby fingers waived a knotted plaid hankie in front of her face. Francesca heard the jingle of coins. Willie looked to be in his forties. His broad chest strained against the faded denim bibs.

"I don't see a car. How'd you get here, Willie?"

"Walked." He squeezed the brim of his hat with both hands.

"As God sits in heaven, your place is a good six miles from here! Did you know the new sheriff was just here? In fact, he was here twice today. He probably passed you on the road."

Willie gnashed his teeth as if he were chewing up his words before he spit them out. "Just a nip then, Dorie. Louie said you—"

"Then go find Louie and see if he'll share his precious stash with you. I can't help you. You have to leave now."

"I see that gutter here needs fixin'. I could do that for you in nothin' flat. That's worth something, huh?" A white chicken with a hat of black feathers on its head strutted near the steps.

"I said I don't have a drop to give you." With that, Dorie tried to close the door, but he stood solidly in the threshold, the bundled coins dangled in the air, the door pressed against his chest and belly. When she realized his bulk prevented the door from latching, she threw her hands up and stomped past Francesca through the porch into the kitchen. Willie stared at them through the screen.

"Do you know when a new batch might be ready then?"

Francesca shook her head. They stared at each other for a moment before he licked his palm, smoothed back his hair and replaced his hat. He stuffed the coins back into his pocket and shuffled down the steps. He favored one leg, she noticed, and the uneven gait reminded her of a seaman on a ship. She watched him as he walked the length of the mucky drive and turned to look back at the house, but by then he was too far away to read his expression.

The chill finally chased her into the kitchen. Dorie sat at the table, her back straight, her delicate hands folded as if in prayer.

"When it's cooled and hard to the touch, you cut it into squares," Dorie said. Her lips barely moved.

"Squares?" What was she talking about?

"You wanted to know how to finish the soap. After you cut it into squares, you pry them out of the box with a knife, wrap them in paper and store it in the cellar where it's cool."

34

Dorie's New Baby

Although the sun won its battle over the clouds, the wind continued to bend bare branches back and forth and spray loose gravel against the windows. When Francesca asked her if the moaning song bothered her, the pitch and tone cresting like a ghostly whine right out of a Christmas tale, Dorie had shrugged and commented that the winds were a good thing because they'd help dry out the wet so the farmers could get into the fields sooner. Francesca had to strain her ears to take in all of Dorie's quiet words. Frankly, Dorie's docile state was more eerie than the winds.

"I need to put my head down for a few minutes." Dorie stood suddenly and left the room, and Francesca, weary with the events of the day, returned to her room and sank into the cool pillow.

How odd the pull of sleep could be so strong with babies at the beginning, and then again, near the end! She must remember to tell Dorie that in just a few weeks she would again be full of vigor. Francesca pictured that in no time at all Dorie would be getting into those fields herself, whatever that meant.

The low golden light painted a warm rectangle across the quilt. Oh, she was so tired, but she couldn't settle in to sleep. The ache in her back that had plagued her all day now forced its way down each leg. Just when she thought she had found the most comfortable position with her mind floating on the edge between the real world and sleep, a twinge would cause her to turn again.

Suddenly, there was a series of booming knocks on the kitchen door. Francesca struggled to sit up as she kicked aside the heavy blanket. She hurried as fast as her bulk would allow through the sitting room, past sleeping Dorie, and into the kitchen. Victor stood inside the porch, shielding his eyes with one hand as he pressed close to the glass, peering through the window. He grinned and waved when he saw Francesca.

She put her finger to her lips as she motioned him into the kitchen. He had worn his great wool coat buttoned to the neck and had one hand splayed across his belly in much the same way as Francesca held the weight of her own baby. What was he hiding?

"Francesca, how are you?" He tipped his head after he had removed his hat and studied her for a moment. "You look so lovely!"

She pushed the loose waves from her face that had come undone during her rest. She felt anything but lovely, but he seemed so sincere she chose to believe him.

"Where's Dorie?" His cheeks flared bright red.

"Shh, sleeping."

"Sleeping? What's going on? She's ill, isn't she?" One of his blond eyebrows crimped.

Francesca shook her head.

"Tell me about your encounter at Evan's."

Before Francesca could answer, Dorie appeared in the kitchen, dragging the shawl behind her.

"Hello, Victor."

Dorie's stupor seemed to have broken. Her cheeks were nearly as pink as Victor's. There was the impression from the upholstery branded high across her cheekbone. One hand smoothed her mussed hair and then checked the buttons on the front of her dress. She didn't take her eyes from Victor.

"You look so full of yourself. I know that look. It usually means trouble." She sounded stern, but she stepped close and allowed him to take her hand in his. Victor ran his thumb over her wrist.

He winked at them and said, "I've brought you a baby, Dorie."

Francesca and Dorie exchanged glances and gasped. Dorie's eyes went wide, and her mouth formed a perfect little circle as if she was either about to whistle or be kissed. Victor tipped his head back and laughed as he undid the top button on his wool coat. Out popped a sleek, black head. It gave a little yelp to announce its arrival.

"Oh, my word, a dog!" Francesca stepped in to take the wiggling puppy from Victor. A male, his coat felt like sealskin. She put one hand on his plump belly and the other between his front paws and examined him. It had been so long since she had been able to hold a dog! Geno and her mother-in-law had strictly forbidden any kind of dog in the house. “Look at those paws! Does he have a name?”

Dorie still stood wide-eyed and silent. The puppy squirmed and whined, forcing Francesca to pull him closer to avoid dropping him. His wet nose skittered up her neck, and he nipped at her earlobe.

“Where did he come from?” Dorie reached out tentatively and stroked his paw. The three of them stood close in a circle around the puppy.

“Ed Gardner’s bitch had a litter. This is the last one.”

“As if I don’t have enough to do around here—now another living thing to take care of.” Francesca and Dorie locked eyes when they realized the double meaning of her words.

“If you don’t want him, I’ll take him back to Ed’s tonight. I just thought you should have someone here to look out for you when I’m not around,” he murmured near her ear.

Francesca watched the black centers of Dorie’s eyes widen in response. Victor held Dorie’s hand, but watching her reaction, it was as if he was touching and kissing her with wild abandon. Francesca blushed now too, feeling awkward and large as an automobile, horrible and obvious. But even more than the urge to disappear or flee from the kitchen, she wished she could respond like that to someone’s touch. The puppy whimpered and squirmed furiously in her arms.

“I think he needs to go outside,” she whispered, surprised at the sound of her hoarse voice, afraid to break their spell. She put her lips to the velvet fur of the dog’s head.

“I’ve got a bit of rope on the porch,” Dorie said, still looking at Victor.

“Let me take care of him,” Victor offered.

“No, no, I want to take him outdoors. Some air will be good for me anyway. I need to clear my head.” Maybe now Dorie can tell Victor about the baby. Maybe they can figure out a way to be together.

A burst of activity followed. Dorie rooted around in the porch until she retrieved a length of rope and a Macintosh coat. She looped the gray, fraying rope into a collar of sorts and tried to slip it around his neck as he twisted his head and opened his mouth to bite the offending restraint. Once it was cinched, the puppy immediately began to chew on the ragged end when she set him on the floor. “Here, put this on.” Dorie held up a battered but warm looking coat.

Francesca's vision blurred with tears as she slipped her arms through the sleeves. She made kissing noises. "Come here, boy. Let's go." He sniffed her feet. "I think you should name him Shane."

Dorie and Victor looked at each other. "Shane?" Victor said.

"I read a book to my boys called *Shane*. It's about a cowboy. The first line of the book is, 'He rode into our valley in the summer of '89.' He dressed all in black, just like this one—very mysterious, of course."

Victor looked at Dorie and shrugged his shoulders. "What do you think, Dorie? Can Shane stay?"

"He'll be needing a dog house. Will that be you, Victor, swinging a hammer in the morning?"

"I've already thought of that. There's one in not too bad shape out at Buzzy's farm. Well, that is, Francesca's place, I guess it is now. If you don't mind, Francesca, could we use it for Shane? I figured if you still want to take a tour of the farm, we could pick it up tomorrow."

Francesca nodded vigorously. "Yes, I want to see it."

Dorie's expression softened then, and a dimple appeared when she raised one eyebrow. "He doesn't look much like a cowboy." The dog whimpered. Dorie and Victor stepped closer together. The look on Victor's face was raw and full of feeling.

Francesca couldn't breathe properly. She took the rope from Victor and ended up half-dragging the puppy across the floor into the porch. She pushed open the screen door into the dim, evening light. The sun had nearly traveled over the edge of this farm world… the pink edges bled into the charcoal sky. The puppy stumbled along, distracted by new smells.

Oh, God, she was just so full of feeling! She missed her boys! Loneliness swelled its way up into her throat. This puppy, who needed warmth and food, for some reason reminded her keenly of their bodies and their smells and how they would clamor into the crevices of her body for comfort, as if it might be possible to crawl directly to that place from where all her feelings of love radiated. The sight of Victor stroking Dorie's wrists and neck made her long for the chance to touch someone or be touched like that. She wanted to be adored in that same way.

The brisk wind whipped the loose hair all around her face, and she breathed as deeply as the baby would allow. The dog hesitated on each step before bravely jumping to the next. When he made it to the ground, she steadied herself on the metal handrail and eased herself down to sit on the bottom step. The dog immediately relieved himself. She patted his soft head. "Good Shane."

She felt so alone under this cloudless, starry sky. She pushed her hands deep into the pockets of the large coat. Shane tugged on the rope and sniffed the ground. Where was Geno? Had he arrived back home in Chicago full of questions and demands? Would he be worried to know she was so far away? She hoped he'd pace the floor and stab a cigar at the ceiling, demanding to know why his beloved wife had been sent to identify Sal's body. Maybe right at this very moment he was in the nursery stroking the children's faces and tucking blankets around their shoulders. She shook her head. That would be Victor's actions, never her husband's. If he arrived home late after a long absence, he would more likely be interested in a bath and a good meal than to sniff the sweet breath of his sleeping children.

She sighed and snuggled deeper into Dorie's coat, smelling the odd combination of a smoky tang and a flowery perfume. Did she expect too much of marriage? Geno provided for her. He gave her children without complaint, even though she knew he used the time of her confinement as an eager excuse to see other women. It was a shock to discover in the early years of their marriage that she would not have the romance portrayed on the postcards she had kept hidden from her tutor. One of her favorites was a reproduction of a painting called The *Intoxication of Love* by Richard Bormeister. It showed a man and a woman out in the woods at night. She was wearing a gauzy, pleated dress, in the style of those times. She arched backward, one arm thrown over a man's neck. His arm wrapped around her tiny waist, and his face was buried in her neck as she looked up at the night sky. Oh, she had nearly forgotten about those cards! What had become of her secret collection?

During her engagement, she predicted a very different sort of marriage from her Uncle Johnny's. She had witnessed his wife, Estelle, sit home alone, growing more dowdy and shrewish with each passing year. At first, she had reasoned it was Estelle's own fault she was left out. She was quite vocal about her distain for the clubs, the dancing, and the threats of danger. Johnny was practically forced to seek out more exciting companionship! When Francesca was sixteen and about to be wed, she believed herself to be more like the young women who appeared on Johnny's arm, smiling knowingly as they smoked and drank as steadily as any man. None of them ever complained about the danger of being a mobster's gal. Why, one of Johnny's girls missed a bullet only because she bent over to adjust her rolled stockings and then laughed gaily when she realized what had nearly happened, or so said the bodyguards. Francesca believed she would be the kind of wife who was elbow to elbow in the action. Now, having been married all these years to Geno, she came to believe that Johnny might have forced Estelle into the shadows.

Her marriage was no scene from an illicit postcard. Instead, she found that Geno seemed to act most in love with her only when an audience was present. He draped her in beautiful things and kept her close as if to announce, "This is mine." Francesca shivered in the damp air and drew the hood of the coat over her head.

She also believed Geno married her to make her the one possession his brother couldn't claim as his own.

She hadn't suffered as much as other women when it came to marriage. She snuck off once to see Margaret Sanger, not because she wanted to limit her own ability to birth children, but because Geno had scoffed and cursed this woman when he read in the papers she was to give a speech. After that tirade, Francesca simply had to see this woman who inspired such anger! She found that it was exciting to be with women who spoke out boldly against their misery and sadness at having children they couldn't care for, many of whom didn't live beyond infancy. She was also deeply embarrassed to realize she had never gone to bed without food or listened to her hungry children sob into their pillows. She slunk away before the meeting ended, because what was she to do about it all?

Shane whimpered at her feet. She picked up his trembling body and placed him inside her coat as Victor had done. His smooth tongue lapped at her chin. Now she wondered how long she should stay outside. How much time had passed? Had they had time to talk? She blushed at the thought of them together, and then secretly cheered their passion. They could be the subject of some artist's next famous photograph or painting! Her nose ran, and she felt ravenous! It had been hours since she shared the noon meal with Steiner. She wanted meats and cheeses and chunks of hearty bread. She decided she would go in the house and prepare something for the three of them. She would show Dorie she could put a meal on the table just like any other farm wife. Wait. What if Dorie and Victor were right at this very moment in a passionate moment in the kitchen? She didn't want to barge in on that, but she couldn't sit on this step much longer either.

Francesca turned when she heard the crunch of gravel. The sound came from behind Victor's automobile. Shane popped his head out of the coat.

"Dorieee," the voice sang. The pitch and melody sounded like the winds that blew earlier in the day.

Francesca gulped. Louie.

"Have you come to take me back?"

He staggered, his hand trailing the metal curves of the car. Francesca attempted to scoot backward up the steps, closer to the porch door, but the heaviness of her own body, the bulk of the long wool coat, and the squirming puppy conspired against her efforts.

"I want to dance with you, my Dorieeee." He stood six feet in front of her, one arm raised, swaying to an imaginary tune. His features were a blur in the dim light. Louie wasn't wearing a coat, just a tattered shirt that billowed and blew away from his waist and hips, thin as a young boy's.

"I'm not Dorie. My name is Francesca."

"I remember that night at Bauer's barn dance. You were the prettiest woman there in that purple dress. You were just itchin' to get out there on the floor! I shoulda quit drinkin' long enough to spin you around the dance floor."

Louie's foot caught on the ground. He was wearing boots this time, but they weren't laced properly and looked too large for his feet. He stumbled and then leaned heavily on the car. "I let Victor take my place."

Francesca pulled the hood from her head so he could see her face. Shane curled up inside the coat.

"Ah, Dorie, you'll always be my sweetie." He pushed himself upright again. "Can I come inside? I need a drink."

Maybe it was the overcoat. Maybe his mind was gone from the drink. He believed she was Dorie. Would he hurt her if he loved her so much?

"I don't feel so good, Dorie. Will you take care of me?" The wind rattled the tin roof on a small building next to the barn. She suddenly wasn't afraid of him any longer. He was just a sad old drunk in love with Dorie. This realization made her bold. Maybe Louie had all the answers to her questions.

"Yes, Louie, it's me, Dorie. Help me remember something. What happened the last night Sal was here drinking?"

"Sal. I like Sal. He's a nice fella. He came all the way from Chicago."

"That's right. Did you fight with him?"

Louie suddenly stopped pitching back and forth as if the memory was a solid thing.

"Did he try to steal my money? Did he want to take over the still?" Then it came to her. She saw a scene playing out before her eyes as if she had been there, because she knew Sal and she knew what happened when he was liquored-up. In that instant she was Dorie pouring drinks in the kitchen. Her heart pounded.

"Did you see Sal try to hurt me?" She paused when she saw she had his attention. "You saw Sal try to force himself on me that night, didn't you Louie?"

Louie pressed both hands to his temples as if he intended to crush his own head.

"Sal tried to kiss me. He had his hands all over me. Isn't that what you saw?"

Louie leaned against the automobile and slid down until he landed heavily on the running board. "Sal said he was my friend."

"But you found out he wasn't your friend. You had to defend me, to save me from him. You hit Sal with a piece of firewood."

"No, no, no," he cried. He tilted his head back and crooned to the dark sky.

"Then tell me what happened, Louie!"

"I saw you in the kitchen. You were tying Sal's shoelaces. Then you and Victor took him for ride." He was breathless with the telling.

Francesca's blood pounded in her ears, and a roar like the winds entered her head. Shane's body radiated warmth. He smelled like dirt and something sweet.

Louie put his hands over his heart and looked up to the black sky before he said, "That's the thing I couldn't figure out. Why would they take him out in the blizzard when he was sleeping?"

35

Victor Offers to Take Francesca to Her Farm

The D'Agostino dining room table was brilliantly lit without benefit of candles or gas lamps or electric lights. Where was the light coming from then? Francesca realized she couldn't see anything beyond the table. Where were the paneled walls, the draped windows, the serving table, or the arched entryway? There was only the white linen tablecloth, the china, and the heavy silver settings glinting in the too-bright glare.

When she looked up, her father-in-law sat at his usual spot at the head of the table, Geno on her left side, and Sal positioned across from her. The men didn't seem concerned about Giovanna's absence. When she looked down, a steaming a bowl of *Pescare'de Mar* appeared. She stirred the tomato broth, thick with mussels, chunks of white fish, spinach, and *ditilini*. Ravenous, it seemed like ages since she'd had the chance to eat her favorite soup. She brought the spoon to her mouth even before she had unfolded her napkin and was surprised when the soup tasted like nothing at all. What kind of trick was this? The men pointed and laughed. She felt the familiar chord tightening against their cruel humor.

"If you think that's odd, try the wine," Geno said.

She hesitated for a moment and picked up the crystal goblet to sip the garnet wine. She tipped the glass back, expecting a rush into her mouth, but it was like drinking air.

Sal laughed so hard he needed to wipe his tears with the back of his broad hand.

"It's all like that," her father-in-law surmised. "The food, the wine—"

"The women," Sal snickered.

"We have all the pleasures before us," her father-in-law continued, "but we cannot enjoy them." He studied the unlit cigar in his hand.

"You have recovered your health," she said to him. "When I left for Osseo, you couldn't speak. The priest had given you Last Rites." Even in the harsh glare he looked as youthful as the day she had first met him, thick white hair, an unlined face.

Francesca ran her hands over her body. Slim. There was no baby in her belly. She looked up in alarm.

"There are no children in this place, Francesca," Geno instructed.

"Where are we?" There was a white glare all around.

"It's complicated," Geno started. "You know how Limbo is for babies that don't get baptized?"

Francesca nodded, trying to wrap her arms around the belly that was no longer there.

"Well, this here is a place for mobsters. We have been given a chance to right our wrongs. We gotta sit here 'til we figure it out."

"I've never heard of that," she said.

"Oh, yeah, it's in the Bible. Sal, who's the guy that says that stuff?"

"Naw, I don't know."

"Maybe that's part of the reason you're here," Francesca shot back.

"Ho-ho. You're a regular vaudeville act. Then why are you here, Miss Frannie?" Why was she here? If Sal's dead and he's here, then this must be some kind of hell. Did that mean Geno and his father were dead too? Had she left the world of the living?

"Now, let's put our heads together on this one, boys." Her father-in-law gestured the question with his hands palms up, still holding the unlit cigar. "What do good people do to make a living?"

She sat in her small bed, gripped the quilt, and thought about that dream. *Then why are you here, Miss Frannie?* The words repeated in her head. It seemed now that the nature of her business here had changed again. First it was just to claim Sal's body and return home. Then it became about saving lovers from the injustice of the law. Now she was past doing things for others. She had to find out what happened to her own husband. If Geno were dead, what would happen to her? Why had she never taken the time to find out if there was a will? She studied the tiny stitches on the quilt, smaller than eyelashes, and wondered if Giovanna would laugh as she threw her only daughter-in-law out on the streets.

She rubbed the end of her braid against her lips. She smelled of Dorie's perfumes now. When she had come back into the house after her encounter with Louie, she was relieved to discover Dorie and Victor had had the good sense to seek the privacy of Dorie's bedroom. Chilled to the bone, she pulled out Dorie's galvanized tub, locked the doors, pulled the drapes, and drew herself a bath. It took forever to heat the water, but she did it without any help at all! She pulled up a chair next to the tub to use as a makeshift table and set out a plate of sliced cheese, roast, and bread. She fed Shane some of the scraps and a saucer of goat's milk. She soaked and ate for the longest time, adding more hot water from the kettle and liberal doses of Dorie's oils. She thought about what Louie had said and wondered how to sort the truth from the lies. When she could no longer keep her eyes open, she put on her dressing gown and climbed into bed with the dog, needing to feel his warmth.

The uncertainty of the previous evening gave way to anger in the morning. Did they both think she was stupid? She certainly felt stupid. She cringed when she thought how she had defended the pair to Steiner. "They showed such kindness to a stranger. They couldn't have done anything wrong." No wonder Steiner thought her a rube. They were both kind to her only because they felt guilty, she realized now. But did she expect a full confession at the train station? *Hello, lovely to meet you. I'm Dorie. This is Victor. In the name of honesty, you should know we murdered your brother-in-law. So sorry, but you of all people should know what a bother he can be.* She shook her head. What really happened? Dorie would have done anything to protect her livelihood. Sal threatened that in some way. Thoughts kept spinning around in her head like a top. Did Dorie kill Sal? Or did Victor kill Sal or did they do it together?

Shane raised his head, wagged his tail and wobbled up the length of her legs for attention. When he started to chew on her thumb with his sharp puppy teeth, she realized he needed to eat and go outside. She closed the front of her dressing gown and helped him down to the floor. Gauzy fragments of the dream clung to her memory. Was this the first time she had dreamt of Geno since his disappearance? She admired the look of his freshly shaved dark skin and his crisp white shirt, although she recalled his tie needed straightening. Why didn't he seem happy to see her? This was a near constant state in her marriage, these moments where she felt a wifely tenderness toward him, but then he would always say something annoying, like commenting on the beauty of another woman, or do something or not do something to stomp over her feelings. She knew it was a little crazy to be angry at his behavior in the dream, but if this was a message from beyond the grave, shouldn't he have had something more to say to his wife?

When she reached the kitchen, she stopped dead in her tracks when she found Victor sitting at the kitchen table. A tuft of hair stood up at the crown of his head making him look like a young boy. She realized she had never seen him when he didn't look perfectly groomed. He was dressed and sipped a steaming cup of coffee. She also noticed that the tub had been drained and put away. He looked up when she entered the room.

He grinned sheepishly. "Francesca, I feel like we abandoned you last night." The puppy scrambled to sniff the cuff of Victor's pants. He tumbled over when Victor scratched his belly.

"You did abandon me." The stove warmed the room. She loved the smells of wood and coffee.

"It wasn't my intention to stay here, to be with Dorie last night. We just never have any time alone together." His voice low and quiet. "When I'm with her it's like jumping off a cliff—all the arm waving and screaming in the world can't stop me from falling."

"Or hitting the ground."

He looked up at her, nodded, then chuckled. She had the urge to smooth down that plaint of hair.

"You haven't offended my sensibilities by spending the night with Dorie, if that's what you're worried about, and I'll forgive you for ignoring me if you bring me a cup of coffee." Be careful, she thought. Don't let his charm fool you. This gentle man, who cared for puppies and pregnant women, might have had a hand in killing Sal. Why did this surprise her? This is the kind of man you already know, she told herself! Remember the contrasting nature of Uncle Johnny.

"I'll do better than that. Let me make you breakfast. I've looked in Dorie's icebox and saw a few potatoes and some sausage. I can go out to the hen house and gather some eggs. You should have something to eat before we drive out to your farm… if you're still wanting to do that."

The farm. The queerest little shiver ran up her spine. Was this what Victor had said to Sal? *I'll drive you out to the farm.* He poured a cup of the blackest coffee and held the steaming mug out to her, still smiling. Her head and mouth felt as if they were stuffed with wet wool. She needed something strong to clear her head and order her thoughts. She said a quick prayer to Saint Drausinus, to protect her against enemy plots.

"My farm. Yes. I would still like to go, except I am expecting Steiner to come by this morning. I'm not sure what time he's due to arrive. He has great concern for my well-being, you know."

"As does anyone who meets you," he said. "Dorie can tell him your whereabouts, or she could send him out there too, I suppose. He won't be happy to hear you're with me. I'm not his favorite person in town." He rubbed the rim of the cup with his thumb.

"Because..."

"The list is long. He's heard enough about the moonshine business from most everyone in these parts. You've probably been told he found Dorie and me stranded together at your farm. Then there's the fact that I was with your brother-in-law when he was killed."

A response stuck in her throat, jammed up by her anger, distrust, and incredulous as it was, by feelings of affection.

"I can see by your face he's been warning you that I'm a shiftless bastard. Excuse such language. Even though I have two good arms and legs, I've never held a job for very long. Is all this ringing true?" He stood up, placed his hands on the back of the chair, and leaned over her. She noticed his shirt was rumpled. Another first.

"Is it true?"

He smiled and held up both hands. "I'm guilty, yes."

Hearing him say "guilty" made her shiver again.

"Will Dorie come with us?"

"She was up before dawn, which is usual for her, but then she came back to bed and fell fast asleep. I couldn't wake her, which worries me. Steiner and the business are wearing on her constitution." He started moving about the kitchen, opening up cupboards, peering into the icebox.

She startled as the coffee scalded her tongue. She set the cup on the red oilcloth. She shook her head. Dorie still hadn't told him about the baby. God in heaven, she was sick of tripping over the trunk full of secrets around here.

"Victor." He turned to look at her as he lifted the skillet. "Dorie is going to have a child. That's why her stomach won't settle. That's why she's tired." She liked the feeling of a release, the power of the secret—it moved through her like a current.

His blue eyes widened in response and then he threw his arms around her, pulling her out of her chair. The weight of the skillet nearly knocked the both of them over. He whooped with delight and spun her in circles, upsetting the bowl of potatoes. The dog yipped in the excitement. Victor's musky and warm scent mixed with Dorie's lavender perfume. She blushed, feeling as if she had climbed into bed with the two of them.

"Why didn't she tell me? How long until she looks like this?" He held his hands out, fingers spread wide on either side of his own belly mimicking Francesca's roundness.

She couldn't help but laugh at his response. "That'll be many months yet. You can't tell her I've told you. She'll be livid if she finds out I've betrayed her secret."

"No, I want her to tell me anyway. I don't want to spoil the surprise." He pushed his blond hair back from his forehead and looked pleased.

A thought struck her. Could Louie be telling tales to get rid of Victor? Maybe he wanted Francesca to run to Steiner and fan the flames of these lies. The confusion of all of these feelings gave her a headache. They both turned when the clock chimed eight times.

"I think it'd be best to get out to the farm early before the mud softens. Listen, Francesca, you get ready while I take care of the dog and make something to eat. Wait though. You shouldn't wear your good skirt and boots. With the melt on, the yard's likely to resemble a muddy battlefield." He looked down at the skillet as if he was unsure how it had gotten into his hand. He set it on the table. "I have an idea."

He went to the porch and retrieved a faded pair of dungarees, Dorie's sweater, and a pair of men's boots. He held the pants up to Francesca, and she saw they bore numerous repairs, reminding her of tiny, white scars. "This is what Dorie wears to muck out the barn or work in the garden. I'll get you some wool socks too."

"It's too much bother. I'll ask Steiner for a tour."

Francesca held her breath and watched his face, waiting for a small movement, his tell.

"If that's what you want. It's up to you." What were the chances of uncovering the truth in Steiner's company? He wouldn't let her out of his automobile, citing some obscure danger. No, she wanted to be with Victor to make him feel guilty, to make him confess. Francesca tried to listen for the voice inside that would tell her what to do, but all she heard was radio static. Could there be some reason for her to be found dead dressed like a beggar?

"I'm sure I won't be able to fasten the pants." She ran her finger over the row of brass buttons.

"I thought of that. Here." He shrugged out of his braces and unbuttoned the clips. He held them out to her. They dangled before her like live snakes. "The braces will keep the pants up."

Watch out. Something is going to happen out at the farm.

"But the dungarees will be, um, open." She tried to speak calmly.

Be brave. He will lead you to the truth.

"When you button up this sweater, no one will be able to see that. You'll thank me for saving your skirt. Take my word, it's bound to be a real mess."

"Victor, did Sal leave any personal effects at my farm?"

His face went smooth. "I'm not sure. We could look, if you want."

"Why did he stay there?"

Victor shook his head and shrugged. "There are always more questions than answers. Get dressed. We'll see what we can figure out."

The baby pushed hard against her ribs, and she rubbed the spot with her fingertips to reassure them both. She gathered the bundle of clothing and moved toward her room.

The chilly air made her rush to dress. Her hands shook, but she consoled her nerves by whispering, "I don't have to go out to the farm. I can say I'm unwell."

This morning, this claim was true enough. A twinge came to her lower back as she bent over to step into the dungarees. The strangeness of donning men's clothes, even if Dorie had worn them, made her giggle out loud, forgetting for a moment her nervousness. She could almost see the boys, especially Joseph, who loved silly costumes, whooping with laughter to see his mother in such a getup. She pulled the braces up over her shoulders and ran her thumbs up and down their length. The happy thought of the boys filled her with calm. All she had to do was find out Geno's whereabouts, and then she could go home in peace. She sat on the bed and, with difficulty, bent to roll a cuff. Francesca startled at the sight of her toes and ankles, fat as *spadini* rolls. She realized then that Victor had neglected to get her a pair of socks.

Francesca headed up the narrow stairs to Dorie's room to borrow some stockings. When Francesca placed her hand on the worn railing, she heard their voices washing down the narrow shaft of stairs.

She crouched on the bottom stair, holding her belly with both hands to relieve the heavy pressure.

"I wish I could go with you, but the room just spins for me."

"Rest now. We won't be gone long. She just wants to see the place. It's such an easy thing to do."

Dorie's voice was muffled. Francesca found herself shifting her weight up one stair to get closer to the words.

"Promise me you'll look. It would mean so much to us now."

"Are you still fixing on that crazy idea?"

The bedsprings creaked, and she couldn't hear any other conversation. Francesca held her breath and counted the ticking from the parlor clock. When she reached twenty, she pictured them kissing again, and wondered if the whole trip might be postponed. Suddenly, she heard Dorie's voice, the tone as clean and clear as crystal hit with a spoon.

"Victor, find that money. I know Geno hid it there someplace."

36

Francesca Sees Her Farm

Victor's car chugged along the long drive that would lead them to her farm. Gray skies cupped the flat brown stretches of churned-up dirt. The moist air pressed into the wool coat she had borrowed from Dorie, but she reveled in its warmth. Francesca began to count the bleached fence posts, only half of which stood upright. The rest leaned this way and that way as if they were too tired to go on with their fencing duties.

"The house and barn are just behind the jack pine," Victor said.

For a minute, Francesca thought he was referring to a person named Jack Pine, a rugged man, she pictured. He would have a white beard, wear plaid shirts and have a saw slung across his shoulder. When she realized the error, she was glad she hadn't commented or asked questions about Jack. Oh, she wasn't thinking clearly at all.

Thirty-five, thirty-six, thirty-seven...

"The barn was built about twenty years ago. There are six sheds, some are in disrepair, and others are in fair shape." He pointed to the right. "There's a small pond back there by the grazing pasture." He said her land ran a hundred acres beyond the stand of trees behind the house. She had no idea what that meant and was too preoccupied to press him for definitions. Victor seemed happy to chat, still in high spirits from his news about Dorie's pregnancy.

Her troubled thoughts circled around and around to Geno—he had been here, in this town, and he had met Dorie, and yet she never let on when Francesca told her tale of her missing husband. Dorie knew enough about his dealings to speculate he had hidden money someplace. If it were true, it seemed logical he would have hidden it at the property owned by his wife even though Francesca knew he had looked at all this flat empty land with distrust and scorn. Why, he must have traveled down this very same road! That thought became a shiver. Had Geno stolen money from Dorie? Had he culled the nerve to pull a bank holdup? Francesca bit her lower lip. No, it was too hard to picture him acting without Sal at his side. What seemed more plausible was that he had continued conning other bootleggers by posing as a federal agent. If he edged his way from Chicago to Osseo, pulling the same scam over and over again, think of how much money he might have collected! Once he arrived here, there was no place to spend it! She nearly laughed out loud to imagine his fury. No clubs, no swank hotels, restaurants, or gambling joints. She counted forty-nine fence posts. Where was Geno now? She held her breath against the pain in her lower back and the confusion in her head.

"This is it," Victor announced, and the car lurched to a stop, pitching Francesca forward against Victor's protective arm.

Francesca surveyed the wide circle of standing water around the car and wondered if this was the pond. Tiny brown birds hopped from the edge of the greening grass, dropped their beaks into the brown water, and then shook themselves to fluff their feathers.

"They lived here? Buzzy and Lois?" Her voice felt thick and broken.

A battered door sat mired in the mud at the foot of the crumbled stairs, the torn screen bobbing in the slight breeze. The yellow color of the house had faded in places to gray to match the skies. Shutters framing the two lower windows cocked at crazy angles. Francesca imagined the whole scene, the fence, the house, the barn, looked like a child's play set, the pieces strewn and destroyed in a fit of temper.

"Of course, you know the place has stood empty for a few years now," Victor said. "There hasn't been anyone around to look after it properly. Can you picture it though? A few coats of paint... wouldn't take someone who's good with a hammer nothing but a few weeks to put it right again."

Francesca squinted, as though blurring her vision would change the scene before her. She couldn't picture her children living here. The farmhouse in her head was stately and white with rows of gleaming windows and a wide porch for receiving visitors. Oh, how Geno and Sal must have snickered when they saw this place! She bet they scoffed at her, and the poor potato-relatives who inflicted this hindrance on them. Why would Sal have stayed here? Now that she had seen this place, it was even more of a mystery. Unless what Dorie had said about the hidden money was true. A shredded curtain billowed out from the second-floor broken window, caught on a shard of glass, and then receded again. Her throat ached at the sadness of this place.

"The barn roof is holding up." He gestured with his head. Francesca spied an enormous rusted thing that looked like the talon of a giant bird, hidden in a tangle of pale, broken grasses waiting for the chance to strike out and impale anyone who tried to escape. Scattered across the yard lay a bedspring, broken bottles, and a lone wheel. Most everything was now the uniform color of dirt.

"Oh, Lord, you're crying." Victor reached into his coat and pushed a handkerchief into her hands.

"This is just not what I pictured." Francesca dabbed at her eyes. "I can't believe they lived here!" She pointed over to the tiny green building to the left of the house. A pitch and force of tears rolled from her.

This cry was for all the nights she had been alone, this was for how much she missed her boys, for how hard it was to move and breathe and bend over, and for that terrible ache in her back. Magically, Victor didn't run from the car or throw up his hands and declare her a nervous case. Instead, he sat quietly and patted her hand and said, "I know." She realized she had never known a man with sapphire eyes.

She couldn't control the pitch of her voice, which rose higher, shrew-like, with her emotions. "When I thought about this farm these last months, I pictured that maybe, one day, I could bring my sons here to live, but this is just an awful place." She could barely catch a breath.

"It could be wonderful," Victor said. "Dorie and I would have perished in that blizzard if it weren't for this house. I found out that she loves me in that parlor. It wasn't until the last couple of months I began to see why Dorie is so attached to that farm of hers. For the first time in my life, I feel like I want to take care of a piece of land."

Francesca swallowed hard and considered the fact that anyone who could be sentimental about this horrible place surely would never scheme to hurt her.

Victor blushed, lifted his hat, and ran his fingers through his hair. "Most fellows around here have a natural feel for the land. I've never so much as owned a proper piece of furniture!"

"Maybe you should buy this place from me then. I think I can charge you a big sum for a place that saved your life. What do you say? I'll sell you this farm, and then I can buy a house that doesn't need so many swings of the hammer. All our problems are solved." She liked joking with him again instead of feeling heavy with suspicion. He wouldn't hurt her. It wasn't in him, but she knew his soul was troubled by a dark secret.

"Miss Francesca, I don't have two-bits to my name. I never saved any of the money I made with Dorie."

"Your still. It's here, isn't it?" She knew it was true even before she looked at his face. She loved that moment of figuring out the puzzle. She had always assumed it was somewhere on Dorie's farm, but Dorie was smarter than that. Of course, this abandoned property made sense as a secret place to set up the still. Unless they were caught red-handed, it was hard to prove who ran the operation.

"I'd bet it's in the cellar." Francesca was breathless with the thrill of this. It seemed as though all her time in this town came down to this moment. The still would have the answers she needed.

Victor shifted in his seat and ran a hand back and forth over the wheel. Finally, he shook his head. "No, it's in the woods there." He pointed to the trees on their right.

"Where? You said you would take me to what has been deeded to me. I want to see it." She knew she sounded like her boys when they begged for sweets or toys, but she didn't care.

"There's not much to see! How about the barn? I'll bet you've never been inside a barn before."

What did a farmer keep in the barn besides animals?

"No, the still," she insisted.

"It'll be muddy out there, worse than this."

"I've boots and trousers." Why was he so reluctant?

"I don't think it would do me any good for our friend Steiner to find me there."

"I'll tell him the truth. I asked for a proper tour of all the property. We're not going to make a batch of moonshine, are we? There's nothing out there that ties you to the still, is there? Or do you have a painted sign—Victor's Kickapoo Joy-Juice Made Here!"

He smiled. "Actually, there might be some of my things left out there, a shaving kit, a few tools. I don't know what else. It's been so long since I've stayed out there to cook a batch." Victor touched the tender looking scar on his eyebrow. This was his tell. Something about the still bothered him more than the mud and cold or a visit from Steiner. Dorie might never tell the truth, but Victor could be broken.

"That settles it. We should go gather your belongings, and then we'll leave. Afterwards, I'll even let you show me the barn."

With that, Victor sighed and stepped out to crank the engine. The smell of gasoline exhaust mixed with the wet air as the engine throttled. They lurched forward, scattering the birds, as the wheels found twin ruts. For a moment she thought he meant to crash into the trees, and then the front of the car found a small opening and nosed forward into a tunnel of green. She clenched her mittens together and held them to her heart, almost feeling the wild beat through the wool.

Dead lower branches scratched at the roof of the car and pushed against the side curtains. Her nose filled with a sharp, clean scent.

"Pine," Victor responded when he noticed her sniffing.

It was dark in this grotto. This place felt like the setting of fairy tales little Joseph begged her to read over and over again. What would jump out and devour them? A wolf? A witch? Forest creatures? She said a quick prayer to Graths of Agosta, the patron saint against dangerous animals. Since she had never made a prayer request to him, it was impossible for her to have used up any graces he might be able to bestow. She fought against a queasy churning of potatoes in her stomach.

The automobile tunneled further into the murky gloom. Victor grimly gripped the wheel, squinting as he pressed on. Francesca squirmed in her seat, anxious for the chance to stretch her cramped legs and back. The baby's head bore down painfully, and she was overcome with the sensation that she might burst at any moment. Francesca wondered again how she would endure the final weeks of pregnancy.

What would she be doing if she were at home in Chicago? Mid-morning might have her supervising lessons with the boys or reviewing the menu for the evening meal, writing letters. If she could sneak away from Giovanna's watchful eye, she could find a quiet place to read or look at a fashion magazine. All of that now seemed like someone else's life, a diary account of a lonely woman living a sleepy life.

When they came up to a place where the narrow path widened, Victor killed the engine. Trees had been cut down, leaving stubby amputations on both sides of the path. Her eyes were drawn to a small building, a crazy quilt of differing lengths of wood with a rusted tin roof.

Francesca opened her door and swung her cramped legs around until her toes dangled over a bed of golden pine needles and a scattering of small brown cones. She turned to look at Victor who sat motionless, his face bleached of color.

"Coming?"

He nodded but didn't move.

She leaned against the door and put a hand to the small of her back to relieve the pressure. The air smelled clean. All around her was a soft rustling sound, like hundreds of whispers. A few feet from the car, she saw a giant kettle perched on a circle of speckled stones. Under the kettle lay chunks of charred wood, and the image reminded her of a witch's cauldron. She half expected to turn to find a cage holding fattened children.

"What's all this?" she called as she moved toward the blackened kettle, still conscious of the feel of trousers brushing against her legs. Francesca pointed to several open barrels that rested behind the fire circle. On the ground, a coil of dulled copper lay bent and kinked. Next to that was a broken shovel.

Victor finally climbed out of the car and stood next to her. He picked up the tubing and tried to bend it. He sighed and threw it to the ground and then kicked at the battered shovel handle.

"This was my condenser. It appears someone has replaced my, what did you call it? 'Kick-a-Poo Joy Juice' sign with one that says *out of business*."

"Tell me how you made the moonshine. I've heard Geno talk some, but the stills he knew about were small. The whole thing happened in an old bathtub."

"One week last summer, we got three hundred gallons." He knocked on the kettle, and it made a short pong sound. "It's not hard—just a lot of waiting. First you put corn and sugar in one of those barrels there and add some warm water. Cover it and leave it for about five days. See, I packed it there around the bottom with manure and old burlap bags."

"Manure?"

"Horsecrap."

"I know what manure is. Why?" Francesca bent over and gave it a sniff, but perhaps it was too cold to smell more than the pine air. She couldn't believe she was trying to smell horse dumplings.

"Helps keep the barrels warm for fermenting. Then after a few days, the sour mash is ready to be dipped out. I strain it through a bed sheet and put it in this kettle. Then I get a fire going, not too hot mind you. That's a dangerous mistake people make. Then the whole thing blows up. Anyway, just get a nice gentle fire and then vapor escapes into the worm—that's the copper tube."

"What does that do?"

"When the alcohol vapor passes through this cold coil, it turns back into a liquid and drains into the jugs. That first run is usually foggy looking because it has too much water and some impurities to it. On the second run, it comes out purified—crystal clear." He stood stock-still and seemed to focus on the trees beyond the clearing. "It got so that when I made a batch, I could shake the bottle and a perfect bead, about the size of a number five shot, would rise up, and then I knew the proof was just right." He kicked at the loose needles on the ground. "I know it's a peculiar thing to be proud of." A chill chased up Francesca's spine.

"Shhh, hear that?" Victor said.

Francesca pulled the edge of the hood away from one ear.

"You can hear the stream that leads to Eagle Lake. It's open now, running full out. Pretty soon the lake will be clear of ice too. It's just over that hill there." He pointed at a place over the hill.

"It's nice by the lake. I spent so much time down here last summer! For days on end I was alone, waiting out a batch. I'd go down and sit by the water. That's when I started thinking of Dorie. I wondered if she could ever find it in her heart to love me. I thought we could have a picnic by the shore. Maybe I'd find an old boat and watch the sun set." His arms mimicked a rowing motion.

"Sounds lovely." She meant that, but his feelings for Dorie were so plaintive and true it hurt her heart to be near it. He was just as romantic as the leading men in the books she read. She could picture him thinking of Dorie as the water lapped at the shore, working these thoughts around and around in his head as the heat of the day beat on. She was sure he would replay little things she said, recall the dress she wore that day, or maybe he'd say her name aloud to the lake just to hear the sound of it. Francesca desperately wanted someone to love her like that.

"Victor, I need to walk around a bit." Her voice caught, and she was ashamed his devotion to Dorie caused her such envy and grief.

He nodded, but she wasn't sure if he was really listening. She probably could have told him she was going off to swim in the lake, and he wouldn't have given her any more notice. He was either thinking of Dorie or visiting whatever ghosts this place held for him. In either case, her legs were nearly numb from the drive and standing in one place. Maybe it was the trousers and the flat boots, but she set out past the last stump as fast as she was able, swinging her arms like a man as Dorie would do.

The trees here were cramped and arthritic looking, larger and bigger around the middle than the ones by the still. A golden sap oozed from various scabs on the trunks. The needles on the ground cushioned each step, and the whispery movement of the trees became louder now, reminding her of the rustling of silk skirts. She pressed on, looking back over her shoulder to mark her distance from the still and saw Victor sitting, hunched over on a crate. The walk in the forest eased the terrible ache in her legs and back, and she felt like a brave explorer. She reasoned if she kept to this walking path she wouldn't get lost, but then decided it would be prudent to leave something to mark her way. She took off one of the red mittens and hung it on the end of a branch.

She walked up and over a slight hill, out of sight of the still now, her lungs burned with effort, and the layers of cotton and wool became damp with sweat. She bent forward to catch her breath, closing her eyes to the hypnotic rustling. The sound of moving water was louder here, and she realized she must be near the stream Victor had mentioned. Suddenly, Francesca was overcome by a powerful thirst and decided to find those waters and squat and drink from cupped hands just like an explorer would do. She started to see other varieties of trees and wished she had a journal to draw sketches to record her discoveries. She particularity liked the slight and tender trees that looked like they were wrapped in white paper, some still bravely clutching their rustling leaves. The white trees appeared not as hearty as the jack pine. Many of them lay on the ground, broken and rotted. The path beneath her feet began to change too, full of black leaves, smelling slick and dark. She tried to memorize all the sights and smells here so she could tell the boys how she bravely surveyed all this that would one day be their forest.

Francesca jumped at a clattering off to her left and saw two gray squirrels in a mad chase around the tree. They stopped overhead long enough to make spitting sounds. Her eyes were drawn farther to the left to an area with more fallen trees. After leaving the other mitten on the ground, she walked off the path through a blanket of wet leaves and sticks, kicking up clumps with her boots. What caught her eye was an enormous pile of jack pine boughs, stacked and ready, it seemed, to burn Joan of Arc at the stake.

Her footsteps made soft rustling sounds, and she moved closer. With a bare hand she yanked one of the branches, the needles now brown and brittle, and several fell away as if woven together, revealing the creamy curved fender.

Geno's car was hidden here in her forest.

It was unmistakable—a 1927 Minerva Torpedo. He had been so proud when he drove it to the house and beeped the horn. The boys had screamed and knocked each other over to be the first one to get a ride. Geno talked about nothing else for months, how it could go seventy-five miles an hour, the special sound the engine made. Even Sal had shown a bit of envy until he purchased a newer, faster Minerva of his own.

Sap from the branches made her fingers sticky. Was Geno inside? Something hot and burning clamored up the back of her throat. Had all these travels brought her to this moment when she would find her husband's body? She wanted to scream for Victor, but the thought that he might have been the one to hide this car stopped her. Could she get to town from here and find Steiner? She backed away, stumbled on a rock, and fell into the wet muck of leaves. If Victor found out she had discovered Geno's car, would he move it? Her fingers went numb from the cold.

This was her chance. Hadn't she prayed to know what happened to Geno? She rolled onto her hands and knees and pushed herself up. The pain in her back throbbed steadily now. She must have strained a muscle when she fell. She could never walk all the way to town!

Look in the car.

With trembling fingers, she held her breath against the pain and her own nerves and pulled the branches away from the canvas top and the windows. Brittle needles fell on the running board. Sap speckled the cream paint finish.

Francesca opened the door and peered into the dank interior. On the passenger seat sat a wine-colored suitcase with the gold-embossed initials: E.A.D. Eugene Anthony D'Agostino.

37

The Fire

A brilliant sun streamed through the stained-glass windows, spilling ribbons of green and blue down the walls of the D'Agostino mansion. Footsteps and voices echoed as the family gathered to send Geno off on his business trip. Francesca stared at a delicate black vein curving on the marble floor, pulled the shawl around her shoulders, and wished his departure was not such a public ceremony. Biaggio plunged his fat fingers into her loose hair, his black eyes crossed as he stared intently at the tendrils. She shifted his bulk on her hip and relished the feeling of his solid thigh in her palm. Oh, in not very long a time he would be too heavy for her to lift!

Giovanna glided into the foyer and threw back her ample shoulders just before she linked arms with her husband. Francesca, under the gaze of her mother-in-law, did her best to look the part of the dutiful, sad wife, and, at the same time, hoped to avoid the discovery of her latest pregnancy. She would have preferred to stay in her room or engage the children in a game to distract them, but her mother-in-law had insisted that everyone be present to send off her eldest son. Joseph whimpered and hiccupped, not having recovered from his morning of tears.

Geno descended the grand staircase, his face glowing after a fresh shave, and the buff cashmere overcoat contrasted his dark looks. She couldn't believe it had already been six years since she had first met him. If he didn't talk or try to touch her, she could remember how his black eyes and glossy hair made her heart quiver. Geno slapped black gloves against his palm, smiled, and paused, standing on the last stair as he surveyed his family. Francesca snorted and then pretended to cough, knowing he deliberately posed that way to appear taller. He relished this passage of power from father to eldest son. He was now a man of authority and importance in the family. Behind him, Bridget struggled down the stairs, two hands gripping the handle of Geno's new leather suitcase. Francesca saw Bridget wince as the corner slammed against her knee. Francesca tapped Geno Junior's shoulder and nodded her head toward the stairs, and he ran to Bridget's aid, first dragging, and finally pushing it across the polished floor. Joseph ran to his father, and a fresh torrent of tears began as he pressed his face into Geno's overcoat. He glanced down at his son, placed a thick hand on his forehead, and pushed him back.

"Be a little man. Quit your belly-achin'." He brushed at the wet spot on the cashmere. Francesca moved in and tried to take Joseph's hand, but he batted her away, his tear-streaked face full of misery. "I'm basking in the love of my great family. This will warm my heart even if the rest of me is cold on my northern journey!" He put a hand across his chest, thumping his fingers, *ba-bump, ba-bump*.

As it was, Francesca could hardly stand to look at Geno since he told her he planned to sell her farm to the first buyer with money in his hand. She rubbed Biaggio's back and put her lips to his temples although he wasn't in need of comfort. She surveyed the scene—her in-laws, the servants, and the boys. Where was Sal?

Giovanna kissed her son and held his face in her hands for a long time. Next, his father hugged and rubbed Geno on the back. When Francesca saw his bent and twisted fingers, she was shocked at how much he had aged in the last months and realized those fingers could no longer pull the trigger of a gun.

"Ah, and my lovely wife." Geno suddenly swooped in, his mouth capturing hers before she had the chance to turn her head away. Oh, she didn't want him to do this in front of the family and the servants! Her heart raced and she flushed. Biaggio fussed and squirmed in her arms, his fingers tangled in her waves. Geno's mouth was wet, and she startled to taste gin at this hour in the morning. His arm went around her, and she panicked to think his fingers would detect her thickening waistline and announce her secret. At first, she had planned to tell him about the spring child as a departure gift, and when he talked so callously of selling her farm, even when she begged him not to, she decided to keep that news from him.

His mouth blocked her nostrils, and she squirmed to break away, desperate for air. Maybe her father-in-law took her struggles as a sign of passion, or he enjoyed her discomfort, for whatever reason, he clapped his gnarled hands together in appreciation.

Francesca felt a sudden steady pressure on her shoulder. It confused her for she mistakenly thought it must be Biaggio, and then deduced it to be Geno's hand, but no, he held her at the waist. A voice boomed behind her, and her husband's mouth broke away from hers. She could feel a wet smear of saliva at the corner of her mouth, but holding Biaggio prevented her from pulling a handkerchief from her skirt pocket.

"Don't let it trouble you, my brother. We will take good care of Francesca here," Sal said.

At first she tried to cover up the Minerva by replacing the branches, but most of them were too heavy to lift, and the ones she could heft slid from the rounded hood as fast as she could pile them. She panted. Her hair had come loose from the pins, and the back of her neck was damp. What was the point of trying to hide the car? With that, she dropped the branches and turned to head back to the bright mitten on the path. The sap from the branches caused her cold fingers to stick to each other.

The baby's head exerted a terrible new pressure, more than his usual weight in his slumbering curve. This one felt lower now, and larger than a new baby should be. Each of the boys had weighed more at birth than the other. What if this new baby was already as large as Biaggio is right now! With hands deep in the pockets of the Mackintosh, Francesca held the hard curve of her belly, hoping for a moment of relief. By the time she bent to retrieve the mitten, she could barely breathe. Fear flickered when she thought she might be growing some abnormally huge circus infant that they would have to cut from her. All of these worries circled in her mind as she headed over the hill back to the still. The rustling made by her footsteps grew louder. Twigs snapped, and birds she couldn't see screeched overhead.

She didn't want to tell Victor about finding the Minerva because, in all likelihood, he was the person who had hidden it in the first place. Who else would have done it? No, it was smarter and safer to alert Steiner and get out of town. Her legs ached as she leaned into the incline, and her lungs felt like they were being poked with sharp sticks.

She walked to a beat, each footstep a word. *Geno is dead. Geno is dead.* The car was proof and something led her here to find it. In her sleepless nights, she had pictured him taking up with another woman, another family, living the fat life in a warm place like Florida. She felt certain he'd marry one of those pale women from the picture shows, the ones with the eyebrows as thin as snippets of embroidery thread. Once she imagined he'd have blond baby girls with curls. Francesca built on these musings, making each one more elaborate than the last. Sometimes they comforted her; other times they infuriated her, but mostly they served to explain the months of silence without letters or telegrams. A darker idea was that Sal had somehow managed to contact his brother and told Geno that he had stepped into his place in the family in every way. Some facets of this theory must be true because how else would Sal have known to search in Osseo?

As she headed down the hill toward the still, she slid in the wet needles, and her arms pinwheeled for balance. Victor was nowhere in sight, and she panicked, thinking she'd been left alone until she saw the automobile parked just where they'd left it.

"Victor, Victor," she called, immediately embarrassed, realizing he might be relieving himself in the woods. With that thought, her own bladder was provoked to ache. Now that she was near the still, the ground was drier than it had been over the hill, and the needles crunched beneath her boot heels. Shadows flickered around her, and she twisted her head this way and that, trying to catch a glimpse of the real or the imagined threat.

"Francesca, I'm in the shed, but don't come in."

"What is it? What's in there?" She stood motionless, the sweat from her exertion cooled to a clammy shiver.

Geno's body. Could it be inside? The door opened a few inches, and she smelled the sharp scent of kerosene. Was he going to burn down the place to hide the body?

"Francesca, get out. Someone soaked the corn and sugar to make sure it can't be used," Victor said as he piled items into a crate that sat at the end of a narrow cot. As her eyes adjusted to the gloom, she saw no body, just bags of spilled corn and sugar, overturned crates, rags, or pieces of clothing scattered and bunched on the floor. There was also the strong odor of animal. Bile rose up in her throat.

He tossed a straight razor and a shaving brush into the crate. "Let's just get out of here and get back to Dorie's. Yeegads, this place stinks." He bent over to cough and held his side with one hand.

"Let me help you." As soon as she stepped inside, the door slammed shut behind her, rattling the hinges. Francesca screamed and stumbled.

"What the hell?" Victor dropped a shaving mirror, ran to the door, and began to pound with both fists. "Hey, open up. What's going on? Who's out there?"

Francesca mimicked Victor's movements, feeling the rough splinters against her palms. The tin roof echoed like thunder. "Let us out!"

She felt the weight of someone pressing against the door from the outside. There was a bitter kerosene taste at the back of her throat.

"Now you can be together! Isn't that what you want?"

Louie! It sounded like his lips were pressed to the crack between the door and frame.

"He thinks I'm Dorie!" Francesca looked at Victor who started kicking at the door.

"Louie, goddammit, Dorie's not here. This is Francesca. Open the door right now."

Francesca whispered to Victor, "Last night when I took Shane outside, Louie came and talked to me. He thought I was Dorie."

Victor pressed his lips together, backed up, and began to throw his shoulder into the door. The whole shack rumbled, and Francesca was reminded of reading "The Three Little Pigs" to the boys, only it was all mixed up, for Louie was like the big, bad wolf trying to keep them inside. Despite the ramshackle look of the place, the door and walls held firm. Victor stood back, breathing hard. He spat behind him.

"Can you feel his spirit? These woods are full of the dead man's spirit."

They heard the fire, the low crackling sound, just before they saw the flames lick under the door. Francesca shrieked and reached out to pound again at the door. Victor gripped her arm and yanked her backward. When smoke began to gather in the tiny space, Victor picked up the quilt and began to beat at the flames. The edges of the fabric quickly caught fire, and Francesca realized that the quilt too must have been doused. Panic swelled in her chest. Oh, her boys, she could see their little faces lined up before her. They were going to be orphans! Who would kiss them and see that they did their lessons?

Smoke scraped her throat, stung her eyes, and she squeezed them shut against the burn. A cough seized her, and her nose ran. She felt it then, a popping sensation, then a burst of warmth ran down her legs, soaking the long johns and dungarees.

The baby was coming now.

But no, no, no. Wait! It's too early. She had weeks until the birth. Then she thought of all the pains she had had the last few days and knew she couldn't deny this occurrence.

Francesca turned to tell Victor, but they were both coughing now. Victor wheezed as he fought to pull in a breath.

"I'm in labor."

"What?" he choked, his face smeared with tears and dirt.

"The water around the baby, it burst."

"Take them off—the dungarees." He held his face in the crook of his elbow.

"What?" she shouted. Was he crazy?

"Press them to your face. It'll help you breathe."

Francesca turned and expected to see a wall of flames behind her, but there was only dark rolling smoke. She fumbled with the buttons at the fly, but finally managed to shimmy out of the pants. When she pressed the cool fabric to her face, the smell was slightly sweet. She held up a trouser leg for him to take, but he shook his head and again began to throw his shoulder against the door. Francesca wanted to plead with Louie, but she couldn't draw a breath deep enough to holler at him.

"Get down!" He pushed her down. "Stay low." He coughed a longer ragged chain.

Francesca dropped to her knees and pitched forward, dropping her forehead into the wet cool dirt. She remembered a nun at St. Cecelia's who prayed for hours on the floor of church in just this position. It felt as if the tongues of fire had ignited her lungs. She understood Joan of Arc's suffering.

"Dorie, Dorie, Dorie," Louie crooned. "I want to be with you."

Her thoughts hurtled, gathering speed as they rolled over her. *Please, God, get me out of here. All the air's gone. Does the baby feel this too? I don't want to die in this horrible place.* She was sad to think she wouldn't be recognized because she was wearing men's clothes. She nearly laughed at that silly thought when she realized her identity would not remain a mystery because of her attire, but rather because she would resemble a stump of charred wood.

Just then she heard a scream outside the door, a horrible high-pitched animal whine. A thumping sound too, but she couldn't open her eyes to see what it was. The last bit of air left in this smoky world felt like the one final drop clinging to the rim of a tipped glass. After that there was no more. She was at a place, one foot poised on this thin line, but she knew if she tried balancing on it, she would fall. It was too thin and fragile to hold her weight.

Confusing sounds roared all around her—shouts, screams, loud crackling sounds. Then it didn't seem to matter so much because she was moving away from the sound. She knew she should be more interested, it had been so important a moment ago, but now she was finally going to meet her mother.

Hadn't she waited for this moment all her life? She put her hands to her face and hair and hoped she looked presentable, her hair in place twisted into a perfect knot at the back of her neck. How would they recognize one another? Francesca never had a picture of her mother, and this stranger-mother had never glimpsed her own child. Oh, she was so anxious to show her this new baby!

Her mother suddenly lifted her up, so fast her head snapped back. She marveled at her surprising strength and wondered why no one ever mentioned this unusual characteristic. She frowned because she still couldn't see her face.

Suddenly there was cold, cold air washing over her raw face. She had the choice then, it seemed, whether to take this air, this clearness back into her body... or not. Where was her mother to tell her what to do? Since there was no one to advise her, Francesca decided to try one tiny sip of air and began pulling wet, clean gulps. She coughed, pushing the heat and the black from her lungs.

When she opened her eyes, Steiner was kneeling over her. Her mother was gone.

When she turned her head, Louie's body lay next to her on the ground. The skin on his face was blistered raw across his cheek and forehead, his eyebrows singed away. His shirt and pants clung to him in charred tatters, a wisp of smoke curling above his head.

38

Giving Birth

When Francesca opened her eyes, she was back in the guest bedroom at Dorie's. There was Dorie's wedding portrait, the tall bureau, the graceful curve of the metal bed frame, and the patchwork quilt across her feet. And for the exhalation of one breath, she believed the fire had been just a terrible dream. But as soon as she inhaled, the horror of the afternoon pressed on her chest with a chain of wheezy coughs. The sweat on her skin, the hair on her pillow, reeked of smoke.

Dorie stood above her, folding a white cloth into three sections. She smiled as she placed the cool cloth against Francesca's forehead.

"Shhh," she said in response to Francesca's cough. "Take it easy. I'm putting a compress soaked in tea to your skin. You've got some burns, but thankfully, no blisters."

A woman appeared on the other side of the bed, and she took Francesca's hand, holding her fingers to the underside of her wrist. Francesca started to speak, but her raw throat and chest seized up with another cough.

"I'm Lenny. I'm training to be a doctor," she said. "Dorie called me because she was worried you might have that baby right in her kitchen. The doc has his hands full with other patients, so I told him I'd help out."

Lenny looked to be about her same age. And a doctor! Who ever heard of that? What kind of name was Lenny for a girl? She had hair the color of wet ocean sand, and it was bobbed in the style of a flapper girl, but instead of donning a beaded dance dress, she had tucked a flannel shirt into slim gray trousers like a boy would wear. For some odd reason she wanted to tell Lenny that she too had donned men's apparel, but when she tried to move the heavy blanket to show her, she found herself wearing a nightdress.

"Do you know what happened to you this afternoon?" Lenny asked.

It was all sounds and smells—the heat, the black rolling smoke, the searing sting in her eyes, Victor thrashing about in the dimness of the shack. Where was Victor now? Was he hurt? Finally, she remembered the last look at Louie's burnt face.

Pain seized her then, fast and hard. It felt like a barbed hook she had seen down at the meat market, caught in the lowest part of her back, rending the muscles from the bone. She grabbed hold of Lenny's hand, clenching against the yawning pain.

"Hang on," Lenny said. When she moved closer, nearly nose-to-nose, Francesca could see curious gold flecks in her green eyes. Oh, she couldn't breathe against this pain. She invoked all the patron saints of childbirth she could remember—Saint Erasmus, Saint Margaret of Antioch, and Saint Ulric—until finally the tension eased. She pictured the pain as a live thing, crouched and panting, waiting for the chance to pounce at her again.

Why did this hurt so much? This was not at all like the labors of the other three boys, even before Dr. Yarusso arrived to give her the Twilight Sleep! Surely something must be wrong with her or the baby. Fear bloomed and filled her chest.

"This is different... what's wrong with me?" she croaked.

"Can you tell me what it's like?" Lenny frowned as she unwound her scarf and handed it to Dorie, never taking her eyes from Francesca.

How to describe this thing? Who would believe it? And her raw throat made it nearly impossible to talk. Lenny bent in close, but all she could whisper was, "My back..."

"Mmm, all right then. I think I know what might be happening. I've seen a delivery like this once before." Lenny moved to stand at the foot of the bed. "I think your baby is trying to get out in not quite the regular way. The baby's face is turned up so the back of the head," Lenny cupped her hand to the rounded curve on the back her own head, "is pressing on your spine, here." She moved her hand to her lower back. "That's why it hurts so much."

"What can we do for her?" Dorie asked as she settled another cool cloth on Francesca's forehead.

Lenny pressed her lips together. "Dorie, I need you to boil water to sterilize the scissors. I'll need lots of clean cloths and oil. Can you make some tea?" Dorie nodded. "Not too strong or hot, but lots of it."

"Yes, of course." Dorie sounded relieved to have something to do.

Lenny called again. "Do you have some combs or something to put up all this hair? I've never seen a woman with so much hair!" She began to roll up the sleeve of her shirt. Francesca watched her slim, freckled fingers efficiently work the buttons and cuffs. She knew she should feel alarmed. No doctor! No blessed whiff of ether! Yet, Lenny was so calm. She had a plan. She would take care of everything. Francesca closed her eyes to rest, listening to the sounds of their preparations.

Her eyes flew open when the talons bit into her back again and began to twist. How long had it been since the last one? Had she dozed? "No, no." She didn't recognize her own voice.

"Quick, let me try something before it gets too bad." Lenny flung back the quilts. "Here, let's get you on all fours. Turn over. Now, up on your knees. Hold yourself up with your hands! Like a dog... that's it!"

She barely had time to think about this crazy request! When no one was watching she would play on the floor like this with the boys, pretending to be wild tigers. The pain came over her again, more intense than the last one. She pressed her face into the smoky smell of the pillow. The fabric scratched against her skin. Nothing was fair. She wasn't supposed to have this baby so far from home! After three other deliveries, she was entitled to an easy birth! A sob escaped from her aching chest as she raged against being left without a husband to take care of her forever. Was Geno watching over her at this moment? A tear leaked out when she realized that even in spirit form, Geno couldn't be bothered to help her deliver his baby.

"Now rock back and forth." She felt the bed shift as Lenny had climbed onto the narrow bed behind her and pushed hard against the small of her back. Oh, Lenny knew exactly where to fight back against the hooks! Suddenly the pillow was snatched away from her face.

"You need to breathe with me and rock. Let's turn this little one around."

Francesca had no words to describe these antics, but the pain had already crested, and she rocked back and forth as Lenny's fist ground against that center, guiding her into a rhythm she could follow.

"Will this work?" Francesca asked when the pain had finally leaked away. She slumped forward, not caring if there was a pillow there or not. She had never been so tired.

"Don't lie down. I want you to keep rocking."

And so they did.

Francesca lost track of the number of times the pain swept through her. Had this gone on for hours or days? It was too much effort to keep her eyes open. She was only aware of their voices, hands stroking the length of her back, swallowing sips of tea. At some point Dorie brushed and braided her hair. When her arms shook and wobbled and could no longer support her own weight, Francesca leaned against Dorie's back for a time, taking in her lavender scent. There might have been snatches of sleep between the twisting pains, but they were filled with images of the fire and Louie's screams.

"I'm burning up!" She pulled at the drenched nightdress that clung to her breasts and back. She suddenly hated the feeling of this fabric twisting up and binding against her skin.

"Could she have a fever?" Dorie asked.

"Here, let's take this off. Get comfortable," Lenny offered.

What was she suggesting? Francesca had never heard of anything so absurd. "But I'll be bare then, unclothed."

"And what of it? It's just the three of us here. No men will be around to help with any of what's to come. It's not a fever. This is normal."

She had never been completely unclothed even in front of her maid or her husband! Perhaps not having grown up with sisters or a mother in the house made her odd in that way. Lenny suggested it like it was the most natural thing in the world. Then, just like that, she suddenly thought, *why not?*

"Oh, fine, let me be rid of this thing then." Together they bunched the sodden nightdress from the ruffle at the bottom and helped her lift her arms and finally get it over her head. The air hitting her skin raised gooseflesh across her arms and breasts. She stared down at her rounded belly as if seeing it for the first time.

Francesca looked at both women. Lenny's hair hung in damp waves around her small face as she wiped her brow on her sleeve, and Dorie's peach-colored dress had sweat stains under both arms and between her shoulder blades. There were dark circles under her eyes, and she worried about Dorie's health.

"Maybe you two should join me?" She smiled weakly, and they laughed.

Another pain started, and she lay back flat on the mattress as it swept through her. She could feel it coil and tighten, but the pain in her back had ceased. This labor she recognized. This felt right.

Dorie and Lenny each held an arm. "Help me get her up. I don't want her flat on the bed."

"It worked. The baby must have moved. The terrible pains in my back are gone now. It's time for the Twilight Sleep." Francesca murmured.

"What's she talking about?" Dorie whispered.

"Twilight Sleep is given to women in hospitals. It's a mix of drugs—morphine for the pain and scopolamine, which is an amnesia drug. The woman forgets most of what's gone on. When the head starts to come out, the doctor puts a few drops of chloroform or ether on a paper cone, and she goes to sleep. Most women who have their babies in the hospitals are doing it that way now."

"Yes, please." Francesca nodded, ready to be released from this agony.

"And then?" Dorie pressed the tea soaked cloth to her own neck.

"The doctor makes an incision, a cut, to open up the birth canal, and then he uses forceps to yank the baby out. Is that how you delivered your other children?"

"Then the doctor must sew up that cut." Dorie looked as though she were a student taking instruction.

Francesca flushed, too embarrassed to tell Lenny and Dorie of Dr. Yarusso's prideful promise to return her to "near virginal condition." She remembered her confusion at his smirking remark but knew she wasn't allowed to ask him any questions.

"I think that incision might be the reason mothers get puerperal fever in the first place. What I'd rather do is stretch that skin with some oil to prevent any tears, and then I won't have any need to make an incision. Anyway, I want you sitting upright. It'll help to speed along the labor. I'm also worried about your lungs because of the fire. I don't want them filling with fluid. Maybe we can put her on the toilet for a while."

"The toilet?" Dorie and Francesca said together.

"What I'm thinking of is called a birthing chair. Women in other countries use them all the time. The bottom of the chair is open. When the woman spreads her legs, it helps open these bones here," she said, pointing to her own narrow hip bones "And then the baby can ease out."

Francesca blushed to hear Lenny talk so casually about a woman intentionally sitting with her legs open, but then her frankness was thrilling at the same time. It all made sense. Why didn't women know more about how their bodies worked?

"I think I might have an idea," Dorie said. "Ages ago, Louie started fixing a chair that belonged to his parents. He pulled off all of the upholstery, the horsehair stuffing and the webbing, but he never got around to finishing it. It's out in the shed. It might work for what you have in mind."

Lenny nodded. "Let's have a try at it."

Dorie gathered up the nightdress. “I’ll fetch the chair and then wash this out for you.” Dorie stood next to the window looking pale and thin as the daylight faded from the room.

“Are you well enough to—?”

Dorie cut her off. “I’m fine. It’s you that’s our concern right now.” She turned and quickly left the room.

“Mmm, something I should know about?” Lenny raised a pale eyebrow. “Never mind, I suppose Dorie will let me know when she’s good and ready.” Lenny walked over to the basin and began to scrub her hands vigorously. “Say, if you’re willing, I’m going to slip my fingers into the birth canal before the next pain starts to find out how long it’ll be until that baby arrives. Then we can start stretching that skin too.”

She had shed her clothes in front of a strange woman and rocked on all fours like an animal. She had agreed to sit in a chair without a bottom. It all seemed reasonable at this point. She shrugged and closed her eyes, thankful for a bit of relief.

“Have you heard about Victor or Louie?” She was getting used to the whiskey sound of her voice. “Dorie must be crazy with worry.” Francesca didn’t say about whom.

“Mmm, no word yet.”

“Why is your name Lenny?”

“I’ll try to be gentle here.” Francesca felt a pressure, but no pain.

“My name’s really Helena. I was the firstborn, and I think my father was wishing for a boy. He got a few eventually, but my nickname had stuck by then.”

“Why are you going to be a doctor?”

“Because I’m smart enough. I was taught that I should use what gifts I have to help others.”

Francesca began to whimper, “Here it comes again.” How much could she stand before it killed her?

“Won’t be much longer now,” Lenny announced as if she were reading her thoughts. She could hear Dr. Yarusso’s voice warning against long labors because he said they caused epilepsy and imbecility. What if Lenny was wrong about all of this? She opened her eyes and watched Lenny’s sure movements and knew it was right to put her trust with this woman.

“Can you sit like this?” Lenny squatted down next to the bed, her knees spread, and then bounced back up again.

"Never in my life," she panted.

"I guess we'll wait for the chair. Say, where are you from?" Lenny asked as she grabbed Francesca's hands. When Lenny smiled, two deep dimples sliced under the apple curve of her cheeks.

"Chicago." She saw the long muscles in Lenny's forearm tense as she held on through the pain, her face smooth and free of worry. Her composure reminded her of the martyr Margaret of Antioch, whose prayers kept her unharmed when they tried to boil her in a cauldron. Francesca shut her eyes just as the wave threatened to crush her.

"Open your eyes. Look at me. Let it out. It's a fine thing to let out a holler if you want. I don't mind at all! How about a curse word or two?"

Francesca did let out a growl that chewed up her raw throat, a sound she had never made before, the sound of animal fury and sadness.

"I'd heard talk about you at Schieffer's. You're famous around here you know."

Francesca knew Lenny was trying to keep her mind occupied as she had used similar distractions with her boys when they were ill, and she wished she could be that easily lead away from this suffering. Oh, her boys. She wanted them to see their newest brother on his birthday! More tears leaked out when she remembered her thoughts of them as the shack filled with smoke. Had she survived the fire only to die in childbirth? Would this baby survive to meet his brothers?

"Can I have some ether?" She longed for this to be over. She had already worked off a thousand days in purgatory by this suffering. She no longer cared how many might be left.

"Even if I had any, I wouldn't give you a dose. We don't want this baby to be born too sleepy."

She opened her eyes and looked at Lenny. "Do you think something is wrong with him? It's early for it to be born, isn't it?"

"Here, have some more tea. You seem like the right size and shape. Some babies are just born when they want to be born. Besides, do you want this baby to have forceps marks on its pretty head?"

She did remember the cruel looking curved brand on Joseph's head and the pinched shape of Biaggio's head that didn't resolve until she prayed to St. Ulrich for healing.

"It was wrong of me to come here. I've put this baby in harm's way. I've had some frights since I arrived here. If something bad happens to this little boy, it'll be my sin." The sky had gone black, and she could see the reflection of the room, her body, and Lenny's movements in the windowpanes. Lenny's arm seemed to pass right through her body. She stared at the roundness of her face, breasts, and belly as if it were an illicit painting.

"Nonsense. Do you think if you cross paths with a fox, your baby will have a snout and tail? You're young and strong. There's no reason for you not to travel. How many children do you have?"

"Three boys." She answered before Lenny tipped the cup to Francesca's mouth. She nearly laughed to see that Dorie had served the tea in a good china cup as if this were an afternoon party. The liquid slid down her parched throat. Her lips felt tender and swollen.

"Then let's not worry about this one yet."

By the time the next pain started, Dorie was busy trying to force the wooden chair frame into the tiny room. She finally settled it under the window near the foot of the bed. Francesca reached out blindly for Lenny's strong hands, relieved when she found the familiar grip.

"We'll be needing those scissors soon, Dorie, and a couple lengths of string too."

At some point, they moved her to the chair. Dorie fussed trying to cover her shoulders or the chair with quilts and sheets, but Francesca welcomed the chilled wood frame against her back and bottom. She obeyed what her body urged. Meanwhile, in between pains Lenny used the oil and the cloths to work at the skin near the birth canal.

Later, the pains came closer together. One chased on the heels of the last. Francesca gripped the rounded arms of the chair and dug her nails into the wood until there was no time for tears or protests. Both Lenny and Dorie were telling her things, touching her, urging her on, but she couldn't hear the words or respond to them. She was deep inside herself, muffled.

Suddenly, a force surged through her. Her head snapped up, and she pressed her back into the wood frame. "It's coming now. I've got to get it out—get it out!"

"Push. You've got the power now. Just take a big breath and bear down."

Francesca bit down on her lower lip and growled a low tone that built and crested as she pushed and pushed until there was no breath left in her body.

"That's it. Do that again!"

She panted. "No, I'm afraid. The baby will fall on the floor."

"Look here. I'm ready with a towel." Lenny squatted at her feet.

"No, no," Francesca said.

"Can't we move her back to the bed?" Dorie asked.

Lenny paused. "If she feels better about that, let's move her. You get on one side, and I'll get on the other." She threw the blanket over her shoulder and reached for Francesca's arm.

Francesca's legs shook like someone with palsy, but she liked the feeling of being flanked by these two women. They cared about her and this baby, even though she was nearly a stranger to them. In her whole life's search, she finally knew what it was like to have friends.

The urge to push came over her again, buckling her knees. "It's coming now. Oh, help me."

"Another step," Lenny hollered to both of them.

She lunged toward the bed, pulling Dorie down with her.

"Turn over," Lenny commanded.

"There's the head," Dorie said. "Oh, my God."

Francesca felt it slip from her, without any push at all. She eased herself up on an elbow to see Lenny gather the tiny blue body into a square of flannel.

It was an impossibly small girl, and she wasn't moving.

Part 2

Mary DesJarlais

39

Francesca's Baby Is Born

Dorie was always an accurate judge of weight. It didn't matter if the purchase was a sack of hayseed or a shank of lamb, she could correctly estimate the weight within a few ounces. She watched as Lenny crooked her finger and snagged the cord that bound the baby's neck and eased the tight coil over the gray face. The length of it lay twisted and glistening across the baby's narrow chest and legs. Lenny scooped up the limp form and placed it directly on Francesca's chest.

This little baby weighed four pounds.

Lenny bent over the tiny body and began to rub the flaccid legs and arms as she blew a stream of breath on the baby's face. There were white clots and smears of blood over her body. The tiny, wrinkled face looked of a creature lost between worlds—an old woman trying to change into a baby for another chance on earth. For a second, Dorie thought she saw movement, but it was only Francesca's silent sobs shaking the tiny body.

"Dorie." Lenny blew again and rushed at the bottom of the breath. "Let's get that quilt up here to cover Francesca and the baby." She inhaled, resuming her tempo.

Dorie stood and gathered the quilt from the floor and covered Francesca's shaking legs, but she couldn't warm the baby because of Lenny's ministering. What else was there to do?

Dorie hated this helpless feeling. She was no different from the weak women she loathed, unable to think of a thing to do but wring their hands. Guilt too, pressed a sharp edge against her chest. Throughout this long birth, Dorie found herself escaping outdoors, to the kitchen, anywhere but that labor room, sweating, heart pounding, unable to draw a decent breath. Staring at this blue infant, Dorie realized Francesca wouldn't be here having this baby in the spare room if she hadn't distilled that first batch of moonshine in the kitchen.

The events of the last two years appeared before her and collapsed on one another. She remembered holding that first glass out to Louie asking if he thought anyone would buy a drink. Hiding tins in the sheds stuffed with rolls of bills. Then there was Victor, leaning against his car, pressing a hand to his bloodied shirt. Slipping Geno's body into the lake. Victor's fever and her fear he might die. Sal appearing at her door to talk about selling the farm, and then his body sprawled on the cellar floor. Francesca, in her mink coat, poised on the train stairs. Now this lifeless baby lay on Francesca's chest, born without a proper attending doctor.

Lenny used a rag to wipe out the baby's tiny mouth. It reminded Dorie of when, as a child, she would force open a rose bud with her thumbs, the petals soft, but tightly bound. Dorie watched the bloodstain grow and darken on the quilt Obeline had made as her wedding gift. What if Francesca died too? She could never face soaking and scrubbing the reminder of Francesca's spilled blood from this quilt. Even if she spread it out in the spring sun for hours, the faint rusty blotches would still be there as a ghostlike reminder. She licked her dry lips and swallowed back against the nausea that plagued her all the time. She hadn't eaten anything for hours, but the smells and textures of most foods made it worse.

"Oh, Holy Innocents," Francesca murmured, "help my baby."

Was she actually praying to the babies murdered by Herod? Dorie shivered at the thought of a legion of babies, still bearing sword wounds, floating above them. Her hand went to her own flat belly often in these last few days, to reassure them both.

"That's it," Lenny said.

Suddenly, the baby gasped. Francesca burst into tears and grabbed Lenny's arm. Dorie marveled once again at Francesca's trusting and adoring nature.

"She needs to nurse right now to get the placenta out."

"It's a miracle. You've saved her. A girl! I can't believe it." Francesca looked up at both of them with a tear-streaked face, her skin bright pink from the fire and exertion of birth. She reached out with trembling fingers to stroke the baby's tiny hand.

"Hand me that scissors and string now, Dorie. We're going to need lots of blankets too." Lenny deftly tied the two lengths of string about an inch apart from one another on the cord about two inches from the baby's belly. Dorie watched Lenny's grave face as she placed the scissors handle in her outstretched palm and understood this proclaimed miracle might be a fleeting one. Lenny began to cut through the cord, her jaw clenched in concentration, reminding Dorie of the effort required to cut through a fat rope. She was thankful she had thought to take the whetstone to the blades.

"She's not very loud, not like the boys at all. Will she be all right?" Francesca sniffled.

"Dorie, can you wrap her up? We need to keep her warm and start her to nurse."

"Geno always insisted on hiring a wet nurse." Francesca opened her bloodshot eyes wide. "I'm not sure I know how it's done."

Dorie laid a square of flannel on the bed and reached for the baby as Lenny finished cutting. The baby's skin was more pink, and most of the blood and mucus had been wiped away. Fine hair, softer than goose down, covered her limbs and chest. Francesca's tiny daughter had pulled her arms and legs in tight so that she resembled a little ball. Her back and buttocks fit in Dorie's palm.

"What about the diaper?"

"Let's not bother with that yet. Let's get her warm and nursing. Wrap the blanket so the head is covered too."

Dorie wrapped the baby, tucked her into the crook of her arm and looked at her stern face. The inverted V-shape of the eyebrows mimicked Francesca's perfectly.

It was impossible for Dorie to imagine what her baby might look like. Most of the time she still couldn't believe the news, a baby of Victor's growing in her own belly! Oh, but the dreams! Last night she was a little child again walking with Grand-père at the Anoka County Fair. He took her by the hand and slipped under the flap of the canvas tent. The thick crowd pushed them along so she could barely breathe in the heat and dense pulse of bodies. Suddenly she was shoved to the front of the throng and saw rows and rows of glass receptacles, larger than canning jars, each containing a baby floating serenely in the clear liquid. Someone parted the canvas, allowing sunshine, bright as a vaudeville spotlight, to filter through the glass, each baby a star for the moment. Some infants had too-large heads or missing limbs. All had skin bleached an unnatural white. The carnie host slapped his stick against one of the jars, and Dorie expected the baby to startle and cry, but of course, it only bobbed, the little nubs of hands folded together in an obscene prayer. As she moved closer, she saw each jar had a canning label affixed to the glass. In fancy script, the last one in the row read: Dorie's Baby. After that point in the dream, Dorie awoke and vomited into the basin by her bed.

Francesca had a drowsy, dreamy look to her. Dorie felt a twinge of admiration for all Francesca had endured to have this child. She was far from Chicago, homesick for her boys, without a doctor and, what had she called it, Twilight Sleep? What would become of her now that she had no husband? Dorie longed to take Francesca's hands in her own and tell her she would take care of her and make amends. But how could she offer that when she didn't know what her own future held? In a matter of months, Dorie would be holding a baby of her own. Would she be poor, having spent all her savings from the business? Would Victor still be in town? What about Louie?

"Oh, Dorie, you look so worried." Francesca's voice sounded like she had swallowed gravel. "Have you heard how Victor is?"

She could only shake her head, fearful if she spoke the tears would start. Steiner's face had been unreadable when he delivered Francesca to her doorstep and told her that Victor, Louie, and Francesca had all been injured in a fire at her still. He had made sure to emphasize that point and let it rot there between them like beef gone bad. She had stared at him, listening to the rush of blood in her ears. Steiner seemed to have forgotten that she was the person who called him when she saw Louie setting off across the field toward Buzzy's place. She would have gone after him herself, anything to avoid involving Steiner, if the furious nausea hadn't kept her bedridden. Steiner and Dorie glared at each other, locked in a silent challenge in the cold March air. Steiner must have been waiting for her to ask about Victor when she should have been inquiring about her husband, but she refused to give him that satisfaction. Finally, he informed her that both Louie and Victor were in town in the infirmary under Doc Pitzer's care because the Doc was unsure if Louie would survive the trip to Northwestern Hospital in Minneapolis. She knew she should go to town, if only to see Victor, but as soon as Steiner had departed, Francesca awoke and announced she was in labor.

Lenny's urgings broke her thoughts. "Dorie, hand the baby to Francesca."

Dorie bent over and handed Francesca the tight bundle that felt more like a purchase of summer sausage than a child. She stared at the baby's tiny mouth and Francesca's large nipple and wondered how this would ever work. Lenny pulled another quilt around Francesca's bare shoulders and helped her to sit up.

"Here, stroke her cheek like this," Lenny said. "Wake her up." After what seemed like a long minute, her dark head finally began to move back and forth, and Lenny adjusted their positions so the baby cupped against Francesca's body.

Then, Dorie's heart felt as if it would tumble over itself when the baby, acting perhaps under the guidance of one of Francesca's favorite saints, opened its little mouth and began to suckle.

"Oh," was all that Francesca could say.

"That's a good sign, if she's strong enough to suck. We still may have to feed her with an eyedropper as well," Lenny said as she pulled back a part of the quilt and began to massage Francesca's belly. Soon Francesca began to whimper as she had during the labor. "Is it another baby?" Her eyes were wide with fear.

"No, the placenta needs to come out. There'll be some more cramping, but just for a little bit. I think you were deeply drugged during this part with your sons." Lenny tugged at the raw end of the cord. After a few minutes there was a brief rush of blood and then the flaccid purple sac spilled out into the waiting burlap bag that she quickly rolled up and handed to Dorie. "She'll need some of the cloths you use for your monthly."

"What was that thing? Am I going to die?" Francesca looked horrified.

As Lenny calmed Francesca's fears and instructed her as to the workings of the female body, Dorie's stomach roiled even though she had seen countless farm animals deliver afterbirths. She ran through the parlor to the kitchen, tossed the burlap bundle on the counter, and leaned over the sink as her stomach clenched and heaved. There was nothing to vomit up but a string of yellow bile. The puppy tumbled out of his peach crate by the stove and nosed her about her ankles, his thin whip of a tail a blur of motion. Dorie pumped a stream of cold water, cupping her hands to rinse out her mouth and splash her face. She rested her wet forehead against her arm, wiped her nose on a flour sack, and waited for the spell to pass. There were so many duties—diapers and blankets to be stitched, the burlap sack to be buried behind the barn, a strong broth to begin simmering on the stove, and a stone to heat for a bed warmer. And what if Francesca wasn't able to make enough milk to feed this child? Should she try to find a wet nurse to help them just in case? The puppy whimpered at her feet.

Shane. She had forgotten about the dog in the excitement of the last hours. He must need to go outside. She went to the pantry and retrieved a loaf of bread wrapped in a towel. Dorie tore off a hunk and crammed it in her mouth. For some reason bread was the only thing that could settle her stomach. She pinched off another bit and dropped it in front of the puppy. Shane happily nosed it before gobbling it down. Dorie sank to the floor, her back pressed against the cabinets, too tired to stop the pup from scrambling into her lap and bracing his paws against her chest as he stood to lick her face.

Had it been two nights ago when Victor had brought the runt of the litter to her? He had been so sure it would please her. What she had come to know about him was that he always made grand, big-hearted gestures, never calculating the work that might be involved. Much to her surprise, the arrival of this puppy had tickled her. Or maybe it was the fact that Victor had spent that night in her bed that had affectionately colored her feelings for Shane. Dorie rubbed her thumbs across his smooth muzzle, and he closed his eyes, breathing a heavy sigh.

The three of them had stood in the kitchen that night, Francesca fussing over the puppy, insisting on naming him after a cowboy, of all silly things, when Victor had started running his hand up and down her back. That evening, Dorie had felt rested and free of stomach upset. His touch sent shivers through her body. It got so that she no longer trusted her knees for support. When Francesca volunteered to take the puppy outside, Dorie had led Victor upstairs.

It never had been her intention to climb into bed with him. After all, Francesca was a guest in the house, and Steiner had used that excuse for an overly liberal visitation schedule. No, all she wanted was a moment in his arms, to feel that perfect fit of her body against his—a moment without looking over her shoulder to see who might be watching. Wordlessly, Victor had followed her, his bulk filling the narrow stairwell in a way that caused Dorie to breathe faster.

Once in the bedroom, Dorie moved, out of habit, to draw the drapes, but Victor put his hand over hers to stop her from blocking the creamy moonlight. He turned and shut the door with a loud click that echoed in the space between them. What she wanted, what she expected, was to be pressed against the wall next to the bureau, to finally feel that perfect Victor kiss that made her toes curl. Instead, Victor leaned in, but then barely grazed her open mouth before he pulled away. He stood close enough for her to feel the heat of him, belly-to-belly, thigh-to-thigh, but he didn't touch her. When she reached out to press her palms to the swell of his chest, he stopped her, threading his fingers through hers, holding her captive. Only then, did he brush his lips along her jaw, his tongue finding her earlobe, before he moved slowly down her neck past the collar of her dress. Dorie tried to pull her fingers from his grasp so she could wrap her arms around his neck, but he'd tightened his grip as his mouth moved to her shoulder, then over the swell of her breast. When she gasped, he answered with a low chuckle, his breath warm through the thin fabric.

She swayed when he knelt, her fingers still locked with his. Oh, how she wanted to cup the back of his neck to pull him closer. His mouth pressed against her belly, pausing, making Dorie think he was about to speak directly to this new baby, but that was absurd for he didn't even know about its existence. It would be so easy to whisper the news to him, but what if he became angry? She had told him she couldn't have children when he inquired about using a French letter. What if he didn't believe it was his? Her worries and arguments were lost at this point because she could barely breathe or stand. She was helpless in this torturous wanting, waiting for his touch.

He proceeded in that same languid fashion, easing open each button when all Dorie wanted was to rip apart the dress, sending a shower of glass fasteners rolling across the floor. *Oh, hurry, hurry, hurry, now.* Did she say that aloud or was it only in her head? If he heard her, he didn't heed her request, but did guide her to the bed after her dress slid to her hips and then the floor. Her bare arms, his face and hands glowed in the bright moonlight. Wordlessly, he instructed her to lie on her stomach before he straddled her, caressing her arms, shoulders, and back, occasionally leaning in to briefly catch her mouth.

This was no longer the room she shared with Louie. He was far, far away from all this. He was barely a flicker in her mind because Louie had never given a touch as simple, as important as one of Victor's. Oh, such a luxury to stretch out in a bed instead of the discomforts they'd experienced at Buzzy's farm! She felt him hard against her and smiled at her own power and his restraint. When his hands finally snaked up under her slip, his fingers felt cool and smooth against her damp skin as he pulled off her undergarments. She arched her back, pushing herself up on her elbows, tilting her head, offering her neck to him. Only then did he accept her bidding, nuzzling her cheek and setting free the coil of hair, cupping her breasts, before he lifted her hips and then, barely entered her. Maddeningly, he moved without surrendering the length of himself to her. Dorie pushed her face into the pillow, sure she would need to muffle a scream that would bring Francesca running. His hands held her hips in guided control, waiting for her, until he knew. Finally, he bent over her, burying his face in her neck as she shuddered against him. "Love, love, love," he had whispered in her ear.

There was a sharp pounding on the porch door. Dorie startled and jumped up as if she had been caught red-handed in that embrace with Victor, causing Shane to flip over and land on his back. He righted himself and gave one sharp bark. Dorie tried to smooth her hair and adjust her dress, but realized it was hopeless—after the sleepless night of Francesca's labor and the vomiting, she knew she looked dreadful. Could it be Victor? Her heart flipped over, her recent intimate thoughts of him so close to the surface.

The pounding resumed as she climbed to her feet and walked through the porch. It was Steiner and not Victor. Her disappointment gave way to distress. What news had he come to tell her? It must be Louie—perhaps he had died. There was a sharp pain in her heart, sad for Louie, the old Louie, but relieved and then embarrassed for her feelings.

Steiner's jacket hung open in the early morning, and she knew the air must be mild. He pushed his way through the door the moment she had released the catch. Two black crows pecked at the gravel drive. In the bright sun, their feathers reflected rainbow colors. She took a deep breath of the cool, bright air.

"I need to speak with Francesca." He pulled his hat from his head and held it by the crown. The pup ran up to smell his boot.

"She just delivered."

"What? Here? Did you and she—?" His face was strained and white. He had missed a morning shave.

"I called for Lenny Erickson. She did a wonderful job." Dorie turned and walked back to the kitchen without asking him to enter. She half expected him to push her aside to get to Francesca's room. For someone so gruff, he seemed to have a special attachment to Francesca. Did he think her beautiful or did he fancy her more like a daughter?

"How is she? The baby?"

"It wasn't an easy birth. Lenny said the girl was turned oddly. She's also a very small infant. It's worrisome."

"A girl. Isn't that something?" He grinned. "I still need to see her."

"She's sleeping after laboring all night." Dorie didn't want him here stirring things up, asking questions about the fire. She was sure now that's why he was here, to say ugly things and spread the blame around.

"I wouldn't think to bother her with something trivial." Steiner had the same smoky smell to him. He's been up all night too, she realized.

"Where is she?" Steiner was all tension, his jaw tight, fists clenched open and closed. She didn't want him telling Francesca anything that would upset her. Would he just barge through the house, room by room, in search of her?

"So how is he?" Dorie asked. "I would have come to town, but I've been busy helping with the birth, you see." That's as much as she would give him. Steiner licked his lips and gave her a wan smile.

"Your *husband* is in very grave condition. I'm not sure if he'll survive the day. Doc Pitzer thinks an infection will be the end of him. I'm not sure you realize, but his health is poor."

He believes me cold and heartless, she thought. Dorie knew he would never extend her the kindness of information about Victor. His disapproval was like a bottled medicine the whole town had been prescribed.

"I need a moment with Francesca. I won't tax her." He squinted at her as if she were standing a great distance away. "You understand, I'm not asking your permission." He tossed his hat on the table, and she saw pink burns on the back of his hand. Did he intentionally show her that he too had been injured in the fire?

"She's in the spare room—just off the parlor." Dorie motioned with a nod of her head.

Dorie strained against the guilt. Part of her wanted to run upstairs to get away from this day, fall into her bed, close her aching eyes, pretending Victor's scent in her pillow meant he was still next to her. The other part wanted to find out what message Steiner needed to impart directly to Francesca. She heard the door creak open, and she rushed after him.

The smells of the small room—sweat, blood, and smoke—rushed at Dorie, and she grabbed the doorframe, digging her nails into the wood to fight the swell that rose in her throat. *Do not give in to this.*

Steiner crouched next to the bed, whispering to Francesca as he held one of her hands. The baby slept encircled in her arms, bundled in additional layers of flannel, her face the size of a small apple. This was the Nativity scene, Steiner as one of the Wise Men, sans gift, kneeling in adoration of the baby. Lenny was a sleepy shepherd, her narrow backside perched on the edge of the chair Francesca had used during the labor. If she moved even an inch, she'd fall off the chair or through the missing seat. Her head was tipped back against the wooden frame. Mouth open, she gave a slight, wet snore.

"It's a girl," Francesca croaked in her ruined voice. This dangerous birth, too, he would catalogue as another of her sins.

"Can you tell me what happened?"

"I asked Victor to give me a tour of my property. I insisted he take me into the woods." Francesca glanced up at Dorie.

"The still," Steiner spelled it out.

"Um, well, yes, the still, but it was my idea. Not Victor's, you see."

"Go on."

Dorie strained to hear Steiner's low voice.

"Louie latched the door to the little building. He thought I was Dorie. He said all kinds of crazy things." She brushed back a tear. "Then he started the fire."

Dorie drew in a sharp breath. Francesca had borrowed Dorie's chore coat and trousers. Louie must have seen them leave or maybe he overheard them talking about going out to Buzzy's.

"It was you that got us out, wasn't it?"

Steiner nodded.

"Victor?"

Dorie held her muscles tight, willing her expression to be smooth as stone.

"Victor is a cat with nine lives. Although I'm not sure how many he has used up at this point."

"I'll send a message to your family. I expect it will be awhile until you can travel. Again, I'd like to extend you the invitation to stay at our home." Lenny opened her eyes and stretched. She nodded to Steiner.

"There's another reason for my visit. I don't want to distress you after your ordeal, but there has been a discovery."

"I know all about it," Francesca said. "I was the one that found it."

"How's that?"

"Geno's car. I found it in the woods."

Dorie had slipped into the room and stood next to Lenny so she could better see Steiner's expressions. At Francesca's words, she felt as if she were floating, hovering inches off the floor.

Steiner nodded and licked his lips. He grimaced against an unseen pain. "Francesca, I am so sorry to tell you this, but I believe it's very likely that your husband's body has been recovered from Eagle Lake."

Dorie knew she should remain silent, but the panic flooded through her making her babble. "Let's not jump to conclusions here and scare this poor thing to death. How do you know it wasn't a hobo or an ice fisherman who went through the ice?"

Steiner turned and addressed Dorie for the first time. “It’s unlikely he’s a local, Dorie. The cold water of Eagle Lake preserved him remarkably well, and he wore an expensive suit.” He pursed his lips and then continued, “And there was also a rope cinched around his ankle as if someone had tried to weigh him down.”

40

Dorie Goes to Town

As Dorie slowed the car to a stop in front of Doc Pitzer's house, she eyed the enamel bowl sitting on the seat and wondered if she would be able to hide it under her coat. Since her treacherous stomach gave her so little warning of its revolt, she had decided to carry a catch basin around with her.

Doc Pitzer had built this Tudor home four years ago, a block south of Main Street. The central part of the house served as living quarters for him and his wife, Marvel. Attached to the south wall was a separate wing that contained an office, a waiting area, and two exam rooms for his patients. The last time Dorie had set foot in this place, Doc had told her she would never bear children. Ah, she couldn't wait to see the look on his face in the summer when she could part her coat, turn demurely, and show him the swell of her pregnancy! The setting sun cast a pinkish tone on the stucco, making it look like it would be warm to the touch. Dorie realized that the days were longer now, a sure sign spring's arrival might be more than just a longing in her heart.

The window shade briefly lifted and then settled. Who was looking at her? Was it Victor? Oh, she so wanted to see his face, hold his hand and make sure he was safe, but not in front of Doc, not with Louie close by.

There was no comfortable refuge in town or even at home.

The thought of an unpleasant encounter with Doc filled her with dread. She didn't want to see him or anyone from Osseo now. Steiner would have begun casting out the net of gossip about the body recovered from the lake. What would her sisters say? Steiner would have cinched her name to the rope around Geno's leg even though he couldn't prove she dumped the body there. Or could he? Had she left behind some damning evidence that would send her to the hangman's noose?

She couldn't bear going home either to see Francesca's slack, vacant face. The newly anointed widow and mother must have loved Geno dearly to be so shaken by the announcement of his death. Dorie had never solicited any details of Francesca's life with her husband. What she knew of Geno—that cold white face, the snow collecting in his hair before she slipped him in the lake—that's as much as she could think about. She didn't want to hear how he brought Francesca specially made frocks, wrote her poetry, or loudly sang Italian ballads, so drunk with love, so lost in her lushness.

She fingered the buttons on her coat and mused that she owed everyone a debt or an apology. They had all lost something. Louie—his health, Francesca—a husband and brother-in-law, and even Victor, who had chanced death three times. Dorie sighed and pushed open the door. She hated wasting time and knew she had to get back home to spell Lenny, who had insisted on staying a few more hours before going back home to her duties.

Sweet, wet air filled Dorie's lungs. If only she could keep the clean green smell in a canning jar for use during those queasy moments! New grass sprouted between the flagstones on the path underfoot, and near the steps to the office door she saw the pointed tongues of tulip leaves thrusting through brittle oak leaves. Dorie knocked at the door, then pushed it open into the waiting room.

"Hello? Hello? Doc Pitzer?" Dorie called to the quiet room. The eight oak chairs lined up on the wall, the hat rack and coat tree were all empty, and it puzzled Dorie for a moment until she remembered the late hour of the day. Voices echoed from behind the closed door to the exam room. Now she hoped no one had heard her call and her stealth would allow her to hear the conversation. She crept across the tapestry rug and pressed her ear to the edge of the door so as not to be seen through the frosted glass.

"When we got married, she was hoppin' mad about our bed—said it was like sleepin' on a bag of rocks. Didn't bother me none, and my parents slept in that bed for years before us—didn't bother them none either. But Dorie, she wouldn't stand for it. Ya know what she did? She went over to Reger's and detassled corn with their crew last summer so she could buy a new mattress. She worked harder than most of—" A coughing spell interrupted Louie's story.

Last summer? Dorie frowned. She had worked with Reger's crew almost ten years ago, and Louie talked about it as a recent event.

"Turn this way, son," Doc Pitzer instructed. "Into the basin."

The fit finally eased. "I've never seen a woman like that," Louie finished.

"Mrs. LaValle, why don't you come in?" Doc invited.

Dorie winced as the door opened. Doc Pitzer had seen her sitting in front of the house. She gazed first at Doc and then at Louie. Not one, but two dying men.

Doc had lost a good deal of weight in recent months. His white shirt sagged about his shoulders and chest, the meat and heft of him seemingly to have melted away like the snow. The thinness was not just of frame, but his face, wrists, and fingers were also skeletal. Even his once glorious head of hair had gone wispy. Cancer. He had it. A death sentence to be sure. Did his patients drop their eyes and turn away as he handed them their little brown bottles of medicine? Dorie knew them to be too mannered to ask, but privately they must be speculating, will he last through the first planting? It surprised her that she felt sadness rather than a real victory over the enemy who had christened her as barren. His hand trembled, causing the bright red blood to slosh dangerously close to the edge of the catch basin.

"See, Doc, I told you my angel would come to me."

Haloed in the golden light of the exam lamp, Louie resembled a newly hatched bird. His bloodshot eyes were opened wide, but he had no eyebrows to speak of, giving him an expectant look. The burns on his face were more severe than Francesca's, and some of the blisters oozed wetly on his jaw line. When he licked his lips, Dorie saw dried blood in little comma shapes at the corners of his mouth. He reached a thickly bandaged hand out to her.

Dorie knew what concern should look like. She ought to pull the stool closer to his bed and sit while looking for a place to touch that wasn't raw or bandaged. But, yeegawds, the smell of him! It brought to mind when Melander's barn burnt to its foundation trapping dozens of sheep. No, it was worse than that—like old brine mixed with outhouse gases. Dorie's stomach started to pitch, and then she realized she had forgotten the enamel bowl. She pulled shallow breaths through her mouth, feeling sweat trickle down her sides.

Doc Pitzer leaned in to whisper. "His mind's gone soft. I understand he's been sampling too much of that poison you make." She stared down at the basin of blood he seemed to be offering her and felt herself swirling into the color. To her horror, she grabbed at him for balance, and her hands curled around an arm that felt like a brittle tree branch. He made no move to offer her a chair, but stared intently at her, his eyes tented by loose folds of skin. They both turned as Louie spoke.

"I'm glad you're here to take me home, my sweet. I want you to fix me up good. Now, what happened to my clothes?" Louie started to fuss with the sheet that covered his legs.

He had wanted to kill her two days ago. He had set fire to the shed believing she would perish there with Victor. She fished in her sleeve for a kerchief to press to her nose.

"A man in better health would heal up these burns in a few weeks. He's vomiting blood and doesn't have the constitution to fight off an infection. Mrs. LaValle, why didn't you bring him in sooner when you noticed he gave up eating for drinking?"

I'm a dreadful wife. He embarrasses me and I wanted him gone. Not dead, just somewhere away from me. Indeed, why hadn't she called Doc? She looked at her husband and shook her head, doubting whether gallons of his special medicine could have worked the miracle Louie required. Her throat closed on her words, and she shook her head and shrugged.

"What's to be done for him now?" Dorie asked. Louie's eyes closed. When his mouth hung open, she saw blackened holes where he had lost a few teeth. The air in the room felt thick with warmth. Dorie wanted to slip out of her coat but then it might appear that she was here for a longer visit, or God forbid, to help with the nursing duties when all she wanted was to run out the door. "Will he be moved to Northwestern Hospital soon?"

Doc Pitzer narrowed his eyes. "I don't think there's much call for that now. Marvel and I will keep him comfortable another day or so. If he lives, then you can take him home." He placed the basin in the sink.

Louie at home meant wounds to clean, meals to prepare, chamber pots to empty. Up and down the stairs dozens of times a day. Another patient to tend. He would be in her bed, the one she had shared with Victor. Her mother would have said, "You reap what you sow." It felt as though parts of her face had gone numb.

"Tell me, did you treat Victor Volk?" She counted the length of his pause by the beat flowing in her ears.

"Ah, yes. In fact, he left here not more than an hour before you arrived." She waited for more details, keeping her face neutral although she had to dab her upper lip. It was hellishly warm in here. Didn't he feel it?

"Victor was well enough to walk out of here on his own two feet."

Dorie closed her eyes to shut out the too bright light and let out a breath of thanks.

"That cousin of his, Ingeborg, picked him up. She was in such a state—ranting and scolding him like he was still in short pants. Once that passed, she took to weeping." Doc frowned at the box of gauze he was trying to open. "He's got a few nasty burns, but I dressed them all. He's also coughing like a man who's spent his life in the mines."

Dorie nodded and started to back out of the room. Louie was asleep, and Victor had gone home. She craved fresh air, a cup of tea, a dark room, and a cool cloth across her forehead.

"You know what I find most curious?" He leaned over Louie and smeared salve on the blistered curve of his ear.

Her stomach hitched again as the creamy medicine dripped, making her think it was a vital fluid leaking directly from Doc's fingers, down to Louie's bony shoulder. She counted his ribs, noting his fast, shallow breaths and knew if she placed a hand there, just under his heart, she would feel the rapid beat like a rabbit just before she slit its throat.

When she didn't respond, he jumped in. "When the sheriff brought the two of them here after the fire, I had to cut their shirts from them. And what do I find?" He made a clucking noise with his tongue. "A pretty pink gunshot scar on Victor's side!" He made a motion with his index finger, pointing to his loose shirt. "My guess is that it happened a month or so ago. I told that new lawman I never dug a bullet out of Victor Volk, but it appears someone else tended to him recently." He grinned.

Dorie stood by the door, her tongue thick and dry in her mouth. Louie snored a low, wet rumble. What could she say? One story might be that Victor had accidentally shot himself cleaning his gun. Would anyone believe that especially after they examine Geno's body? No, it seemed wiser to match his silence than to argue or deny Victor's injury.

"Mrs. LaValle, you are unusually quiet today. It's been my experience that you are always itching to get in the last word." He unwound a length of gauze and snipped it with a scissors.

"I've had to manage the farm alone. I'm tired. This has all been such a shock." She didn't bother to say she'd been busy delivering a baby.

"But certainly you see how you brought on all your own troubles." The roll of gauze tumbled from his fingers and rolled across the floor.

Dorie lifted her chin when she spoke. "I didn't force the glass to his lips."

"Did you call Father Caouette?"

"Excuse me?" What did the priest have to do with the notion that she encouraged Louie's drunkenness?

"Extreme Unction. Your husband should be given last rights." He wound the bandage around Louie's head to cover the blisters on his chin and ear before tying a knot.

"No, I haven't called St. Vincent's." Another failure. She hadn't properly cared for his body or his immortal soul. If he up and died, would he suffer in purgatory for an eternity? Why was she responsible for everything?

All these accusations and events pulled and weighed on her arms, shoulders and across her neck, reminding Dorie of the days when she would walk behind Louie's plow to gather the large boulders the blade had heaved to the surface. With every new furrow and each plodding step, the stone grew heavier.

It seemed like a lifetime ago when Victor had invited her to leave town. She wished she had had the courage to pack her bags and turn her back on Louie and this whole mess. Staying hadn't solved any problems! Her business was finished. She felt responsible for Louie, yet she had left him to his own devices. If she had left weeks ago, Francesca would have returned home to her sons, crying into a pillow miles away from here.

Find Victor and tell him about the baby. She would count all the money in the tins, pack a satchel and drive to St. Paul. She could pay Lenny to nurse Francesca and the baby for a few weeks. Hell's bells, she could pay her double to care for Louie as well. Perhaps one day after they were settled, she could invite Francesca to St. Paul for a visit. Lenny could come too. She hoped she'd be back in medical school by that time. Dorie's baby would sit on her lap. A boy she pictured, blond and serene. Francesca's daughter would be walking by then, holding her mother's fingers as she took wobbly steps across the room. The women would laugh and cry as they relived the story of her March birth ordeal.

Dorie's peaceful vision of these events shattered with Louie's screams. "Fire. My arm's on fire! Put it out! Put it out!" He batted at the imaginary flames with the thick bandages. "Can't you see it? Throw water on me. Hurry, Dorie, do something."

She backed out of the exam room, her heart skittering as she ran the path to the car.

41

The Confession

The engine roared as the beams from the headlamps burst through the fog that floated low and silky over the road and pastures. When Dorie was a child, Jeanette whispered that these were ghostly apparitions of the recently dead who stubbornly clung to the earth, and even now she couldn't shake the notion that she was blasting through a brigade of lost souls. Her foot pressed the gas pedal, and she hunched over the wheel, urging the car on to put the necessary miles between her and Louie. The plan to leave town had begun to take shape in her mind. There were trunks to pack, but what if her clothes weren't smart enough for St. Paul? The last thing she wanted to do was be pegged as a poor farmer's wife.

Then there was the matter of her farm. She could lease the land to Obeline's oldest son for more than a fair price. Art had just turned eighteen and was anxious to strike out on his own. Her nephew had spent summers with them years ago and had a better feel for farming at the age of fourteen than Louie had in his whole life. If anyone could turn this place around, Art stood first in line as the likely candidate. Besides, if Louie died, then Art could buy it outright from her. Dorie startled each time a mailbox loomed out of the mist, but without benefit of barns and houses, she depended solely on those landmarks to guide her home.

There was so much to do once she arrived home even if Francesca and the baby were doing well—diapers to be sewn, bed linens to boil. Despite her fatigue, she welcomed chores where she could get lost in the pure physical nature of the work—pulling the lever back and forth above the steaming water until her shoulders burned, feeding the sopping linens through the wringer until they lay in heavy, cramped bundles in the basket. She wanted something to stop her thoughts from circling around the image of Geno's body being pulled from the lake. What would he look like after all these weeks in the water? In her mind she kept going back to the first summer of her marriage when she had stood on the east shore as the setting sun burned a brilliant orange, watching as Will DeWeese and his eldest son rowed back and forth in Cattail Bay, trolling a grappling hook attached to a rope. By the time Will finally snagged his youngest daughter's body, she had already bloated up to twice her three-year-old size, and they speculated a muskellunge was responsible for taking her hands.

Dorie pulled hard at the wheel, fist over fist, to follow the wide bend of the road, and in this movement, she found her breasts to be full and tender. Everything about her body felt different these last days. Oddly, her dress hung loosely at the waist, but then again she hadn't eaten enough over the last four weeks to keep a bird alive. At the thought of food, her stomach ground against itself in a way that made her realize she was truly hungry for the first time in days! Certainly, this had to be a good sign of health!

Then there was the matter of telling Victor about the baby. How would he react?

After that last night they had spent together, she woke feeling sure of his feelings, but as the hours slipped away from the moment of their last kiss, so did her confidence in his happy reaction to this announcement. Oh, everything must be just perfect when she told him! She would wear her finest dress and cook a meal of all his favorites, and when he was in her bed again, she would place his hand on her belly and all would be right with the world. Wasn't it her turn to live the nice dream?

She had passed Dubay's mailbox a few minutes ago, and she squinted, watching for the one that marked the turn to her drive. Creamy fog settled in now, making it even more difficult to navigate, and she was thankful when her oversized mailbox reflected in the light, the largest script-style "L" Louie had painted was unmistakable in height and girth next to the letters that shrank smaller and smaller as he ran out of room on the dull aluminum.

As Dorie pulled into the drive, she noted with alarm that the Erickson truck was not parked where Lenny had left it next to the storage shed. Had she gone for help? Dorie braked abruptly, lurching against the wheel as the car stalled out. She didn't even bother to shut the car door or stop to untie the pup that whined and yelped at the end of the rope. Dorie flew through the porch and kitchen, picturing the sheet pulled over Francesca's head. What had happened? Maybe she had continued to bleed or her lungs and heart had failed after the fire and the hard birth. Or maybe she would find the baby, already cold and blue, swaddled in that length of yellow flannel Dorie had intended for a new nightdress. She heard singing coming from the guest room as she crossed the parlor floor. Why did it always seem as if she were lurking on the other side of doors like a war spy? To her surprise, it was Victor's voice. He must have hidden his car in the barn. If he and Francesca had heard her arrival, they gave no notice. She smiled wistfully when she realized she had never known his musical ability.

If you're needin' me,
Like I've been needin' you.
Just drop me a line,
Sayin', baby, you'll be mine.
Write me in care of Mr. Blues.
Hopin' you've been missin' me,
Like I've been missin' you.
I should've never let you go
'Cause, baby, I love you so.
Write me in care of Mr. Blues.

Victor perched on the frame of the wooden chair and held the new baby against his chest. He tipped his head to the side so that her dark head nestled against his neck. With fingers splayed, his right hand dwarfed the width of her tiny body as he rhythmically patted her back. His left hand, bandaged in the same manner as Louie's, looked like the head of a pussy willow.

As he finished the song, Dorie pressed her hand to the door, her throat full of love and relief. She waited to compose herself or risk the rush of tears. He was here and safe, and he held that baby in a way that Dorie knew all would be wonderful.

Instead, it was Francesca who started to cry. At some point her hair had come loose from the ribbon, and it spread across the pillow in a dark tangle. She turned her face to the pillow, and Dorie couldn't hear her muffled words.

Victor sprang from the chair and sat on the bed. His back was to Dorie now, curved over Francesca's prone form, and she focused on the way the hair grew on the top of the baby's head in a perfect swirl.

"What an entertaining song! Look at her, little Victoria loves the sound of your voice!"

Victoria! She had named the baby after Victor! Dorie bristled with annoyance for reasons she couldn't name. Wouldn't it be more proper for Francesca to consider a family name? Dorie caught a glimpse of Francesca's face. There were dark circles under her eyes that only served to make her look more tragic and lovely. Dorie wanted to push open the door, but her feet stayed rooted because suddenly she felt like an intruder.

"Besides being the loveliest creature, she's also very smart. I think she's sleeping so she doesn't have to listen to me!" Victor chuckled.

"Ah, Victor, these are all the things I wanted in my life with Geno. Someone to declare this child the most beautiful baby ever born, and to bring me plates of, what did you call it? *Spaetzel*? A man to sing comfort to us." Francesca's voice sounded sleepy and sad. Dorie's throat ached.

Dorie leaned to her right side just in time to see Victor tuck his namesake in Francesca's arms. He pulled the blankets to her shoulders and smoothed back the hair from her face. Dorie watched as he knelt on the floor and put his head in his arms. She held her breath. Was he having some kind of attack?

"It's my fault your husband's dead, Francesca. I shot him." Victor's voice sounded strangled.

No, no, no, don't say anything, Dorie wanted to shout, but the words stayed locked inside.

"What are you telling me?" Francesca pulled an arm free from the covers and placed it on his shoulder.

"No one knows this. I haven't even told Dorie. For the longest time I couldn't remember any bit of what happened. It was hidden from me, and whenever I thought about it too hard, it all went gray." He made a sound that was part wheezy gasp, part sob. "The day we went out to the shack, that's when I remembered it all."

The parlor clock chimed seven times, drowning Francesca's response.

"I was out at the still, loading up to bring a batch here. I remember it was so warm out for a February day! I had a case in my hands, and when I looked up there was this fella standing there, not more than thirty feet away. I called out, 'Hey there,' but he didn't answer me." Victor started coughing. He reached into his pocket for a handkerchief and spat into it.

"I remember thinking, he's too well-dressed to be a bum or gypsy. Then it hit me that he was probably a fed, and I cursed myself for not watching, not being careful like Dorie always lectured me. It was strange because he kept grinning at me, not saying a word. He smiled like we were old pals, and I wondered if I had met him before, and then he pointed a gun at me. I reached for mine, but it wasn't in the waistband of my pants. Then I remembered I had set it on the running board because it jabbed me when I stooped over."

As the baby made mewing sounds, Dorie wondered if Geno's grin resembled his brother's lopsided sneer. Francesca's large, unblinking eyes locked on Victor.

"I leaned over to grab my gun. That's when I heard the shots. The first one splintered the case, shattering a jug. The hootch ran all down my trouser leg just like I'd pissed myself. The second shot took me here." Victor motioned to his side. "God Almighty, it was worse than being kicked by any horse. It pushed me backward, and I slid down the car. I started thinking all kinds of crazy things like *Don't drop any more bottles or Dorie will be sore,* and then when I saw the blood on my shirt, I thought, *Oh, Christ on a crutch, this was a brand spankin' new shirt!* Why was I thinking about ruining my clothes or making Dorie mad in what might have been my last gasps on earth?" Victor looked up at Francesca and shrugged his shoulders and then set his forehead against his arm again as if he were too weary to go on.

Francesca patted his shoulder and then the top of his head as she might have comforted one of her young sons.

"He stood over me then with his gun pointed at my head, and I couldn't breathe or say anything to make him stop, so I pulled the trigger."

At the sound of his sobbing, Dorie felt something crack open and break loose in her chest.

"Francesca, I killed your Geno. This baby will never meet her father because of me."

Dorie stood sweating and lightheaded, staring at the scuffed hallway floor.

"He turned around and started walking toward the creek. He staggered and then he fell. I got into my car and somehow made it here to Dorie's. She put his body in the lake to protect me."

Dorie bit her lip against her shock. Did he want to put a noose around both of their necks? Geno was dead long before Francesca came to town, so what was the point of this confession? Besides, if Victor's story were true, then Geno fired the first shots. Victor had only acted in self-defense.

Dorie burst into the room before he topped off his confession with the story of Sal's death. She stood there, breathing fast, unable to collect her thoughts as they both stared at her.

"Dorie, is it true?" Francesca asked.

Dorie stared at Francesca and said nothing.

"I saw you standing there, just outside the door. You heard Victor, clearly. Did you put my husband's body in the lake?" Tears ran from Francesca's large brown eyes, and there was Victor offering another of his pressed handkerchiefs.

"It wasn't like that," Dorie started. She couldn't go on when she realized it was exactly like that. She had found Geno's body out at the still, and she had tied a rope to his leg and dumped him into the lake. How could she explain her terror at being found out by the sheriff or the feds and losing her business and then her home?

The heat rose in her face, and her tongue felt thick and uncooperative in her mouth. If confession felt good for Victor's soul, it did nothing for hers.

Victor rose and took her hand. She watched that round muscle in his jaw flex. Oh, the rush of feelings—relief, love, shame, and sitting on top of all that was a simmering anger.

"All those times I told you I needed to know what happened to my husband, and you never breathed a word." Francesca sniffled.

"All of this happened before I knew you! What good would have come from telling you this? You heard Victor. He shot Geno to save his own life. We're not criminals, and I don't intend to confess to being one."

"Dorie, I needed to know! Geno's family may disown me now that he's dead. What if they won't let me see my boys? What will I do?" Dorie watched as baby Victoria's face scrunched and contorted, her tiny mouth pursed into a bud.

There it was. She and Francesca were not so different after all. Both of them were worried about how they would support themselves and their children. Maybe Francesca's tears weren't so much spilled over lost love, but lost security.

"And now that you know, how does that change things?"

Tears leaked out of Francesca's eyes and ran down her cheeks. "I don't know," she whispered, "but you should have told me the truth—it was the right thing to do."

Dorie felt a laugh well up and nearly burst through her throat. "What has doing the right thing ever done for me? I tried to be a good potato-farmer's wife, and I nearly starved to death. Since I've stopped that nonsense, I finally made enough money to keep food on the table and pay the taxes. Hell, I've made more money than anyone around here. And I found a man I love." Dorie glanced at Victor. "After years of waiting with empty arms, I'll get the baby I always wanted." Her pulse thudded in her ears.

There, her secret was out—not the way she had pictured, but then when did anything work that way? From the look on Victor's face it was apparent this wasn't recently hatched news. Francesca must have blabbed to him in the name of their newfound closeness. In a rush of breath, she realized his reaction was a happy one. He stood and moved to stand next to her, squeezed her hand, and nuzzled her temple.

The baby squirmed and began to bleat a tiny cry again, and those eyebrows, so like her mother's, furrowed her disapproval.

"She needs to nurse," Dorie announced, dropping Victor's hand. She was relieved to be speaking of practical duties and not mortal sins.

"Victor, Francesca needs privacy. Unless you two are now so cozy with each other that Francesca doesn't mind if you watch." When he flushed and cast his eyes to the floor, she was instantly ashamed. Victor was only following his pure heart with his confession, and she usually loved him for that. A few dried *spaetzel* lay curled up on themselves like slugs on the greasy plate. Ingeborg's doing, no doubt.

She handed him the plate and whispered, "I need to talk to you." He gave her a wary, wounded look, and she realized for all their love and passionate moments, they didn't know each other well at all. Her remorse and sadness at this fact made her ache. She wanted to apologize and knew she should beg forgiveness, but the words jammed in a stew of anger and confusion. Why was it that just when she had thoughts and plans of perfect clarity, something always happened to clutter it all up?

42

Francesca Tells Dorie Her Theory

Dorie pulled the quilt over her shoulder and snuggled under Victor's arm. A breath of musky air escaped from under the covers into the cool of the bedroom. She felt the caress of the gauze bandage as he moved a hand across the top of her fingers. Dorie liked to press her face to the warm, smooth skin of his chest and listen to the inner workings of his body, the whooshing beat of his heart and the stirring of a stomach already clamoring for eggs and biscuits. The curtain to the window she had cracked open last night lifted and billowed, revealing the gray light of dawn, and then pressed against the sill as if the house itself were breathing.

"Victor, are you awake?" Clearly he wasn't, but Dorie felt bright and tightly coiled and pleased her stomach felt settled.

He mumbled something and kissed the top of her head. They had spent the night that way, talking and then slipping back into slumber. They whispered details of far off plans as if the outlook for the immediate future was settled and serene. They both laughed at each other when they discovered Victor was sure their baby would be a dark, petite girl, while Dorie knew for certain she was carrying a stocky, blond boy. All the angry feelings of the past evening had evaporated in the healing balm of their touch.

"How is it you know so much about women?" Dorie couldn't think of the right way to assemble the words to express her question. How did he know how to touch her in all the ways that made her weak for him? She blushed at the thought of even speaking these words aloud, thankful to be tucked under his arm in a position where he couldn't watch her reaction.

She tickled him between the ribs with her thumb. Had he fallen back to sleep?

"Hmm?" She heard him clear his throat and then lick his lips.

"Where did you learn what women like?" That wasn't the right way to ask either. Now, unfortunately, she pictured a long line of women lounging in undergarments that he had serviced during his apprenticeship.

He barked a raw, dry cough. "I was raised by women. Women are wonderful."

"No, I mean, here, when we're alone under the sheets, like this." She spoke in a halting cadence. Was she wrong to assume it was a secret puzzle that most men didn't bother to solve? Of course, she only knew about her physical life with Louie. Did other women have men more like Louie or Victor? Who knew? Her sisters never talked of such things. And lovely Francesca, what had her love life with Geno been like?

"Ah, I see," Victor said. Dorie swore she could hear him smile.

"Well, when I was seventeen years old, I worked in the stockyards in St. Paul for a butcher, Helmut, his name was Helmut Kuettel. One of my jobs was to select the best livers and the kidneys out of the barrels to make sausage. I think to make that stinky job bearable, Helmut showed me how a woman would most like to have her breasts touched by demonstrating with those livers! Believe me, I practiced the whole summer!" Victor chuckled and yawned. "Anyway, I started watching Helmut and saw that all the women loved him! They sought him out, young brides, old widows, spinsters, all of them had questions about cuts of meat it seemed, and in turn, he asked for their advice on romance, cooking, or business. I can still see how they looked at him through downcast lashes, blushing, laughing and smiling. They adored him, I figured out, because he *listened* to them."

Dorie laughed to think of a young Victor tenderly fondling livers. Still, this didn't truly answer her questions, but it was another bit of information about him to tuck away for later.

"I didn't know you lived in St. Paul."

"Mmm? Yeah, years ago." When he shifted his weight to stretch, the bed springs creaked. His hair spiked up on one side from the waxy pomade.

"Victor, let's go there, to St. Paul. Why don't we pack what we need and just leave today?" Dorie sat up, pulling the covers to her neck while she looked at him.

"What? Are you dreaming? We can't. Not now!" Victor pushed himself up on an elbow and punched the pillow up against the headboard. He reclined and crooked an arm over his head. Dorie stared at the curve of his muscle, the pallid skin of his underarm.

"Then, how about California? Remember when you asked me to go to California? I'm answering now, and I say yes!"

He reached for Dorie, tugged her arm, and when she fell against him, her fingertips found the raised surface of the scar on his side.

"Don't you see how everything's changed?" Victor asked.

Changed? Was he kidding? She saw ruin—her business and the sad remainder of her reputation, and yet in all this misery she had found love and was carrying a child. Yes, everything had changed. She wanted to press her lips to that smooth chest and feel muscle and sinew under his bare skin.

As if to answer that question, they heard noises downstairs and the wail of baby Victoria. "She needs us. She's entitled to that much," Victor said. Dorie was unsure if he were referring to Francesca or her child.

"You see, I've thought that all through," Dorie said. "We can hire Lenny to care for her until she's well enough to travel home. I can pay for that. What, say two weeks to a month is all. Besides, Lenny needs the money in order to return to medical school." Thankfully, he hadn't mentioned Louie.

"What about Osseo's dedicated sheriff, Dorie? Do you want to be looking over your shoulder for the rest of your days, catching a glimpse of Steiner in every stranger? Thinking, this is it—he finally found me."

"What makes you think he is after you, Victor?" Dorie sat up and started to braid her snarled hair. There would be no more kisses this morning, not with the baby awake and Steiner's presence as real in the room as if he were leaning against the wall.

"I'm up to my neck in all of this, Dorie, and he knows it. The bad part is that his theory probably puts more stink on me than the truth."

"He can't prove it."

"And what makes you so sure?"

Dorie didn't answer as she shrugged into her dressing gown and strained to hear any more sounds from the baby or any movement downstairs. Now that she was away from Victor's warmth, the air in the room chilled her. She moved to the window, struggling with the stubborn sash and finally succeeded in slamming it shut with a loud thump.

"What about Geno's gun, Dorie?"

She turned to look at him in the pink-gray morning light. The sheet bunched low, baring the arc of his hipbone. Dorie's body registered a crazy mix of desire and panic.

"What happened to the gun?" Victor pressed.

In an instant, she saw herself standing above Geno's body as the snow fell in the failing daylight. The gun, as black as his hair, lay inches from his curled palm. She had slipped it into the deep pocket of his overcoat just before she hefted the body onto the sled. Had she ever revealed that fact to Victor?

"What does that matter now?"

"Fingerprints." He held his left hand out and one by one touched the tips of each finger with the index finger of his right hand.

"Fingerprints," she repeated idiotically.

"You know, each person has a unique pattern of whorls and loops. No two fingerprints are the same. The oil on your skin helps make a mark on a hard surface." Victor had swung his legs from the bed and gathered the sheet to his waist as he moved to the window. He moved the curtain aside and pressed his hand to the cold glass. When he pulled his hand away, she watched the ghost of the imprint dissipate. "Look here," he leaned in and exhaled a long breath against the place on the window he had touched. The handprint flared to life. He wrapped an arm around her and stroked her cheek with the chilled fingertip.

"Did you know that a man named Thomas Jennings broke into someone's home and shot the owner? He left four fingerprints in some wet paint, and they convicted him. That was nearly twenty years ago." Victor leaned his forehead against the glass and exhaled again.

How did Victor know these things? She pressed against him, relief flooding her body. "Then what are you worried about? Your fingerprints won't be on Geno's gun."

"But what about yours, Dorie? Did you handle Geno's gun?"

Nausea seized her. Downstairs, the baby wailed.

Dorie crammed some dry heels of bread she had intended for bread pudding into the pocket of her dressing gown. She turned her back to Victor, who was busying himself starting the stove fire, and gnawed on the largest chunk. She chewed quickly hoping to ease the nausea, as she had no wish for him to see her head hanging over the sink.

"Dorie? Dorie!" Francesca called from the bedroom. Shane yipped in response.

"Do you want me to go?" Victor asked.

Dorie concentrated on making each breath as shallow as possible. "She probably wants a cup of tea. I'll see to her."

"How's the stomach?"

Dorie blinked. He knew of her discomfort. Of course, hadn't they just discussed Victor's understanding of women? Somewhere, some poor pregnant woman had unleashed a litany of complaints to him, the vomiting, the fatigue, the raw tenderness of her whole body and her mind too, and he had cocked his head, nodding sympathetically, and then offered some small comfort, most likely more consideration than the father who had given his seed. Dorie waggled her piece of stale bread at him. "This helps."

"I'll put on some tea for the both of you, unless you want coffee. I'll put him out too." Victor bent to scratch Shane's head.

Tea is fine."

As she crossed the parlor, Dorie's heart ached with her feelings for Victor, for this chance to be with someone who understood her, a true partner in this life. This is what she deserved. It felt just within her grasp, but at the same time something too delicate to possess.

Dorie pushed open the bedroom door to find Francesca standing next to the bed, and the baby, naked in the midst of tangled bed linens, flannels, and diapers. Victoria frowned as her bottom lip vibrated with her staccato cry, her spindly arms and legs pulled in tight to her body. Dorie pulled a clean, folded flannel from the dresser and rushed to the baby, placing a hand on her clammy torso. The string tied to the stump of her cord was stiff with dried blood.

"Francesca, she's cold!" Dorie wrapped the tiny form in the blanket and hugged the baby to her body.

"She's wet. We're both drenched!"

Francesca pulled the sodden dressing gown away from where it clung to her breasts and belly.

"I got up, but such a dizziness came over me, I thought I might fall. Then I tried to take care of Victoria, but, well, she's sopping. I didn't know where to start." Francesca wiped her eyes with the back of her hand, still plucking at the offending wet gown with the other.

As Dorie swayed her body, the baby quieted. Lost in her own thoughts, she had forgotten that Francesca was unaccustomed to managing without servants.

"Your milk has come in," Dorie said. Still holding the baby, she knelt as she reached for the enamel basin under the bed.

"What?" Francesca sniffed.

"That's why you're wet. Your milk's come in." Dorie dropped the wet, twisted flannels into the basin. The baby needed a bath now. She would get

Victor to put on some more water. Dorie wrinkled her nose. The room was thick with stale air, sweat, and ammonia. Her stomach lunged, and she took small breaths through her mouth. "Can you manage on a bedpan again?"

Francesca looked out the window, frowned, and nodded.

Dorie moved to the dresser and opened the top drawer. "Here, put this on. I bleached your gown as best I could." Dorie tugged at the quilt and bed linens, but it was too difficult to manage stripping the bed with the baby in one arm. "Has she nursed yet?"

"Yes."

"Then I'll hand this one off to Victor until we get you settled here." Dorie took in the sweet baby smell as her face nestled against her collarbone. She stroked the curve of Victoria's head, reminded of the lighter-than-air feel of pulling out the silk from a milkweed pod.

Francesca threw herself on the bed and proceeded to weep into the damp quilt. Dorie was surprised by the magnitude of the outburst—great choking sobs and wails, thankfully muffled by the bedding. Good Lord, what was this about?

"What's wrong?" Dorie hesitated, but touched Francesca's shoulder and then watched her recoil. Dorie pulled her hand back and cupped Victoria's head. Why did she ask when she already knew?

"Look, I'm sorry I didn't tell you about Geno. How could I? You were a stranger, and then you were here in my house, and... I don't know. It was a secret I planned to take to my grave. I'm sorry the man you love is dead, but he shot at Victor first." Dorie wiped tears away with the back of her hand.

"Victor, I've forgiven. He confessed from his heart."

Of course, Victor is absolved. It was always that easy for him, Dorie thought.

Francesca looked up through a tangled mass of curls and flashed a dangerous look that Dorie had never seen before. "I dreamt of Geno this morning, Dorie. He tried to put his arms around me, but he was wet and cold. He wanted to take the baby with him, and I knew I had to stop him, but when I hit his chest my hands went through him like rotten fruit." Francesca smiled then, as if she had told a bawdy story and raised her eyebrows. "Do you ever dream of him?"

Dorie shuddered and blinked. This tone unnerved her more than the crying. She shrugged her shoulders.

"Dorie do you know how to tell the truth? I'll show you how it's done. I'll tell you something I've never told anyone else." Francesca sat up, wiping her tears and runny nose on the hem of the nightdress. "I'm not surprised that son-of-a- bitch is dead. It was only a matter of time. He was a two-bit gangster, and not a very smart one at that. He relied on his brother to get by in life. I realize now, I didn't love him. When I see you and Victor together, how you are with each other, I know Geno must not have loved me either." More tears flowed down her cheeks, and Dorie wished she could offer a fresh handkerchief, as Victor was always able to do. "I don't love Geno, but I love the children he gave me."

She pushed the curls from her face and stuck her chin out. "There, that's the first of my secrets. Women shouldn't keep things from each other, Dorie. We need each other too much."

Dorie took a heel of bread from her pocket but couldn't bear to put a bite in her dry mouth. She sat on the bed next to Francesca. "I haven't been close to another woman. I have five sisters who barely speak to me. The women in this town turn their noses up when they see me because I sell liquor to their husbands." Her voice came out in a whisper, and her chest felt tight as if an invisible hand were cinching a rope tighter and tighter.

Francesca chuckled. "Fine, Dorie, that is a good start, but it's no secret—not even to a stranger here in town." The baby squirmed in Dorie's arms as Francesca started to speak again. "Okay, we have some things in common. I lost my mother. I have no sisters and grew up in a house of gangsters and bodyguards. Giovanna and the maids resent me. You see, we are not so different." Francesca's lovely hands fluttered around her as she talked.

Francesca tucked an arm under her head. "The men in my life never looked at me as something of value. They only saw me as something pretty to touch. Someone to bear children, not run a business. I will need to support myself like you do, Dorie. I think we can be useful to each other."

Useful? What did she mean? Dorie wanted to remind her that she no longer had a business to run, but held her tongue.

"Why are you worried about money? Won't Geno's family take care of you?" Dorie turned to look at the door when she heard clanking noises in the kitchen. The puppy barked, and Victor howled back like a wolf. They smiled at each other.

"Years ago, Giovanna made her disapproval of me very clear. I was a bad match for her son, you see. With Sal gone, and my father-in-law on death's doorstep, she'll do as she pleases." Her dark eyes filled with tears. "I'm worried she'll try to keep the boys from me."

Dorie kissed the baby's cheek. The love for this little mite in her arms and the baby she carried swelled to an ache. She couldn't imagine someone trying to take either one away. Victor was right. They were duty-bound to find a way to take care of Francesca.

Francesca sat up and shrugged out of the damp gown and tossed it into the basin. Her breasts were full and heavy looking now. No need for a wet nurse. Francesca pushed her head through the neck opening, freed her long hair, and then began to work the tiny buttons on the bodice. Despite Dorie's laundering, the faint outline of a bloodstain could be seen down the front. Francesca ran her fingertips along the edges.

"I'm sorry I couldn't get it all out. If I could put it in the sun for a few days..."

Francesca continued to follow the edge of the stain. "For me, it's like a medal from a war. Maybe I will show this to Victoria when she is older to remind her of what her mother lived through. I will tell her the story of the two brave women who helped bring her into the world." Francesca smiled and pulled on Dorie's elbow to sit on the bed.

"Now, try again. Tell me your secrets, Dorie."

Dorie locked eyes with Francesca's. The three of them sat close enough to hear each other breathe. Francesca rubbed Dorie's shoulders and arms. There was a power here that made gooseflesh rise over her body. It felt like standing on the porch when the summer sky turned green and the world would go still before a tornado blew in. She recalled Victor's tearful confession, right here on this bed.

"Sal. He came here late one night after the regulars had left. He was drunk. He tried... he wanted to... to force himself on me." Dorie's voice cracked. "Victor arrived in time to fight with Sal, and then he fell down the cellar stairs and broke his neck. We set it up to look like an accident in the blizzard." The words came out of her in a whoosh at the very bottom of a breath. There was a moment when she wondered if it were possible to breathe again. And then Dorie gasped so deep and fast it hurt.

Francesca nodded sagely, part gypsy, part priest. "See? That's how women share the secrets of their hearts."

"You said we could be useful to each other. What did you mean, Francesca?"

She let go of Dorie's arms, pulled the mass of hair from her neck, and piled it on top of her head for a moment before she let it fall.

"I know where it is, Dorie, the money you think Geno hid. It's out at the still. Geno put it where no one would ever think to look. I'm sure of it." She leaned in close enough for their foreheads to touch and whispered, "Hopefully, it's enough money to save us both."

43

Dorie Goes Back to the Still

Time played tricks on Dorie's mind. As she surveyed the scene of the fire, she remembered that morning in her kitchen when the idea to start a business had begun to form. It seemed so recent, but it really must have been over two years ago. She remembered standing over the sink in the kitchen. After Dorie gouged out the black spots and sprouts from the potatoes, she began to dice the remnants, cursing the ratio of rotten pieces to good ones. Why, there might not be enough to make a batch of Poor Man's Oyster Soup, meant to feed the two of them for the week. Her mouth watered for some pink cured ham, but she'd be damned before she'd stick her nose in Hackemuler's shop with an empty pocketbook. Oh, she cringed to think of Charles offering the soup bones he was known to wrap up for the hard-luck cases.

"Ack, potatoes," Dorie spat. Fried, boiled, scrambled with eggs, every meal, day after day. She should be thankful Louie never complained about what was on his plate. Then again, she wished he were fed up enough to get off the back stoop and figure out how to make enough money to put food on the table. Dorie squeezed the last green-tinged potato until her hand ached and then flung it out the window into the yard, scattering the wrens that pecked in the gravel drive. She laughed, marched outside, and dumped all the diced pieces to the goat. Breathing hard, she thought for a second, and then pitched the cracked bowl too. She was done, done, done with potatoes, old bowls, mended dresses and stockings, and that God-awful lye soap. Dorie was done doing without. She would figure out a smarter way to make money.

Now as she sniffed the air, heavy with the tang of scorched wood and sap, she realized she hadn't been out to the still since the day Victor got shot, and yet that day felt like another lifetime!

Bent tin panels, heaps of white ash, and stubs of charred lumber were all that remained of Victor's shack. Dorie poked at the debris with her shovel until she uncovered the blackened door handle with two nails still dangling from the mounting holes. When a puff of smoke rose and curled, she realized the ruins still smoldered with the hot memory of the fire. Dorie shuddered to think how close Victor and Francesca had come to perishing here. And baby Victoria too! Why, their bones would be indistinguishable from the materials used to build this place.

Dorie stared up at the blackened skeleton of the charred tree. How different this place felt during the warm months when the woods were filled with blooming columbine, thallictrum, and delicate ferns. Now a cold whispery feeling crawled along her neck. It had become a Grimm's fairy tale forest, full of lurking goblins and ghosts. Good Lord, she sounded like Louie now, but standing on the pine needles where Geno and Victor had spilled their blood, was it so crazy to think that the air and the soil of these woods, host to so many living things, might become tainted by Geno's evil and Louie's jealous rage? Maybe this place had drawn hostile creatures and lost souls to taunt her. *You made the poison that rotted your husband's brain. Your sin for another man made him crazy! You are the reason Geno's children are fatherless.*

The handle of her shovel, split into fissures of age, scraped against her palm. She hoisted it on her shoulder and walked over to the fermenting pots.

"I know where the money is hidden," Francesca had whispered. "I didn't think of it when Victor and I were in the woods, but I've had time to figure it out. Geno always hid his loot in things that people didn't want to touch—that was his trademark. Once, he hid money from a heist in a coffin, and months later when he thought it was safe, he dug it up. Another time, he hid diamonds in a dead man's mouth. That didn't work too well because the jaws locked up tighter than a safe. Oh, there was such a terrible fight with the undertaker, but he finally cut him a split and all was well." She had said this all matter of fact as she nursed the baby, stopping to croon and caress the baby's puckered face. "Dorie, I think the money is hidden in the manure Victor used to pack the fermenting pots."

Dorie's hands trembled. How much money might there be? Francesca had said Geno pretended to be a fed and then grabbed all the money and the booze too. Francesca said it was his plan to sell the moonshine to the next town down the line and then repeat the process all over again.

Dorie kicked at the kinked copper tubing Victor had used to condense the steam. Someone had bent it so it couldn't be used. Who was responsible? Steiner? Geno? Her anger churned. Why did they have to ruin it all? She surveyed the fermenting pots. The manure, dried and cracked now, had been packed around each pot in layer after layer. When she pried at an edge of the nearest one with the shovel, it fell away in thick, rounded pieces reminding her of broken crocks. What would Geno have put the money in to protect it from the wet and stink? Would he have divided it up to store in jars or kept it all together?

The light dimmed, and Dorie pushed herself to work faster, each movement bringing her hope of discovery and then disappointment as she failed to find the stash. According to Francesca, Dorie should pray to dear Saint Anthony to find Geno's money, but Dorie didn't think saints were interested in aiding the discovery of stolen loot. She squinted now at the shadowy movements around her. She clenched her teeth, angry she had forgotten how dark it got here in the woods, but the thought of finding this money made her lose all threads of common sense. Dorie had slipped out of the house as Francesca and the baby slept, and who knew when her next chance to search alone might come?

The wind picked up, the tops of the restless pines whooshed, drowning out the twitter of birds. As Dorie dug around the last pot, the long sound of the metal scraping metal made her shiver. She shrugged shoulders against the tightness and rubbed a tender spot in the middle of her palm that foretold of a blister.

It must be here.

Francesca had seemed so confident in her deduction. Suddenly, something tumbled against her shoulder and Dorie dropped the shovel, brushing furiously at her coat. She screamed and kicked at the round body as it hit the ground before she realized it wasn't a bat, but merely a pinecone. Her legs shuddered as if her center had melted like lard in a skillet. She bent to retrieve the handle and scraped at the last of the packed manure with the blunt head.

There was no stash of money packed around the fermenting pots. Francesca had been wrong.

Dorie leaned over the shovel, breathing hard, and closed her eyes as a strange ache rippled through her body. What if Geno had put the money in the shack? It would be lost to them all now. She could picture him squatting on the dirt floor as he stuffed handfuls of bills into the sacks of corn or sugar or maybe he had ripped open the seams of the quilt Victor kept folded at the end of the cot and pushed rolls of bills into the goose-down filling. If that was the case, the money was gone now, that is if it was ever here in the first place. Of course, any number of people could have made off with the stash. Why had she allowed Francesca to send her on this crazy chase? A sob escaped from deep in her chest. What she craved most at this moment surprised her, for it was the feel of baby Victoria's body molding to her own aching curves.

Dusk settled in. Just over the hill from where the stream fed into the lake, a light winked. Victor? A gypsy? Could it just be someone from town coming to snoop the scene of the fire? The shovel would be her only weapon against a robber. As Dorie stumbled backward, her heel caught on the pine tree roots.

Numbness started at the crown of her head and moved down her body. She couldn't swallow the thickness at the back of her throat. He moved quickly, more shadow than man, the beam of light slashing slivers out of the dark.

"Dorie LaValle, is that you?" The voice boomed, not Victor's.

No one knew she was out here. She thought again of the ghosts who might hold court in this place. The dull feeling spread down her legs and feet, curiously reminding her of the deadening reaction of moonshine. She couldn't run. The crunch and crack of needles and sticks made a great racket.

Suddenly he was upon her, the lantern held high next to the side of his head, his face a mask of shadows and bleached light. Steiner. How long had he watched her from the top of the hill?

He gestured to her shovel. "I heard a scream. What are you doing out here at this hour?"

"Francesca lost a bracelet. I told her I'd see if I could find it."

"And you expect to find it in the dark." He dropped his arm so the lantern hung at knee level, but she could see the thin press of his lips. In his other hand he held a suitcase.

"The afternoon got away from me."

"Funny, Francesca didn't know where you'd gone. When she woke up alone, she guessed you'd gone to visit Louie."

Damn. Steiner had been to the house. What did he want now? Did he expect Francesca to identify the bloated body of her husband? An idea tumbled around in her head. Perhaps there was another reason for his incessant visits. It struck Dorie suddenly that Steiner might have feelings for Francesca. Dorie tried to imagine Steiner's brittle arms attempting to enfold Francesca's lushness.

"What are *you* doing out here?" Her tongue certainly wasn't as numb as the rest of her. Where did the suitcase come from? That's what she wanted to ask instead.

"Francesca told me she discovered her husband's car hidden here in the woods, just a bit over that hill." He pointed with the lantern to the area where she had first spotted the light. "I was going to drive it into town, but it won't turn over—been sitting too long, I expect."

Dorie was breathing hard. Why hadn't Francesca said anything about finding Geno's car? What other secrets had she told Steiner? Dorie flashed to the bedside confidences she had shared with Francesca. Was this all Steiner's idea? *Get Dorie to confess, she should pay for what happened to your family.*

"Ah, yes the car," Dorie said neutrally as if she knew about it. She swallowed something bitter.

"I found this on the seat." Steiner swung the suitcase up for her to see. "Geno's I guess, from the initials here by the handle. Hopefully, there's a change of clothes in here suitable enough to dress the body before it ships home."

What if the money is in the suitcase? Maybe Geno never got a chance to bury it the day he ran into Victor!

"You're sure it's him—Geno."

Steiner leaned the case against his leg and fished in his inner pocket until he found what he was looking for.

"Francesca lent me this portrait. I'll ask Doc Pitzer to verify, but just from looking at this, I'd say the body is Geno D'Agostino." He dangled his evidence in front of her as if to ask her opinion too. Dorie was thankful for the dark. The last thing she wanted was a glimpse of Geno beaming with good health. She frowned. How could Steiner be so sure?

"The water was very cold. It preserved him, you know. I'm venturing he looked near the same as when he went into the lake." He paused, hiking the lantern high again and squinted at her, "bullet hole and all."

Dorie's fear felt like a fist in her throat. He knew! He knew everything. This was Francesca's perfect revenge. *I'll get both of them to confess*, she must have bragged to Steiner. And then turn them over to you. Francesca's plan didn't end there. She would also get Dorie to find the missing money. Steiner, serving his bittersweet love and odd sense of justice, would let Francesca keep the money, reasoning it was impossible to return it to its rightful owners. Why hadn't Dorie seen all this sooner?

"What do you want?" she asked.

"It's all going to stop now. The moonshine, the mob," he gestured to the ruined shack. "Your little business has brought nothing to my town but robbing, shooting, and general mayhem that'll lead to more of the same." A fleck of his spit landed below her left eye. Fear arched some place high in her chest making it hard to breath. She had never seen him like this before.

He just wanted her to stop making moonshine! She would tell him what he needed to hear. "Fine. I won't run the business anymore."

It was over. She had known this for months now, but she felt a stab of hatred for the D'Agostino brothers. Things were fine until they came to town to ruin everything. Dorie backed up against a tree and touched the sticky bark.

Steiner set the lantern down again and fished around in his pocket and pulled out a cigarette. He flicked a match on his belt buckle and curved his hands around the flame as it caught. He squinted at her as he blew out the match. The smell of tobacco comforted Dorie, reminding her of her Grand-père Madore. She and Steiner would strike a deal. No more moonshine business, and then he'd leave her alone. Steiner picked a bit of tobacco from his tongue. "Do you think you can just go on as if nothing has happened?"

She blinked as the smoke pricked the back of her throat. Why did it sound like he was accusing her of something more sinister? "Why, I..."

"Do you know anything about the D'Agostino family?" He exhaled a long stream of smoke and went on before she had a chance to reply. "Well, I found out plenty. I'm surprised more of those murdering thugs haven't already arrived here now that word of Geno's death has reached Chicago. Sal found his way to your door. How long will it take this time for someone else to come?"

"They brought their own trouble. It wasn't my fault. I've done nothing wrong." Would they come after her if she had Francesca in her care?

"Do you know Calvin Perriott was found dead this morning?"

Dorie struggled to remember the last time she had seen Calvin, and finally singled out a sleety afternoon when he had stopped by to pick up an order.

"I haven't seen Calvin since January. What's that got to do with me?" The winds quieted now, and she knew he thought it had everything to do with her.

"His wife, Marie, went to live with her sister in Minneapolis, saying he preferred the drink to her. Calvin's brother said he had lost interest in his place after that. Cows died because he forgot to care for them. Looks like he got desperate enough to drink some ethanol and wandered outside and froze to death.

"You must be wrong. It wasn't cold enough last night for anyone to freeze to death."

"I didn't say he died *last* night, now did I? Seems Calvin had been dead for a while when they found him."

Dorie pushed her shoulders hard against the rough bark of the tree. A cramp spread through her lower belly and into her back.

"You look so surprised. I would think you'd know first-hand what that stuff can do to a man." Steiner said and inhaled deeply.

Louie. Her belly felt as if it were full of rusty metal. She would never be free of this mess. Hatred for Louie, for Steiner, twisted through her. With a good swing of the shovel, she could catch him across the side of his head. She could grab the suitcase, and then she and Victor could leave town tonight. Her hands flexed around the handle. *One swing, do it now, when he's looking for another match.* Dorie's breath came in funny little hitches.

The baby. Victor's baby. *His mother murdered the sheriff…* the biddies in town wouldn't even bother to lower their voices… *and they hanged her by the neck just after his birth. That orphan baby will turn out just like her, just wait and see.* One of her sisters, probably Jeanette, would take him in only because it was her duty, but she would treat him like a burden, another mouth to feed. That poor boy would grow up never able to look another soul straight in the eye. A great sob, that was part sorrow, part anger, escaped from deep in her chest.

"So now you understand," Steiner said. "I want you to confess or I plan to arrest Victor on murder charges."

"Confess to murder? I didn't murder anyone." Dorie swallowed a dry mass at the back of her throat when she remembered Victor's lesson on fingerprints.

"You've misunderstood me. I want you to confess to the bootlegging. Did you know that Coolidge just signed a bill that changed the prison term for first offenders from six months to five years? Oh, and the fines have been raised from one thousand to ten thousand dollars. I figure, by the time you serve your jail sentence and pay off all that money, my town will be as dry as a bone. Steiner ran his tongue over his top lip, tasting this trump card he had played. "It's your choice."

44

Things Escalate at Home

"I don't know what to do," Francesca sobbed as Dorie pulled her arm out of the sleeve of her coat. The brightly lit kitchen was a wild array of pots and pans, overturned cups, and piles of tangled flannels. Shane whined and bounced at her feet. Chilled and reeling from Steiner's threats, Dorie blinked and put her hands up to shield her face. After the gloom of the woods, this brightness gouged her eyes. The kitchen smelled of soiled diapers, burnt wood, and wet fur. The sour mix of odors sent her stomach pitching once more. In the parlor, the clock chimed six times.

Francesca paced in a circle around the table, holding baby Victoria high on her shoulder. When her hip nudged the table, a glass fell to the floor with a crash, but the baby didn't startle or cry out. "I want Lenny here," Francesca moaned.

Dorie blocked her path and put her hand to Victoria's head. Immediately the heat of a fever filled the curve of her palm.

"How long has she been like this?"

Francesca shrugged as she swayed back and forth. "I don't know." Her breath hitched and she repeated herself. "I don't know. When I woke, you were gone." She sniffed and used her shoulder to blot tears that ran along her jaw. "By the time Steiner arrived, she'd been crying for what seemed like such a long time! After he left, it was one diaper after another. I used the last of the clean flannels." Francesca's fingers fluttered across the baby's back.

"But how long has she been feverish?"

"You told me to keep her warm," Francesca said accusingly. "I kept her wrapped in blankets." She maneuvered around Dorie and continued circling the table.

"It's not from the blankets. Victoria's ill, Francesca. Has she nursed?"

"Yes, well, she cried so much. I'm not sure if she got any. How am I to know this? There's no way to tell how much is in her belly."

Dorie clenched her jaw. Not so long ago, it seemed the biggest challenge was bringing Victoria safely into this world. She had shut her mind to all the sad things that happened to babies after their births. Dorie remembered walking through the St. Vincent de Paul cemetery, and while her mother tended the graves of relatives, Dorie busied herself by counting headstones of infants. She kept a tally in her head of how many died at birth. The next categories were how many lived to three months, six months, and then a year. Dorie also kept track of how many families lost more than one child. She knew all their stories, those that died of measles, diphtheria, fires, infections, and those babies that died for what seemed no good reason at all. The year the flu took her mother, and the upkeep of graves had passed to her daughters, Dorie counted fourteen new headstones, most featuring carved images of sleeping angels.

"Where were you? I've never been left all alone with a baby before. Now look what happened!" Francesca eased herself down onto one of the kitchen chairs, but continued to move her torso back and forth, rocking her silent infant.

Dorie stopped to consider this point. In Francesca's other life she had a number of servants who could step in and diaper the baby and bring her tea. She thought of her sister Jeanette who, all alone, had managed her six children, feeding the farm hands, and upkeep of the house.

Irritation burned through Dorie, working its way through the numbness that hung over her shoulders. "I was looking for Geno's money. You were wrong. He didn't hide it in the packed manure. I looked at every single fermenting pot." She drew out her last words for emphasis—"The money's not there."

Francesca's unfocused gaze made Dorie shiver. She didn't seem to hear Dorie at all.

"She's so still. How do I know if she's breathing?" Francesca set Victoria in her lap and frantically undid the layers of blankets, exposing her thin torso. The baby's skin, red and angry in the hours after birth, was now white in the bright light, nearly transparent. Dark-blue veins, like morning glory vines, twisted and sprawled under her skin that rose and fell with so many panting breaths. Each inhalation exposed the twin fans of delicate ribs. It reminded Dorie of the time she picked up a baby sparrow that had fallen from its nest above the barn light. Eyes closed, the rounded breast moved under her thumbs in the same fluttery manner until the breaths began to slow and then finally stilled. Dorie rubbed her cold hands over her own belly to soothe an ache of worry and fear.

Francesca seemed relieved by her discovery. "That's good, isn't it? She's breathing fine."

"Yes," a lie certainly. Dorie's eyes locked on Victoria's face. Were her eyelids fluttering in some sort of fit? Was there a bluish tinge around her mouth? Dorie's throat closed around what she felt for this child. How was it possible to fiercely love this new baby, a child not even of her own blood, from the moment of her first breath?

Dorie sighed, realizing that either this baby was strong enough to fight this sickness or she would die within a matter of days. The headstone inscription flashed in Dorie's mind. *Baby Victoria 1928 Our Angel.* Francesca began to mouth silent words, hopefully inviting one of her saints who cared for afflicted infants.

"If I go to the attic and get a bolt of flannel, will you cut some more diapers?" Dorie pumped water to boil as she spoke. The splash in the pot matched the whooshing sounds in her head. "I'll wash the soiled things."

"What about her?"

"She's probably worn herself out from crying. We can keep an eye on her here in the kitchen. As long as she's sleeping, you can nestle her into a bushel basket."

Francesca gathered the baby closer as if Dorie had suggested flinging the baby into the barnyard. "No, I mean can Lenny come back? I would feel better with her advice."

Dorie sighed. Would Lenny have a potion or a modern medicine to dispense to help this tiny baby? How many times could she call upon Lenny for help? Just as she laced both hands around the kettle handle and lifted, a sharp twinge, like the plucking of a fiddle string, resonated up through her belly. Leaning against the stove, she panted, waiting, but it was gone, just as quickly as it had come. She pushed out a slow breath through parted lips. When all seemed quiet in her body, she struck a match to light the kindling. The flame shuddered in her trembling hands. What did that pain mean? Only nerves and overexertion, she told herself. The kindling caught and flared. Don't think about it. It's nothing. She blew out the match to snuff her panic.

Dorie caught her thin reflection in the kitchen window, and she leaned over to touch the glass as Victor had done, feeling the cold March air press back against the panes. Where was the money now? At this very moment, Steiner could be opening the suitcase. Dorie looked down to see the pup relieve himself under a kitchen chair. Between the soiled flannels and the dog, her house would end up smelling no better than the barnyard.

"Why don't you call Steiner? He's always concerned about your welfare. Maybe he knows what to do for your baby." Dorie bent and used a dirty flannel to blot up the puddle. The anger she felt in the woods swung in a wide arc at Francesca.

"Steiner?" Francesca's eyebrows pulled together in puzzlement. "He's not trained as a doctor."

"A good sheriff, one that's worth his weight, knows enough about doctoring to get by."

"It's Lenny I want. She knows about babies—my baby." Her voice thick with tears broke as she turned her face away from Dorie's. "I'm a burden to you. That's why you're angry with me."

Dorie ground her teeth hard enough to make a squeaking noise. Traitor, she thought to herself. Burdens and duty, she understood. Traitors she didn't. Maybe her reluctance to call upon Lenny had more to do with the sharp edge of spite than feelings of indebtedness.

"Where's Victor?" Francesca sniffed and wiped a tear from the corner of her eye. The baby began to squirm and fuss. Francesca jumped up and jostled her with big, rough movements. Francesca's stringy hair fell across her face, and she made no movement to brush it back.

Dorie looked out to the yard as if the glance could make him appear in the drive. He'd been gone for hours and should have returned by now unless something had happened. Had Steiner gone ahead and arrested Victor?

"Haven't you guessed Victor's whereabouts, Francesca? After all, you told Steiner all our secrets and then sent him into the woods to threaten me." Her words leaped out in a high pitch. "Do you know he wants to arrest Victor for murder? Wait. Of course you do. Steiner clued you in on his plan. He probably even rehearsed his speech with you." Breathless with effort, she slammed the lid down on the kettle.

It was pointless to argue with Francesca. What Dorie needed was the soothing rhythm of chores to dull the noise in her head. First task—laundry. Dorie walked to the porch to retrieve the washstand, but the leg had tangled in some rope causing a pile of crates to upset. The dog began to yip again.

While Dorie dragged the stand across the floor, Francesca aimlessly tugged at the sodden blankets around the baby, her wet face full of misery. "I didn't tell your secrets to Steiner. I would never do such a thing. I only told Steiner that Geno's car was hidden in the woods. I found it before the fire. That's when I knew he was dead."

Dorie stopped, and an ache rippled through her. Did she believe Francesca? Where was the truth hiding? The baby's dark head lolled back, and Dorie feared Francesca, in this state, might drop her.

"We need to cool her down, to ease the fever," Dorie said, placing her hand on Victoria again. The hot skin made her queasy.

"No," Francesca argued. "When Joseph had a fever, Bridget stoked up a great fire and then closed off the kitchen. She held him like this," Francesca pressed the baby close to her body, "all night to sweat out the fever. It worked, I tell you. By morning, the fever had broken."

"Feel her skin, Francesca. She's on fire. Maybe sweating it out works for older children, but Victoria is too small to endure that." Dorie pinched the skin on the back of her tiny hand as Lenny had shown her when Victor was so ill. Victor, where are you? I need you here. Surely he could reason with Francesca.

"Don't hurt her!"

"Look how the skin sags back slowly when I press it."

"Please, let's call Lenny." Francesca burst into a fresh torrent of tears.

"When Victor had an infection from the gunshot wound, we had to cool him down to save him. Please believe me when I tell you this is the only way."

"Lenny. The baby needs Lenny," Francesca said and bit down stubbornly on her bottom lip. "I see it in your eyes. You think I'm like a spoiled child. I tell you, Dorie, this is what you'll do for your baby, the one, there, in your belly. You'll do anything possible to save it!"

Victoria stirred again and opened her mouth but emitted only a feeble croaking sound. They both stared at her, and Dorie held her breath waiting for the tears that didn't come. The top of her head, where the bones had yet to come together was sunken as if a force was pulling from the inside. Dorie saw the spot pulse a fast beat, galloping as fast as her own heart.

Silently, Dorie walked over to pick up the receiver and held it to her ear. Francesca followed, and to Dorie's surprise, leaned in pressing her forehead against the space between Dorie's shoulder blades. Her hands felt wet and sticky as she turned the crank.

"Claudia, Dorie here. Ring me the Erickson farm." The weight and rank smell of the bodies pushed against her, and she braced a hand to the wall to steady herself. Please put the call through, Dorie invoked. Claudia's protests of Dorie's business came in the form of dead phone lines and mysteriously severed connections. "There's a sick baby here at the farm," she said quickly, knowing Claudia had heard all about Francesca's stay at the farm. When Dorie heard the connection go through, she let out a long breath and began to count six, seven rings. Finally, one of the younger Erickson boys, Gunnar or Willus, answered and told Dorie between sobs that his mother had taken a turn for the worse, and Lenny couldn't talk now. Dorie held the receiver tight against her ear to prevent Francesca from overhearing the news. In all of the recent illness and misery she had nearly forgotten Lenny's burden.

"We'll see you as soon as you're able then," Dorie said to the dead connection.

Francesca's voice muffled prayers to a saint against Dorie's back. The lid on the pot rattled.

Dorie pulled away and grabbed an enamel pan from under the sink. She pumped enough water to fill the bottom and used a soup ladle to transfer some of the heated water.

"Get her out of those soiled flannels. Maybe the water will wake her enough so that she'll want to nurse. You can sponge her down while I retrieve that bolt in the attic."

"I think we should wait for Lenny."

How to tell her it might be days before Lenny arrived? It might be too late by then. She began to take breaths by mouth, as the collective human odors gathered.

She was startled to see the back door ease slowly open, not having heard an automobile pull into the drive. Doc Pitzer leaned against the door frame, panting, a hand pressed to his chest, and it confused her for a moment because at first she thought Claudia might have called him when she heard about the sick baby. He gulped a few breaths and tapped his chest as if he needed to remind his heart to keep beating. Dorie heard a commotion behind him on the porch. Doc Pitzer wasn't alone.

Doc moved aside and let Sam pass into the kitchen. Sam smiled hard enough to reveal his missing back teeth. He held Louie in his arms like a bride. Why, the bandages around his head resembled a lacy veil! Part of his face was turned against Sam's wide chest, and he fixed on her with one unblinking eye.

"I've brought him home to you, Dorie." Sam nodded. "Back where he belongs."

45

Louie at Home

Following Doc Pitzer's directions, Dorie cut away the dressings wrapped around Louie's head. Their bedroom was quiet except for the heavy whooshing, snipping sounds of the blades. The handle of the scissors dug into the tender web of her thumb, reminding her of yesterday's chore of cutting a fat bolt of flannel into a stack of diapers.

Curled up tight in the middle of the bed, Louie now claimed the last place in this house where she had felt Victor's arms around her, that only haven of restful sleep. Last night, well after midnight when she finally settled in on the hard settee in the parlor, Dorie dreamt she was in the midst of packing the contents of the house onto the hay wagon. Quilts and sets of dishes, jugs of moonshine, chairs heaped on one another, trunks, and crates of chickens were all stacked until the staggering piles passed the roofline of the barn. When she couldn't find the mule in the penned area, she balanced the yoke on her shoulders, strained forward, biting her lower lip until she tasted coppery blood, and then finally she felt the wheels give and the cart begin to roll forward. Not more than a few feet down the drive, the load began to sway and then topple, spilling all her possessions in the dirt and mud of the driveway. She was forced to repack, and this time she wedged in Francesca and the baby. She had barely made it to the main road when the wheel wobbled off the axle and once again the cargo tipped. Where was Victor, she wondered? He would know how to fix this cart. When she woke, her shoulders and hands cramped, and she wondered if it had all been true.

Thankfully, Louie slept most of the time since his return, not demanding much of her attention other than an occasional holler for a bedpan.

Whoosh. Snip. She dropped the sticky sections of gauze into the basin, revealing weepy, open sores across his temples and forehead, the burns more angry looking than when she had first seen them at the infirmary days ago. The last section, stained yellow with pus, stuck stubbornly to the top curve of his ear when she tried to remove it. While she puzzled over how to best loosen it, one of Louie's lids snapped open and fixed on her. The other eye remained closed, and Dorie wondered if it had been seared in its socket, useless and dried up like a currant.

"I remember the first fall after we got hitched," his ruined voice whispered. "I saw you come across the yard with your apron full of those bitter little apples from the good-for-nothin' tree behind the barn, even though I'd warned you they weren't fit for pig food. And when I came in for the noon meal you was standing in the same spot as my ma did, usin' her bowls and rolling pin. It appeared you was set on making a pie, and it warmed my heart to see you using my ma's things, so I didn't say nothin'." He snaked his hand out from under the covers and scratched at his forearm.

Sweat dampened her dress and neck, and she wondered if Louie was able to conduct some leftover heat of the fire in his intense gaze. She pulled her eyes from his to concentrate on freeing the gauze from his ear.

"I thought that pie would be a mouthful of misery, but I knew better than to say so because I watched you work that pie crust like you were mad at it or something. I didn't want none of that wrath turned on me." His ragged, uncut nails raised red welts across his arm. "And then I was ashamed for those thoughts because that pie was the finest thing I'd ever tasted, flakier crust than ma ever made in her fifty years. I can just about taste it now loaded with enough cinnamon and sugar to tame those wayward apples."

Louie reached up and, without flinching, yanked the gauze patch from his ear and handed it to her. Dorie stared in horror at the blackened stub on the bandage and then at the rounded edge missing from the top curve of his ear. She felt the bile rise up and burn the back of her throat.

"That's when I knew I'd found the wife for me. Yes, ma'am." Dorie hastily folded more gauze from the roll and tried to press it to his ear, but he started flailing around now, gouging at his arms until bloody tracks appeared. "Get those potato bugs offa me!" His voice was ragged. "They're crawling under my skin."

"Stop it," she hissed at him. She meant for him to stop all of it—the talking of their marriage, the scratching, and the screaming. And darkly, she held a lungful of air until it burned, as if this act could stop his breathing.

Louie pulled back the blankets and sheets to expose his legs. "My God, swat them!"

Dorie leaned in, squinting to see what kind of infestation he had brought to their bed.

"Look here, on the back of my hand." He yanked off the bandage, held a shaking hand to her, and made a keening noise. Tears rolled down his cheeks into the silver stubble on his chin. There was nothing there. No potato bugs. What was wrong with him?

She heard heavy footsteps coming up the stairs. Doc Pitzer was long gone, which meant it must be Victor, and this filled her first with longing, and then dread. Please don't come into the room, she plead silently. Seeing Victor would only upset Louie further. She glanced at the bureau, remembering the medicine Doc Pitzer had left and his instructions. *Give him a dropperful under his tongue if the pain gets too bad.* The brown bottle sat on the dresser scarf next to her brush and comb. With shaking hands, she unscrewed the cap and filled the dropper with a clear, sweet smelling liquid.

"Louie, here, take this."

He shook his head back and forth, his hands a blur of motion.

"Louie, it's a new batch of moonshine. Come taste."

He stopped and turned toward her. She slipped the dropper into the pocket of his cheek and squeezed the bulb. He moved again, and some of the laudanum dribbled down his cheek, making it hard to tell how much he had swallowed. How much was too much?

"Look at me, Louie," she said not believing she was asking to be the focus of that awful one-eyed gaze. She placed a hand on his leg to quiet his movements, but he pushed her hand away. The calm she felt over the last day fled as she watched him scratch his limbs to a bloody mess over non-existent bugs. She hated Doc Pitzer for dropping him on her porch like this. It was punishment, she knew, for the moonshine, for Victor.

Louie was beyond her words now. Kicking and rolling, he fell from the bed with a thud that knocked over a framed picture on the bureau. She turned to see Victor push open the door, but she shook her head at him when he stepped over the threshold. When he held up a hand in greeting, she had to turn away or risk running sobbing into his arms, begging to be rescued from all this. Dorie's eyes filled with tears when she looked out the window and remembered how they had stood together at this very spot and how she had pressed against his warm, bare shoulder.

Dorie searched for the words to that tune Louie liked Freddy to play. She hummed until she had his attention and he stared and bobbed his head to the tune until his movements slowed and then ceased. Louie laid his head on the floor, closed that one terrible eye, and slept.

Although she wanted to run from the room and leave him there, she unwound a length of gauze and started to redress his burns. After she finished, Victor squatted down to pick Louie up, his spindly arms and legs resembling an armful of kindling, and settled him back into the bed. Dorie pulled the quilt up to his chin, struck by the irony that this was how they might someday put their own child to bed.

Victor's movements cast long shadows across the braided rug as the light eased from the parlor. Dorie drowsed. Her eyelids closed and snapped open as she watched the back of Victor's rumpled shirt as he walked the length of the room and then spun on his heel like a soldier, holding the baby and a chilled water bottle against his chest. The quiet of the house was glorious, and Dorie's body buzzed with fatigue that was nearly a sound.

"She seems cooler, don't you think?" Victor squatted down in front of the rocking chair, putting his hand over Dorie's, as they lay cupped in her lap. His hair fell across one eye as he pursed his lips in a way that looked like an exaggerated kiss, an expression that was all Victor and never failed to make her heart skitter. He studied Victoria, looking at her from odd angles, the way someone did when they were about to purchase cattle or a piece of farm equipment. Dorie wanted to check the baby's forehead for fever, but she liked his warmth and the way his thumb stroked the long curve of her palm too much to pull away. Even after these long hours of nursing and cooking and cleaning, she felt a stir of desire at his touch.

"What were you spooning into her mouth?" he asked.

"Willow bark tea. I gave some to Francesca too."

"Why Francesca?" Victor settled himself on the floor with the baby nestled in his lap. He plopped the water bottle on the floor, propped his hands behind him, and leaned back.

"Mastitis. The baby hasn't nursed properly for a few days, and the ducts are clogged. She's miserable."

"Oh," he said and flushed so that the scar on his eyebrow contrasted white. Dorie was again reminded that he wasn't raised on a farm. "Well, what does that tea do?"

"It helps with pain, reduces a fever. I didn't know what else to do for them." Dorie shrugged.

"How do you know about willow bark?"

"When my sister Minnie moved to Ely, she had an old Indian woman living with her. She taught Minnie about things in the woods that can cure…" Dorie paused, "…or kill. That reminds me—that damned Doc Pitzer, he's about as useful as lips on a fish."

"What?" Victor snorted, causing the baby to stir and open her eyes.

"Do you know what he said about her?"

"Victoria?"

"When he dumped Louie on my doorstep, I asked him what to do for Victoria. Do you know what he said to me?"

Victor shook his head.

"He took one look at her and said, 'Either she'll live or die.' Now what's the good in that? Francesca cried herself to sleep when she overheard him." Dorie ground her teeth every time he came to mind.

"You're doing a fine job, Dorie. You know that, don't you?" Victor broke in and squeezed her hand. "Louie, Francesca, this sick little baby. Hell, we'd all be lost without you."

Dorie's eyes filled with tears, and it hurt to swallow. She didn't want to cry in front of him. He thought she was so strong, but it was all a lie. If he knew her darker impulses, where she had willed Louie to stop breathing, would he think her so fine and wonderful then? Could she tell him that yesterday she sat on the stairs unable to catch her breath when it all pressed against her?

"Don't you want to leave all of this behind?" Her voice cracked on the last words as she gestured to the baby and the spare bedroom where Francesca slept.

"I want to stay here, right in the middle of all of this, more than you'll ever know." He leaned forward and rested his cheek against her knee. His fierce look frightened her.

"Steiner threatened me." Dorie whispered. "He said if I didn't confess to the bootlegging charges, he was going to charge you with murder." The room blurred, and those unwanted tears spilled over her cheeks.

Victor moved his large hand to Victoria's head and paused for a minute. Dorie heard the puppy bark outside and wondered if Shane was signaling a visitor. "I think the fever's down," Victor said.

His avoidance was maddening. "Don't distract me with talk of the fever. Listen, I think Francesca told Steiner about when you shot Geno at the still. That's why he's so bold."

"It's her right to tell what truth she knows," he said slowly. "She swore to me that this wasn't the case, but Geno was her husband—"

"When did she say that?"

"Just a bit ago, when you were tending to Louie."

"I think you should go, Victor. Leave this town. I'll follow you later, when it's safe."

"And when would that be? I told you, I don't want to spend my life running from Steiner or maybe even the FBI. He would call them, you know."

"What if we go to California or Canada?"

"You know you'll never leave this place, Dorie. Our baby will be coming, and then you won't be able to travel so far..." He grinned and shook his head at her. "You're in this place for life." Victoria began to fuss in earnest now. Her cry was lustier than it had been in two days.

"I can't sit here and wait. It'll drive me crazy. There's something you're not telling me," she said over the baby's cries. She wiped her face with her palms. God, she must look dreadful, streaky face, a soiled dress. What must her hair look like? Why did he want to stay?

"I have something for you. Let me go get it." He stood up, balancing the baby on his inner forearm.

"Take the baby to Francesca. She needs to nurse. It'll be good for the both of them."

When Victor left the room, Dorie made her way to the kitchen to put together a supper for all of them. There would be nothing fancy tonight, just hardboiled eggs, cold ham, a bit of cheese, and bread. She was thankful her appetite was back. She was slicing the eggs when Victor slipped behind her and put a hand over her eyes, the other hand pressed against her belly. Dorie closed her eyes and leaned against him, believing she could stand just like that forever. When she turned around to kiss him, an egg fell from the counter to the floor. Her hands ran under his dress shirt and then pulled at his undershirt to get at his skin. He responded by pressing his hips against her. Where could they go to be alone and get rid of all of these clothes?

When he pulled his mouth from hers, she staggered forward. "Don't you want to see what I've brought you?" he asked.

"I thought this was your surprise." She reached on tiptoes for another kiss.

"Look here, on the table."

She turned to see a bolt of dark-green wool, the hat she had ordered and forgotten to pick up, and a bottle of perfume. He had gathered all of her favorite things. Expensive things… she couldn't stop herself from calculating the totals.

She picked up the hat and stroked the cream-colored velvet trim and admired the tiny stitches.

"Put it on. I want to remember you in this hat today."

"My hair—"

"Just put it on… for me."

She couldn't resist his request, and when she tied the bow under her chin, she saw a look of such pain in his eye. She pulled him to her to kiss away his misery.

46

Victor's Plan

The next morning, Dorie slipped Victor's white shirt on and walked barefoot to the kitchen to start coffee while Victor slept under the quilts they had spread on the parlor rug. Dorie's back and hips ached from sleeping on the floor, but it reminded her of her best memories of the blizzard, so she didn't complain.

The cold water from the pump splashed the front of the shirt. Her pink skin shone through where the wet fabric went transparent. She loved the feeling of the soft cotton, how the shirttails tickled the backs of her bare thighs when she walked. Dorie brought the sleeve to her nose and inhaled his scent. Like Lenny, maybe she would take to donning men's clothes as her belly grew bigger. She closed her eyes against the happiness that felt too bright, like staring into the sun.

Maybe this was the tradeoff. She was forced out of business and saddled with a houseful of sick people, but if she still got to spend her days and nights with Victor, didn't that make it all bearable? Just before midnight, as they had settled in together on the parlor floor, and Dorie had closed her eyes to the day, she felt him bury his face in her hair, murmuring words she couldn't quite hear.

While waiting for the coffee to brew, she sat at the table, sharpened a pencil with a paring knife, and composed a list of things to purchase in town. Francesca and the baby were better now that the fever had broken, she was sure of it. In any case, Victor could look after them. She could give Louie another dose of the laudanum just before she left in case he might be a bother. Maybe she should stop by Doc's and ask him for a larger bottle of the sleep mixture. She touched the lead to her tongue and began to write her list: *coffee, flour, roasts, cheeses, baby shirts, and booties.*

She stopped and pressed her fingers against her eyes. What would it be like to go to town now? Even though she had provided them with ample gossip between the discovery of Geno's body and the fire at the still, it seemed hard to imagine getting treated any worse than usual. Shane yipped outside and scratched at the door. Dorie let him in along with the damp morning air, deciding to serve him the plate of scraps indoors since her legs and feet were bare. His tongue lolled out of his mouth when he bounced at her feet. Lordy, he had grown. Time was passing, and everything was changing.

They both startled when they heard an engine roar into the drive. Dorie cursed at whoever was coming to interrupt her tranquil morning. Shane ran to the door, barking a high-pitched alarm. Dorie lifted the curtain and peered out in the yard as fine droplets of rain sprayed the windows.

Steiner again.

He was here to press her for a decision. Dorie touched the front of Victor's shirt and realized she couldn't answer the door in this state. If she changed in her room she ran the risk of waking Louie. Maybe she wouldn't answer the door at all. How long could she shut out the world?

When she backed away from the window, she turned as Victor wrapped a quilt over her shoulders. He was nearly dressed—undershirt, trousers, his braces dangled across his hips, everything except his dress shirt.

"Come here, kiss me quick," he said. He tugged on the quilt to pull her closer. "Don't be angry with me." He held her chin and tilted her face upward before he pressed his mouth to her temple.

Dorie pulled back. "Angry?"

Steiner was already banging on the porch door, his hat pitched at an angle against the rain.

"Let me handle him," Dorie warned over the dog's barks. "God, I'm going to give him a piece of my mind if he wakes the baby or Louie at this hour." Francesca shuffled into the kitchen holding the baby. Her eyes were swollen.

"How are you?" Dorie and Victor both said together.

"My legs, they feel weak, but I'm better, thank you. She's better too." She kissed Victoria's head and smiled, but leaned against the table for support.

"Steiner's here," Dorie announced.

"I know," Francesca said and nodded. She dabbed at her cheeks with one of Victor's handkerchiefs.

A queasy feeling crawled over Dorie, a cold sweat that started at the crown of her head and washed down throughout her body. As Dorie went to the door, she glanced over to see a fat tear spill down Francesca's cheek.

"Morning, Dorie." Steiner removed his hat and slapped it against his thigh. He smelled of tobacco and wet leather. Dorie rocked back on her heels and hated the fact that she wasn't dressed for this encounter. It made her feel weak and unprepared.

"Sheriff." That was as much of a greeting as she would give him. "Early for a visit, isn't it?"

"I'm here at the appointed time, I believe." He squinted at his pocket watch as he followed her into the kitchen.

Dorie's chest tightened around the sharp fear. She had no story, no line to fall back on. Grit from the porch floor bit into her feet.

"I'm sorry, Dorie. I haven't got much choice." Steiner pursed his lips.

Dorie trembled. *He's going to arrest me*, she thought. She stared at Steiner, holding her breath against his next words. His face blurred. Victor kissed Francesca's hand and nuzzled the baby.

"Be well, Victor. I'll pray to the saints in your name."

"What's going on?" Dorie demanded. Shane tugged at an edge of the quilt. Dorie fought to keep her shoulders covered. "Stop it," she said to the dog, but the command was directed at all of them.

"I'm arresting Victor on bootlegging charges. First he'll go to my jail cell, and then be moved to St. Cloud prison after the county judge sentences him."

St. Cloud prison? Steiner's tone was as casual as if they were discussing the price of feed or when the ice would go out on the lake.

Victor buttoned his overcoat, eyeing each button with exaggerated concentration. *Your shirt*, she wanted to call out to him. *You can't leave without your shirt.*

"Wait. What about a trial?" *Why were they all so calm?*

"There won't be a trial. Victor signed a confession. I gave him some time to put things in order as part of our agreement."

"You agreed to this how long ago?" It sounded like an accusation. "And you knew about this too?" She pointed her finger at Francesca. "I suppose even the dog was told. Everyone but me." There was not enough air in the room.

"Dorie, he's doing it for you." Francesca stepped forward and touched her arm.

"No, no, no. This isn't right." Dorie held every muscle tight to prevent her collapse to the floor.

"I offered Victor the same deal as you. Either he could admit to bootlegging charges, or I told him I'd arrest you for the murders of the D'Agostino brothers. Frankly, it didn't matter to me one way or another which one of you confessed." Steiner licked his chapped lips. "Anyway, I guess Victor wanted to spare you the humiliation of the trial, especially considering your delicate condition." Steiner's gaze flicked around the room, as if following an insect's flight.

Dorie stared at the three of them. She cringed to think of Victor telling Steiner about their baby and flashed to that first meeting when he had found them together at Buzzy's farm after the blizzard.

Dorie stared into Steiner's queer, gray eyes and her hatred for him felt like a metal thing residing in her chest. He was too polite to voice his thoughts, but she knew he believed her to be a selfish and immoral creature. Did she imagine she saw his lip curl into a sneer?

"Steiner, there's no cause for telling her these things." Victor stepped toward Steiner.

"Why didn't you tell me? Why did I have to find out like this?" Dorie's voice was full of tears, and she cursed that disadvantage. Victor reached for her, but she pulled away from him, tripping over the dog and the quilt. He lunged and caught her just as her forehead smacked the back of the chair.

"Dorie!" Francesca called out.

She wrenched out of Victor's hold, turned her back to them, and stared out the window as the wind buffeted the tree branches. She pressed her palm against the pain. Her eyes and throat burned. Why would he do this? Why didn't he just leave town like she suggested? A knot above her eye started to form and throb, tightening the skin.

"Victor, if you're ready. Your things?" Steiner asked.

"I have a satchel out front."

He had packed! In the reflection of the window, she saw Steiner put his hat on and move toward the door. Victor turned and raised a hand to her as if he were merely going out on a brief errand.

"Say goodbye. Tell him you love him," Francesca whispered as she edged closer.

No words came to her. She was to be left alone with Louie and this new baby.

Victor mouthed goodbye as the dog whined and tried to follow them. Steiner used his foot to block Shane's escape from the porch. When he shut the door, Dorie heard their heavy steps shuffling down the stairs. A few wet leaves stuck to the gray porch floor.

Francesca gripped her arm through the quilt, and Victoria started to wail. How could he still love her when she had never once considered making that sacrifice for him?

47

After Victor Leaves

There was no time to wallow in her sadness and shock. Louie's sheets needed washing, the baby was nearly out of flannels again, and then there was the matter of meals. Dorie scrubbed floors, sewed tiny kimonos for Victoria, not pausing between tasks to think of Victor sitting in the jail cell. She worried that her memories of his kisses might wear out and fade in their loveliness from too much use.

She drew a bath for Francesca and washed her nightclothes, spinning like a dervish despite Francesca's pleas for her to stop.

"I need to show you something! Please stop and talk with me," Francesca pleaded.

Dorie ignored her. All she needed was Francesca announcing their newly minted sisterhood, now that they were both women without men to take care of them.

He knew he was leaving, and he hadn't said a word.

She burned to think of her ignorance. The gifts, the fiercely silent way he had held her. Now it made sense. If only he had trusted her enough to tell her! She knew she could have convinced him to run far away if only she'd worked harder to put a real plan in place with maps and train schedules and names of people he could stay with. Maybe Victor never understood that she had enough money stashed to keep him safe. She should have never talked so much about needing Geno's money.

Dorie rested for a moment at the sink to catch her breath and stared out the window into the yard. A weak afternoon sun broke through the gray sky staining the clouds a pale yellow. The break in the weather and the strong wind was her chance to pin bedding to the line. Dorie got down on one knee next to the bushel basket full of wet sheets that sat in front of the stove. As she stood and hefted the load to her hips, she felt a tearing pain burn through her belly and down her thighs. She screamed and dropped the basket as she fell to her knees. The sheets and Victor's shirt slapped against the floor.

Dorie slumped over on her side and curled up against the pain. When she squeezed her eyes shut, lights and colors sprinted across the blackness.

"Dorie, what's wrong?" She heard Francesca's shuffling footsteps and her frantic voice. Tears spilled over the bridge of Dorie's nose. The pain twisted tighter, low and fierce. She couldn't take a breath to answer Francesca, but sensed it when she knelt next to her. "Dorie, is it the baby?" she whispered.

The baby.

A miscarriage? Her throat swelled against that possibility, but the cramps felt like a sprung bear trap. She tried to draw herself tighter to hold it in. Francesca was wrong. What did she know? It was just a pain, like the other day when she moved the kettle, like the ache she experienced that night in the woods. It wouldn't last. It was from shock, too many chores, and the brutal news that Victor was leaving. A common enough reaction, wasn't it?

"I'll ring Lenny. She'll know what to do. I'll call over to the jail too. Victor should know."

She saw the big, blond baby waving chubby hands as he sat on a blanket. When he squinted up at her and grinned, she spied four tiny teeth that looked like delicate pearls of sweet corn. He reached out with both arms to be held.

Dorie bit her lip and rocked her head against the floor. Not Victor. He mustn't know. "No, don't call," she managed to whisper. Her nose ran.

"Can you move? Let me help you to my bed."

A fresh cramp seized her, and she hissed through clenched teeth. Pain like this could only be punishment from God, retribution for the business, for Geno and Sal, for Victor. Francesca tried to tug at her arm and then sat back on her haunches. When Dorie started to shake with chills that erupted from her core, Francesca ran from the room.

Dorie's head throbbed, and she concentrated on taking tiny breaths through clenched teeth, willing the pain to leave. Suddenly she remembered standing at the far end of Minnie's yard, near a shady place where two blue-spruce trees grew. Dorie was probably twelve years old. Minnie was describing the darkest parts of the woods where she had found the lady's slippers that bloomed under the spruce when Dorie pointed out the three round, pink-tinged stones set evenly between the tree trunks. Minnie hugged herself and explained that each stone marked the spot where she had buried her lost children. Dorie remembered her confusion. Lost children? They had just sent all the boys out to work in the field after the noon meal! She waited, not wanting to ask, but not able to puzzle out Minnie's meaning. Finally, she told her, these were the children born too early, too small to live in this world. Were they girls or boys? Were they buried in tiny caskets? Dorie wanted to know, but Minnie didn't offer any other details.

What did her baby look like? How big was it?

Francesca returned dragging an armful of bedding and wedged a pillow under Dorie's head. She draped the quilt over Dorie's shoulder, knelt on the floor behind her, and began to murmur. The blankets smelled of milk and Francesca's salty-sweat smell.

"Which patron saint are you praying to?" Dorie managed to say once the cramp loosened its clenched grip. "For dead babies or barren women?" Dorie croaked and moved her hands to cover her wet face.

"Catherine of Siena will find the best way to help you," Francesca said quietly. "You have always been so strong and sure, like she was."

If she didn't move at all, if she barely breathed, this might stop the storm that raged in her body. Francesca pushed the hair from Dorie's face and stroked the back of her head. *I'll do anything*, she bargained with God, *if you let this pass*. Had God spared Francesca's baby only to take her own?

"Can one of your saints stop this?"

"The saints know what it was like to be human. It does no harm to ask."

Francesca stayed with Dorie on the kitchen floor, offering her sips of water, sometimes nursing Victoria as the daylight dimmed and the room grew dark. At some point Dorie drifted into an uneasy sleep where she argued with Louie about why they couldn't keep the baby in one of his birdhouses. Louie just whistled and smiled at her. His skin was pink and clear. He pushed a planer over and over the same board until fat curls of pine covered the table and what remained of the wood was as thin as a piece of paper.

She opened her eyes when she felt Francesca's cool hand on her cheek and nearly wept for this kindness, grateful not to be left alone. After these hours spent on the floor, comforted by her soothing words and touch, Dorie would never again question Francesca's devotion.

For a moment, she existed in the calm where there was no line drawn between what was a dream and what was real. When Dorie struggled to sit upright, she felt a gush of blood in her undergarments and knew for certain Francesca's saints had turned their backs and marched out the door.

48

Five Years Later, 1933, Francesca

Shane greeted Francesca at the end of the dusty driveway, tail wagging, his pink, curled tongue slung out the side of his mouth as he loped and jumped so close to the car she could see the raw deer fly bites on his ears. After Lenny had taught her how to drive, she was scared to death she would run him over, but now she was accustomed to his antics.

Francesca set the brake and secured the towel around the plate of fresh *pizelles*. She liked this part of the day the best, when the insects got noisy and the people got quiet. She and Dorie had gotten into the habit this summer of sitting together on the porch, drinking lemonade or root beer, sometimes sharing a cigarette and talking. Other nights they sat in silence watching the sunset and the dark roll in, and then Francesca would head home to Lenny and the children.

After she scratched Shane's ears, she said, "Wait here. I'll be right back."

She let herself in the porch door and walked through the kitchen, leaving the plate on the counter next to the jars of tomatoes Dorie had put up that day. She headed back to the bedroom where she heard voices.

"Don't read from the book. Those aren't good stories!" Ann complained. "Tell me one of your stories. No, wait! Tell me how I came to be your little girl."

Francesca smiled as she heard Dorie sigh and close the book. Dorie told tales of a girl who sometimes built rafts and sailed down the Mississippi River. Frequently the heroine saved abandoned babies floating in baskets or built forts and lived with the wild animals or fought off creatures that lived in the murky waters. Part Tom Sawyer, part Old Testament, packed with danger and excitement, Dorie's stories were always about one girl, alone in the world. Francesca loved to hear them as much as all the children did, but tonight Ann wanted to hear her favorite story—how she came to live with Dorie.

"Come in, Frannie," Dorie called. Francesca pushed open the door and saw Dorie sitting on the bed next to Ann, her back resting against the headboard. A fan on the bureau purred back and forth, ruffling the hem of Dorie's dress with each pass.

Francesca walked to the bed and leaned over to tickle Ann's bare feet.

"How are you, my sweet?" Francesca asked.

Ann nodded and giggled. "We heard you come, Frannie." Her red hair, plaited and slick from her bath, looked dark against the white pillowcase. "My story, Dorie?"

"Prayers first?" Francesca pressed her hands together.

Ann scrambled off the bed onto her knees. Her movements always reminded Francesca of mercury from a broken thermometer racing across the floor.

"Prayers to Saint Osmund, to heal my mother's mind. May Saint Dymphna look over our families, Francesca." Ann squinted open one eye and smiled. "For Dorie, Lenny, the boys, and Victoria. And please, Mark the Evangelist, watch over Victor and bring him home to us. Amen. Oh, wait. May the eternal fires of hell lick at the soles of my father's feet. Amen again." Ann made a hasty sign of the cross as she boosted herself back on the bed.

"I can see you've been advising her prayers," Dorie said.

"And you've added your own two-cents' worth as well."

As Dorie shrugged her shoulders with exaggerated movements, Ann patted her hand with urgency.

"You know the story. You tell it to *me*," Dorie said.

"No," Ann shook her head. "It's better when you do it."

"All right then." Dorie crossed her ankles and began, "It was the middle of the night. You were a new baby nursing in your mother's arms. Cousin Agnes liked to sit in the rocking chair next to the window that looked down over the yard and the barn. When she heard noises outside, she peered into the blue moonlight and saw your father swing his suitcase into the back of the truck and then drive off down the road." Dorie's arm curled around Ann's shoulders. "Days later when Albert hadn't shown up for his shifts at the mill, Sheriff Steiner stopped over. Your brothers and sisters were wandering the farm, eating carrots and radishes they had pulled from the garden. He found your mother in her room with the shades drawn. He said, at first she was so still, he took her for dead. Then she had whispered, 'Albert's gone.' Steiner said you were in the crib in her room. Your diaper was full and when you cried, there weren't any tears."

Francesca saw Ann bunch each sheet in her hands. The little girl rushed to finish the story for Dorie. "And when Sheriff Steiner told you about me, you marched over to your nephew's farm and said, 'I'll take that baby girl and raise her like she was my own!'"

"Yes." Dorie nodded and kissed Ann's head as she reached for the light switch. "Like my own."

The two stories of Francesca's life in Osseo that would always stay sharp in her mind were the birth of her youngest and last child and the day Dorie lost her baby. Those two accounts, life and death of two babies continued to seep into Francesca's dreams.

After Francesca had covered Dorie with a blanket that rainy afternoon, she moaned and cried in her sleep. Sometimes she jerked as if pinched by invisible fingers. When Francesca had finally reached Lenny, she didn't ask for help when she heard Lenny's mother was dying, even though she craved Lenny's practical directives and her calm manner. Lenny was needed at home, and there wasn't anything to do but wait.

Who could ever have imagined what came next? When Dorie pushed herself up and flung back the blanket, the lower half of her dress was dark with blood. Francesca's hand flew to her mouth, but she couldn't stifle her gasp. Dorie plucked at the wet fabric, trying to pull it from her legs and then stared at her sticky hands.

"He's gone from me." Dorie said as she slumped against Francesca's chest and then sobbed. Francesca held her until the smeared blood on the back of her hands dried and her skin itched. Did she mean the baby or Victor? Francesca didn't ask.

When she realized there was no one to help, not Lenny or Victor, and certainly she didn't dare call Steiner for fear of Dorie's reaction. Francesca became one of them that day—a woman like Dorie and Lenny who could do whatever was necessary without complaint of leaky, sore breasts or her own achy discomfort or her terror. Francesca rolled up her sleeves, heated water on the stove, and removed Dorie's sodden dress and undergarments. That day she became a woman strong enough to rinse away the clots and all traces of Dorie's baby.

Dorie took to the bed that night and seemed determined to stay there. She refused food, turning her face to the wall the time when Francesca had mentioned calling in Doc Pitzer.

As Dorie grew thin and pale, Francesca's strength blossomed. When Steiner offered to escort her home to Chicago, she refused, claiming she was needed here. After a few arguments, Steiner gave in, brought over a rollaway cot, a bassinette, and stews and breads prepared by his wife. When Steiner asked how she would manage taking care of two sick people and a baby, Francesca showed him how she figured out how to tie a sheet around her shoulder and waist to bind the baby against her body, leaving her hands free.

Francesca even took care of Louie. She didn't discourage him when he mistook her for the Virgin Mary, and after that she was certain to have the baby with her whenever she went to his room. It alarmed her that his sores seemed to grow larger each time she removed his bandages. Most of the time, his demeanor continued to be sweet except when he asked after Dorie, and then he just seemed sad.

Finally, when she couldn't stand Dorie's stillness another day, she opened the shades and sat next to her on the bed.

"Dorie, I need to read you something," she began.

Dorie didn't move, but Francesca saw her brow furrow.

"Victor left you a letter. I want to read it to you." Francesca's mouth suddenly felt dry, but she pushed on, pulled the folded paper from her apron pocket and read his neatly printed message.

> My darling Dorie,
>
> I haven't written much of anything since my days at the Osseo schoolhouse, so this letter might not reach your heart the way I intend. When you read this, I know you'll be hopping mad at me for turning myself in to Steiner, and I love you for believing in another answer, but, frankly, I can't find my way to what that might be. In my whole life, I never found a job I much cared for. I didn't attach much affection to a place or a woman, but that all changed this past year. With your love, everything had meaning, Francesca, the baby, the farm, even the Schumacher brothers make me smile. I loved all of

> it. That's why I want to do the right thing and put these mistakes I've made behind us. Nothing will be right until I go to prison.
>
> It's not my place to act as husband to you or a father to our child, circumstances being what they are. I don't even think to hope for things to change because I know what that means for Louie. In a day, I think about you more times than I can count. I'm glad for the time I got to spend with Victoria because I will know the feeling of a newborn baby in my arms. Please know our days together were the best of my life.
>
> I know you will continue to take good care of all who need you. Lastly, money always ran through my foolish fingers and has never meant much more to me than the paper it's printed on, so it's strange that I was the one who found Geno's stash in the shack the day of the fire. Since I can't provide for you the way a proper husband should and since I'm responsible for Francesca's life as a widow, I'm turning over this money to the two of you to make amends. The rest of my life is love for you.
>
> Victor

When she finished reading the letter aloud, Francesca pulled a flour sack from under the bed and heaved it up, spilling the bundles of money tied with twine across Dorie's quilt. Dorie stared at the pile for a full minute before she asked, "How much?"

"How do you know I counted it?"

Dorie shrugged.

"There's over five thousand dollars."

"Victor could have taken it all and left town." She paused and wiped her eyes with the sheet. "You could have done the same. It's yours rightfully."

"I know," Francesca answered. "That's not what Victor wanted."

A few days later, as Francesca was dressing the baby for the day, she heard noises in the kitchen, and found Dorie washing a tub of bed linens, as if nothing had happened. The weather warmed, lilacs outside the porch windows produced tight buds that plumped, and then overnight bloomed a dark-purple perfume.

As spring gave way to summer, Dorie worked from sunup to well after dark, painting, cooking, cleaning, mending fences, putting in a garden, even patching the porch roof. She cut off any attempts by Francesca to offer words of sympathy or mention of Victor or the pregnancy. Victor's goodbye letter remained for months on the nightstand, unfolded where Francesca had put it until it finally disappeared. New letters from him began to arrive in July, but they sat unopened on the buffet, one stacked on top of another. Francesca suggested writing back to Victor, but she knew better than to bring that up again after Dorie's frosty response.

Francesca was too busy at that point to campaign on Victor's behalf. With her half of the money, she paid off the back taxes and hired two of Lenny's brothers to fix up her farmhouse. She wrote long letters to Giovanna, pleading to let the boys come north for a visit. Of course, Giovanna recognized that this visit would not be a temporary one, so she refused. Francesca missed her children fiercely, but the lawyer she consulted in Anoka told her it was unlikely a judge would allow the boys to be removed from a wealthy home only to live on a farm with their mother who had no means of support. However, circumstances would change, he advised, if she were to remarry. As much as she ached for the boys, she couldn't bring herself to move back to that dreary mansion under Giovanna's thumb. She wrote them long letters each week, talking about their new sister and the farm she was preparing for their arrival. Victoria grew, but her health was fragile. She was plagued with colds and fevers and coughs that rattled her tiny lungs. Francesca was afraid to travel with her and equally afraid to leave her in Osseo. Even though she was torn about leaving Victoria, she was more reluctant to part with Lenny.

That summer she had helped Lenny mind the Erickson household of motherless children. To her surprise, she learned how to cook meals and enjoyed taking a bushel of raw ingredients and turning it into meals to feed so many mouths. She liked lining up all the children for haircuts and baths, scrubbing the dirt from their elbows and fingernails. At night she mended their clothes and made sure to spend time with the small ones on her lap. The baby cooed and laughed around Lenny's siblings, and in so many of those moments, the children listening to the Goodrich Zipper Banjo Ensemble on the radio while Lenny studied her textbooks, preparing for school in the fall, Francesca felt a warmth and love for Lenny and this life grow in a way she didn't quite understand and was reluctant to examine too deeply.

Louie lingered in a place between living and dying. His burns healed slowly, but because of the months he spent in bed, he lost the use of his legs. His mind seemed locked in the past, and he talked about Dorie as his new bride. Louie ranted a list of chores he planned to accomplish the next day when his legs felt up to it. The memories of the moonshine business, the D'Agostino brothers, and Victor had vanished. Dorie quietly attended to his needs, patient with his childish moods. She grew thin and lean that summer, taking on the look of the hired hands at the Erickson farm. Her arms grew muscular, and her collarbones jutted out starkly from Louie's old undershirts. She no longer wore jewelry of any kind or used her lavender soaps and lotions. Her palms calloused, and her arms and shoulders browned in the sun.

Late in August, Francesca stopped over at Dorie's one morning and was surprised to find Dorie wearing nothing more than Victor's shirt. Before Francesca could tell her that she missed him too, Dorie stormed upstairs and slammed her bedroom door shut. Months later, Francesca hunted for the shirt in the closets and drawers, craving proof that Dorie loved still loved him, but she never found it.

Just when Francesca believed Dorie was forever lost to sadness, she rescued Ann. Dorie softened overnight, singing songs, rocking this baby who, in her first few weeks at Dorie's, screamed for hours each night until Dorie figured out how to soothe her by binding her tightly like a papoose. The baby grew plump and lovely, a fair contrast to Victoria's dark, serious looks, and fussed each time Dorie left the room.

Late that fall, Francesca received word from the solicitor that Giovanna had suddenly died, stomach tumor, he wrote. No one even knew she was ill. Francesca traveled back home for the funeral, and after endless wrangling with the lawyers, brought the boys to live in her farmhouse in Osseo. Most of the money from the sale of the house was put into a trust for the boys. A stipend was allotted each month toward food and clothes for the children. Giovanna's fury and bitterness was evident in her will stipulations. No money was set aside for Francesca as Geno's widow. Francesca was unsure if Giovanna's anger stemmed from the fact that she refused to leave Osseo, the place that had claimed her only sons or that she hid her last pregnancy. In any case, Francesca was overjoyed to be with her boys again, but sometimes felt guilty she couldn't work up any feeling of sadness toward Giovanna's passing.

As the boys settled into their new home, Francesca took to writing Victor. She copied down the address from the growing stack at Dorie's and composed long letters about the children and the house. To her joy, Victor wrote her back giving brief details of his daily life, and he usually offered her good advice about raising boys. She outlined details of Dorie's life and vowed to get Dorie to return a letter.

They celebrated their first Christmas in Osseo. The boys received sleds and spent hours on the hill by the lake. Lenny was on a holiday break from school, and they celebrated at the Erickson house with all of Lenny's brothers and sisters, and Francesca's four children, along with Dorie and Ann. Francesca spent hours reading cookbooks sent from Chicago and then days cooking the meal. As they gathered around the table for the blessing, Francesca couldn't remember a time when she was happier. It took only a glimpse of Dorie's haunted face to make Francesca realize that not everyone felt such joy that day.

The next full year was a whirlwind of snowstorms, chicken pox outbreaks, and growing babies. Francesca leased out her acres to Dorie's nephew and cooked pies for Schieffer's Diner. Dorie seemed determined to run her farm by herself, but switched from growing potatoes to producing what she called a truck garden—cabbage, cauliflower, peppers, tomatoes, and squash. Dorie would get up at 3:00 in the morning and take Joseph with her to the Minneapolis market. Francesca learned much later that she let Joseph drive most of the way home so she could sleep.

It was only after the stock market crash in October of '29 that life changed for them all. Dorie's habit of hording money in tins served her well, as most of the banks failed and people lost fortunes of varying sizes. Francesca still had money left over from Geno's heists. Two years after the crash, Francesca purchased Schieffer's Diner for pennies on the dollar. Business was slow, but Dorie convinced her that things would improve and people would have more money in their pockets for a meal out.

The same year Francesca took over the diner, Louie died quietly one morning in his wheelchair, carving another toy for Ann. The funeral was well attended, and most of the town came to pay their respects and tell stories of Louie's kindness and woodcarving talents. After his death, Dorie leased out her farm and ended up buying property closer to town—a small house with eight cabins that she rented out to migrant farmers or men who had lost their families and had nowhere to go. She didn't earn as much money as she did during the moonshine days, but she confided in Francesca that a legitimate business was less worrisome to run.

With Ann in tow, Dorie painted, cleaned, made repairs, and collected rents. At first Francesca was skeptical of Dorie's methods. More times than not, Ann wore blue dungarees rather than dresses, and Francesca discovered Ann kept a knife nestled between her sock and her boot, just in case, they both said. Then one day shortly after Ann's fifth birthday, Francesca overheard Dorie quizzing Ann as they took turns beating the rugs.

"If the rent is two dollars a week, Ann, how much is that in a month? In six months? Now how much will it be if I increase rents by fifty cents a week from June until the end of the year?" Ann could compute these sums in her head as quickly as Dorie could fire off the questions. "Clever girl," Dorie said. "You'll be ready to take care of yourself soon." From then on, Francesca never doubted Dorie's wisdom in raising children.

Francesca and Dorie stood in the gloom of Ann's room, watching the sky's pink edges warm and deepen in color. Francesca knew that Dorie watched over Ann like this each night until she passed into slumber, her promise that Ann would never be left alone again.

"Did you bring those *pizelles* like you promised?" Dorie whispered.

Francesca's heart fluttered. Standing this close to Dorie, she smelled of tobacco, shoe polish, and Dorie's unique spicy scent. For months, this surprise had seemed like such a good idea, and now Francesca had misgivings. Sweat gathered on her upper lip.

"Dorie, come outside with me. There's someone here to see you."

"A renter? Tell 'em I'm full up for now."

"No. Not a renter."

"Have you been meddling about with my sisters again?" At least this time there was no edge to Dorie's voice regarding Francesca's attempts to mend her stormy relationships with her sisters.

"No, well, not this week anyway."

Dorie brushed past her as she left the bedroom, and Francesca kept close on her heels. Yesterday, the news had seemed so easy to deliver. Now the words stuck to her tongue like flour paste. She always should remember the picture in her head never matched the real world.

"Is it Lenny? Are the two of you going to the lake to cool off?"

Dorie lifted the corner of the towel and pulled out a *pizelle*, snapped it in two pieces, and nibbled.

"No, it's not Lenny." Francesca took a deep breath. "It's Victor. He's out now." Her voice went high like Biaggio's did when he tried to tell a fib.

Dorie whirled around, eyes wide. A crumb of cookie clung to her lower lip.

"This was your idea, wasn't it, to bring him here?"

"He wants to see you."

"Why? He can't. He shouldn't—"

"Victor loves you, Dorie. He never stopped for a moment, not in all these years."

"That's what your silly romantic heart wants to believe."

"We've been writing to each other for ages. He's the one with the romantic heart."

She watched Dorie press her lips together before she said, "Proving once again that I'm not suited to him as a companion."

Dorie pulled open the kitchen curtain and saw him sitting on the running board as Shane pranced back and forth, licking Victor's chin and ears.

Dorie whirled around. One hand lifted the hair from the back of her neck, and the other clutched her throat. "Why didn't you give me more warning? I look dreadful! I could have—"

"Could have what? Locked the door? Driven off with Ann? Hidden in the barn?"

"That's mean spirited."

"That's the truth."

Francesca thought Dorie looked anything but dreadful. When she was working, she braided her hair, but around the house she wore it long and unpinned, and it fell in waves, lightened by the sun, across her back. Her skin had a healthy golden color, making her eyes look violet in this light. Even the slight fan of lines around her eyes made her look lovely.

Dorie pumped some water and splashed it on her face and neck. She drank from her cupped palm. She leaned against the sink and continued to look out the window at Victor. "How is he?"

How could Francesca answer that one? *Heartbroken? He thinks you don't love him. Lonely. Older. Sad, oh so sad. I don't know what will become of him if you turn him away.*

"He's fine."

"What about the baby?" Dorie whispered.

"He's known for years you lost the baby." Francesca couldn't look at Dorie, but concentrated on arranging the jars of tomatoes in a perfect line.

"Ann?" Dorie paced around the large kitchen. She adjusted the belt on her dress.

Francesca nodded and smiled. "He'd like the chance to meet Ann."

"He'll never forgive me."

"There was nothing to forgive. He loves you."

Outside the crickets chirped. Francesca wanted to shoo her out the door, but she saw the set of Dorie's shoulders, how she held her chin up in that stubborn way, and knew better than to hurry her. In the pink evening light, Shane fetched a stick, crouching and running along the path that led to the yellow cabins.

"He's hungry. I know that for sure. He didn't take the last dinner there at the prison. He just wanted to come straight here."

There were only a few tiny fibs. Victor commented he was too wound up to eat every time Francesca slowed and offered to stop at diners they passed on the trip from St. Cloud. When she mentioned going to Dorie's, he'd looked wild-eyed with panic. "She's got on fine without me. I got the message loud and clear," he had said.

Dorie headed toward the door, but paused with her hand on the latch. "I can't turn him away hungry. I can cook something for him. That's the least I can do."

"He should see the house too."

"The house. Of course."

Dorie headed out the back door and crossed the yard to where Victor stood with his hands on his hips watching the dog. He turned then, even though Francesca was certain she didn't call out, and she watched Dorie walk to him. She couldn't make out his expression, but he stood stock-still. He didn't raise a hand in greeting or open his arms to her. Dorie stopped in front of him, and their forms became one dark shadow. Shane sat, stick in his mouth, waiting. Francesca turned off the light, sweating in the heavy air of the kitchen, craving the cool breeze of the porch, but not daring to move. In the blue dusk wrap she saw the blur of Victor's shirt around Dorie's shoulders and waist, and exhaled.

Acknowledgements

Gratitude to Jonis Agee who urged a young undergraduate to consider a life as a writer, and years later, gave encouragement to turn a writing exercise into a novel. Thanks to the support of the Blue Moon Writing group who reviewed this manuscript over many bottles of wine. To Jewell Gaspard, the lovely French woman pictured on the cover, who represents Dorie's spirit and private anguish.

Finally, to the all the strong women in my life, especially my mother Clare, who taught me to be self-reliant. Over the years, I have reveled in the love and care of my life-long friends and the labor women--your grit, loyalty and intellect supported me through the death of two husbands and a breast cancer diagnosis. As writers are prone to do, I gathered parts from all of you to create the characters of Dorie and Francesca, in all of their imperfect and wonderful glory.

About the Author

Mary DesJarlais accomplished it all in the Midwest. Born, educated, twice married, twice widowed, she raised two lively daughters, survived a breast cancer siege, and launched a career as a fiction writer with her first novel, *Dorie LaValle*, in 2011. DesJarlais is excited to have been acquired by Calumet Editions, which has released this revised edition of *Dorie LaValle* and will be publishing her new novel, *Written on the River*, a story of survival, grief and adoption gone awry. Mary lives and works in St. Paul, Minnesota.